MW01277877

Marx Joyce
Abbott Hardy Machiavelli Chesterton Cooper Emerson Austen
Defoe Melville Montaigne Haggard Molière Hugo Grimm
Stoker Christie Carroll Maupassant Byron Eliot
Wilde Garnett Einstein Fitzgerald Engels Schiller
Goethe Hawthorne Smith Kafka
Baum Cotton Henry Dostoyevsky Hall Willis
Leslie Dumas Kipling Doyle
Flaubert Nietzsche
Stockton Turgenev Balzac
Burroughs Vatsyayana Crane
Curtis Tocqueville Verne
Homer Widger Tolstoy Whitman Gogol Vinci
Darwin Thoreau Busch
Potter Freud Zola Twain Scott
Kant Jowett Stevenson Lawrence Plato Harte
Andersen Dickens Burton Hesse
London Descartes
Poe Aristotle Wells Cervantes
Hale James Hastings Voltaire Cooke
Bunner Shakespeare Irving
Richter Chambers
Doré Swift Dante Chekhov da Shaw Wodehouse Benedict Pushkin Alcott
Newton

**tredition**®

tredition was established in 2006 by Sandra Latusseck and Soenke Schulz. Based in Hamburg, Germany, tredition offers publishing solutions to authors and publishing houses, combined with world-wide distribution of printed and digital book content. tredition is uniquely positioned to enable authors and publishing houses to create books on their own terms and without conventional manu-facturing risks.

For more information please visit: www.tredition.com

## TREDITION CLASSICS

This book is part of the TREDITION CLASSICS series. The creators of this series are united by passion for literature and driven by the intention of making all public domain books available in printed format again - worldwide. Most TREDITION CLASSICS titles have been out of print and off the bookstore shelves for decades. At tredi-tion we believe that a great book never goes out of style and that its value is eternal. Several mostly non-profit literature projects pro-vide content to tredition. To support their good work, tredition donates a portion of the proceeds from each sold copy. As a reader of a TREDITION CLASSICS book, you support our mission to save many of the amazing works of world literature from oblivion. See all available books at www.tredition.com.

 Project Gutenberg

The content for this book has been graciously provided by Project Gutenberg. Project Gutenberg is a non-profit organization founded by Michael Hart in 1971 at the University of Illinois. The mission of Project Gutenberg is simple: To encourage the creation and distribu-tion of eBooks. Project Gutenberg is the first and largest collection of public domain eBooks.

# An English Grammar

William Malone Baskervill

# Imprint

This book is part of TREDITION CLASSICS

Author: William Malone Baskervill
Cover design: Buchgut, Berlin – Germany

Publisher: tredition GmbH, Hamburg - Germany
ISBN: 978-3-8424-7476-5

www.tredition.com
www.tredition.de

# PREFACE.

Of making many English grammars there is no end; nor should there be till theoretical scholarship and actual practice are more happily wedded. In this field much valuable work has already been accomplished; but it has been done largely by workers accustomed to take the scholar's point of view, and their writings are addressed rather to trained minds than to immature learners. To find an advanced grammar unencumbered with hard words, abstruse thoughts, and difficult principles, is not altogether an easy matter. These things enhance the difficulty which an ordinary youth experiences in grasping and assimilating the facts of grammar, and create a distaste for the study. It is therefore the leading object of this book to be both as scholarly and as practical as possible. In it there is an attempt to present grammatical facts as simply, and to lead the student to assimilate them as thoroughly, as possible, and at the same time to do away with confusing difficulties as far as may be.

To attain these ends it is necessary to keep ever in the foreground the *real basis of grammar*; that is, good literature. Abundant quotations from standard authors have been given to show the student that he is dealing with the facts of the language, and not with the theories of grammarians. It is also suggested that in preparing written exercises the student use English classics instead of "making up" sentences. But it is not intended that the use of literary masterpieces for grammatical purposes should supplant or even interfere with their proper use and real value as works of art. It will, however, doubtless be found helpful to alternate the regular reading and æsthetic study of literature with a grammatical study, so that, while the mind is being enriched and the artistic sense quickened, there may also be the useful acquisition of arousing a keen observation of all grammatical forms and usages. Now and then it has been deemed best to omit explanations, and to withhold personal preferences, in order that the student may, by actual contact with the sources of grammatical laws, discover for himself the better way in regarding given data. It is not the grammarian's business to "correct:" it is simply to record and to arrange the usages of language, and to point the way to the arbiters of usage in all disputed cases.

Free expression within the lines of good usage should have widest range.

It has been our aim to make a grammar of as wide a scope as is consistent with the proper definition of the word. Therefore, in addition to recording and classifying the facts of language, we have endeavored to attain two other objects, — to cultivate mental skill and power, and to induce the student to prosecute further studies in this field. It is not supposable that in so delicate and difficult an undertaking there should be an entire freedom from errors and oversights. We shall gratefully accept any assistance in helping to correct mistakes.

Though endeavoring to get our material as much as possible at first hand, and to make an independent use of it, we desire to express our obligation to the following books and articles: —

Meiklejohn's "English Language," Longmans' "School Grammar," West's "English Grammar," Bain's "Higher English Grammar" and "Composition Grammar," Sweet's "Primer of Spoken English" and "New English Grammar," etc., Hodgson's "Errors in the Use of English," Morris's "Elementary Lessons in Historical English Grammar," Lounsbury's "English Language," Champney's "History of English," Emerson's "History of the English Language," Kellner's "Historical Outlines of English Syntax," Earle's "English Prose," and Matzner's "Englische Grammatik." Allen's "Subjunctive Mood in English," Battler's articles on "Prepositions" in the "Anglia," and many other valuable papers, have also been helpful and suggestive.

We desire to express special thanks to Professor W.D. Mooney of Wall & Mooney's Battle-Ground Academy, Franklin, Tenn., for a critical examination of the first draft of the manuscript, and to Professor Jno. M. Webb of Webb Bros. School, Bell Buckle, Tenn., and Professor W.R. Garrett of the University of Nashville, for many valuable suggestions and helpful criticism.

W.M. BASKERVILL.

J.W. SEWELL.

NASHVILLE, TENN., January, 1896.

# CONTENTS.

**PART III.**
*SYNTAX*

**INTRODUCTORY.**
**NOUNS.**
**PRONOUNS.**
**ADJECTIVES.**
**ARTICLES.**
**VERBS.**
**INDIRECT DISCOURSE.**
**VERBALS.**
**INFINITIVES.**
**ADVERBS.**
**CONJUNCTIONS.**
**PREPOSITIONS**

# INTRODUCTION.

So many slighting remarks have been made of late on the use of teaching grammar as compared with teaching science, that it is plain the fact has been lost sight of that grammar is itself a science. The object we have, or should have, in teaching science, is not to fill a child's mind with a vast number of facts that may or may not prove useful to him hereafter, but to draw out and exercise his powers of observation, and to show him how to make use of what he observes.... And here the teacher of grammar has a great advantage over the teacher of other sciences, in that the facts he has to call attention to lie ready at hand for every pupil to observe without the use of apparatus of any kind while the use of them also lies within the personal experience of every one. — Dr Richard Morris.

The proper study of a language is an intellectual discipline of the highest order. If I except discussions on the comparative merits of Popery and Protestantism, English grammar was the most important discipline of my boyhood. — John Tyndall.

## INTRODUCTION.

What various opinions writers on English grammar have given in answer to the question, *What is grammar?* may be shown by the following —

*Definitions of grammar.*

English grammar is a description of the usages of the English language by good speakers and writers of the present day. — Whitney

A description of account of the nature, build, constitution, or make of a language is called its grammar — Meiklejohn

Grammar teaches the laws of language, and the right method of using it in speaking and writing. — Patterson

Grammar is the science of *letter*; hence the science of using words correctly. — Abbott

The English word *grammar* relates only to the laws which govern the significant forms of words, and the construction of the sentence. — Richard Grant White

These are sufficient to suggest several distinct notions about English grammar—

*Synopsis of the above.*

(1) It makes rules to tell us how to use words.

(2) It is a record of usage which we ought to follow.

(3) It is concerned with the *forms* of the language.

(4) English *has* no grammar in the sense of forms, or inflections, but takes account merely of the nature and the uses of words in sentences.

*The older idea and its origin.*

Fierce discussions have raged over these opinions, and numerous works have been written to uphold the theories. The first of them remained popular for a very long time. It originated from the etymology of the word *grammar* (Greek *gramma*, writing, a letter), and from an effort to build up a treatise on English grammar by using classical grammar as a model.

Perhaps a combination of (1) and (3) has been still more popular, though there has been vastly more classification than there are forms.

*The opposite view.*

During recent years, (2) and (4) have been gaining ground, but they have had hard work to displace the older and more popular theories. It is insisted by many that the student's time should be used in studying general literature, and thus learning the fluent and correct use of his mother tongue. It is also insisted that the study and discussion of forms and inflections is an inexcusable imitation of classical treatises.

*The difficulty.*

Which view shall the student of English accept? Before this is answered, we should decide whether some one of the above theories must be taken as the right one, and the rest disregarded.

The real reason for the diversity of views is a confusion of two distinct things, — what the *definition* of grammar should be, and what the *purpose* of grammar should be.

### *The material of grammar.*

The province of English grammar is, rightly considered, wider than is indicated by any one of the above definitions; and the student ought to have a clear idea of the ground to be covered.

### *Few inflections.*

It must be admitted that the language has very few inflections at present, as compared with Latin or Greek; so that a small grammar will hold them all.

### *Making rules is risky.*

It is also evident, to those who have studied the language historically, that it is very hazardous to make rules in grammar: what is at present regarded as correct may not be so twenty years from now, even if our rules are founded on the keenest scrutiny of the "standard" writers of our time. Usage is varied as our way of thinking changes. In Chaucer's time two or three negatives were used to strengthen a negation; as, "Ther *nas no* man *nowher* so vertuous" (There never was no man nowhere so virtuous). And Shakespeare used good English when he said *more elder* ("Merchant of Venice") and *most unkindest* ("Julius Cæsar"); but this is bad English now.

If, however, we have tabulated the inflections of the language, and stated what syntax is the most used in certain troublesome places, there is still much for the grammarian to do.

### *A broader view.*

Surely our noble language, with its enormous vocabulary, its peculiar and abundant idioms, its numerous periphrastic forms to express every possible shade of meaning, is worthy of serious study, apart from the mere memorizing of inflections and formulation of rules.

### *Mental training. An æsthetic benefit.*

Grammar is eminently a means of mental training; and while it will train the student in subtle and acute reasoning, it will at the same time, if rightly presented, lay the foundation of a keen observation and a correct literary taste. The continued contact with the highest thoughts of the best minds will create a thirst for the "well of English undefiled."

*What grammar is.*

Coming back, then, from the question, *What ground should grammar cover?* we come to answer the question, *What should grammar teach?* and we give as an answer the definition, —

*English grammar is the science which treats of the nature of words, their forms, and their uses and relations in the sentence.*

*The work it will cover.*

This will take in the usual divisions, "The Parts of Speech" (with their inflections), "Analysis," and "Syntax." It will also require a discussion of any points that will clear up difficulties, assist the classification of kindred expressions, or draw the attention of the student to everyday idioms and phrases, and thus incite his observation.

*Authority as a basis.*

A few words here as to the *authority* upon which grammar rests.

*Literary English.*

The statements given will be substantiated by quotations from the leading or "standard" literature of modern times; that is, from the eighteenth century on. This *literary English* is considered the foundation on which grammar must rest.

*Spoken English.*

Here and there also will be quoted words and phrases from *spoken* or *colloquial English*, by which is meant the free, unstudied expressions of ordinary conversation and communication among intelligent people.

These quotations will often throw light on obscure constructions, since they preserve turns of expressions that have long since perished from the literary or standard English.

*Vulgar English.*

Occasionally, too, reference will be made to *vulgar English,* — the speech of the uneducated and ignorant, — which will serve to illustrate points of syntax once correct, or standard, but now undoubtedly bad grammar.

The following pages will cover, then, three divisions: —

Part I. The Parts of Speech, and Inflections.

Part II. Analysis of Sentences.

Part III. The Uses of Words, or Syntax.

# PART I.

# *THE PARTS OF SPEECH.*

## NOUNS.

**1.** In the more simple *state* of the *Arabs*, the *nation* is free, because each of her *sons* disdains a base *submission* to the *will* of a *master.* — Gibbon.

*Name words*

By examining this sentence we notice several words used as names. The plainest name is *Arabs*, which belongs to a people; but, besides this one, the words *sons* and *master* name objects, and may belong to any of those objects. The words *state, submission,* and *will* are evidently names of a different kind, as they stand for ideas, not objects; and the word *nation* stands for a whole group.

When the meaning of each of these words has once been understood, the word naming it will always call up the thing or idea itself. Such words are called **nouns**.

*Definition.*

**2.** A noun is a name word, representing directly to the mind an object, substance, or idea.

*Classes of nouns.*

**3.** Nouns are classified as follows: —

(1) **Proper.**

(2) **Common.** (a) CLASS NAMES: i. Individual.
ii. Collective.
(b) MATERIAL.

(3) **Abstract.** (a) ATTRIBUTE.
(b) VERBAL

*Names for special objects.*

**4.** A **proper noun** is a name applied to a particular object, whether person, place, or thing.

It specializes or limits the thing to which it is applied, reducing it to a narrow application. Thus, *city* is a word applied to any one of its kind; but *Chicago* names one city, and fixes the attention upon that particular city. *King* may be applied to any ruler of a kingdom, but *Alfred the Great* is the name of one king only.

The word *proper* is from a Latin word meaning *limited, belonging to one*. This does not imply, however, that a proper name can be applied to only one object, but that each time such a name is applied it is fixed or proper to that object. Even if there are several Bostons or Manchesters, the name of each is an individual or proper name.

*Name for any individual of a class.*

**5.** A **common noun** is a name possessed by *any* one of a class of persons, animals, or things.

*Common*, as here used, is from a Latin word which means *general, possessed by all*.

For instance, *road* is a word that names *any* highway outside of cities; *wagon* is a term that names *any* vehicle of a certain kind used for hauling: the words are of the widest application. We may say, *the man here*, or *the man in front of you*, but the word *man* is here hedged in by other words or word groups: the name itself is of general application.

*Name for a group or collection of objects.*

Besides considering persons, animals, and things separately, we may think of them in groups, and appropriate names to the groups.

Thus, men in groups may be called a *crowd*, or a *mob*, a *committee*, or a *council*, or a *congress*, etc.

These are called **COLLECTIVE NOUNS**. They properly belong under common nouns, because each group is considered as a unit, and the name applied to it belongs to any group of its class.

*Names for things thought of in mass.*

**6.** The definition given for common nouns applies more strictly to class nouns. It may, however, be correctly used for another group of nouns detailed below; for they are common nouns in the sense that the names apply to *every particle of similar substance*, instead of to each individual or separate object.

They are called **MATERIAL NOUNS**. Such are *glass, iron, clay, frost, rain, snow, wheat, wine, tea, sugar*, etc.

They may be placed in groups as follows: —

(1) The metals: *iron, gold, platinum*, etc.

(2) Products spoken of in bulk: *tea, sugar, rice, wheat*, etc.

(3) Geological bodies: *mud, sand, granite, rock, stone*, etc.

(4) Natural phenomena: *rain, dew, cloud, frost, mist*, etc.

(5) Various manufactures: *cloth* (and the different kinds of cloth), *potash, soap, rubber, paint, celluloid*, etc.

**7. NOTE.** — There are some nouns, such as *sun, moon, earth*, which seem to be the names of particular individual objects, but which are not called proper names.

*Words naturally of limited application not proper.*

The reason is, that in proper names the intention is *to exclude* all other individuals of the same class, and fasten a special name to the object considered, as in calling a city *Cincinnati*; but in the words *sun, earth*, etc., there is no such intention. If several bodies like the center of our solar system are known, they also are called *suns* by a natural extension of the term: so with the words *earth, world*, etc. They remain common class names.

*Names of ideas, not things.*

**8. Abstract nouns** are names of qualities, conditions, or actions, considered abstractly, or apart from their natural connection.

When we speak of a *wise man*, we recognize in him an attribute or quality. If we wish to think simply of that quality without describing the person, we speak of the *wisdom* of the man. The quality is still there as much as before, but it is taken merely as a name. So *poverty* would express the condition of a poor person; *proof* means the act of proving, or that which shows a thing has been proved; and so on.

Again, we may say, "*Painting* is a fine art," "*Learning* is hard to acquire," "a man of *understanding*."

**9.** There are two chief divisions of abstract nouns:—

(1) ATTRIBUTE NOUNS, expressing attributes or qualities.

(2) VERBAL NOUNS, expressing state, condition, or action.

*Attribute abstract nouns.*

**10.** The ATTRIBUTE ABSTRACT NOUNS are derived from adjectives and from common nouns. Thus, (1) *prudence* from *prudent, height* from *high, redness* from *red, stupidity* from *stupid,* etc.; (2) *peerage* from *peer, childhood* from *child, mastery* from *master, kingship* from *king,* etc.

*Verbal abstract nouns.*

**II.** The VERBAL ABSTRACT NOUNS Originate in verbs, as their name implies. They may be—

(1) Of the same form as the simple verb. The verb, by altering its function, is used as a noun; as in the expressions, "a long *run*" "a bold *move*," "a brisk *walk*."

(2) Derived from verbs by changing the ending or adding a suffix: *motion* from *move, speech* from *speak, theft* from *thieve, action* from *act, service* from *serve.*

*Caution.*

(3) Derived from verbs by adding -*ing* to the simple verb. It must be remembered that these words are *free from any verbal function.* They cannot govern a word, and they cannot *express* action, but are merely *names* of actions. They are only the husks of verbs, and are to be rigidly distinguished from *gerunds* (Secs. 272, 273).

To avoid difficulty, study carefully these examples:

The best thoughts and *sayings* of the Greeks; the moon caused fearful *forebodings*; in the *beginning* of his life; he spread his *blessings* over the land; the great Puritan *awakening*; our birth is but a sleep and a *forgetting*; a *wedding* or a festival; the rude *drawings* of the book; masterpieces of the Socratic *reasoning*; the *teachings* of the High Spirit; those opinions and *feelings*; there is time for such *reasonings*; the *well-being* of her subjects; her *longing* for their favor; *feelings* which their original *meaning* will by no means justify; the main *bearings* of this matter.

*Underived abstract nouns.*

**12.** Some abstract nouns were not derived from any other part of speech, but were framed directly for the expression of certain ideas or phenomena. Such are *beauty, joy, hope, ease, energy; day, night, summer, winter; shadow, lightning, thunder*, etc.

The adjectives or verbs corresponding to these are either themselves derived from the nouns or are totally different words; as *glad — joy, hopeful — hope*, etc.

**Exercises.**

1. From your reading bring up sentences containing ten common nouns, five proper, five abstract.

NOTE. — Remember that all sentences are to be *selected* from standard literature.

2. Under what class of nouns would you place (*a*) the names of diseases, as *pneumonia, pleurisy, catarrh, typhus, diphtheria*; (*b*) branches of knowledge, as *physics, algebra, geology, mathematics*?

3. Mention collective nouns that will embrace groups of each of the following individual nouns: —

- man
- horse
- bird
- fish
- partridge
- pupil
- bee
- soldier
- book

- sailor
- child
- sheep
- ship
- ruffian

4. Using a dictionary, tell from what word each of these abstract nouns is derived:—

- sight
- speech
- motion
- pleasure
- patience
- friendship
- deceit
- bravery
- height
- width
- wisdom
- regularity
- advice
- seizure
- nobility
- relief
- death
- raid
- honesty
- judgment
- belief
- occupation
- justice
- service
- trail
- feeling
- choice

- simplicity

## SPECIAL USES OF NOUNS.

*Nouns change by use.*

**13.** By being used so as to vary their usual meaning, nouns of one class may be made to approach another class, or to go over to it entirely. Since words alter their meaning so rapidly by a widening or narrowing of their application, we shall find numerous examples of this shifting from class to class; but most of them are in the following groups. For further discussion see the remarks on articles (p. 119).

*Proper names transferred to common use.*

**14. Proper nouns are used as common** in either of two ways: —

(1) *The origin of a thing is used for the thing itself*: that is, the name of the inventor may be applied to the thing invented, as a *davy*, meaning the miner's lamp invented by Sir Humphry Davy; the *guillotine*, from the name of Dr. Guillotin, who was its inventor. Or the name of the country or city from which an article is derived is used for the article: as *china*, from China; *arras*, from a town in France; *port* (wine), from Oporto, in Portugal; *levant* and *morocco* (leather).

Some of this class have become worn by use so that at present we can scarcely discover the derivation from the form of the word; for example, the word *port*, above. Others of similar character are *calico*, from Calicut; *damask*, from Damascus; *currants*, from Corinth; etc.

(2) *The name of a person or place noted for certain qualities is transferred to any person or place possessing those qualities*; thus, —

Hercules and Samson were noted for their strength, and we call a very strong man *a Hercules* or *a Samson*. Sodom was famous for wickedness, and a similar place is called *a Sodom* of sin.

*A Daniel* come to judgment! — Shakespeare.

If it prove a mind of uncommon activity and power, *a Locke, a Lavoisier, a Hutton, a Bentham, a Fourier*, it imposes its classification on other men, and lo! a new system. — Emerson.

*Names for things in bulk altered for separate portions.*

**15. Material nouns may be used as class names.** Instead of considering the whole body of material of which certain uses are made, one can speak of particular uses or phases of the substance; as—

(1) *Of individual objects* made from metals or other substances capable of being wrought into various shapes. We know a number of objects made of iron. The material *iron* embraces the metal contained in them all; but we may say, "The cook made the *irons* hot," referring to flat-irons; or, "The sailor was put in *irons*" meaning chains of iron. So also we may speak of *a glass* to drink from or to look into; *a steel* to whet a knife on; *a rubber* for erasing marks; and so on.

(2) *Of classes* or *kinds* of the same substance. These are the same in material, but differ in strength, purity, etc. Hence it shortens speech to make the nouns plural, and say *teas, tobaccos, paints, oils, candies, clays, coals.*

(3) *By poetical use*, of certain words necessarily singular in idea, which are made plural, or used as class nouns, as in the following:—

The lone and level *sands* stretch far away.


From all around—
Earth and her *waters*, and the depths of air—
Comes a still voice.
—Bryant.


Their airy ears
*The winds* have stationed on the mountain peaks.
—Percival.


(4) *Of detached portions* of matter used as class names; as *stones, slates, papers, tins, clouds, mists,* etc.

*Personification of abstract ideas.*

**16. Abstract nouns are frequently used as proper names** by being personified; that is, the ideas are spoken of as residing in living beings. This is a poetic usage, though not confined to verse.

> Next *Anger* rushed; his eyes, on fire,
> In lightnings owned his secret stings.
> — Collins.

*Freedom's* fame finds wings on every wind. — Byron.

*Death*, his mask melting like a nightmare dream, smiled. — Hayne.

*Traffic* has lain down to rest; and only *Vice* and *Misery*, to prowl or to moan like night birds, are abroad. — Carlyle.

*A halfway class of words. Class nouns in use, abstract in meaning.*

**17. Abstract nouns are made half abstract** by being spoken of in the plural.

They are not then pure abstract nouns, nor are they common class nouns. For example, examine this: —

The *arts* differ from the *sciences* in this, that their power is founded not merely on *facts* which can be communicated, but on *dispositions* which require to be created. — Ruskin.

When it is said that *art* differs from *science*, that the power of art is founded on *fact*, that *disposition* is the thing to be created, the words italicized are pure abstract nouns; but in case *an art* or *a science*, or *the arts* and *sciences*, be spoken of, the abstract idea is partly lost. The words preceded by the article *a*, or made plural, are still names of abstract ideas, not material things; but they widen the application to separate kinds of *art* or different branches of *science*. They are neither class nouns nor pure abstract nouns: they are more properly called *half abstract*.

Test this in the following sentences: —

Let us, if we must have great *actions*, make our own so. — Emerson.

And still, as each repeated *pleasure* tired, Succeeding *sports* the mirthful band inspired. — Goldsmith.

But ah! those *pleasures*, *loves*, and *joys*
Which I too keenly taste,
The Solitary can despise.
—Burns.


All these, however, were mere *terrors* of the night. —Irving.

*By ellipses, nouns used to modify.*

**18. Nouns used as descriptive terms.** Sometimes a noun is attached to another noun to add to its meaning, or describe it; for example, "a *family* quarrel," "a *New York* bank," "the *State Bank Tax* bill," "a *morning* walk."

It is evident that these approach very near to the function of adjectives. But it is better to consider them as nouns, for these reasons: they do not give up their identity as nouns; they do not express quality; they cannot be compared, as descriptive adjectives are.

They are more like the possessive noun, which belongs to another word, but is still a noun. They may be regarded as elliptical expressions, meaning a walk *in the morning*, a bank *in New York*, a bill *as to tax on the banks*, etc.

NOTE.—If the descriptive word be a *material* noun, it may be regarded as changed to an adjective. The term "*gold* pen" conveys the same idea as "*golden* pen," which contains a pure adjective.

### WORDS AND WORD GROUPS USED AS NOUNS.

*The noun may borrow from any part of speech, or from any expression.*

**19.** Owing to the scarcity of distinctive forms, and to the consequent flexibility of English speech, words which are usually other parts of speech are often used as nouns; and various word groups may take the place of nouns by being used as nouns.

*Adjectives, Conjunctions, Adverbs.*

(1) *Other parts of speech* used as nouns:—

*The great*, *the wealthy*, fear thy blow. —Burns.

Every *why* hath a *wherefore*. —Shakespeare.

When I was young? Ah, woeful *When*!
Ah! for the change 'twixt *Now* and *Then*!
— Coleridge.

(2) *Certain word groups* used like single nouns: —

*Too swift* arrives as tardy as *too slow*. —Shakespeare.

Then comes the *"Why, sir!"* and the *"What then, sir?"* and the *"No, sir!"* and the *"You don't see your way through the question, sir!"* — Macaulay

(3) Any part of speech may be considered merely as a word, without reference to its function in the sentence; also titles of books are treated as simple nouns.

The *it*, at the beginning, is ambiguous, whether it mean the sun or the cold. — Dr BLAIR

In this definition, is the word *"just,"* or *"legal,"* finally to stand? — Ruskin.

There was also a book of Defoe's called an *"Essay on Projects,"* and another of Dr. Mather's called *"Essays to do Good."* — B. FRANKLIN.

*Caution.*

**20.** It is to be remembered, however, that the above cases are shiftings of the *use*, of words rather than of their *meaning*. We seldom find instances of complete conversion of one part of speech into another.

When, in a sentence above, the terms *the great, the wealthy*, are used, they are not names only: we have in mind the idea of persons and the quality of being *great* or *wealthy*. The words are used in the sentence where nouns are used, but have an adjectival meaning.

In the other sentences, *why* and *wherefore, When, Now*, and *Then*, are spoken of as if pure nouns; but still the reader considers this not a natural application of them as name words, but as a figure of speech.

NOTE. — These remarks do not apply, of course, to such words as become pure nouns by use. There are many of these. The adjective *good* has no claim on the noun *goods*; so, too, in speaking of the *principal* of a school, or a state *secret*, or a faithful *domestic*, or a *criminal*, etc., the words are entirely independent of any adjective force.

**Exercise.**

Pick out the nouns in the following sentences, and tell to which class each belongs. Notice if any have shifted from one class to another.

1. Hope springs eternal in the human breast.

2. Heaven from all creatures hides the book of Fate.

3.

Stone walls do not a prison make.
Nor iron bars a cage.

4. Truth-teller was our England's Alfred named.

5. A great deal of talent is lost to the world for want of a little courage.

6.

Power laid his rod aside,
And Ceremony doff'd her pride.

7. She sweeps it through the court with troops of ladies.

8. Learning, that cobweb of the brain.

9.

A little weeping would ease my heart;
But in their briny bed
My tears must stop, for every drop
Hinders needle and thread.

10. A fool speaks all his mind, but a wise man reserves something for hereafter.

11. Knowledge is proud that he has learned so much; Wisdom is humble that he knows no more.

12. Music hath charms to soothe the savage breast.

13.

> And see, he cried, the welcome,
> Fair guests, that waits you here.

14. The fleet, shattered and disabled, returned to Spain.

15. One To-day is worth two To-morrows.

16. Vessels carrying coal are constantly moving.

17.

> Some mute inglorious Milton here may rest,
> Some Cromwell guiltless of his country's blood.

18. And oft we trod a waste of pearly sands.

19.

> A man he seems of cheerful yesterdays
> And confident to-morrows.

20. The hours glide by; the silver moon is gone.

21. Her robes of silk and velvet came from over the sea.

22. My soldier cousin was once only a drummer boy.

23.

But pleasures are like poppies spread,
You seize the flower, its bloom is shed.


24. All that thou canst call thine own Lies in thy To-day.

# INFLECTIONS OF NOUNS.

# GENDER.

**21.** In Latin, Greek, German, and many other languages, some general rules are given that names of male beings are usually masculine, and names of females are usually feminine. There are exceptions even to this general statement, but not so in English. Male beings are, in English grammar, always masculine; female, always feminine.

When, however, *inanimate* things are spoken of, these languages are totally unlike our own in determining the gender of words. For instance: in Latin, *hortus* (garden) is masculine, *mensa* (table) is feminine, *corpus* (body) is neuter; in German, *das Messer* (knife) is neuter, *der Tisch* (table) is masculine, *die Gabel* (fork) is feminine.

The great difference is, that in English the gender follows the *meaning* of the word, in other languages gender follows the *form*; that is, in English, gender depends on *sex*: if a thing spoken of is of the male sex, the *name* of it is masculine; if of the female sex, the *name* of it is feminine. Hence:

*Definition.*

**22. Gender** is the mode of distinguishing sex by words, or additions to words.

**23.** It is evident from this that English can have but two genders, — **masculine** and **feminine**.

*Gender nouns. Neuter nouns.*

All nouns, then, must be divided into two principal classes, — **gender nouns**, those distinguishing the sex of the object; and **neuter nouns**, those which do not distinguish sex, or names of things without life, and consequently without sex.

Gender nouns include names of persons and some names of animals; neuter nouns include some animals and all inanimate objects.

*Some words either gender or neuter nouns, according to use.*

**24.** Some words may be either gender nouns or neuter nouns, according to their use. Thus, the word *child* is neuter in the sentence, "A little *child* shall lead them," but is masculine in the sentence from Wordsworth, —

> I have seen
> A curious *child* ... applying to *his* ear
> The convolutions of a smooth-lipped shell.

Of animals, those with which man comes in contact often, or which arouse his interest most, are named by gender nouns, as in these sentences: —

Before the barn door strutted the gallant *cock*, that pattern of a husband, ... clapping *his* burnished wings. — Irving.

*Gunpowder* ... came to a stand just by the bridge, with a suddenness that had nearly sent *his* rider sprawling over *his* head — *Id.*

Other animals are not distinguished as to sex, but are spoken of as neuter, the sex being of no consequence.

Not a *turkey* but he [Ichabod] beheld daintily trussed up, with *its* gizzard under *its* wing. — Irving.

He next stooped down to feel the *pig*, if there were any signs of life in *it*. — Lamb.

*No "common gender."*

**25.** According to the definition, there can be no such thing as "common gender:" words either distinguish sex (or the sex is distinguished by the context) or else they do not distinguish sex.

If such words as *parent, servant, teacher, ruler, relative, cousin, domestic*, etc., do not show the sex to which the persons belong, they are neuter words.

**26.** Put in convenient form, the division of words according to sex, or the lack of it, is, —

(MASCULINE: Male beings.
**Gender nouns** {
(FEMININE: Female beings.

**Neuter nouns:** Names of inanimate things, or of living beings whose sex cannot be determined.

**27.** The inflections for gender belong, of course, only to masculine and feminine nouns. *Forms* would be a more accurate word than *inflections*, since inflection applies only to the *case* of nouns.

There are three ways to distinguish the genders: —

(1) By prefixing a gender word to another word.

(2) By adding a suffix, generally to a masculine word.

(3) By using a different word for each gender.

# I. Gender shown by Prefixes.

*Very few of class I.*

**28.** Usually the gender words *he* and *she* are prefixed to neuter words; as *he-goat—she-goat, cock sparrow—hen sparrow, he-bear—she-bear*.

One feminine, *woman*, puts a prefix before the masculine *man*. *Woman* is a short way of writing *wifeman*.

## II. Gender shown by Suffixes.

**29.** By far the largest number of gender words are those marked by suffixes. In this particular the native endings have been largely supplanted by foreign suffixes.

*Native suffixes.*

The **native suffixes** to indicate the feminine were *-en* and *-ster*. These remain in *vixen* and *spinster*, though both words have lost their original meanings.

The word *vixen* was once used as the feminine of *fox* by the Southern-English. For *fox* they said *vox*; for *from* they said *vram*; and for the older word *fat* they said *vat*, as in *wine vat*. Hence *vixen* is for *fyxen*, from the masculine *fox*.

*Spinster* is a relic of a large class of words that existed in Old and Middle English, [1] but have now lost their original force as feminines. The old masculine answering to *spinster* was *spinner*; but *spinster* has now no connection with it.

The **foreign suffixes** are of two kinds: —

*Foreign suffixes. Unaltered and little used.*

(1) Those belonging to borrowed words, as *czarina, señorita, executrix, donna*. These are attached to foreign words, and are never used for words recognized as English.

*Slightly changed and widely used.*

(2) That regarded as the standard or regular termination of the feminine, *-ess* (French *esse*, Low Latin *issa*), the one most used. The corresponding masculine may have the ending *-er (-or)*, but in most cases it has not. Whenever we adopt a new masculine word, the feminine is formed by adding this termination *-ess*.

Sometimes the *-ess* has been added to a word already feminine by the ending *-ster*; as *seam-str-ess, song-str-ess*. The ending *-ster* had then lost its force as a feminine suffix; it has none now in the words *huckster, gamester, trickster, punster*.

*Ending of masculine not changed.*

**30.** The ending *-ess* is added to many words without changing the ending of the masculine; as, —

- baron — baroness
- count — countess
- lion — lioness
- Jew — Jewess
- heir — heiress
- host — hostess
- priest — priestess
- giant — giantess

*Masculine ending dropped.*

The masculine ending may be dropped before the feminine *-ess* is added; as, —

- abbot — abbess
- negro — negress
- murderer — murderess
- sorcerer — sorceress

*Vowel dropped before adding* -ess.

The feminine may discard a vowel which appears in the masculine; as in —

- actor — actress
- master — mistress
- benefactor — benefactress
- emperor — empress
- tiger — tigress
- enchanter — enchantress

*Empress* has been cut down from *emperice* (twelfth century) and *emperesse* (thirteenth century), from Latin *imperatricem*.

*Master* and *mistress* were in Middle English *maister — maistresse*, from the Old French *maistre — maistresse*.

**31.** When the older *-en* and *-ster* went out of use as the distinctive mark of the feminine, the ending *-ess*, from the French *-esse*, sprang into a popularity much greater than at present.

*Ending* -ess *less used now than formerly.*

Instead of saying *doctress, fosteress, wagoness*, as was said in the sixteenth century, or *servauntesse, teacheresse, neighboresse, frendesse*, as in the fourteenth century, we have dispensed with the ending in many cases, and either use a prefix word or leave the masculine to do work for the feminine also.

Thus, we say *doctor* (masculine and feminine) or *woman doctor, teacher* or *lady teacher, neighbor* (masculine and feminine), etc. We frequently use such words as *author, editor, chairman*, to represent persons of either sex.

NOTE. — There is perhaps this distinction observed: when we speak of a female *as an active agent* merely, we use the masculine termination, as, "George Eliot is the *author* of 'Adam Bede;'" but when we speak purposely *to denote a distinction from a male*, we use the feminine, as, "George Eliot is an eminent *authoress*."

# III. Gender shown by Different Words.

**32.** In some of these pairs, the feminine and the masculine are entirely different words; others have in their origin the same root. Some of them have an interesting history, and will be noted below: —

- bachelor — maid
- boy — girl
- brother — sister
- drake — duck
- earl — countess
- father — mother
- gander — goose
- hart — roe
- horse — mare
- husband — wife
- king — queen
- lord — lady
- wizard — witch
- nephew — niece
- ram — ewe
- sir — madam
- son — daughter
- uncle — aunt
- bull — cow
- boar — sow

**Girl** originally meant a child of either sex, and was used for male or female until about the fifteenth century.

**Drake** is peculiar in that it is formed from a corresponding feminine which is no longer used. It is not connected historically with our word *duck*, but is derived from *ened* (duck) and an obsolete suffix *rake* (king). Three letters of *ened* have fallen away, leaving our word *drake*.

**Gander** and **goose** were originally from the same root word. *Goose* has various cognate forms in the languages akin to English (German *Gans*, Icelandic *gás*, Danish *gaas*, etc.). The masculine was formed by adding *-a*, the old sign of the masculine. This *gansa* was modified into *gan-ra*, *gand-ra*, finally *gander*; the *d* being inserted to make pronunciation easy, as in many other words.

**Mare**, in Old English *mere*, had the masculine *mearh* (horse), but this has long been obsolete.

**Husband** and **wife** are not connected in origin. *Husband* is a Scandinavian word (Anglo-Saxon *hūsbonda* from Icelandic *hús-bóndi*, probably meaning house dweller); *wife* was used in Old and Middle English to mean woman in general.

**King** and **queen** are said by some (Skeat, among others) to be from the same root word, but the German etymologist Kluge says they are not.

**Lord** is said to be a worn-down form of the Old English *hlāf-weard* (loaf keeper), written *loverd*, *lhauerd*, or *lauerd* in Middle English. **Lady** is from *hlæfdige* (*hlæf* meaning loaf, and *dige* being of uncertain origin and meaning).

**Witch** is the Old English *wicce*, but **wizard** is from the Old French *guiscart* (prudent), not immediately connected with *witch*, though both are ultimately from the same root.

**Sir** is worn down from the Old French *sire* (Latin *senior*). **Madam** is the French *ma dame*, from Latin *mea domina*.

*Two masculines from feminines.*

**33.** Besides *gander* and *drake*, there are two other masculine words that were formed from the feminine: —

**Bridegroom,** from Old English *brȳd-guma* (bride's man). The *r* in *groom* has crept in from confusion with the word *groom*.

**Widower,** from the weakening of the ending *-a* in Old English to *-e* in Middle English. The older forms, *widuwa — widuwe*, became identical, and a new masculine ending was therefore added to distinguish the masculine from the feminine (compare Middle English *widuer — widewe*).

# Personification.

**34.** Just as abstract ideas are personified (Sec. 16), material objects may be spoken of like gender nouns; for example, —

"Now, where the swift *Rhone* cleaves *his* way."
—Byron.

The *Sun* now rose upon the right:
Out of the sea came *he*.
—Coleridge.

And haply the *Queen Moon* is on *her* throne,
Clustered around by all her starry Fays.
—Keats.

*Britannia* needs no bulwarks,
No towers along the steep;
*Her* march is o'er the mountain waves,
*Her* home is on the deep.
—Campbell.

This is not exclusively a poetic use. In ordinary speech personification is very frequent: the pilot speaks of his boat as feminine; the engineer speaks so of his engine; etc.

*Effect of personification.*

In such cases the gender is marked by the pronoun, and not by the form of the noun. But the fact that in English the distinction of gender is confined to difference of sex makes these departures more effective.

# NUMBER.

*Definition.*

**35.** In nouns, number means the mode of indicating whether we are speaking of one thing or of more than one.

**36.** Our language has two numbers, — *singular* and *plural*. The singular number denotes that one thing is spoken of; the plural, more than one.

**37.** There are three ways of changing the singular form to the plural: —

(1) By adding *-en.*

(2) By changing the root vowel.

(3) By adding *-s* (or *-es*).

The first two methods prevailed, together with the third, in Old English, but in modern English *-s* or *-es* has come to be the "standard" ending; that is, whenever we adopt a new word, we make its plural by adding *-s* or *-es.*

# I. Plurals formed by the Suffix -*en*.

*The* -en *inflection.*

**38.** This inflection remains only in the word **oxen**, though it was quite common in Old and Middle English; for instance, *eyen* (eyes), *treen* (trees), *shoon* (shoes), which last is still used in Lowland Scotch. *Hosen* is found in the King James version of the Bible, and *housen* is still common in the provincial speech in England.

**39.** But other words were inflected afterwards, in imitation of the old words in -*en* by making a double plural.

-En *inflection imitated by other words.*

**Brethren** has passed through three stages. The old plural was *brothru*, then *brothre* or *brethre*, finally *brethren*. The weakening of inflections led to this addition.

**Children** has passed through the same history, though the intermediate form *childer* lasted till the seventeenth century in literary English, and is still found in dialects; as, —

"God bless me! so then, after all, you'll have a chance to see your *childer* get up like, and get settled." — Quoted By De Quincey.

**Kine** is another double plural, but has now no singular.

In spite of wandering *kine* and other adverse circumstance. — Thoreau.

## II. Plurals formed by Vowel Change.

**40.** Examples of this inflection are, —

- man — men
- foot — feet
- goose — geese
- louse — lice
- mouse — mice
- tooth — teeth

Some other words — as *book, turf, wight, borough* — formerly had the same inflection, but they now add the ending *-s*.

**41.** Akin to this class are some words, originally neuter, that have the singular and plural alike; such as *deer, sheep, swine*, etc.

Other words following the same usage are, *pair, brace, dozen*, after numerals (if not after numerals, or if preceded by the prepositions *in, by*, etc, they add *-s*): also *trout, salmon; head, sail; cannon; heathen, folk, people*.

The words *horse* and *foot*, when they mean soldiery, retain the same form for plural meaning; as, —

> The *foot* are fourscore thousand,
> The *horse* are thousands ten.
> — Macaulay.

> Lee marched over the mountain wall, —
> Over the mountains winding down,
> *Horse* and *foot*, into Frederick town.
> — Whittier.

# III. Plurals formed by Adding -s or -es.

**42.** Instead of *-s*, the ending *-es* is added —

(1) If a word ends in a letter which cannot add *-s* and be pronounced. Such are *box, cross, ditch, glass, lens, quartz*, etc.

*-Es added in certain cases.*

If the word ends in a *sound* which cannot add *-s*, a new syllable is made; as, *niche — niches, race — races, house — houses, prize — prizes, chaise — chaises*, etc.

*-Es* is also added to a few words ending in *-o*, though this sound combines readily with *-s*, and does not make an extra syllable: *cargo — cargoes, negro — negroes, hero — heroes, volcano — volcanoes*, etc.

Usage differs somewhat in other words of this class, some adding *-s*, and some *-es*.

(2) If a word ends in *-y* preceded by a consonant (the *y* being then changed to *i*); e.g., *fancies, allies, daisies, fairies*.

*Words in -ies.*

Formerly, however, these words ended in *-ie*, and the real ending is therefore *-s*. Notice these from Chaucer (fourteenth century): —

*Their old form.*

> The *lilie* on hir stalke grene.
> Of *maladie* the which he hadde endured.

And these from Spenser (sixteenth century): —

> Be well aware, quoth then that *ladie* milde.
> At last fair Hesperus in highest *skie*
> Had spent his lampe.

(3) In the case of some **words ending in *-f* or *-fe*** , which have the plural in *-ves*: *calf — calves, half — halves, knife — knives, shelf — shelves,* etc.

# Special Lists.

**43. Material nouns** and **abstract nouns** are always singular. When such words take a plural ending, they lose their identity, and go over to other classes (Secs. 15 and 17).

**44. Proper nouns** are regularly singular, but may be made plural when we wish to speak of several persons or things bearing the same name; e.g., *the Washingtons, the Americas.*

**45.** Some words are **usually singular**, though they are plural in form. Examples of these are, *optics, economics, physics, mathematics, politics,* and many branches of learning; also *news, pains* (care), *molasses, summons, means*: as, —

*Politics,* in its widest extent, is both the science and the art of government. — *Century Dictionary.*

So live, that when thy *summons comes,* etc. — Bryant.

It served simply as *a means* of sight. — Prof. Dana.

Means *plural.*

Two words, **means** and **politics**, *may be plural* in their construction with verbs and adjectives: —

Words, by strongly conveying the passions, by *those means* which we have already mentioned, fully compensate for their weakness in other respects. — Burke.

With great dexterity *these means* were now applied. — Motley.

By *these means,* I say, riches will accumulate. — Goldsmith.

Politics *plural.*

Cultivating a feeling that *politics* are tiresome. — G. W. Curtis.

The *politics* in which he took the keenest interest *were politics* scarcely deserving of the name. — Macaulay.

Now I read all the *politics* that *come* out. — Goldsmith.

**46.** Some words have **no corresponding singular**.

- aborigines
- amends
- annals
- assets
- antipodes
- scissors
- thanks
- spectacles
- vespers
- victuals
- matins
- nuptials
- oats
- obsequies
- premises
- bellows
- billiards
- dregs
- gallows
- tongs

*Occasionally singular words.*

Sometimes, however, a few of these words have the construction of singular nouns. Notice the following: —

They cannot get on without each other any more than one blade of *a scissors* can cut without the other. — J. L. Laughlin.

A relic which, if I recollect right, he pronounced to have been *a tongs*. — Irving.

Besides this, it is furnished with *a forceps*. — Goldsmith.

The air, — was it subdued when...the wind was trained only to turn a windmill, carry off chaff, or work in *a bellows*? — Prof. Dana.

In Early Modern English *thank* is found.

What *thank* have ye? — *Bible*

**47.** Three words were *originally singular*, the present ending *-s* not being really a plural inflection, but they are regularly construed as plural: *alms, eaves, riches*.

*two plurals.*

**48.** A few nouns have **two plurals** differing in meaning.

- brother — brothers (by blood), brethren (of a society or church).
- cloth — cloths (kinds of cloth), clothes (garments).
- die — dies (stamps for coins, etc.), dice (for gaming).
- fish — fish (collectively), fishes (individuals or kinds).
- genius — geniuses (men of genius), genii (spirits).
- index — indexes (to books), indices (signs in algebra).
- pea — peas (separately), pease (collectively).
- penny — pennies (separately), pence (collectively).
- shot — shot (collective balls), shots (number of times fired).

In speaking of coins, *twopence, sixpence*, etc., may add *-s*, making a double plural, as two *sixpences*.

*One plural, two meanings.*

**49.** Other words have **one plural form with two meanings**, — one corresponding to the singular, the other unlike it.

- custom — customs: (1) habits, ways; (2) revenue duties.
- letter — letters: (1) the alphabet, or epistles; (2) literature.
- number — numbers: (1) figures; (2) poetry, as in the lines, —

I lisped in *numbers*, for the numbers came.
— Pope.


Tell me not, in mournful *numbers*.
— Longfellow.

*Numbers* also means issues, or copies, of a periodical.

- pain — pains: (1) suffering; (2) care, trouble,
- part — parts: (1) divisions; (2) abilities, faculties.

*Two classes of compound words.*

**50. Compound words** may be divided into two classes: —

(1) *Those whose parts are so closely joined as to constitute one word.* These make the last part plural.

- courtyard
- dormouse
- Englishman
- fellow-servant
- fisherman
- Frenchman
- forget-me-not
- goosequill
- handful
- mouthful
- cupful
- maidservant
- pianoforte
- stepson
- spoonful
- titmouse

(2) *Those groups in which the first part is the principal one, followed by a word or phrase making a modifier.* The chief member adds *-s* in the plural.

- aid-de-camp
- attorney at law
- billet-doux
- commander in chief

- court-martial
- cousin-german
- father-in-law
- knight-errant
- hanger-on

NOTE. — Some words ending in -*man* are not compounds of the English word *man*, but add -*s*; such as *talisman, firman, Brahman, German, Norman, Mussulman, Ottoman.*

**51.** Some groups pluralize both parts of the group; as *man singer, manservant, woman servant, woman singer.*

*Two methods in use for names with titles.*

**52.** As to plurals of **names with titles**, there is some disagreement among English writers. The title may be plural, as *the Messrs. Allen, the Drs. Brown, the Misses Rich*; or the name may be pluralized.

The former is perhaps more common in present-day use, though the latter is often found; for example, —

Then came Mr. and Mrs. Briggs, and then *the three Miss Spinneys*, then Silas Peckham. — Dr. Holmes.

Our immortal Fielding was of the younger branch of the *Earls of Denbigh*, who drew their origin from the *Counts of Hapsburgh*. — Gibbon.

The *Miss Flamboroughs* were reckoned the best dancers in the parish. — Goldsmith.

The *Misses Nettengall's* young ladies come to the Cathedral too. — Dickens.

The *Messrs. Harper* have done the more than generous thing by Mr. Du Maurier. — *The Critic.*

**53.** A number of **foreign words** have been adopted into English without change of form. These are said to be *domesticated,* and retain their foreign plurals.

Others have been adopted, and by long use have altered their power so as to conform to English words. They are then said to be *naturalized,* or *Anglicized,* or *Englished.*

*Domesticated words.*

The domesticated words may retain the original plural. Some of them have a secondary English plural in *-s* or *-es*.

**Exercise.**

Find in the dictionary the plurals of these words: —

I. FROM THE LATIN.

- apparatus
- appendix
- axis
- datum
- erratum
- focus
- formula
- genus
- larva
- medium
- memorandum
- nebula
- radius
- series
- species
- stratum
- terminus
- vertex

II. FROM THE GREEK.

- analysis
- antithesis
- automaton
- basis
- crisis
- ellipsis

- hypothesis
- parenthesis
- phenomenon
- thesis

*Anglicized words.*

When the foreign words are fully naturalized, they form their plurals in the regular way; as, —

- bandits
- cherubs
- dogmas
- encomiums
- enigmas
- focuses
- formulas
- geniuses
- herbariums
- indexes
- seraphs
- apexes

*Usage varies in plurals of letters, figures, etc.*

**54. Letters, figures, etc.,** form their plurals by adding *-s* or *'s*. Words quoted merely as words, without reference to their meaning, also add *-s* or *'s*; as, "His *9's* (or *9s*) look like *7's* (or *7s*)," "Avoid using too many *and's* (or *ands*)," "Change the *+'s* (or *+s*) to *-'s* (or *-s*)."

# CASE.

*Definition.*

**55.** Case is an inflection or use of a noun (or pronoun) to show its relation to other words in the sentence.

In the sentence, "He sleeps in a felon's cell," the word *felon's* modifies *cell*, and expresses a relation akin to possession; *cell* has another relation, helping to express the idea of place with the word *in*.

**56.** In the general wearing-away of inflections, the number of case forms has been greatly reduced.

*Only two* case forms.

There are now only two case forms of English nouns, — one for the *nominative* and *objective*, one for the *possessive*: consequently the matter of inflection is a very easy thing to handle in learning about cases.

*Reasons for speaking of* three cases *of nouns.*

But there are reasons why grammars treat of *three* cases of nouns when there are only two forms: —

(1) Because the relations of all words, whether inflected or not, must be understood for purposes of analysis.

(2) Because pronouns still have three case forms as well as three case relations.

**57.** Nouns, then, may be said to have three cases, — the **nominative**, the **objective**, and the **possessive**.

# I. Uses of the Nominative.

**58.** The nominative case is used as follows: —

(1) *As the subject of a verb*: "*Water* seeks its level."

(2) *As a predicate noun*, completing a verb, and referring to or explaining the subject: "A bent twig makes a crooked *tree*."

(3) *In apposition* with some other nominative word, adding to the meaning of that word: "The reaper *Death* with his sickle keen."

(4) *In direct address*: "*Lord Angus*, thou hast lied!"

(5) *With a participle in an absolute or independent phrase* (there is some discussion whether this is a true nominative): "The *work* done, they returned to their homes."

(6) *With an infinitive in exclamations*: "*David* to die!"

### Exercise.

Pick out the nouns in the nominative case, and tell which use of the nominative each one has.

> 1. Moderate lamentation is the right of the dead; excessive grief, the enemy of the living.
>
> 2.
>
>> Excuses are clothes which, when asked unawares,
>> Good Breeding to naked Necessity spares.
>
> 3. Human experience is the great test of truth.
>
> 4. Cheerfulness and content are great beautifiers.
>
> 5. Three properties belong to wisdom, — nature, learning, and experience; three things characterize man, — person, fate, and merit.
>
> 6.

But of all plagues, good Heaven, thy wrath can send,
Save, save, oh save me from the candid friend!


7. Conscience, her first law broken, wounded lies.

8. They charged, sword in hand and visor down.

9.

O sleep! O gentle sleep!
Nature's soft nurse, how have I frighted thee?

# II. Uses of the Objective.

**59.** The objective case is used as follows: —

(1) *As the direct object of a verb*, naming the person or thing directly receiving the action of the verb: "Woodman, spare that *tree!*"

(2) *As the indirect object of a verb*, naming the person or thing indirectly affected by the action of the verb: "Give the *devil* his due."

(3) *Adverbially*, defining the action of a verb by denoting *time, measure, distance,* etc. (in the older stages of the language, this took the regular accusative inflection): "Full *fathom* five thy father lies;" "Cowards die many *times* before their deaths."

(4) *As the second object*, completing the verb, and thus becoming part of the predicate in acting upon an object: "Time makes the worst enemies *friends*;" "Thou makest the storm a *calm*." In these sentences the real predicates are *makes friends*, taking the object *enemies*, and being equivalent to one verb, *reconciles*; and *makest a calm*, taking the object *storm*, and meaning calmest. This is also called the *predicate objective* or the *factitive object*.

(5) *As the object of a preposition*, the word toward which the preposition points, and which it joins to another word: "He must have a long spoon that would eat with the *devil*."

The preposition sometimes takes the *possessive* case of a noun, as will be seen in Sec. 68.

(6) *In apposition with another objective*: "The opinions of this junto were completely controlled by Nicholas Vedder, a *patriarch* of the village, and *landlord* of the inn."

### Exercise.

Point out the nouns in the objective case in these sentences, and tell which use each has: —

    1. Tender men sometimes have strong wills.

    2. Necessity is the certain connection between cause and effect.

3. Set a high price on your leisure moments; they are sands of precious gold.

4. But the flood came howling one day.

5. I found the urchin Cupid sleeping.

6. Five times every year he was to be exposed in the pillory.

7. The noblest mind the best contentment has.

8. Multitudes came every summer to visit that famous natural curiosity, the Great Stone Face.

9.

> And whirling plate, and forfeits paid,
> His winter task a pastime made.

10.

> He broke the ice on the streamlet's brink,
> And gave the leper to eat and drink.

# III. Uses of the Possessive.

**60.** The possessive case always modifies another word, expressed or understood. There are three forms of possessive showing how a word is related in sense to the modified word: —

(1) *Appositional possessive*, as in these expressions, —

The blind old man of *Scio's* rocky isle. — Byron.

Beside a pumice isle in *Baiæ's* bay. — Shelley.

In these sentences the phrases are equivalent to *of the rocky isle [of] Scio*, and *in the bay [of] Baiæ*, the possessive being really equivalent here to an appositional objective. It is a poetic expression, the equivalent phrase being used in prose.

(2) *Objective possessive*, as shown in the sentences, —

Ann Turner had taught her the secret before this last good lady had been hanged for *Sir Thomas Overbury's* murder. — Hawthorne.

He passes to-day in building an air castle for to-morrow, or in writing *yesterday's* elegy. — Thackeray

In these the possessives are equivalent to an objective after a verbal expression: as, *for murdering Sir Thomas Overbury*; *an elegy to commemorate yesterday*. For this reason the use of the possessive here is called objective.

(3) *Subjective possessive*, the most common of all; as, —

> The unwearied sun, from day to day,
> Does his Creator's power display.
> — Addison.

If this were expanded into *the power which his Creator possesses*, the word *Creator* would be the subject of the verb: hence it is called a subjective possessive.

**61.** This last-named possessive expresses a variety of relations. *Possession* in some sense is the most common. The kind of relation may usually be found by expanding the possessive into an equivalent phrase: for example, "*Winter's* rude tempests are gathering now" (i.e., tempests that winter is likely to have); "His beard was of *several days'* growth" (i.e., growth which several days had developed); "The *forest's* leaping panther shall yield his spotted hide" (i.e., the panther which the forest hides); "Whoso sheddeth *man's* blood" (blood that man possesses).

*How the possessive is formed.*

**62.** As said before (Sec. 56), there are only two case forms. One is the simple form of a word, expressing the relations of nominative and objective; the other is formed by adding *'s* to the simple form, making the possessive singular. To form the possessive plural, only the apostrophe is added if the plural nominative ends in -*s*; the *'s* is added if the plural nominative does not end in -*s*.

# Case Inflection.

*Declension or inflection of nouns.*

**63.** The full declension of nouns is as follows:—

|  | SINGULAR. | PLURAL. |
|---|---|---|
| 1. *Nom. and Obj.* | lady | ladies |
| *Poss.* | lady's | ladies' |
| 2. *Nom. and Obj.* | child | children |
| *Poss.* | child's | children's |

*A suggestion.*

NOTE.—The difficulty that some students have in writing the possessive plural would be lessened if they would remember there are two steps to be taken:—

(1) Form the nominative plural according to Secs 39-53

(2) Follow the rule given in Sec. 62.

# Special Remarks on the Possessive Case.

*Origin of the possessive with its apostrophe.*

**64.** In Old English a large number of words had in the genitive case singular the ending *-es*; in Middle English still more words took this ending: for example, in Chaucer, "From every *schires* ende," "Full worthi was he in his *lordes* werre [war]," "at his *beddes* syde," "*mannes* herte [heart]," etc.

*A false theory.*

By the end of the seventeenth century the present way of indicating the possessive had become general. The use of the apostrophe, however, was not then regarded as standing for the omitted vowel of the genitive (as *lord's* for *lordes*): by a false theory the ending was thought to be a contraction of *his*, as schoolboys sometimes write, "George Jones *his* book."

*Use of the apostrophe.*

Though this opinion was untrue, the apostrophe has proved a great convenience, since otherwise words with a plural in -*s* would have three forms alike. To the eye all the forms are now distinct, but to the ear all may be alike, and the connection must tell us what form is intended.

The use of the apostrophe in the plural also began in the seventeenth century, from thinking that *s* was not a possessive sign, and from a desire to have distinct forms.

*Sometimes s is left out in the possessive singular.*

**65.** Occasionally the *s* is dropped in the possessive singular if the word ends in a hissing sound and another hissing sound follows, but the apostrophe remains to mark the possessive; as, *for goodness' sake, Cervantes' satirical work.*

In other cases the *s* is seldom omitted. Notice these three examples from Thackeray's writings: "Harry ran upstairs to his *mistress's* apartment;" "A postscript is added, as by the *countess's* command;" "I saw what the *governess's* views were of the matter."

*Possessive with compound expressions.*

**66.** In compound expressions, containing words in apposition, a word with a phrase, etc., the possessive sign is usually last, though instances are found with both appositional words marked.

Compare the following examples of literary usage: —

Do not the Miss Prys, my neighbors, know the amount of my income, the items of my *son's, Captain Scrapegrace's,* tailor's bill — Thackeray.

The world's pomp and power sits there on this hand: on that, stands up for God's truth one man, the *poor miner Hans Luther's* son. — Carlyle.

They invited me in the *emperor their master's* name. — Swift.

I had naturally possessed myself of *Richardson the painter's* thick octavo volumes of notes on the "Paradise Lost." — DE QUINCEY.

They will go to Sunday schools to teach classes of little children the age of Methuselah or the dimensions of *Og the king of Bashan's* bedstead. — Holmes.

More common still is the practice of turning the possessive into an equivalent phrase; as, *in the name of the emperor their master*, instead of *the emperor their master's name*.

*Possessive and no noun limited.*

**67.** The possessive is sometimes used without belonging to any noun in the sentence; some such word as *house, store, church, dwelling*, etc., being understood with it: for example, —

Here at the *fruiterer's* the Madonna has a tabernacle of fresh laurel leaves. — Ruskin.

It is very common for people to say that they are disappointed in the first sight of *St. Peter's.* — Lowell.

I remember him in his cradle at *St. James's.* — Thackeray.

Kate saw that; and she walked off from the *don's.* — De Quincey.

*The double possessive.*

**68.** A peculiar form, a double possessive, has grown up and become a fixed idiom in modern English.

In most cases, a possessive relation was expressed in Old English by the inflection *-es*, corresponding to *'s*. The same relation was expressed in French by a phrase corresponding to *of* and its object. Both of these are now used side by side; sometimes they are used together, as one modifier, making a double possessive. For this there are several reasons: —

*Its advantages: Euphony.*

(1) When a word is modified by *a, the, this, that, every, no, any, each*, etc., and at the same time by a possessive noun, it is distasteful to place the possessive before the modified noun, and it would also alter the meaning: we place it after the modified noun with *of*.

*Emphasis.*

(2) It is more emphatic than the simple possessive, especially when used with *this* or *that*, for it brings out the modified word in strong relief.

*Clearness.*

(3) It prevents ambiguity. For example, in such a sentence as, "This introduction *of Atterbury's* has all these advantages" (Dr. Blair), the statement clearly means only one thing, — the introduction which Atterbury made. If, however, we use the phrase *of Atterbury*, the sentence *might* be understood as just explained, or it might mean this act of introducing Atterbury. (See also Sec. 87.)

The following are some instances of double possessives: —

This Hall *of Tinville's* is dark, ill-lighted except where she stands. — Carlyle.

Those lectures *of Lowell's* had a great influence with me, and I used to like whatever they bade me like. — Howells

Niebuhr remarks that no pointed sentences *of Cæsar's* can have come down to us. — Froude.

Besides these famous books *of Scott's and Johnson's*, there is a copious "Life" by Thomas Sheridan. — Thackeray

Always afterwards on occasions of ceremony, he wore that quaint old French sword *of the Commodore's*. — E. E. Hale.

**Exercises.**

(*a*) Pick out the possessive nouns, and tell whether each is appositional, objective, or subjective.

(*b*) Rewrite the sentence, turning the possessives into equivalent phrases.

> 1. I don't choose a hornet's nest about my ears.

> 2. Shall Rome stand under one man's awe?

> 3. I must not see thee Osman's bride.

> 4.

>> At lovers' perjuries,
>> They say, Jove laughs.

> 5. The world has all its eyes on Cato's son.

> 6. My quarrel and the English queen's are one.

> 7.

>> Now the bright morning star, day's harbinger,
>> Comes dancing from the East.

> 8. A man's nature runs either to herbs or weeds; therefore, let him seasonably water the one, and destroy the other.

> 9.

>> 'Tis all men's office to speak patience
>> To those that wring under the load of sorrow.

> 10.

>> A jest's prosperity lies in the ear
>> Of him that hears it, never in the tongue

Of him that makes it.

11. No more the juice of Egypt's grape shall moist his lip.

12.

There Shakespeare's self, with every garland crowned,
Flew to those fairy climes his fancy sheen.

13.

What supports me? dost thou ask?
The conscience, Friend, to have lost them [his eyes]
overplied
In liberty's defence.

14.

Or where Campania's plain forsaken lies,
A weary waste expanding to the skies.

15.

Nature herself, it seemed, would raise
A minster to her Maker's praise!

# HOW TO PARSE NOUNS.

**69. Parsing** a word is putting together all the facts about its form and its relations to other words in the sentence.

In parsing, some idioms — the double possessive, for example — do not come under regular grammatical rules, and are to be spoken of merely as idioms.

**70.** Hence, in parsing a noun, we state, —

(1) The class to which it belongs, — common, proper, etc.

(2) Whether a neuter or a gender noun; if the latter, which gender.

(3) Whether singular or plural number.

(4) Its office in the sentence, determining its case.

*The correct method.*

**71.** In parsing any word, the following method should always be followed: tell the facts about what the word *does*, then make the grammatical statements as to its class, inflections, and relations.

# MODEL FOR PARSING.

"What is bolder than a miller's neckcloth, which takes a thief by the throat every morning?"

*Miller's* is a name applied to every individual of its class, hence it is a common noun; it is the name of a male being, hence it is a gender noun, masculine; it denotes only one person, therefore singular number; it expresses possession or ownership, and limits *neckcloth*, therefore possessive case.

*Neckcloth*, like *miller's*, is a common class noun; it has no sex, therefore neuter; names one thing, therefore singular number; subject of the verb *is* understood, and therefore nominative case.

*Thief* is a common class noun; the connection shows a male is meant, therefore masculine gender; singular number; object of the verb *takes*, hence objective case.

*Throat* is neuter, of the same class and number as the word *neckcloth*; it is the object of the preposition *by*, hence it is objective case.

NOTE. — The preposition sometimes takes the possessive case (see Sec. 68).

*Morning* is like *throat* and *neckcloth* as to class, gender, and number; as to case, it expresses time, has no governing word, but is the adverbial objective.

**Exercise.**

Follow the model above in parsing all the nouns in the following sentences: —

1. To raise a monument to departed worth is to perpetuate virtue.

2. The greatest pleasure I know is to do a good action by stealth, and to have it found out by accident.

3. An old cloak makes a new jerkin; a withered serving man, a fresh tapster.

4.

That in the captain's but a choleric word,
Which in the soldier is flat blasphemy.


5. Now, blessings light on him that first invented ... sleep!

6. Necker, financial minister to Louis XVI., and his daughter, Madame de Staël, were natives of Geneva.

7. He giveth his beloved sleep.

8. Time makes the worst enemies friends.

9. A few miles from this point, where the Rhone enters the lake, stands the famous Castle of Chillon, connected with the shore by a drawbridge, — palace, castle, and prison, all in one.

10.

Wretches! ye loved her for her wealth,
And hated her for her pride.



11. Mrs. Jarley's back being towards him, the military gentleman shook his forefinger.

## PRONOUNS.

*The need of pronouns.*

**72.** When we wish to speak of a name several times in succession, it is clumsy and tiresome to repeat the noun. For instance, instead of saying, "*The pupil* will succeed in *the pupil's* efforts if *the pupil* is ambitious," we improve the sentence by shortening it thus, "The pupil will succeed in *his* efforts if *he* is ambitious."

Again, if we wish to know about the ownership of a house, we evidently cannot state the owner's name, but by a question we say, "*Whose* house is that?" thus placing a word instead of the name till we learn the name.

This is not to be understood as implying that pronouns were *invented* because nouns were tiresome, since history shows that pronouns are as old as nouns and verbs. The use of pronouns must have sprung up naturally, from a necessity for short, definite, and representative words.

*Definition.*

A **pronoun** is a reference word, standing for a name, or for a person or thing, or for a group of persons or things.

*Classes of pronouns.*

**73.** Pronouns may be grouped in five classes: —

(1) **Personal pronouns**, which distinguish person by their form (Sec. 76).

(2) **Interrogative pronouns**, which are used to ask questions about persons or things.

(3) **Relative pronouns**, which relate or refer to a noun, pronoun, or other word or expression, and at the same time connect two statements They are also called **conjunctive**.

(4) **Adjective pronouns**, words, primarily adjectives, which are classed as adjectives when they modify nouns, but as pronouns when they stand for nouns.

(5) **Indefinite pronouns**, which cannot be used as adjectives, but stand for an indefinite number of persons or things.

Numerous examples of all these will be given under the separate classes hereafter treated.

# PERSONAL PRONOUNS..

*Person in grammar.*

**74.** Since pronouns stand for persons as well as names, they must represent the person talking, the person or thing spoken to, and the person or thing talked about.

This gives rise to a new term, "the distinction of *person*."

Person *of nouns.*

**75.** This distinction was not needed in discussing nouns, as nouns have the *same form*, whether representing persons and things spoken to or spoken of. It is evident that a noun could not represent the person speaking, even if it had a special form.

From analogy to pronouns, which have *forms* for person, nouns are sometimes spoken of as first or second person by their *use*; that is, if they are in apposition with a pronoun of the first or second person, they are said to have person by agreement.

But usually nouns represent something spoken of.

*Three persons of pronouns.*

**76.** Pronouns naturally are of three persons: —

(1) First person, representing the person speaking.

(2) Second person, representing a person or thing spoken to.

(3) Third person, standing for a person or thing spoken of.

# FORMS OF PERSONAL PRONOUNS.

**77.** Personal pronouns are inflected thus: —

## FIRST PERSON.

|  | *Singular.* | *Plural.* |
|---|---|---|
| *Nom.* | I | we |
| *Poss.* | mine, my | our, ours |
| *Obj.* | me | us |

## SECOND PERSON.

*Singular.*

|  | *Old Form* | *Common Form.* |
|---|---|---|
| *Nom.* | thou | you |
| *Poss.* | thine, thy | your, yours |
| *Obj.* | thee | you |

*Plural.*

|  | | |
|---|---|---|
| *Nom.* | ye | you |
| *Poss.* | your, yours | your, yours |
| *Obj.* | you | you |

## THIRD PERSON.

*Singular.*

|        | *Masc.* | *Fem.*    | *Neut..* |
|--------|---------|-----------|----------|
| *Nom.* | he      | she       | it       |
| *Poss.*| his     | her, hers | its      |
| *Obj.* | him     | her       | it       |

*Plur. of all Three.*

|        |               |
|--------|---------------|
| *Nom.* | they          |
| *Poss.*| their, theirs |
| *Obj.* | them          |

# Remarks on These Forms.

*First and second persons without gender.*

**78.** It will be noticed that the pronouns of the first and second persons have no forms to distinguish gender. The speaker may be either male or female, or, by personification, neuter; so also with the person or thing spoken to.

*Third person* singular *has gender.*

But the third person has, in the singular, a separate form for each gender, and also for the neuter.

*Old forms.*

In Old English these three were formed from the same root; namely, masculine *hē*, feminine *hēo*, neuter *hit*.

The form *hit* (for *it*) is still heard in vulgar English, and *hoo* (for *hēo*) in some dialects of England.

The plurals were *hī*, *heora*, *heom*, in Old English; the forms *they*, *their*, *them*, perhaps being from the English demonstrative, though influenced by the cognate Norse forms.

*Second person always plural in ordinary English.*

**79.** *Thou, thee*, etc., are old forms which are now out of use in ordinary speech. The consequence is, that we have no singular pronoun of the second person in ordinary speech or prose, but make the plural *you* do duty for the singular. We use it with a plural verb always, even when referring to a single object.

*Two uses of the old singulars.*

**80.** There are, however, two modern uses of *thou, thy*, etc.: —

(1) *In elevated style*, especially in poetry; as, —

> With *thy* clear keen joyance
> Languor cannot be;
> Shadow of annoyance
> Never came near *thee*;

*Thou* lovest; but ne'er knew love's sad satiety.
—Shelley.

(2) *In addressing the Deity*, as in prayers, etc.; for example, —

Oh, *thou* Shepherd of Israel, that didst comfort *thy* people of old, to *thy* care we commit the helpless. — Beecher.

*The form* its.

**81.** It is worth while to consider the possessive *its*. This is of comparatively recent growth. The old form was *his* (from the nominative *hit*), and this continued in use till the sixteenth century. The transition from the old *his* to the modern *its* is shown in these sentences: —

1 He anointed the altar and all *his* vessels. — *Bible*

Here *his* refers to *altar*, which is a neuter noun. The quotation represents the usage of the early sixteenth century.

2 It's had *it* head bit off by *it* young — Shakespeare

Shakespeare uses *his*, *it*, and sometimes *its*, as possessive of *it*.

In Milton's poetry (seventeenth century) *its* occurs only three times.

3 See heaven *its* sparkling portals wide display — Pope

*A relic of the olden time.*

**82.** We have an interesting relic in such sentences as this from Thackeray: "One of the ways to know '*em* is to watch the scared looks of the ogres' wives and children."

As shown above, the Old English objective was *hem* (or *heom*), which was often sounded with the *h* silent, just as we now say, "I saw '*im* yesterday" when the word *him* is not emphatic. In spoken English, this form '*em* has survived side by side with the literary *them*.

*Use of the pronouns in personification.*

**83.** The pronouns *he* and *she* are often used in poetry, and sometimes in ordinary speech, to personify objects (Sec. 34).

# CASES OF PERSONAL PRONOUNS.

# I The Nominative.

*Nominative forms.*

**84.** The nominative forms of personal pronouns have the same uses as the nominative of nouns (see Sec. 58). The case of most of these pronouns can be determined more easily than the case of nouns, for, besides a nominative *use*, they have a nominative form. The words *I, thou, he, she, we, ye, they*, are very rarely anything but nominative in literary English, though *ye* is occasionally used as objective.

*Additional nominatives in spoken English.*

**85.** In spoken English, however, there are some others that are added to the list of nominatives: they are, *me, him, her, us, them*, when they occur in the *predicate position*. That is, in such a sentence as, "I am sure it was *him*," the literary language would require *he* after *was*; but colloquial English regularly uses as predicate nominatives the forms *me, him, her, us, them*, though those named in Sec. 84 are always subjects. Yet careful speakers avoid this, and follow the usage of literary English.

# II. The Possessive.

*Not a separate class.*

**86.** The forms *my, thy, his, her, its, our, your, their,* are sometimes grouped separately as POSSESSIVE PRONOUNS, but it is better to speak of them as the possessive case of personal pronouns, just as we speak of the possessive case of nouns, and not make more classes.

Absolute *personal pronouns.*

The forms *mine, thine, yours, hers, theirs,* sometimes *his* and *its,* have a peculiar use, standing apart from the words they modify instead of immediately before them. From this use they are called ABSOLUTE PERSONAL PRONOUNS, or, some say, ABSOLUTE POSSESSIVES.

As instances of the use of absolute pronouns, note the following: —

'Twas *mine,* 'tis *his,* and has been slave to thousands. — Shakespeare.

And since thou own'st that praise, I spare thee *mine.* — Cowper.

My arm better than *theirs* can ward it off. — Landor.

*Thine* are the city and the people of Granada. — Bulwer.

*Old use of* mine *and* thine.

Formerly *mine* and *thine* stood before their nouns, if the nouns began with a vowel or *h* silent; thus, —

Shall I not take *mine* ease in *mine* inn? — Shakespeare.

Give every man *thine* ear, but few thy voice. — *Id.*

If *thine* eye offend thee, pluck it out. — *Bible.*

My greatest apprehension was for *mine* eyes. — Swift.

This usage is still preserved in poetry.

*Double and triple possessives.*

**87.** The forms *hers, ours, yours, theirs,* are really double possessives, since they add the possessive *s* to what is already a regular
possessive inflection.

Besides this, we have, as in nouns, a possessive phrase made up
of the preposition *of* with these double possessives, *hers, ours, yours,
theirs,* and with *mine, thine, his,* sometimes *its.*

*Their uses.*

Like the noun possessives, they have several uses: —

(1) *To prevent ambiguity,* as in the following: —

I have often contrasted the habitual qualities of that gloomy
friend *of theirs* with the astounding spirits of Thackeray and Dickens. — J. T. Fields.

No words *of ours* can describe the fury of the conflict. — J. F.
Cooper.

(2) *To bring emphasis,* as in these sentences: —

This thing *of yours* that you call a Pardon of Sins, it is a bit of rag-
paper with ink. — Carlyle.

This ancient silver bowl *of mine,* it tells of good old times. —
Holmes.

(3) *To express contempt, anger, or satire*; for example, —

"Do you know the charges that unhappy sister *of mine* and her
family have put me to already?" says the Master. — Thackeray.

He [John Knox] had his pipe of Bordeaux too, we find, in that old
Edinburgh house *of his.* — Carlyle.

"Hold thy peace, Long Allen," said Henry Woodstall, "I tell thee
that tongue *of thine* is not the shortest limb about *thee*." — Scott.

(4) *To make a noun less limited in application*; thus, —

A favorite liar and servant *of mine* was a man I once had to drive a
brougham. — Thackeray.

In New York I read a newspaper criticism one day, commenting
upon a letter *of mine.* — *Id.*

What would the last two sentences mean if the word *my* were written instead of *of mine*, and preceded the nouns?

*About the case of absolute pronouns.*

**88.** In their function, or use in a sentence, the absolute possessive forms of the personal pronouns are very much like adjectives used as nouns.

In such sentences as, "*The good* alone are great," "None but *the brave* deserves *the fair*," the words italicized have an adjective force and also a noun force, as shown in Sec. 20.

So in the sentences illustrating absolute pronouns in Sec. 86: *mine* stands for *my property*, *his* for *his property*, in the first sentence; *mine* stands for *my praise* in the second. But the first two have a nominative use, and *mine* in the second has an objective use.

They may be spoken of as possessive in form, but nominative or objective in use, according as the modified word is in the nominative or the objective.

# III. The Objective.

*The old* dative *case.*

**89.** In Old English there was one case which survives in use, but not in form. In such a sentence as this one from Thackeray, "Pick *me* out a whip-cord thong with some dainty knots in it," the word *me* is evidently not the direct object of the verb, but expresses *for whom, for whose benefit,* the thing is done. In pronouns, this **dative** use, as it is called, was marked by a separate case.

*Now the objective.*

In Modern English the same *use* is frequently seen, but the *form* is the same as the objective. For this reason a word thus used is called a **dative-objective**.

The following are examples of the dative-objective: —

Give *me* neither poverty nor riches. — *Bible.*

Curse *me* this people. — *Id.*

Both joined in making *him* a present. — Macaulay

Is it not enough that you have *burnt me* down three houses with your dog's tricks, and be hanged to you! — Lamb

I give *thee* this to wear at the collar. — Scott

*Other uses of the objective.*

**90.** Besides this use of the objective, there are others: —

(1) *As the direct object of a verb.*

They all handled *it.* — Lamb

(2) *As the object of a preposition.*

Time is behind *them* and before *them.* — Carlyle.

(3) *In apposition.*

She sate all last summer by the bedside of the blind beggar, *him* that so often and so gladly I talked with. — De Quincey.

# SPECIAL USES OF PERSONAL PRONOUNS.

*Indefinite use of* you *and* your.

**91.** The word *you*, and its possessive case *yours* are sometimes used without reference to a particular person spoken to. They approach the indefinite pronoun in use.

*Your* mere puny stripling, that winced at the least flourish of the rod, was passed by with indulgence. — Irving

To empty here, *you* must condense there. — Emerson.

The peasants take off their hats as *you* pass; *you* sneeze, and they cry, "God bless you!" The thrifty housewife shows *you* into her best chamber. *You* have oaten cakes baked some months before. — Longfellow

*Uses of* it.

**92.** The pronoun *it* has a number of uses: —

(1) *To refer to some single word preceding*; as, —

Ferdinand ordered the *army* to recommence *its* march. — Bulwer.

*Society*, in this century, has not made *its* progress, like Chinese skill, by a greater acuteness of ingenuity in trifles. — D. Webster.

(2) *To refer to a preceding word group*; thus, —

If any man should do wrong merely out of ill nature, why, yet *it* is but like the thorn or brier, which prick and scratch because they can do no other. — Bacon.

Here *it* refers back to the whole sentence before it, or to the idea, "any man's doing wrong merely out of ill nature."

(3) *As a grammatical subject, to stand for the real, logical subject, which follows the verb*; as in the sentences, —

*It* is easy in the world *to live after the world's opinion.* — Emerson.

*It* is this *haziness* of intellectual vision which is the malady of all classes of men by nature. — Newman.

*It* is a pity *that he has so much learning, or that he has not a great deal more.* — Addison.

(4) *As an impersonal subject in certain expressions which need no other subject*; as, —

*It* is finger-cold, and prudent farmers get in their barreled apples. — Thoreau.

And when I awoke, *it* rained. — Coleridge.

For when *it* dawned, they dropped their arms. — *Id.*

*It* was late and after midnight. — De Quincey.

(5) *As an impersonal or indefinite object of a verb or a preposition*; as in the following sentences: —

(*a*) Michael Paw, who *lorded it* over the fair regions of ancient Pavonia. — Irving.

I made up my mind *to foot it.* — Hawthorne.

A sturdy lad ... who in turn tries all the professions, who *teams it, farms it, peddles it*, keeps a school. — Emerson.

(*b*) "Thy mistress leads thee a dog's life *of it*." — Irving.

There was nothing *for it* but to return. — Scott.

An editor has only to say "respectfully declined," and there is an end *of it*. — Holmes.

Poor Christian was hard put *to it*. — Bunyan.

*Reflexive use of the personal pronouns.*

**93.** The personal pronouns in the objective case are often used *reflexively*; that is, referring to the same person as the subject of the accompanying verb. For example, we use such expressions as, "I found *me* a good book," "He bought *him* a horse," etc. This reflexive use of the *dative*-objective is very common in spoken and in literary English.

The personal pronouns are not often used reflexively, however, when they are *direct* objects. This occurs in poetry, but seldom in prose; as, —

Now I lay *me* down to sleep. — Anon.

I set *me* down and sigh. — Burns.

And millions in those solitudes, since first
The flight of years began, have laid *them* down
In their last sleep.
— Bryant.

# REFLEXIVE OR COMPOUND PERSONAL PRONOUNS.

*Composed of the personal pronouns with* -self, -selves.

**94.** The REFLEXIVE PRONOUNS, or COMPOUND PERSONAL, as they are also called, are formed from the personal pronouns by adding the word *self,* and its plural *selves.*

They are *myself, (ourself), ourselves, yourself, (thyself), yourselves, himself, herself, itself, themselves.*

Of the two forms in parentheses, the second is the old form of the second person, used in poetry.

*Ourself* is used to follow the word *we* when this represents a single person, especially in the speech of rulers; as, —

> Methinks he seems no better than a girl;
> As girls were once, as we *ourself* have been.
> — Tennyson.

*Origin of these reflexives.*

**95.** The question might arise, Why are *himself* and *themselves* not *hisself* and *theirselves,* as in vulgar English, after the analogy of *myself, ourselves,* etc.?

The history of these words shows they are made up of the dative-objective forms, not the possessive forms, with *self.* In Middle English the forms *meself, theself,* were changed into the possessive *myself, thyself,* and the others were formed by analogy with these. *Himself* and *themselves* are the only ones retaining a distinct objective form.

In the forms *yourself* and *yourselves* we have the possessive *your* marked as singular as well as plural.

*Use of the reflexives.*

**96.** There are three uses of reflexive pronouns: —

(1) *As object of a verb or preposition, and referring to the same person or thing as the subject;* as in these sentences from Emerson: —

He who offers *himself* a candidate for that covenant comes up like an Olympian.

I should hate *myself* if then I made my other friends my asylum.

We fill *ourselves* with ancient learning.

What do we know of nature or of *ourselves*?

(2) *To emphasize a noun or pronoun*; for example, —

The great globe *itself* ... shall dissolve. — Shakespeare.

> Threats to all;
> To *you yourself*, to us, to every one.
> — *Id.*


> Who would not sing for Lycidas! he knew
> *Himself* to sing, and build the lofty rhyme.
> — Milton.


NOTE. — In such sentences the pronoun is sometimes omitted, and the reflexive modifies the pronoun understood; for example, —

Only *itself* can inspire whom it will. — Emerson.

My hands are full of blossoms plucked before, Held dead within them till *myself* shall die. — E. B. Browning.

As if it were *thyself* that's here, I shrink with pain. — Wordsworth.

(3) *As the precise equivalent of a personal pronoun*; as, —

Lord Altamont designed to take his son and *myself*. — De Quincey.

Victories that neither *myself* nor my cause always deserved. — B. Franklin.

For what else have our forefathers and *ourselves* been taxed? — Landor.

Years ago, Arcturus and *myself* met a gentleman from China who knew the language. — Thackeray.

**Exercises on Personal Pronouns.**

(*a*) Bring up sentences containing ten personal pronouns, some each of masculine, feminine, and neuter.

(*b*) Bring up sentences containing five personal pronouns in the possessive, some of them being double possessives.

(*c*) Tell which use each *it* has in the following sentences: —

1.

> Come and trip it as we go,
> On the light fantastic toe.

2. Infancy conforms to nobody; all conform to it.

3. It is an ill wind that blows nobody good.

4. Courage, father, fight it out.

5. And it grew wondrous cold.

6. To know what is best to do, and how to do it, is wisdom.

7. If any phenomenon remains brute and dark, it is because the corresponding faculty in the observer is not yet active.

8. But if a man do not speak from within the veil, where the word is one with that it tells of, let him lowly confess it.

9. It behooved him to keep on good terms with his pupils.

10. Biscuit is about the best thing I know; but it is the soonest spoiled; and one would like to hear counsel on one point, why it is that a touch of water utterly ruins it.

# INTERROGATIVE PRONOUNS.

*Three now in use.*

**97.** The interrogative pronouns now in use are *who* (with the forms *whose* and *whom*), *which*, and *what*.

*One obsolete.*

There is an old word, *whether*, used formerly to mean which of two, but now obsolete. Examples from the Bible: —

*Whether* of them twain did the will of his father?

*Whether* is greater, the gold, or the temple?

From Steele (eighteenth century): —

It may be a question *whether* of these unfortunate persons had the greater soul.

*Use of* who *and its forms.*

**98.** The use of *who*, with its possessive and objective, is seen in these sentences: —

*Who* is she in bloody coronation robes from Rheims? — De Quincey.

> *Whose* was that gentle voice, that, whispering sweet,
> Promised, methought, long days of bliss sincere?
> — Bowles.

What doth she look on? *Whom* doth she behold? — Wordsworth.

From these sentences it will be seen that interrogative *who* refers to *persons only*; that it is not inflected for gender or number, but for case alone, having three forms; it is always third person, as it always asks *about* somebody.

*Use of* which.

**99.** Examples of the use of interrogative *which*: —

*Which* of these had speed enough to sweep between the question and the answer, and divide the one from the other? — De Quincey.

*Which* of you, shall we say, doth love us most? — Shakespeare.

*Which* of them [the sisters] shall I take? — *Id.*

As shown here, *which* is not inflected for gender, number, or case; it refers to either persons or things; it is selective, that is, picks out one or more from a number of known persons or objects.

*Use of* what.

**100.** Sentences showing the use of interrogative *what*: —

> Since I from Smaylho'me tower have been,
> *What* did thy lady do?
> — Scott.


*What* is so rare as a day in June? — Lowell.

*What* wouldst thou do, old man? — Shakespeare.

These show that *what* is not inflected for case; that it is always singular and neuter, referring to things, ideas, actions, etc., not to persons.

# DECLENSION OF INTERROGATIVE PRO-
NOUNS.

**101.** The following are all the interrogative forms: —

|        | SING. AND PLUR. | SING. AND PLUR. | SINGULAR |
|--------|-----------------|-----------------|----------|
| *Nom.* | who?            | which?          | what?    |
| *Poss.*| whose?          | —               | —        |
| *Obj.* | whom?           | which?          | what?    |

In spoken English, *who* is used as objective instead of *whom*; as, "*Who* did you see?" "*Who* did he speak to?"

*To tell the case of interrogatives.*

**102.** The interrogative *who* has a separate form for each case, consequently the case can be told by the form of the word; but the case of *which* and *what* must be determined exactly as in nouns, — by the *use* of the words.

For instance, in Sec. 99, *which* is nominative in the first sentence, since it is subject of the verb *had*; nominative in the second also, subject of *doth love*; objective in the last, being the direct object of the verb *shall take*.

*Further treatment of* who, which *and* what.

**103.** *Who, which,* and *what* are also relative pronouns; *which* and *what* are sometimes adjectives; *what* may be an adverb in some expressions.

They will be spoken of again in the proper places, especially in the treatment of indirect questions (Sec. 127).

# RELATIVE PRONOUNS.

*Function of the relative pronoun.*

**104. Relative pronouns** differ from both personal and interrogative pronouns in referring to an antecedent, and also in having a conjunctive use. The advantage in using them is to unite short statements into longer sentences, and so to make smoother discourse. Thus we may say, "The last of all the Bards was he. These bards sang of Border chivalry." Or, it may be shortened into, —

> "The last of all the Bards was he,
> *Who* sung of Border chivalry."

In the latter sentence, *who* evidently refers to *Bards*, which is called the **antecedent** of the relative.

*The antecedent.*

**105.** The **antecedent** of a pronoun is the noun, pronoun, or other word or expression, for which the pronoun stands. It usually precedes the pronoun.

Personal pronouns of the third person may have antecedents also, as they take the place usually of a word already used; as, —

The priest hath *his* fee who comes and shrives us. — Lowell

In this, both *his* and *who* have the antecedent *priest*.

The pronoun *which* may have its antecedent following, and the antecedent may be a word or a group of words, as will be shown in the remarks on *which* below.

*Two kinds.*

**106.** Relatives may be SIMPLE or INDEFINITE.

When the word *relative* is used, a simple relative is meant. Indefinite relatives, and the indefinite use of simple relatives, will be discussed further on.

The SIMPLE RELATIVES are *who, which, that, what.*

Who *and its forms.*

**107.** Examples of the relative *who* and its forms: —

1. Has a man gained anything *who* has received a hundred favors and rendered none? — Emerson.

2. That man is little to be envied *whose* patriotism would not gain force upon the plain of Marathon. — Dr Johnson.

3.

> For her enchanting son,
> *Whom* universal nature did lament.
> — Milton.

4. The nurse came to us, *who* were sitting in an adjoining apartment. — Thackeray.

5.

> Ye mariners of England,
> That guard our native seas;
> *Whose* flag has braved, a thousand years,
> The battle and the breeze!
> — Campbell.

6. The men *whom* men respect, the women *whom* women approve, are the men and women *who* bless their species. — Parton

Which *and its forms.*

**108.** Examples of the relative *which* and its forms: —

1. They had not their own luster, but the look *which* is not of the earth. — Byron.

2.

> The embattled portal arch he pass'd,
> *Whose* ponderous grate and massy bar

Had oft roll'd back the tide of war.
— Scott.

3. Generally speaking, the dogs *which* stray around the butcher shops restrain their appetites. — Cox.

4. The origin of language is divine, in the same sense in *which* man's nature, with all its capabilities ..., is a divine creation. — W. D. Whitney.

5.

(*a*) This gradation ... ought to be kept in view; else this description will seem exaggerated, *which* it certainly is not. — Burke.

(*b*) The snow was three inches deep and still falling, *which* prevented him from taking his usual ride. — Irving.

That.

**109.** Examples of the relative *that*: —

1.

The man *that* hath no music in himself,...
Is fit for treasons, stratagems, and spoils.
— Shakespeare

2. The judge ... bought up all the pigs *that* could be had. — Lamb

3. Nature and books belong to the eyes *that* see them. — Emerson.

4. For the sake of country a man is told to yield everything *that* makes the land honorable. — H. W. Beecher

5. Reader, *that* do not pretend to have leisure for very much scholarship, you will not be angry with me for telling you. — De Quincey.

6. The Tree Igdrasil, *that* has its roots down in the kingdoms of Hela and Death, and whose boughs overspread the highest heaven! — Carlyle.

What.

**110.** Examples of the use of the relative *what*: —

1. Its net to entangle the enemy seems to be *what* it chiefly trusts to, and *what* it takes most pains to render as complete as possible. — Goldsmith.

2. For *what* he sought below is passed above, Already done is all that he would do. — Margaret Fuller.

3. Some of our readers may have seen in India a crowd of crows picking a sick vulture to death, no bad type of *what* often happens in that country. — Macaulay

[*To the Teacher.* — If pupils work over the above sentences carefully, and test every remark in the following paragraphs, they will get a much better understanding of the relatives.]

# REMARKS ON THE RELATIVE PRONOUNS.

**Who.**

**111.** By reading carefully the sentences in Sec. 107, the following facts will be noticed about the relative *who*: —

(1) It usually refers to persons: thus, in the first sentence, Sec. 107, *a man...who*; in the second, *that man...whose*; in the third, *son, whom*; and so on.

(2) It has three case forms, — *who, whose, whom.*

(3) The forms do not change for person or number of the antecedent. In sentence 4, *who* is first person; in 5, *whose* is second person; the others are all third person. In 1, 2, and 3, the relatives are singular; in 4, 5, and 6, they are plural.

Who *referring to animals.*

**112.** Though in most cases *who* refers to persons there are instances found where it refers to animals. It has been seen (Sec. 24) that animals are referred to by personal pronouns when their characteristics or habits are such as to render them important or interesting to man. Probably on the same principle the personal relative *who* is used not infrequently in literature, referring to animals.

Witness the following examples: —

And you, warm little housekeeper [the cricket], *who* class With those who think the candles come too soon. — Leigh Hunt.

The robins...have succeeded in driving off the bluejays *who* used to build in our pines. — Lowell.

The little gorilla, *whose* wound I had dressed, flung its arms around my neck. — Thackeray.

A lake frequented by every fowl *whom* Nature has taught to dip the wing in water. — Dr. Johnson.

While we had such plenty of domestic insects *who* infinitely excelled the former, because they understood how to weave as well as to spin. — Swift.

My horse, *who*, under his former rider had hunted the buffalo, seemed as much excited as myself. — Irving.

Other examples might be quoted from Burke, Kingsley, Smollett, Scott, Cooper, Gibbon, and others.

Which.

**113.** The sentences in Sec. 108 show that—

(1) *Which* refers to animals, things, or ideas, not persons.

(2) It is not inflected for gender or number.

(3) It is nearly always third person, rarely second (an example of its use as second person is given in sentence 32, p. 96).

(4) It has two case forms, — *which* for the nominative and objective, *whose* for the possessive.

*Examples of* whose, *possessive case of* which.

**114.** Grammarians sometimes object to the statement that *whose* is the possessive of *which*, saying that the phrase *of which* should always be used instead; yet a search in literature shows that the possessive form *whose* is quite common in prose as well as in poetry: for example, —

I swept the horizon, and saw at one glance the glorious elevations, on *whose* tops the sun kindled all the melodies and harmonies of light. — Beecher.

Men may be ready to fight to the death, and to persecute without pity, for a religion *whose* creed they do not understand, and *whose* precepts they habitually disobey. — Macaulay

Beneath these sluggish waves lay the once proud cities of the plain, *whose* grave was dug by the thunder of the heavens. — Scott.

Many great and opulent cities *whose* population now exceeds that of Virginia during the Revolution, and *whose* names are spoken in the remotest corner of the civilized world. — Mcmaster.

Through the heavy door *whose* bronze network closes the place of his rest, let us enter the church itself. — Ruskin.

This moribund '61, *whose* career of life is just coming to its terminus. — Thackeray.

So in Matthew Arnold, Kingsley, Burke, and numerous others.

Which *and its antecedents*.

**115.** The last two sentences in Sec. 108 show that *which* may have other antecedents than nouns and pronouns. In 5 (*a*) there is a participial adjective used as the antecedent; in 5 (*b*) there is a complete clause employed as antecedent. This often occurs.

Sometimes, too, the antecedent follows *which*; thus, —

> And, which is worse, *all you have done*
> *Hath been but for a wayward son.*
> — Shakespeare.


Primarily, which is very notable and curious, I observe that *men of business rarely know the meaning of the word "rich."* — Ruskin.

I demurred to this honorary title upon two grounds, — first, as being one toward which I had no natural aptitudes or predisposing advantages; secondly (which made her stare), *as carrying with it no real or enviable distinction.* — De Quincey.

That.

**116.** In the sentences of Sec. 109, we notice that —

(1) *That* refers to persons, animals, and things.

(2) It has only one case form, no possessive.

(3) It is the same form for first, second, and third persons.

(4) It has the same form for singular and plural.

It sometimes borrows the possessive *whose*, as in sentence 6, Sec. 109, but this is not sanctioned as good usage.

What.

**117.** The sentences of Sec. 110 show that —

(1) *What* always refers to things; is always neuter.

(2) It is used almost entirely in the singular.

(3) Its antecedent is hardly ever expressed. When expressed, it usually follows, and is emphatic; as, for example, —

What I would, *that* do I not; but what I hate, *that* do I. — *Bible*

What fates impose, *that* men must needs abide. —Shakespeare.

What a man does, *that* he has. — Emerson.

Compare this: —

Alas! is *it* not too true, what we said? — Carlyle.

# DECLENSION OF RELATIVE PRONOUNS.

**118.** These are the forms of the simple relatives: —

SINGULAR AND PLURAL.

| | | | | |
|------|-------|-------|------|------|
| *Nom.* | who | which | that | what |
| *Poss.* | whose | whose | — | — |
| *Obj.* | whom | which | that | what |

# HOW TO PARSE RELATIVES.

**119.** The *gender, number,* and *person* of the relatives *who, which,* and *that* must be determined by those of the antecedent; the *case* depends upon the function of the relative in its own clause.

For example, consider the following sentence:

"He uttered truths *that* wrought upon and molded the lives of those *who* heard him."

Since the relatives hold the sentence together, we can, by taking them out, let the sentence fall apart into three divisions: (1) "He uttered truths;" (2) "The truths wrought upon and molded the lives of the people;" (3) "These people heard him."

*That* evidently refers to *truths,* consequently is neuter, third person, plural number. *Who* plainly stands for *those* or *the people,* either of which would be neuter, third person, plural number. Here the relative agrees with its antecedent.

We cannot say the relative agrees with its antecedent in *case.* *Truths* in sentence (2), above, is subject of *wrought upon and molded;* in (1), it is object of *uttered.* In (2), *people* is the object of the preposition *of;* in (3), it is subject of the verb *heard.* Now, *that* takes the case of *the truths* in (2), not of *truths* which is expressed in the sentence: consequently *that* is in the nominative case. In the same way *who,* standing for *the people* understood, subject of *heard,* is in the nominative case.

### Exercise.

First find the antecedents, then parse the relatives, in the following sentences: —

1. How superior it is in these respects to the pear, whose blossoms are neither colored nor fragrant!

2. Some gnarly apple which I pick up in the road reminds me by its fragrance of all the wealth of Pomona.

3. Perhaps I talk with one who is selecting some choice barrels for filling an order.

4. Ill blows the wind that profits nobody.

5. Alas! it is we ourselves that are getting buried alive under this avalanche of earthly impertinences.

6. This method also forces upon us the necessity of thinking, which is, after all, the highest result of all education.

7. I know that there are many excellent people who object to the reading of novels as a waste of time.

8. I think they are trying to outwit nature, who is sure to be cunninger than they.

*Parsing* what, *the simple relative.*

**120.** The relative *what* is handled differently, because it has usually no antecedent, but is singular, neuter, third person. Its case is determined exactly as that of other relatives. In the sentence, "What can't be cured must be endured," the verb *must be endured* is the predicate of something. What must be endured? Answer, *What can't be cured.* The whole expression is its subject. The word *what*, however, is subject of the verb *can't be cured*, and hence is in the nominative case.

"What we call nature is a certain self-regulated motion or change." Here the subject of *is*, etc., is *what we call nature*; but of this, *we* is the subject, and *what* is the direct object of the verb *call*, so is in the objective case.

*Another way.*

Some prefer another method of treatment. As shown by the following sentences, *what* is equivalent to *that which*: —

It has been said that "common souls pay with *what* they do, nobler souls with *that which* they are." — Emerson.

*That which* is pleasant often appears under the name of evil; and *what* is disagreeable to nature is called good and virtuous. — Burke.

Hence some take *what* as a double relative, and parse *that* in the first clause, and *which* in the second clause; that is, "common souls pay with *that* [singular, object of *with*] *which* [singular, object of *do*] they do."

# INDEFINITE RELATIVES.

**121.** INDEFINITE RELATIVES are, by meaning and use, not as direct as the simple relatives.

They are *whoever, whichever, whatever, whatsoever;* less common are *whoso, whosoever, whichsoever, whatsoever.* The simple relatives *who, which,* and *what* may also be used as indefinite relatives. Examples of indefinite relatives (from Emerson): —

1. *Whoever* has flattered his friend successfully must at once think himself a knave, and his friend a fool.

2. It is no proof of a man's understanding, to be able to affirm *whatever* he pleases.

3. They sit in a chair or sprawl with children on the floor, or stand on their head, or *what* else *soever*, in a new and original way.

4. *Whoso* is heroic will always find crises to try his edge.

5. Only itself can inspire *whom* it will.

6. God offers to every mind its choice between truth and repose. Take *which* you please, — you cannot have both.

7. Do *what* we can, summer will have its flies.

*Meaning and use.*

**122.** The fitness of the term *indefinite* here cannot be shown better than by examining the following sentences: —

1. There is something so overruling in *whatever* inspires us with awe, in *all things which* belong ever so remotely to terror, that nothing else can stand in their presence. — Burke.

2. Death is there associated, not with *everything that* is most endearing in social and domestic charities, but with *whatever* is darkest in human nature and in human destiny. — Macaulay.

It is clear that in 1, *whatever* is equivalent to *all things which*, and in 2, to *everything that*; no certain antecedent, no particular thing, being referred to. So with the other indefinites.

What *simple relative and* what *indefinite relative.*

**123.** The above helps us to discriminate between *what* as a simple and *what* as an indefinite relative.

As shown in Sec. 120, the simple relative *what* is equivalent to *that which* or the *thing which,*—some particular thing; as shown by the last sentence in Sec. 121, *what* means *anything that, everything that* (or *everything which*). The difference must be seen by the meaning of the sentence, as *what* hardly ever has an antecedent.

The examples in sentences 5 and 6, Sec. 121, show that *who* and *which* have no antecedent expressed, but mean *any one whom, either one that,* etc.

# OTHER WORDS USED AS RELATIVES.

*But and* as.

**124.** Two words, **but** and **as**, are used with the force of relative pronouns in some expressions; for example, —

1. There is not a leaf rotting on the highway *but* has force in it: how else could it rot? — Carlyle.

2. This, amongst such other troubles *as* most men meet with in this life, has been my heaviest affliction. — De Quincey.

*Proof that they have the force of relatives.*

Compare with these the two following sentences: —

3. There is nothing *but* is related to us, nothing *that* does *not* interest us. — Emerson.

4. There were articles of comfort and luxury such *as* Hester never ceased to use, but *which* only wealth could have purchased. — Hawthorne.

Sentence 3 shows that *but* is equivalent to the relative *that* with *not*, and that *as* after *such* is equivalent to *which*.

For *as* after *same* see "Syntax" (Sec. 417).

*Former use of* as.

**125.** In early modern English, *as* was used just as we use *that* or *which*, not following the word *such*; thus, —

> I have not from your eyes that gentleness
> And show of love *as* I was wont to have.
> — Shakespeare


This still survives in vulgar English in England; for example, —

"Don't you mind Lucy Passmore, *as* charmed your warts for you when you was a boy? " — Kingsley

This is frequently illustrated in Dickens's works.

*Other substitutes.*

**126.** Instead of the phrases *in which, upon which, by which*, etc., the conjunctions *wherein, whereupon, whereby*, etc., are used.

A man is the facade of a temple *wherein* all wisdom and good abide. — Emerson.

The sovereignty of this nature *whereof* we speak. — *Id.*

> The dear home faces *whereupon*
> That fitful firelight paled and shone.
> — Whittier.

# PRONOUNS IN INDIRECT QUESTIONS.

*Special caution needed here.*

**127.** It is sometimes hard for the student to tell a relative from an interrogative pronoun. In the regular direct question the interrogative is easily recognized; so is the relative when an antecedent is close by. But compare the following in pairs: —

1.

(*a*) Like a gentleman of leisure *who* is strolling out for pleasure.

(*b*) Well we knew *who* stood behind, though the earthwork hid them.

2.

(*a*) But *what* you gain in time is perhaps lost in power.

(*b*) But *what* had become of them they knew not.

3.

(*a*) These are the lines *which* heaven-commanded Toil shows on his deed.

(*b*) And since that time I thought it not amiss To judge *which* were the best of all these three.

In sentences 1 (*a*), 2 (*a*) and 3 (*a*) the regular relative use is seen; *who* having the antecedent *gentleman*, *what* having the double use of pronoun and antecedent, *which* having the antecedent *lines*.

But in 1 (*b*), 2 (*b*), and 3 (*b*), there are two points of difference from the others considered: first, no antecedent is expressed, which would indicate that they are not relatives; second, a question is disguised in each sentence, although each sentence as a whole is declarative in form. Thus, 1 (*b*), if expanded, would be, "Who stood behind? We knew," etc., showing that *who* is plainly interrogative. So in 2 (*b*), *what* is interrogative, the full expression being, "But what had become of them? They knew not." Likewise with *which* in 3 (*b*).

*How to decide.*

In studying such sentences, (1) see whether there is an antecedent of *who* or *which*, and whether *what* = *that* + *which* (if so, it is a simple relative; if not, it is either an indefinite relative or an interrogative pronoun); (2) see if the pronoun introduces an indirect question (if it does, it is an interrogative; if not, it is an indefinite relative).

*Another caution.*

**128.** On the other hand, care must be taken to see whether the pronoun is the word that really *asks the question* in an interrogative sentence. Examine the following: —

1.

Sweet rose! whence is this hue
*Which* doth all hues excel?
— Drummond

2.

And then what wonders shall you do
*Whose* dawning beauty warms us so?
— Walker

3.

Is this a romance? Or is it a faithful picture of *what* has lately been in a neighboring land? — Macaulay

These are interrogative sentences, but in none of them does the pronoun ask the question. In the first, *whence* is the interrogative word, *which* has the antecedent *hue*. In the second, *whose* has the antecedent *you*, and asks no question. In the third, the question is asked by the verb.

# OMISSION OF THE RELATIVES.

*Relative omitted when* object.

**129.** The relative is frequently omitted in spoken and in literary English when it would be the object of a preposition or a verb. Hardly a writer can be found who does not leave out relatives in this way when they can be readily supplied in the mind of the reader. Thus, —

These are the sounds we feed upon. — Fletcher.

I visited many other apartments, but shall not trouble my reader with all the curiosities I observed. — Swift.

**Exercise**.

Put in the relatives *who*, *which*, or *that* where they are omitted from the following sentences, and see whether the sentences are any smoother or clearer: —

1. The insect I am now describing lived three years, — Goldsmith.

2. They will go to Sunday schools through storms their brothers are afraid of. — Holmes.

3. He opened the volume he first took from the shelf. — G. Eliot.

4. He could give the coals in that queer coal scuttle we read of to his poor neighbor. — Thackeray.

5. When Goldsmith died, half the unpaid bill he owed to Mr. William Filby was for clothes supplied to his nephew. — Forster

6. The thing I want to see is not Redbook Lists, and Court Calendars, but the life of man in England. — Carlyle.

7. The material they had to work upon was already democratical by instinct and habitude. — Lowell.

*Relative omitted when* subject.

**130.** We often hear in spoken English expressions like these: —

There isn't one here ˏ knows how to play ball.

There was such a crowd ˏ went, the house was full.

Here the omitted relative would be in the nominative case. Also in literary English we find the same omission. It is rare in prose, and comparatively so in poetry. Examples are, —

The silent truth that it was she was superior. — Thackeray

I have a mind presages me such thrift. — Shakespeare.

> There is a nun in Dryburgh bower,
> Ne'er looks upon the sun.
> — Scott.

> And you may gather garlands there
> Would grace a summer queen.
> — Id.

'Tis distance lends enchantment to the view. — Campbell.

### Exercises on the Relative Pronoun.

(*a*) Bring up sentences containing ten instances of the relatives *who*, *which*, *that*, and *what*.

(*b*) Bring up sentences having five indefinite relatives.

(*c*) Bring up five sentences having indirect questions introduced by pronouns.

(*d*) Tell whether the pronouns in the following are interrogatives, simple relatives, or indefinite relatives: —

> 1. He ushered him into one of the wherries which lay ready to attend the Queen's barge, which was already proceeding.

> 2. The nobles looked at each other, but more with the purpose to see what each thought of the news, than to exchange any remarks on what had happened.

> 3. Gracious Heaven! who was this that knew the word?

> 4. It needed to be ascertained which was the strongest kind of men; who were to be rulers over whom.

5. He went on speaking to who would listen to him.

6. What kept me silent was the thought of my mother.

# ADJECTIVE PRONOUNS.

*Function of adjective pronouns.*

**131.** Most of the words how to be considered are capable of a double use,—they may be pure modifiers of nouns, or they may stand for nouns. In the first use they are adjectives; in the second they retain an adjective *meaning*, but have lost their adjective *use*. Primarily they are adjectives, but in this function, or use, they are properly classed as adjective pronouns.

The following are some examples of these:—

*Some* say that the place was bewitched.—Irving.

> That mysterious realm where *each* shall take
> His chamber in the silent halls of death.
> —Bryant.

> How happy is he born or taught
> That serveth not *another's* will.
> —Wotton

*That* is more than any martyr can stand.—Emerson.

*Caution.*

*Adjectives, not pronouns.*

Hence these words are like adjectives used as nouns, which we have seen in such expressions as, "*The dead* are there;" that is, a word, in order to be an adjective pronoun, *must not modify any word, expressed or understood*. It must come under the requirement of pronouns, and *stand for a noun*. For instance, in the following sentences—"The cubes are of stainless ivory, and on *each* is written, in letters of gold, '*Truth*;'" "You needs must play such pranks as *these*;" "They will always have one bank to sun themselves upon, and *another* to get cool under;" "Where two men ride on a horse, *one* must ride behind"—the words italicized modify nouns understood, necessarily thought of: thus, in the first, "each *cube*;" in the second, "these *pranks*," in the others, "another *bank*," "one *man*."

*Classes of adjective pronouns.*

**132.** Adjective pronouns are divided into three classes:—

(1) DEMONSTRATIVE PRONOUNS, such as *this*, *that*, *the former*, etc.

(2) DISTRIBUTIVE PRONOUNS, such as *each*, *either*, *neither*, etc.

(3) NUMERAL PRONOUNS, as *some*, *any*, *few*, *many*, *none*, *all*, etc.

# DEMONSTRATIVE PRONOUNS

*Definition and examples.*

**133.** A DEMONSTRATIVE PRONOUN is one that definitely points out what persons or things are alluded to in the sentence.

The person or thing alluded to by the demonstrative may be in another sentence, or may be the whole of a sentence. For example, "Be *that* as it may" could refer to a sentiment in a sentence, or an argument in a paragraph; but the demonstrative clearly points to that thing.

The following are examples of demonstratives: —

I did not say *this* in so many words.

All *these* he saw; but what he fain had seen He could not see.

Beyond *that* I seek not to penetrate the veil.

How much we forgive in *those* who yield us the rare spectacle of heroic manners!

The correspondence of Bonaparte with his brother Joseph, when *the latter* was the King of Spain.

*Such* are a few isolated instances, accidentally preserved.

Even as I have seen, they that plow iniquity, and sow wickedness, reap *the same*.

They know that patriotism has its glorious opportunities and its sacred duties. They have not shunned *the one*, and they have well performed *the other*.

NOTE. — It will be noticed in the first four sentences that *this* and *that* are inflected for number.

## Exercises.

(*a*) Find six sentences using demonstrative adjective pronouns.

(*b*) In which of the following is *these* a pronoun? —

1. Formerly the duty of a librarian was to keep people as much as possible from the books, and to hand *these* over to his successor as little worn as he could. — Lowell.

2. They had fewer books, but *these* were of the best. — *Id.*

3. A man inspires affection and honor, because he was not lying in wait for *these*. — Emerson

4. Souls such as *these* treat you as gods would. — *Id.*

5. *These* are the first mountains that broke the uniform level of the earth's surface. — Agassiz

# DISTRIBUTIVE PRONOUNS.

*Definition and examples.*

**134.** The DISTRIBUTIVE PRONOUNS are those which stand for the names of persons or things considered singly.

*Simple.*

Some of these are *simple* pronouns; for example, —

They stood, or sat, or reclined, as seemed good to *each.*

As two yoke devils sworn to *other's* purpose.

Their minds accorded into one strain, and made delightful music which *neither* could have claimed as all his own.

*Compound.*

Two are compound pronouns, — *each other, one another.* They may be separated into two adjective pronouns; as,

We violated our reverence *each* for *the other's* soul. — Hawthorne.

More frequently they are considered as one pronoun.

They led one another, as it were, into a high pavilion of their thoughts. — Hawthorne.

Men take each other's measure when they react. — Emerson.

**Exercise.** — Find sentences containing three distributive pronouns.

# NUMERAL PRONOUNS.

*Definition and examples.*

**135.** The NUMERAL PRONOUNS are those which stand for an uncertain number or quantity of persons or things.

The following sentences contain numeral pronouns: —

Trusting too much to *others'* care is the ruin of *many.*

'Tis of no importance how large his house, you quickly come to the end of *all.*

*Another* opposes him with sound argument.

It is as if *one* should be so enthusiastic a lover of poetry as to care nothing for Homer or Milton.

There were plenty *more* for him to fall in company with, as *some* of the rangers had gone astray.

The Soldan, imbued, as *most* were, with the superstitions of his time, paused over a horoscope.

If those [taxes] were the only *ones* we had to pay, we might the more easily discharge them.

*Much* might be said on both sides.

> If hand of mine *another's* task has lightened.
> It felt the guidance that it does not claim.
> So perish *all* whose breast ne'er learned to glow
> For *others'* good, or melt for *others'* woe.

*None* shall rule but the humble.

*Some inflected.*

It will be noticed that some of these are inflected for case and number; such as *one other, another.*

The word *one* has a reflexive form; for example, —

One *reflexive.*

The best way to punish *oneself* for doing ill seems to me to go and do good. — Kingsley.

The lines sound so prettily to *one's self*. — Holmes.

Exercise. — Find sentences containing ten numeral pronouns.

# INDEFINITE PRONOUNS.

*Definition and examples.*

**136. Indefinite pronouns** are words which stand for an indefinite number or quantity of persons or things; but, unlike adjective pronouns, they are never used as adjectives.

Most of them are compounds of two or more words: —

*List.*

*Somebody, some one, something; anybody, any one* (or *anyone*), *anything; everybody, every one* (or *everyone*), *everything; nobody, no one, nothing; somebody else, anyone else, everybody else, every one else,* etc.; also *aught, naught;* and *somewhat, what,* and *they.*

The following sentences contain indefinite pronouns: —

As he had them of all hues, he hoped to fit *everybody's* fancy.

*Every one* knows how laborious the usual method is of attaining to arts and sciences.

*Nothing* sheds more honor on our early history than the impression which these measures everywhere produced in America.

Let us also perform *something* worthy to be remembered.

William of Orange was more than *anything else* a religious man.

Frederick was discerned to be a purchaser of *everything* that *nobody else* would buy.

These other souls draw me as *nothing else* can.

The genius that created it now creates *somewhat else.*

*Every one else* stood still at his post.

That is perfectly true: I did not want *anybody else's* authority to write as I did.

*They* indefinite means people in general; as, —

At lovers' perjuries, *they* say, Jove laughs. — Shakespeare.

*What* indefinite is used in the expression "I tell you *what.*" It means *something,* and was indefinite in Old English.

Now, in building of chaises, I tell you *what*,
There is always somewhere a weakest spot.


**Exercise.** — Find sentences with six indefinite pronouns.

**137.** Some indefinite pronouns are inflected for case, as shown in the words *everybody's*, *anybody else's*, etc.

See also "Syntax" (Sec. 426) as to the possessive case of the forms with *else*.

# HOW TO PARSE PRONOUNS.

*A reminder.*

**138.** In **parsing** pronouns the student will need particularly to guard against the mistake of parsing words according to *form* instead of according to function or use.

### Exercise.

Parse in full the pronouns in the following sentences: —

1. She could not help laughing at the vile English into which they were translated.

2. Our readers probably remember what Mrs. Hutchinson tells us of herself.

3. Whoever deals with M. de Witt must go the plain way that he pretends to, in his negotiations.

4. Some of them from whom nothing was to be got, were suffered to depart; but those from whom it was thought that anything could be extorted were treated with execrable cruelty.

5. All was now ready for action.

6. Scarcely had the mutiny broken up when he was himself again.

7. He came back determined to put everything to the hazard.

8. Nothing is more clear than that a general ought to be the servant of his government, and of no other.

9. Others did the same thing, but not to quite so enormous an extent.

10. On reaching the approach to this about sunset of a beautiful evening in June, I first found myself among the mountains, — a feature of natural scenery for which, from my earliest days, it was not extravagant to say that I hungered and thirsted.

11. I speak of that part which chiefly it is that I know.

12. A smaller sum I had given to my friend the attorney (who was connected with the money lenders as their lawyer), to which, indeed, he was entitled for his unfurnished lodgings.

13. Whatever power the law gave them would be enforced against me to the utmost.

14. O thou that rollest above, round as the shield of my fathers!

15. But there are more than you ever heard of who die of grief in this island of ours.

16. But amongst themselves is no voice nor sound.

17. For this did God send her a great reward.

18. The table was good; but that was exactly what Kate cared little about.

19. Who and what was Milton? That is to say, what is the place which he fills in his own vernacular literature?

20. These hopes are mine as much as theirs.

21. What else am I who laughed or wept yesterday, who slept last night like a corpse?

22. I who alone am, I who see nothing in nature whose existence I can affirm with equal evidence to my own, behold now the semblance of my being, in all its height, variety, and curiosity reiterated in a foreign form.

23.

> What hand but would a garland cull
> For thee who art so beautiful?

24.

> And I had done a hellish thing,
> And it would work 'em woe.

25. Whatever he knows and thinks, whatever in his apprehension is worth doing, that let him communicate.

26. Rip Van Winkle was one of those foolish, well-oiled dispositions, who take the world easy, eat white bread or brown, whichever can be got with least thought or trouble.

27.

> And will your mother pity me,
> Who am a maiden most forlorn?

28.

> They know not I knew thee,
> Who knew thee too well.

29.

> I did remind thee of our own dear Lake,
> By the old Hall which may be mine no more.

30.

> He sate him down, and seized a pen, and traced
> Words which I could not guess of.

31.

Time writes no wrinkle on thine azure brow:
Such as creation's dawn beheld, thou rollest now.


32.

Wild Spirit which art moving everywhere;
Destroyer and preserver; hear, oh, hear!


33. A smile of hers was like an act of grace.

34. No man can learn what he has not preparation for learning.

35. What can we see or acquire but what we are?

36. He teaches who gives, and he learns who receives.

37. We are by nature observers; that is our permanent state.

38. He knew not what to do, and so he read.

39. Who hears me, who understands me, becomes mine.

40. The men who carry their points do not need to inquire of their constituents what they should say.

41. Higher natures overpower lower ones by affecting them with a certain sleep.

42. Those who live to the future must always appear selfish to those who live to the present.

43. I am sorry when my independence is invaded or when a gift comes from such as do not know my spirit.

44. Here I began to howl and scream abominably, which was no bad step towards my liberation.

45. The only aim of the war is to see which is the stronger of the two — which is the master.

# ADJECTIVES.

*Office of Adjectives.*

**139.** Nouns are seldom used as names of objects without additional words joined to them to add to their meaning. For example, if we wish to speak of a friend's house, we cannot guide one to it by merely calling it *a house.* We need to add some words to tell its color, size, position, etc., if we are at a distance; and if we are near, we need some word to point out the house we speak of, so that no other will be mistaken for it. So with any object, or with persons.

As to the kind of words used, we may begin with the common adjectives telling the *characteristics* of an object. If a chemist discovers a new substance, he cannot describe it to others without telling its qualities: he will say it is *solid,* or *liquid,* or *gaseous; heavy* or *light; brittle* or *tough; white* or *red;* etc.

Again, in *pointing out* an object, adjectives are used; such as in the expressions "*this* man," "*that* house," "*yonder* hill," etc.

Instead of using nouns indefinitely, the *number* is limited by adjectives; as, "*one* hat," "*some* cities," "*a hundred* men."

The office of an adjective, then, is to narrow down or limit the application of a noun. It may have this office alone, or it may at the same time add to the meaning of the noun.

*Substantives.*

**140.** Nouns are not, however, the only words limited by adjectives: pronouns and other words and expressions also have adjectives joined to them. Any word or word group that performs the same office as a noun may be modified by adjectives.

To make this clear, notice the following sentences: —

*Pronoun.*

If *he* be *thankful* for small benefits, it shows that he weighs men's minds, and their trash. — Bacon.

*Infinitives.*

*To err* is *human; to forgive, divine.* — Pope.

With exception of the "and then," the "and there," and the still less *significant "and so,"* they constitute all his connections. — Coleridge.

*Definition.*

**141.** An **adjective** is a word joined to a noun or other substantive word or expression, to describe it or to limit its application.

*Classes of adjectives.*

**142.** Adjectives are divided into four classes: —

(1) **Descriptive adjectives**, which describe by expressing qualities or attributes of a substantive.

(2) **Adjectives of quantity**, used to tell how many things are spoken of, or how much of a thing.

(3) **Demonstrative adjectives**, pointing out particular things.

(4) **Pronominal adjectives**, words primarily pronouns, but used adjectively sometimes in modifying nouns instead of standing for them. They include relative and interrogative words.

# DESCRIPTIVE ADJECTIVES.

**143.** This large class includes several kinds of words: —

(1) SIMPLE ADJECTIVES expressing quality; such as *safe, happy, deep, fair, rash, beautiful, remotest, terrible*, etc.

(2) COMPOUND ADJECTIVES, made up of various words thrown together to make descriptive epithets. Examples are, "*Heaven-derived* power," "this *life-giving* book," "his spirit wrapt and *wonder-struck*," "*ice-cold* water," "*half-dead* traveler," "*unlooked-for* burden," "*next-door* neighbor," "*ivory-handled* pistols," "the *cold-shudder-inspiring* Woman in White."

(3) PROPER ADJECTIVES, derived from proper nouns; such as, "an old *English* manuscript," "the *Christian* pearl of charity," "the well-curb had a *Chinese* roof," "the *Roman* writer Palladius."

(4) PARTICIPIAL ADJECTIVES, which are either pure participles used to describe, or participles which have lost all verbal force and have no function except to express quality. Examples are, —

*Pure participial adjectives*: "The *healing* power of the Messiah," "The *shattering* sway of one strong arm," "*trailing* clouds," "The *shattered* squares have opened into line," "It came on like the *rolling* simoom," "God tempers the wind to the *shorn* lamb."

*Faded participial adjectives*: "Sleep is a *blessed* thing;" "One is hungry, and another is *drunken*;" "under the *fitting* drapery of the jagged and trailing clouds;" "The clearness and quickness are *amazing*;" "an *aged* man;" "a *charming* sight."

*Caution.*

**144.** Care is needed, in studying these last-named words, to distinguish between a participle that forms part of a verb, and a participle or participial adjective that belongs to a noun.

For instance: in the sentence, "The work was well and rapidly accomplished," *was accomplished* is a verb; in this, "No man of his day was more brilliant or more accomplished," *was* is the verb, and *accomplished* is an adjective.

**Exercises.**

1. Bring up sentences with twenty descriptive adjectives, having some of each subclass named in Sec. 143.

2. Is the italicized word an adjective in this? —

The old sources of intellectual excitement seem to be well-nigh *exhausted*.

# ADJECTIVES OF QUANTITY.

**145.** Adjectives of quantity tell *how much* or *how many*. They have these three subdivisions:—

*How much.*

(1) QUANTITY IN BULK: such words as *little, much, some, no, any, considerable,* sometimes *small,* joined usually to singular nouns to express an indefinite measure of the thing spoken of.

The following examples are from Kingsley:—

> So he parted with *much* weeping of the lady.
> Which we began to do with *great* labor and *little* profit.
> Because I had *some* knowledge of surgery and blood-letting.
> But ever she looked on Mr. Oxenham, and seemed to take *no* care as long as he was by.

Examples of *small* an adjective of quantity:—

"The deil's in it but I bude to anger him!" said the woman, and walked away with a laugh of *small* satisfaction.—Macdonald.

'Tis midnight, but *small* thoughts have I of sleep.—Coleridge.

It gives *small* idea of Coleridge's way of talking.—Carlyle.

When *some, any, no,* are used with plural nouns, they come under the next division of adjectives.

*How many.*

(2) QUANTITY IN NUMBER, which may be expressed exactly by numbers or remotely designated by words expressing indefinite amounts. Hence the natural division into—

(*a*) *Definite numerals;* as, "*one* blaze of musketry;" "He found in the pathway *fourteen* Spaniards;" "I have lost *one* brother, but I have gained *fourscore;*" "*a dozen* volunteers."

(*b*) *Indefinite numerals,* as the following from Kingsley: "We gave *several* thousand pounds for it;" "In came some five and twenty more, and with them *a few* negroes;" "Then we wandered for *many* days;" "Amyas had evidently *more* schemes in his head;" "He had lived by hunting for *some* months;" "That light is far too red to be the reflection of *any* beams of hers."

*Single ones of any number of changes.*

(3) DISTRIBUTIVE NUMERALS, which occupy a place midway between the last two subdivisions of numeral adjectives; for they are indefinite in telling how many objects are spoken of, but definite in referring to the objects one at a time. Thus, —

*Every* town had its fair; *every* village, its wake. — Thackeray.

An arrow was quivering in *each* body. — Kingsley.

Few on *either* side but had their shrewd scratch to show. — *Id.*

> Before I taught my tongue to wound
> My conscience with a sinful sound,
> Or had the black art to dispense
> A *several* sin to *every* sense.
> — Vaughan.

**Exercise.** — Bring up sentences with ten adjectives of quantity.

# DEMONSTRATIVE ADJECTIVES.

*Not primarily pronouns.*

**146.** The words of this list are placed here instead of among pronominal adjectives, for the reason that they are felt to be primarily adjectives; their pronominal use being evidently a shortening, by which the words point out but stand for words omitted, instead of modifying them. Their natural and original use is to be joined to a noun following or in close connection.

*The list.*

The **demonstrative adjectives** are *this*, *that*, (plural *these*, *those*), *yonder* (or *yon*), *former*, *latter*; also the pairs *one* (or *the one*) — *the other*, *the former* — *the latter*, used to refer to two things which have been already named in a sentence.

*Examples.*

The following sentences present some examples: —

The bashful virgin's sidelong looks of love, The matron's glance that would *those* looks reprove. — Goldsmith.

These were thy charms...but all *these* charms are fled. — *Id.*

About *this* time I met with an odd volume of the "Spectator." — B. Franklin.

*Yonder* proud ships are not means of annoyance to you. — D. Webster.

*Yon* cloud with *that* long purple cleft. — Wordsworth.

I chose for the students of Kensington two characteristic examples of early art, of equal skill; but in *the one* case, skill which was progressive — in *the other*, skill which was at pause. — Ruskin.

**Exercise.** — Find sentences with five demonstrative adjectives.

*Ordinal numerals classed under demonstratives.*

**147.** The class of numerals known as **ordinals** must be placed here, as having the same function as demonstrative adjectives. They point out which thing is meant among a series of things mentioned. The following are examples: —

The *first* regular provincial newspapers appear to have been created in the last decade of the *seventeenth* century, and by the middle of the *eighteenth* century almost every important provincial town had its local organ. — Bancroft.

These do not, like the other numerals, tell *how many* things are meant. When we speak of the seventeenth century, we imply nothing as to how many centuries there may be.

# PRONOMINAL ADJECTIVES.

*Definition.*

**148.** As has been said, **pronominal adjectives** are primarily pronouns; but, when they *modify* words instead of referring to them as antecedents, they are changed to adjectives. They are of two kinds, — RELATIVE and INTERROGATIVE, — and are used to join sentences or to ask questions, just as the corresponding pronouns do.

*Modify names of persons or things.*

**149.** The RELATIVE ADJECTIVES are *which* and *what*; for example, —

It matters not *what* rank he has, *what* revenues or garnitures. — Carlyle.

The silver and laughing Xenil, careless *what* lord should possess the banks that bloomed by its everlasting course. — Bulwer.

The taking of *which* bark. I verily believe, was the ruin of every mother's son of us. — Kingsley.

In *which* evil strait Mr. Oxenham fought desperately. — Id.

*Indefinite relative adjectives.*

**150.** The INDEFINITE RELATIVE adjectives are *what, whatever, whatsoever, whichever, whichsoever*. Examples of their use are, —

He in his turn tasted some of its flavor, which, make *what* sour mouths he would for pretense, proved not altogether displeasing to him. — Lamb.

*Whatever* correction of our popular views from insight, nature will be sure to bear us out in. — Emerson.

*Whatsoever* kind of man he is, you at least give him full authority over your son. — Ruskin.

Was there, as it rather seemed, a circle of ominous shadow moving along with his deformity, *whichever* way he turned himself? — Hawthorne.

New torments I behold, and new tormented
Around me, *whichsoever* way I move,
And *whichsoever* way I turn, and gaze.
—Longfellow (From Dante).


**151.** The INTERROGATIVE ADJECTIVES are *which* and *what.*
They may be used in direct and indirect questions. As in the pronouns, *which* is selective among what is known; *what* inquires about
things or persons not known.

*In direct questions.*

Sentences with *which* and *what* in direct questions:—

*Which* debt must I pay first, the debt to the rich, or the debt to the
poor?—Emerson.

But when the Trojan war comes, *which* side will you take? —
Thackeray.

But *what* books in the circulating library circulate?—Lowell.

*What* beckoning ghost along the moonlight shade
Invites my steps, and points to yonder glade?
—Pope.


*In indirect questions.*

Sentences with *which* and *what* in indirect questions:—

His head...looked like a weathercock perched upon his spindle
neck to tell *which* way the wind blew.—Irving.

A lady once remarked, he [Coleridge] could never fix *which* side
of the garden walk would suit him best.—Carlyle.

He was turned before long into all the universe, where it was uncertain *what* game you would catch, or whether any.— *Id.*

At *what* rate these materials would be distributed and precipitat-
ed in regular strata, it is impossible to determine.—Agassiz.

*Adjective* what *in exclamations.*

**152.** In exclamatory expressions, *what* (or *what a*) has a force somewhat like a descriptive adjective. It is neither relative nor interrogative, but might be called an EXCLAMATORY ADJECTIVE; as, —

Oh, *what a* revolution! and *what a* heart must I have, to contemplate without emotion that elevation and that fall! — Burke.

*What a* piece of work is man! — Shakespeare.

And yet, alas, the making of it right, *what a* business for long time to come! — Carlyle

Through *what* hardships it may attain to bear a sweet fruit! — Thoreau.

**Exercise.** — Find ten sentences containing pronominal adjectives.

# INFLECTIONS OF ADJECTIVES.

**153** .Adjectives have two inflections, — **number** and **comparison**.

**NUMBER**. — *This* , *That* .

*History of* this — these *and* that — those.

**154.** The only adjectives having a plural form are *this* and *that* (plural *these, those*).

*This* is the old demonstrative; *that* being borrowed from the forms of the definite article, which was fully inflected in Old English. The article *that* was used with neuter nouns.

In Middle English the plural of *this* was *this* or *thise*, which changed its spelling to the modern form *these*.

Those *borrowed from* this.

But *this* had also another plural, *thās* (modern *those*). The old plural of *that* was *tha* (Middle English *tho* or *thow*): consequently *tho* (plural of *that*) and *those* (plural of *this*) became confused, and it was forgotten that *those* was really the plural of *this*; and in Modern English we speak of *these* as the plural of *this*, and *those* as the plural of *that*.

# COMPARISON.

**155.** Comparison is an inflection not possessed by nouns and pronouns: it belongs to adjectives and adverbs.

*Meaning of comparison.*

When we place two objects side by side, we notice some differences between them as to size, weight, color, etc. Thus, it is said that a cow is *larger* than a sheep, gold is *heavier* than iron, a sapphire is *bluer* than the sky. All these have certain qualities; and when we compare the objects, we do so by means of their qualities, — cow and sheep by the quality of largeness, or size; gold and iron by the quality of heaviness, or weight, etc., — but not the same degree, or amount, of the quality.

The degrees belong to any beings or ideas that may be known or conceived of as possessing quality; as, "untamed thought, great, giant-like, enormous;" "the commonest speech;" "It is a nobler valor;" "the largest soul."

Also words of quantity may be compared: for example, "more matter, with less wit;" "no fewer than a hundred."

*Words that cannot be compared.*

**156.** There are some descriptive words whose meaning is such as not to admit of comparison; for example, —

His company became very agreeable to the brave old professor of arms, whose *favorite* pupil he was. — Thackeray.

A *main* difference betwixt men is, whether they attend their own affair or not. — Emerson

It was his business to administer the law in its *final* and closest application to the offender — Hawthorne.

Freedom is a *perpetual, organic, universal* institution, in harmony with the Constitution of the United States. — Seward.

So with the words *sole, sufficient, infinite, immemorial, indefatigable, indomitable, supreme,* and many others.

It is true that words of comparison are sometimes prefixed to them, but, strictly considered, they are not compared.

*Definition.*

**157. Comparison** means the changes that words undergo to express degrees in quality, or amounts in quantity.

*The two forms.*

**158.** There are two forms for this inflection: the **comparative**, expressing a greater degree of quality; and the **superlative**, expressing the greatest degree of quality.

These are called **degrees of comparison**.

These are properly the only degrees, though the simple, uninflected form is usually called the **positive degree**.

**159.** The comparative is formed by adding *-er*, and the superlative by adding *-est*, to the simple form; as, *red, redder, reddest; blue, bluer, bluest; easy, easier, easiest.*

*Substitute for inflection in comparison.*

**160.** Side by side with these inflected forms are found comparative and superlative expressions making use of the adverbs **more** and **most**. These are often useful as alternative with the inflected forms, but in most cases are used before adjectives that are never inflected.

They came into use about the thirteenth century, but were not common until a century later.

*Which rule, — -er and -est or more and most?*

**161.** The English is somewhat capricious in choosing between the inflected forms and those with *more* and *most*, so that no inflexible rule can be given as to the formation of the comparative and the superlative.

The general rule is, that monosyllables and easily pronounced words of two syllables add *-er* and *-est*; and other words are preceded by *more* and *most*.

But room must be left in such a rule for pleasantness of sound and for variety of expression.

To see how literary English overrides any rule that could be given, examine the following taken at random: —

From Thackeray: "The *handsomest* wives;" "the *immensest* quantity of thrashing;" "the *wonderfulest* little shoes;" "*more odd, strange,* and yet familiar;" "*more austere* and *holy.*"

From Ruskin: "The sharpest, finest chiseling, and *patientest* fusing;" "*distantest* relationships;" "*sorrowfulest* spectacles."

Carlyle uses *beautifulest, mournfulest, honestest, admirablest, indisputablest, peaceablest, most small,* etc.

These long, harsh forms are usually avoided, but *more* and *most* are frequently used with monosyllables.

**162.** Expressions are often met with in which a superlative form does not carry the superlative meaning. These are equivalent usually to *very* with the positive degree; as, —

To this the Count offers a *most wordy* declaration of the benefits conferred by Spain. — *The Nation,* No 1507

In all formulas that Johnson could stand by, there needed to be a *most genuine* substance. — Carlyle

A gentleman, who, though born in no very high degree, was *most finished, polished, witty, easy, quiet.* — Thackeray

He had actually nothing else save a rope around his neck, which hung behind in the *queerest* way. — *Id.*

"So help me God, madam, I will," said Henry Esmond, falling on his knees, and kissing the hand of his *dearest* mistress. — *Id.*

*Adjectives irregularly compared.*

**163.** Among the variously derived adjectives now in our language there are some which may always be recognized as native English. These are adjectives **irregularly compared**.

Most of them have worn down or become confused with similar words, but they are essentially the same forms that have lived for so many centuries.

The following lists include the majority of them: —

## LIST I.

| 1. | Good or well | Better | Best |
|----|----|----|----|
| 2. | Evil, bad, ill | Worse | Worst |
| 3. | Little | Less, lesser | Least |
| 4. | Much or many | More | Most |
| 5. | Old | Elder, older | Eldest, oldest |
| 6. | Nigh | Nigher | Nighest, next |
| 7. | Near | Nearer | Nearest |
| 8. | Far | Farther, further | Farthest, furthest |
| 9. | Late | Later, latter | Latest, last |
| 10. | Hind | Hinder | Hindmost, hindermost |

## LIST II.

These have no adjective positive: —

| 1. | [In] | Inner | Inmost, innermost |
|----|----|----|----|
| 2. | [Out] | Outer, utter | Outmost, outermost<br>Utmost, uttermost |
| 3. | [Up] | Upper | Upmost, uppermost |

## LIST III.

A few of comparative form but not comparative meaning: —

After        Over        Under            Nether

# Remarks on Irregular Adjectives.

*List I.*

**164.** (1) The word good has no comparative or superlative, but takes the place of a positive to *better* and *best*. There was an old comparative *bet*, which has gone out of use; as in the sentence (14th century), "Ich singe *bet* than thu dest" (I sing better than thou dost). The superlative I form was *betst*, which has softened to the modern *best*.

(2) In Old English, **evil** was the positive to *worse, worst*; but later *bad* and *ill* were borrowed from the Norse, and used as positives to the same comparative and superlative. *Worser* was once used, a double comparative; as in Shakespeare, —

O, throw away the *worser* part of it. — Hamlet.

(3) **Little** is used as positive to *less, least*, though from a different root. A double comparative, *lesser*, is often used; as, —

We have it in a much *lesser* degree. — Matthew Arnold.

Thrust the *lesser* half by main force into the fists of Ho-ti. — Lamb.

(4) The words **much** and **many** now express quantity; but in former times *much* was used in the sense of *large, great*, and was the same word that is found in the proverb, "Many a little makes *a mickle*." Its spelling has been *micel, muchel, moche, much*, the parallel form *mickle* being rarely used.

The meanings *greater, greatest*, are shown in such phrases as, —

The *more* part being of one mind, to England we sailed. — Kingsley.

The *most* part kept a stolid indifference. — *Id*.

The latter, meaning *the largest part*, is quite common.

(5) The forms **elder, eldest**, are earlier than *older, oldest*. A few other words with the vowel *o* had similar change in the comparative and superlative, as *long, strong*, etc.; but these have followed *old* by keeping the same vowel *o* in all the forms, instead of *lenger, strenger*, etc., the old forms.

(6) and (7) Both **nigh** and **near** seem regular in Modern English, except the form *next*; but originally the comparison was *nigh, near, next*. In the same way the word **high** had in Middle English the superlative *hexte*.

By and by the comparative *near* was regarded as a positive form, and on it were built a double comparative *nearer*, and the superlative *nearest*, which adds *-est* to what is really a comparative instead of a simple adjective.

(8) These words also show confusion and consequent modification, coming about as follows: **further** really belongs to another series, — *forth, further, first*. **First** became entirely detached from the series, and *furthest* began to be used to follow the comparative *further*; then these were used as comparative and superlative of *far*.

The word **far** had formerly the comparative and superlative *farrer, farrest*. In imitation of *further, furthest, th* came into the others, making the modern *farther, farthest*. Between the two sets as they now stand, there is scarcely any distinction, except perhaps *further* is more used than *farther* in the sense of *additional*; as, for example, —

When that evil principle was left with no *further* material to support it. — Hawthorne.

(9) **Latter** and **last** are the older forms. Since *later, latest*, came into use, a distinction has grown up between the two series. *Later* and *latest* have the true comparative and superlative force, and refer to time; *latter* and *last* are used in speaking of succession, or series, and are hardly thought of as connected in meaning with the word *late*.

(10) **Hinder** is comparative in form, but not in meaning. The form *hindmost* is really a double superlative, since the *m* is for *-ma*, an old superlative ending, to which is added *-ost*, doubling the inflection. *Hind-er-m-ost* presents the combination comparative + superlative + superlative.

*List II.*

**165.** In List II. (Sec. 163) the comparatives and superlatives are adjectives, but they have no adjective positives.

The comparatives are so in form, but not in their meaning.

The superlatives show examples again of double inflection, and of comparative added to double-superlative inflection.

Examples (from Carlyle) of the use of these adjectives: "revealing the *inner* splendor to him;" "a mind that has penetrated into the *inmost* heart of a thing;" "This of painting is one of the *outermost* developments of a man;" "The *outer* is of the day;" "far-seeing as the sun, the *upper* light of the world;" "the *innermost* moral soul;" "their *utmost* exertion."

-Most *added to other words.*

**166.** The ending -*most* is added to some words that are not usually adjectives, or have no comparative forms.

There, on the very *topmost* twig, sits that ridiculous but sweet-singing bobolink. — H. W. Beecher.

Decidedly handsome, having such a skin as became a young woman of family in *northernmost* Spain. — De Quincey.

Highest and *midmost*, was descried The royal banner floating wide. — Scott.

*List III.*

**167.** The adjectives in List III. are like the comparative forms in List II. in having no adjective positives. They have no superlatives, and have no comparative force, being merely descriptive.

Her bows were deep in the water, but her *after* deck was still dry. — Kingsley.

Her, by the by, in *after* years I vainly endeavored to trace. — De Quincey.

The upper and the *under* side of the medal of Jove. — Emerson.

Have you ever considered what a deep *under* meaning there lies in our custom of strewing flowers? — Ruskin.

Perhaps he rose out of some *nether* region. — Hawthorne.

*Over* is rarely used separately as an adjective.

# CAUTION FOR ANALYZING OR PARSING.

*Think what each adjective belongs to.*

**168.** Some care must be taken to decide what word is modified by an adjective. In a series of adjectives in the same sentence, all may belong to the same noun, or each may modify a different word or group of words.

For example, in this sentence, "The young pastor's voice was tremulously sweet, rich, deep, and broken," it is clear that all four adjectives after *was* modify the noun *voice*. But in this sentence, "She showed her usual prudence and her usual incomparable decision," *decision* is modified by the adjective *incomparable*; *usual* modifies *incomparable decision*, not *decision* alone; and the pronoun *her* limits *usual incomparable decision*.

Adjectives modifying the same noun are said to be of the *same rank*; those modifying different words or word groups are said to be adjectives of *different rank*. This distinction is valuable in a study of punctuation.

**Exercise.**

In the following quotations, tell what each adjective modifies: —

1. Whenever that look appeared in her wild, bright, deeply black eyes, it invested them with a strange remoteness and intangibility. — Hawthorne.

2. It may still be argued, that in the present divided state of Christendom a college which is positively Christian must be controlled by some religious denomination. — Noah Porter.

3. Every quaking leaf and fluttering shadow sent the blood backward to her heart. — Mrs. Stowe.

4. This, our new government, is the first in the history of the world based upon this great physical, philosophical, and moral truth. — A. H. Stephens

5. May we not, therefore, look with confidence to the ultimate universal acknowledgment of the truths upon which our system rests? — *Id.*

6. A few improper jests and a volley of good, round, solid, satisfactory, and heaven-defying oaths. — Hawthorne.

7. It is well known that the announcement at any private rural entertainment that there is to be ice cream produces an immediate and profound impression. — Holmes.

# ADVERBS USED AS ADJECTIVES.

**169.** By a convenient brevity, adverbs are sometimes used as adjectives; as, instead of saying, "the one who was then king," in which *then* is an adverb, we may say "the *then* king," making *then* an adjective. Other instances are, —

My *then* favorite, in prose, Richard Hooker. — Ruskin.

Our *sometime* sister, now our queen. — Shakespeare

Messrs. Bradbury and Evans, the *then* and *still* owners. — Trollope.

The *seldom* use of it. — Trench.

For thy stomach's sake, and thine *often* infirmities. — *Bible.*

# HOW TO PARSE ADJECTIVES.

*What to tell in parsing.*

**170.** Since adjectives have no gender, person, or case, and very few have number, the method of parsing is simple.

In **parsing** an adjective, tell —

(1) The class and subclass to which it belongs.

(2) Its number, if it has number.

(3) Its degree of comparison, if it can be compared.

(4) What word or words it modifies.

# MODEL FOR PARSING.

These truths are not unfamiliar to your thoughts.

*These* points out *what* truths, therefore demonstrative; plural number, having a singular, *this*; cannot be compared; modifies the word *truths*.

*Unfamiliar* describes *truths*, therefore descriptive; not inflected for number; compared by prefixing *more* and *most*; positive degree; modifies *truths*.

**Exercise.**

Parse in full each adjective in these sentences: —

1. A thousand lives seemed concentrated in that one moment to Eliza.

2. The huge green fragment of ice on which she alighted pitched and creaked.

3. I ask nothing of you, then, but that you proceed to your end by a direct, frank, manly way.

4. She made no reply, and I waited for none.

5. A herd of thirty or forty tall ungainly figures took their way, with awkward but rapid pace, across the plain.

6. Gallantly did the lion struggle in the folds of his terrible enemy, whose grasp each moment grew more fierce and secure, and most astounding were those frightful yells.

7. This gave the young people entire freedom, and they enjoyed it to the fullest extent.

8. I will be as harsh as truth and as uncompromising as justice.

9. To every Roman citizen he gives, To every several man, seventy-five drachmas.

10. Each member was permitted to entertain all the rest on his or her birthday, on which occasion the elders of the family were bound to be absent.

11. Instantly the mind inquires whether these fishes under the bridge, yonder oxen in the pasture, those dogs in the yard, are immutably fishes, oxen, and dogs.

12. I know not what course others may take.

13. With every third step, the tomahawk fell.

14. What a ruthless business this war of extermination is!

15. I was just emerging from that many-formed crystal country.

16. On what shore has not the prow of your ships dashed?

17. The laws and institutions of his country ought to have been more to him than all the men in his country.

18. Like most gifted men, he won affections with ease.

19. His letters aim to elicit the inmost experience and outward fortunes of those he loves, yet are remarkably self-forgetful.

20. Their name was the last word upon his lips.

21. The captain said it was the last stick he had seen.

22. Before sunrise the next morning they let us out again.

23. He was curious to know to what sect we belonged.

24. Two hours elapsed, during which time I waited.

25. In music especially, you will soon find what personal benefit there is in being serviceable.

26. To say what good of fashion we can, it rests on reality, and hates nothing so much as pretenders.

27. Here lay two great roads, not so much for travelers that were few, as for armies that were too many by half.

28. On whichever side of the border chance had thrown Joanna, the same love to France would have been nurtured.

29. What advantage was open to him above the English boy?

30. Nearer to our own times, and therefore more interesting to us, is the settlement of our own country.

31. Even the topmost branches spread out and drooped in all directions, and many poles supported the lower ones.

32. Most fruits depend entirely on our care.

33. Even the sourest and crabbedest apple, growing in the most unfavorable position, suggests such thoughts as these, it is so noble a fruit.

34. Let him live in what pomps and prosperities he like, he is no literary man.

35. Through what hardships it may bear a sweet fruit!

36. Whatsoever power exists will have itself organized.

37. A hard-struggling, weary-hearted man was he.

## ARTICLES.

**171.** There is a class of words having always an adjectival use in general, but with such subtle functions and various meanings that they deserve separate treatment. In the sentence, "He passes an ordinary brick house on the road, with an ordinary little garden," the words *the* and *an* belong to nouns, just as adjectives do; but they cannot be accurately placed under any class of adjectives. They are nearest to demonstrative and numeral adjectives.

*Their origin.*

172. The article **the** comes from an old demonstrative adjective (*sē, sēo, ðat,* later *thē, thēo, that*) which was also an article in Old English. In Middle English *the* became an article, and *that* remained a demonstrative adjective.

**An** or a came from the old numeral *ān,* meaning *one.*

*Two relics.*

Our expressions *the one, the other,* were formerly *that one, that other;* the latter is still preserved in the expression, in vulgar English, *the tother.* Not only this is kept in the Scotch dialect, but the former is used, these occurring as *the tane, the tother,* or *the tane, the tither;* for example, —

We ca' her sometimes *the tane,* sometimes *the tother.* — Scott.

An *before vowel sounds,* a *before consonant sounds.*

**173.** Ordinarily *an* is used before vowel sounds, and *a* before consonant sounds. Remember that a *vowel sound* does not necessarily mean beginning with a vowel, nor does *consonant sound* mean beginning with a consonant, because English spelling does not coincide closely with the sound of words. Examples: "*a* house," "*an* orange," "*a* European," "*an* honor," "*a* yelling crowd."

An *with consonant sounds.*

**174.** Many writers use *an* before *h*, even when not silent, when the word is not accented on the first syllable.

*An* historian, such as we have been attempting to describe, would indeed be an intellectual prodigy. — Macaulay.

The Persians were *an* heroic people like the Greeks. — Brewer.

He [Rip] evinced *an* hereditary disposition to attend to anything else but his business. — Irving.

*An* habitual submission of the understanding to mere events and images. — Coleridge.

*An* hereditary tenure of these offices. — Thomas Jefferson.

*Definition.*

**175.** An **article** is a limiting word, not descriptive, which cannot be used alone, but always joins to a substantive word to denote a particular thing, or a group or class of things, or any individual of a group or class.

*Kinds.*

**176.** Articles are either **definite** or **indefinite**.

**The** is the definite article, since it points out a particular individual, or group, or class.

**An** or **a** is the indefinite article, because it refers to any one of a group or class of things.

**An** and **a** are different forms of the same word, the older *ān*.

# USES OF THE DEFINITE ARTICLE.

*Reference to a known object.*

**177.** The most common use of the definite article is to refer to an object that the listener or reader is already acquainted with; as in the sentence, —

Don't you remember how, when *the* dragon was infesting *the* neighborhood of Babylon, *the* citizens used to walk dismally out of evenings, and look at *the* valleys round about strewed with *the* bones? — Thackeray.

NOTE. — This use is noticed when, on opening a story, a person is introduced by *a*, and afterwards referred to by *the*: —

By and by *a* giant came out of the dark north, and lay down on the ice near Audhumla.... *The* giant frowned when he saw the glitter of the golden hair. — *Heroes Of Asgard.*

*With names of rivers.*

**178.** *The* is often prefixed to the names of rivers; and when the word *river* is omitted, as "*the* Mississippi," "*the* Ohio," the article indicates clearly that a river, and not a state or other geographical division, is referred to.

No wonder I could face *the* Mississippi with so much courage supplied to me. — Thackeray.

The Dakota tribes, doubtless, then occupied the country south-west of *the* Missouri. — G. Bancroft.

*To call attention to attributes.*

**179.** When *the* is prefixed to a proper name, it alters the force of the noun by directing attention to *certain qualities* possessed by the person or thing spoken of; thus, —

*The* Bacon, *the* Spinoza, *the* Hume, Schelling, Kant, or whosoever propounds to you a philosophy of the mind, is only a more or less awkward translator of things in your consciousness. — Emerson.

*With plural of abstract nouns.*

**180.** *The*, when placed before the pluralized abstract noun, marks it as half abstract or a common noun.

*Common.*

His messages to *the* provincial *authorities.* — Motley.

*Half abstract.*

He was probably skilled in *the subtleties* of Italian statesmanship. — *Id.*

*With adjectives used as nouns.*

**181.** When *the* precedes adjectives of the positive degree used substantively, it marks their use as common and plural nouns when they refer to persons, and as singular and abstract when they refer to qualities.

1. *The simple* rise as by specific levity, not into a particular virtue, but into the region of all the virtues. — Emerson.

2. If *the good* is there, so is *the evil.* — *Id.*

*Caution.*

NOTE. — This is not to be confused with words that have shifted from adjectives and become pure nouns; as, —

As she hesitated to pass on, *the gallant*, throwing his cloak from his shoulders, laid it on the miry spot. — Scott.

But De Soto was no longer able to abate the confidence or punish the temerity of *the natives.* — G. Bancroft.

*One thing for its class.*

**182.** *The* before class nouns may mark one thing as a representative of the class to which it belongs; for example, —

The faint, silvery warblings heard over the partially bare and moist fields from *the bluebird, the song sparrow,* and *the redwing,* as if the last flakes of winter tinkled as they fell! — Thoreau.

In the sands of Africa and Arabia *the camel* is a sacred and precious gift. — Gibbon.

*For possessive person pronouns.*

**183.** *The* is frequently used instead of the possessive case of the personal pronouns *his, her,* etc.

More than one hinted that a cord twined around *the head,* or a match put between *the fingers,* would speedily extract the required information. — Kingsley.

*The* mouth, and the region of the mouth, were about the strongest features in Wordsworth's face. — De Quincey.

The *for* a.

**184.** In England and Scotland *the* is often used where we use *a,* in speaking of measure and price; as, —

Wheat, the price of which necessarily varied, averaged in the middle of the fourteenth century tenpence *the bushel,* barley averaging at the same time three shillings *the quarter.* — Froude.

*A very strong restrictive.*

**185.** Sometimes *the* has a strong force, almost equivalent to a descriptive adjective in emphasizing a word, —

No doubt but ye are *the* people, and wisdom shall die with you. — *Bible.*

As for New Orleans, it seemed to me *the* city of the world where you can eat and drink the most and suffer the least. — Thackeray.

He was *the* man in all Europe that could (if any could) have driven six-in-hand full gallop over Al Sirat. — De Quincey.

*Mark of a substantive.*

**186.** *The,* since it belongs distinctively to substantives, is a sure indication that a word of verbal form is not used participially, but substantively.

In the hills of Sacramento there is gold for *the gathering.* — Emerson.

I thought *the writing* excellent, and wished, if possible, to imitate it. — Franklin.

*Caution.*

**187.** There is one use of *the* which is different from all the above. It is an adverbial use, and is spoken of more fully in Sec. 283. Compare this sentence with those above: —

There was something ugly and evil in his face, which they had not previously noticed, and which grew still *the more obvious* to the sight *the oftener* they looked upon him. — Hawthorne.

**Exercise.** — Find sentences with five uses of the definite article.

# USES OF THE INDEFINITE ARTICLE.

*Denotes any one of a class.*

**188.** The most frequent use of the indefinite article is to denote any one of a class or group of objects: consequently it belongs to singular words; as in the sentence, —

Near the churchyard gate stands *a* poor-box, fastened to *a* post by iron bands and secured by *a* padlock, with *a* sloping wooden roof to keep off the rain. — Longfellow

*Widens the scope of proper nouns.*

**189.** When the indefinite article precedes proper names, it alters them to class names. The qualities or attributes of the object are made prominent, and transferred to any one possessing them; as, —

The vulgar riot and debauchery, which scarcely disgraced *an Alcibiades* or *a Cæsar*, have been exchanged for the higher ideals of *a Bayard* or *a Sydney.* — Pearson

*With abstract nouns.*

**190.** *An* or *a* before abstract nouns often changes them to half abstract: the idea of quality remains, but the word now denotes only one instance or example of things possessing the quality.

*Become half abstract.*

The simple perception of natural forms is *a delight.* — Emerson

If thou hadst *a sorrow* of thine own, the brook might tell thee of it. — Hawthorne

In the first sentence, instead of the general abstract notion of delight, which cannot be singular or plural, *a delight* means one thing delightful, and implies others having the same quality.

So *a sorrow* means one cause of sorrow, implying that there are other things that bring sorrow.

*Become pure class nouns.*

NOTE. — Some abstract nouns become common class nouns with the indefinite article, referring simply to persons; thus, —

If the poet of the "Rape of the Lock" be not *a wit*, who deserves to be called so? — Thackeray.

He had a little brother in London with him at this time, — as great *a beauty*, as great a dandy, as great a villain. — *Id.*

*A youth* to fortune and to fame unknown. — Gray.

*Changes material to class nouns.*

**191.** *An* or *a* before a material noun indicates the change to a class noun, meaning one kind or a detached portion; as, —

> They that dwell up in the steeple,...
> Feel a glory in so rolling
> On the human heart *a stone*.
> — Poe.


> When God at first made man,
> Having *a glass* of blessings standing by.
> — Herbert.


The roofs were turned into arches of massy stone, joined by *a cement* that grew harder by time. — Johnson.

*Like the numeral adjective* one.

**192.** In some cases *an* or *a* has the full force of the numeral adjective *one*. It is shown in the following: —

To every room there was *an* open and *a* secret passage. — Johnson.

In a short time these become a small tree, *an* inverted pyramid resting on the apex of the other. — Thoreau.

All men are at last of *a* size. — Emerson.

At the approach of spring the red squirrels got under my house, two at *a* time. — Thoreau.

*Equivalent to the word* each *or* every.

**193.** Often, also, the indefinite article has the force of *each* or *every*, particularly to express measure or frequency.

It would be so much more pleasant to live at his ease than to work eight or ten hours *a day.* — Bulwer

*Compare to Sec. 184.*

Strong beer, such as we now buy for eighteenpence *a gallon,* was then a penny *a gallon.* — Froude

*With* such, many, what.

**194.** *An* or *a* is added to the adjectives *such, many,* and *what,* and may be considered a part of these in modifying substantives.

How was I to pay *such a* debt? — Thackeray.

*Many a* one you and I have had here below. — Thackeray.

*What a* world of merriment then melody foretells! — Poe.

*With* not *and* many.

**195.** *Not* and *never* with *a* or *an* are numeral adjectives, instead of adverbs, which they are in general.

*Not a* drum was heard, *not a* funeral note. — Wolfe

My Lord Duke was as hot as a flame at this salute, but said *never a* word. — Thackeray.

NOTE. — All these have the function of adjectives; but in the last analysis of the expressions, *such, many, not,* etc., might be considered as adverbs modifying the article.

*With* few *or* little.

**196.** The adjectives *few* and *little* have the negative meaning of *not much, not many,* without the article; but when *a* is put before them, they have the positive meaning of *some.* Notice the contrast in the following sentences: —

Of the country beyond the Mississippi *little* more was known than of the heart of Africa. — Mcmaster

To both must I of necessity cling, supported always by the hope that when *a little* time, *a few* years, shall have tried me more fully in their esteem, I may be able to bring them together.— *Keats's Letters.*

*Few* of the great characters of history have been so differently judged as Alexander. — Smith, *History of Greece*

*With adjectives, changed to nouns.*

**197.** When *the* is used before adjectives with no substantive following (Sec. 181 and note), these words are adjectives used as nouns, or pure nouns; but when *an* or *a* precedes such words, they are always nouns, having the regular use and inflections of nouns; for example, —

Such are the words *a brave* should use. — Cooper.

In the great society of wits, John Gay deserves to be *a favorite*, and to have a good place. — Thackeray

Only the name of one obscure epigrammatist has been embalmed for use in the verses of *a rival.* — Pearson.

**Exercise.** — Bring up sentences with five uses of the indefinite article.

# HOW TO PARSE ARTICLES.

**198.** In parsing the article, tell —

(1) What word it limits.

(2) Which of the above uses it has.

**Exercise.**

Parse the articles in the following: —

1. It is like gathering a few pebbles off the ground, or bottling a little air in a phial, when the whole earth and the whole atmosphere are ours.

2. Aristeides landed on the island with a body of Hoplites, defeated the Persians and cut them to pieces to a man.

3. The wild fire that lit the eye of an Achilles can gleam no more.

4. But it is not merely the neighborhood of the cathedral that is mediæval; the whole city is of a piece.

5. To the herdsman among his cattle in remote woods, to the craftsman in his rude workshop, to the great and to the little, a new light has arisen.

6. When the manners of Loo are heard of, the stupid become intelligent, and the wavering, determined.

7. The student is to read history actively, and not passively.

8. This resistance was the labor of his life.

9. There was always a hope, even in the darkest hour.

10. The child had a native grace that does not invariably coexist with faultless beauty.

11. I think a mere gent (which I take to be the lowest form of civilization) better than a howling, whistling, clucking, stamping, jumping, tearing savage.

12. Every fowl whom Nature has taught to dip the wing in water.

13. They seem to be lines pretty much of a length.

14. Only yesterday, but what a gulf between now and then!

15. Not a brick was made but some man had to think of the making of that brick.

16. The class of power, the working heroes, the Cortes, the Nelson, the Napoleon, see that this is the festivity and permanent celebration of such as they; that fashion is funded talent.

## VERBS AND VERBALS..

### VERBS.

*Verb, — the word of the sentence.*

**199.** The term *verb* is from the Latin *verbum* meaning *word*: hence it is *the* word of a sentence. A thought cannot be expressed without a verb. When the child cries, "Apple!" it means, *See* the apple! or I *have* an apple! In the mariner's shout, "A sail!" the meaning is, "Yonder *is* a sail!"

Sentences are in the form of declarations, questions, or commands; and none of these can be put before the mind without the use of a verb.

*One group or a group of words.*

**200.** The verb may not always be a single word. On account of the lack of inflections, *verb phrases* are very frequent. Hence the verb may consist of:

(1) *One word*; as, "The young man *obeyed*."

(2) *Several words of verbal nature, making one expression*; as, (*a*) "Some day it *may be considered* reasonable," (*b*) "Fearing lest he *might have been anticipated*."

(3) *One or more verbal words united with other words to compose one verb phrase*: as in the sentences, (*a*) "They knew well that this woman *ruled over* thirty millions of subjects;" (*b*) "If all the flummery and extravagance of an army *were done away with*, the money could be made to go much further;" (*c*) "It is idle cant to pretend anxiety for the better distribution of wealth until we can devise means by

which this preying upon people of small incomes *can be put a stop to.*"

In (*a*), a verb and a preposition are used as one verb; in (*b*), a verb, an adverb, and a preposition unite as a verb; in (*c*), an article, a noun, a preposition, are united with verbs as one verb phrase.

*Definition and caution.*

**201.** A **verb** is a word used as a predicate, to say something to or about some person or thing. In giving a definition, we consider a verb as one word.

Now, it is indispensable to the nature of a verb that it is "a word used as a predicate." Examine the sentences in Sec. 200: In (1), *obeyed* is a predicate; in (2, *a*), *may be considered* is a unit in doing the work of one predicate; in (2, *b*), *might have been anticipated* is also one predicate, but *fearing* is not a predicate, hence is not a verb; in (3, *b*), *to go* is no predicate, and not a verb; in (3, *c*), *to pretend* and *preying* have something of verbal nature in expressing action in a faint and general way, but cannot be predicates.

In the sentence, "*Put* money in thy purse," *put* is the predicate, with some word understood; as, "Put *thou* money in thy purse."

# VERBS CLASSIFIED ACCORDING TO MEANING AND USE.

## TRANSITIVE AND INTRANSITIVE VERBS.

*The nature of the transitive verb.*

**202.** By examining a few verbs, it may be seen that not all verbs are used alike. All do not express action: some denote state or condition. Of those expressing action, all do not express it in the same way; for example, in this sentence from Bulwer,—"The proud lone *took* care to conceal the anguish she *endured*; and the pride of woman *has* an hypocrisy which *can deceive* the most penetrating, and *shame* the most astute,"—every one of the verbs in Italics has one or more words before or after it, representing something which it influences or controls. In the first, lone *took* what? answer, *care; endured* what? *anguish;* etc. Each influences some object, which may be a person, or a material thing, or an idea. *Has* takes the object *hypocrisy; can deceive* has an object, *the most penetrating;* (can) *shame* also has an object, *the most astute.*

In each case, the word following, or the object, is necessary to the completion of the action expressed in the verb.

All these are called transitive verbs, from the Latin *transire,* which means *to go over.* Hence

*Definition.*

**203.** A transitive verb is one which must have an object to complete its meaning, and to receive the action expressed.

*The nature of intransitive verbs.*

**204.** Examine the verbs in the following paragraph:—

She *sprang up* at that thought, and, taking the staff which always guided her steps, she *hastened* to the neighboring shrine of Isis. Till she *had been* under the guardianship of the kindly Greek, that staff *had sufficed* to conduct the poor blind girl from corner to corner of Pompeii.—Bulwer

In this there are some verbs unlike those that have been examined. *Sprang*, or *sprang up*, expresses action, but it is complete in itself, does not affect an object; *hastened* is similar in use; *had been* expresses condition, or state of being, and can have no object; *had sufficed* means *had been sufficient*, and from its meaning cannot have an object.

Such verbs are called intransitive (not crossing over). Hence

*Definition.*

**205.** An intransitive verb is one which is complete in itself, or which is completed by other words without requiring an object.

*Study* use, *not* form, *of verbs here.*

206. Many verbs can be either transitive or intransitive, according to their use in the sentence, It can be said, "The boy *walked* for two hours," or "The boy *walked* the horse;" "The rains *swelled* the river," or "The river *swelled* because of the rain;" etc.

The important thing to observe is, many words must be distinguished as transitive or intransitive by *use*, not by *form*.

**207.** Also verbs are sometimes made transitive by prepositions. These may be (1) compounded with the verb; or (2) may follow the verb, and be used as an integral part of it: for example, —

Asking her pardon for having *withstood* her. — Scott.

I can wish myself no worse than to have it all to *undergo* a second time. — Kingsley.

A weary gloom in the deep caverns of his eyes, as of a child that has *outgrown* its playthings. — Hawthorne.

It is amusing to walk up and down the pier and *look at* the countenances passing by. — B. Taylor.

He was at once so out of the way, and yet so sensible, that I loved, *laughed at*, and pitied him. — Goldsmith.

My little nurse told me the whole matter, which she had cunningly *picked out* from her mother. — Swift.

**Exercises.**

(*a*) Pick out the transitive and the intransitive verbs in the following: —

1. The women and children collected together at a distance.

2. The path to the fountain led through a grassy savanna.

3. As soon as I recovered my senses and strength from so sudden a surprise, I started back out of his reach where I stood to view him; he lay quiet whilst I surveyed him.

4. At first they lay a floor of this kind of tempered mortar on the ground, upon which they deposit a layer of eggs.

5. I ran my bark on shore at one of their landing places, which was a sort of neck or little dock, from which ascended a sloping path or road up to the edge of the meadow, where their nests were; most of them were deserted, and the great thick whitish eggshells lay broken and scattered upon the ground.

6. Accordingly I got everything on board, charged my gun, set sail cautiously, along shore. As I passed by Battle Lagoon, I began to tremble.

7. I seized my gun, and went cautiously from my camp: when I had advanced about thirty yards, I halted behind a coppice of orange trees, and soon perceived two very large bears, which had made their way through the water and had landed in the grove, and were advancing toward me.

(*b*) Bring up sentences with five transitive and five intransitive verbs.

# VOICE, ACTIVE AND PASSIVE.

*Meaning of active voice.*

**208.** As has been seen, transitive verbs are the only kind that can express action so as to go over to an object. This implies three things, — the agent, or person or thing acting; the verb representing the action; the person or object receiving the act.

In the sentence, "We reached the village of Sorgues by dusk, and accepted the invitation of an old dame to lodge at her inn," these three things are found: the actor, or agent, is expressed by *we*; the action is asserted by *reached* and *accepted*; the things acted upon are *village* and *invitation*. Here the subject is represented as doing something. The same word is the subject and the agent. This use of a transitive verb is called the **active voice**.

*Definition.*

**209.** The **active voice** is that form of a verb which represents the subject as acting; or

The active voice is that form of a transitive verb which makes the *subject* and the *agent* the same word.

*A question.*

**210.** Intransitive verbs are *always active voice*. Let the student explain why.

*Meaning of passive voice.*

**211.** In the assertion of an action, it would be natural to suppose, that, instead of always representing the subject as acting upon some person or thing, it must often happen that the subject is spoken of as *acted upon*; and the person or thing acting may or may not be expressed in the sentence: for example, —

All infractions of love and equity in our social relations are speedily punished. They are punished by fear. — Emerson.

Here the subject *infractions* does nothing: it represents the object toward which the action of *are punished* is directed, yet it is the subject of the same verb. In the first sentence the agent is not expressed; in the second, *fear* is the agent of the same action.

So that in this case, instead of having the agent and subject the same word, we have the *object* and *subject* the same word, and the agent may be omitted from the statement of the action.

*Passive* is from the Latin word *patior*, meaning *to endure* or *suffer*; but in ordinary grammatical use *passive* means *receiving an action*.

Definition.

**212.** The passive voice is that form of the verb which represents the subject as being acted upon; or —

The passive voice is that form of the verb which represents the *subject* and the *object* by the same word.

**Exercises.**

(*a*) Pick out the verbs in the active and the passive voice: —

1. In the large room some forty or fifty students were walking about while the parties were preparing.

2. This was done by taking off the coat and vest and binding a great thick leather garment on, which reached to the knees.

3. They then put on a leather glove reaching nearly to the shoulder, tied a thick cravat around the throat, and drew on a cap with a large visor.

4. This done, they were walked about the room a short time; their faces all this time betrayed considerable anxiety.

5. We joined the crowd, and used our lungs as well as any.

6. The lakes were soon covered with merry skaters, and every afternoon the banks were crowded with spectators.

7. People were setting up torches and lengthening the rafts which had been already formed.

8. The water was first brought in barrels drawn by horses, till some officer came and opened the fire plug.

9. The exclusive in fashionable life does not see that he excludes himself from enjoyment, in the attempt to appropriate it.

(*b*) Find sentences with five verbs in the active and five in the passive voice.

# MOOD.

**213.** The word *mood* is from the Latin *modus*, meaning *manner, way, method*. Hence, when applied to verbs, —

**Mood** means the manner of conceiving and expressing action or being of some subject.

*The three ways.*

**214.** There are three chief ways of expressing action or being: —

(1) As a fact; this may be a question, statement, or assumption.

(2) As doubtful, or merely conceived of in the mind.

(3) As urged or commanded.

# INDICATIVE MOOD.

*Deals with facts.*

**215.** The term *indicative* is from the Latin *indicare* (to declare, or assert). The indicative represents something as a fact, —

*Affirms or denies.*

(1) *By declaring a thing to be true or not to be true*; thus, —

Distinction *is* the consequence, never the object, of a great mind. — Allston.

I *do not remember* when or by whom I *was taught* to read; because I *cannot* and never *could recollect* a time when I *could not read* my Bible. — D. Webster.

*Assumed as a fact.*

*Caution.*

(2) *By assuming a thing to be true* without declaring it to be so. This kind of indicative clause is usually introduced by *if* (meaning *admitting that, granting that*, etc.), *though, although*, etc. Notice that the action is not merely conceived as possible; it is assumed to be a fact: for example, —

If the penalties of rebellion hung over an unsuccessful contest; if America was yet in the cradle of her political existence; if her population little exceeded two millions; if she was without government, without fleets or armies, arsenals or magazines, without military knowledge, — still her citizens had a just and elevated sense of her rights. — A. Hamilton.

(3) *By asking a question to find out some fact*; as, —

Is private credit the friend and patron of industry? — Hamilton.

With respect to novels what shall I say? — N. Webster.

*Definition.*

**216** .The **indicative mood** is that form of a verb which represents a thing as a fact, or inquires about some fact.

# SUBJUNCTIVE MOOD.

*Meaning of the word.*

**217.** *Subjunctive* means *subjoined,* or joined as dependent or sub-ordinate to something else.

*This meaning is misleading.*

If its original meaning be closely adhered to, we must expect every dependent clause to have its verb in the subjunctive mood, and every clause *not* dependent to have its verb in some other mood.

But this is not the case. In the quotation from Hamilton (Sec. 215, 2) several subjoined clauses introduced by *if* have the indicative mood, and also independent clauses are often found having the verb in the subjunctive mood.

*Cautions.*

Three cautions will be laid down which must be observed by a student who wishes to understand and use the English subjunctive: —

(1) You cannot tell it always by the form of the word. The main difference is, that the subjunctive has no *-s* as the ending of the present tense, third person singular; as, "If he *come.*"

(2) The fact that its clause is dependent or is introduced by certain words will not be a safe rule to guide you.

(3) The *meaning* of the verb itself must be keenly studied.

*Definition.*

**218.** The subjunctive mood is that form or use of the verb which expresses action or being, not as a fact, but as merely conceived of in the mind.

# Subjunctive in Independent Clauses.

## I. Expressing a Wish.

**219.** The following are examples of this use: —

Heaven *rest* her soul! — Moore.

God *grant* you find one face there You loved when all was young. — Kingsley.

Now *tremble* dimples on your cheek, Sweet *be* your lips to taste and speak. — Beddoes.

Long *die* thy happy days before thy death. — Shakespeare.

## II. A Contingent Declaration or Question.

**220.** This really amounts to the conclusion, or principal clause, in a sentence, of which the condition is omitted.

Our chosen specimen of the hero as literary man [if we were to choose one] *would be* this Goethe. — Carlyle.

> I *could lie* down like a tired child,
> And *weep* away the life of care
> Which I have borne and yet must bear.
> — Shelley.

Most excellent stranger, as you come to the lakes simply to see their loveliness, *might* it not *be* as well to ask after the most beautiful road, rather than the shortest? — De Quincey.

# Subjunctive in Dependent Clauses.

## I. Condition or Supposition.

**221.** The most common way of representing the action or being as merely thought of, is by putting it into the form of a *supposition* or *condition*; as, —

Now, if the fire of electricity and that of lightning *be* the same, this pasteboard and these scales may represent electrified clouds. — Franklin.

Here no assertion is made that the two things *are* the same; but, if the reader merely *conceives* them for the moment to be the same, the writer can make the statement following. Again, —

If it *be* Sunday [supposing it to be Sunday], the peasants sit on the church steps and con their psalm books. — Longfellow.

# STUDY OF CONDITIONAL SENTENCES.

**222.** There are three kinds of conditional sentences: —

*Real or true.*

(1) Those in which an assumed or admitted fact is placed before the mind in the form of a condition (see Sec. 215, 2); for example, —

If they *were* unacquainted with the works of philosophers and poets, they were deeply read in the oracles of God. If their names *were not found* in the registers of heralds, they were recorded in the Book of Life. — Macaulay.

*Ideal, — may or may not be true.*

(2) Those in which the condition depends on something uncertain, and *may or may not be regarded true, or be fulfilled*; as, —

If, in our case, the representative system ultimately *fail*, popular government must be pronounced impossible. — D. Webster.

If this *be* the glory of Julius, the first great founder of the Empire, so it is also the glory of Charlemagne, the second founder. — Bryce.

If any man *consider* the present aspects of what is called by distinction society, he will see the need of these ethics. — Emerson.

*Unreal — cannot be true.*

(3) Suppositions *contrary to fact*, which cannot be true, or conditions that cannot be fulfilled, but are presented only in order to suggest what *might be* or *might have been* true; thus, —

If these things *were* true, society could not hold together. — Lowell.

*Did not* my writings *produce* me some solid pudding, the great deficiency of praise would have quite discouraged me. — Franklin.

*Had* he for once *cast* all such feelings aside, and *striven* energetically to save Ney, it *would have cast* such an enhancing light over all his glories, that we cannot but regret its absence. — Bayne.

NOTE. — Conditional sentences are usually introduced by *if, though, except, unless,* etc.; but when the verb precedes the subject, the conjunction is often omitted: for example, *"Were I bidden to say how the highest genius could be most advantageously employed,"* etc.

### Exercise.

In the following conditional clauses, tell whether each verb is indicative or subjunctive, and what kind of condition: —

1. The voice, if he speak to you, is of similar physiognomy, clear, melodious, and sonorous. — Carlyle.

2. Were you so distinguished from your neighbors, would you, do you think, be any the happier? — Thackeray.

3. Epaminondas, if he was the man I take him for, would have sat still with joy and peace, if his lot had been mine. — Emerson.

4. If a damsel had the least smattering of literature, she was regarded as a prodigy. — Macaulay.

5. I told him, although it were the custom of our learned in Europe to steal inventions from each other,... yet I would take such caution that he should have the honor entire. — Swift.

6. If he had reason to dislike him, he had better not have written, since he [Byron] was dead. — N. P. Willis.

7. If it were prostrated to the ground by a profane hand, what native of the city would not mourn over its fall? — Gayarre.

8. But in no case could it be justified, except it be for a failure of the association or union to effect the object for which it was created. — Calhoun.

## II. Subjunctive of Purpose.

**223.** The subjunctive, especially *be, may, might,* and *should,* is used to express purpose, the clause being introduced by *that* or *lest;* as, —

It was necessary, he supposed, to drink strong beer, that he *might be* strong to labor. — Franklin.

I have been the more particular...that you *may compare* such unlikely beginnings with the figure I have since made there. — *Id.*

He [Roderick] with sudden impulse that way rode, To tell of what had passed, lest in the strife They *should engage* with Julian's men. — Southey.

## III. Subjunctive of Result.

**224.** The subjunctive may represent the result toward which an action tends: —

> So many thoughts move to and fro,
> That vain it *were* her eyes to close.
> — Coleridge.

> So live, that when thy summons comes to join
> The innumerable caravan...
> Thou *go* not, like the quarry-slave at night.
> — Bryant.

# IV. In Temporal Clauses.

**225.** The English subjunctive, like the Latin, is sometimes used in a clause to express the time when an action is to take place.

Let it rise, till it *meet* the sun in his coming. — D. Webster.

Rise up, before it *be* too late! — Hawthorne.

> But it will not be long
> Ere this *be thrown* aside.
> — Wordsworth.

# V. In Indirect Questions.

**226.** The subjunctive is often found in indirect questions, the answer being regarded as doubtful.

Ask the great man if there *be* none greater. — Emerson

What the best arrangement *were*, none of us could say. — Carlyle.

Whether it *were* morning or whether it *were* afternoon, in her confusion she had not distinctly known. — De Quincey.

# VI. Expressing a Wish.

**227.** After a verb of wishing, the subjunctive is regularly used in the dependent clause.

The transmigiation of souls is no fable. I would it *were*! — Emerson.

Bright star! Would I *were* steadfast as thou art! — Keats.

> I've wished that little isle *had* wings,
> And we, within its fairy bowers,
> *Were wafted* off to seas unknown.
> — Moore.

# VII. In a Noun Clause.

*Subject.*

**228.** The noun clause, in its various uses as subject, object, in apposition, etc., often contains a subjunctive.

The essence of originality is not that it *be* new. — Carlyle

*Apposition or logical subject.*

To appreciate the wild and sharp flavors of those October fruits, it is necessary that you *be breathing* the sharp October or November air. — Thoreau.

*Complement.*

The first merit, that which admits neither substitute nor equivalent, is, that everything *be* in its place. — Coleridge.

*Object.*

As sure as Heaven shall rescue me, I have no thought what men they *be*. — Coleridge.

Some might lament that I *were* cold. — Shelley.

*After verbs of commanding.*

This subjunctive is very frequent after verbs of *commanding*.

See that there *be* no traitors in your camp. — Tennyson.

> Come, tell me all that thou hast seen,
> And look thou *tell* me true.
> —Scott.

See that thy scepter *be* heavy on his head. — De Quincey.

# VIII. Concessive Clauses.

**229.** The concession may be expressed —

(1) In the nature of the verb; for example, —

*Be* the matter how it may, Gabriel Grub was afflicted with rheumatism to the end of his days. — Dickens.

*Be* the appeal *made* to the understanding or the heart, the sentence is the same — that rejects it. — Brougham

(2) By an indefinite relative word, which may be

(*a*) *Pronoun.*

> Whatever *betide*, we'll turn aside,
> And see the Braes of Yarrow.
> — Wordsworth.

(*b*) *Adjective.*

That hunger of applause, of cash, or whatsoever victual it *may be*, is the ultimate fact of man's life. — Carlyle.

(*c*) *Adverb.*

> Wherever he *dream* under mountain or stream,
> The spirit he loves remains.
> — Shelley.

# Prevalence of the Subjunctive Mood.

**230.** As shown by the wide range of literature from which these examples are selected, the subjunctive is very much used in literary English, especially by those who are artistic and exact in the expression of their thought.

At the present day, however, the subjunctive is becoming less and less used. Very many of the sentences illustrating the use of the subjunctive mood could be replaced by numerous others using the indicative to express the same thoughts.

The three uses of the subjunctive now most frequent are, to express a wish, a concession, and condition contrary to fact.

In spoken English, the subjunctive *were* is much used in a wish or a condition contrary to fact, but hardly any other subjunctive forms are.

It must be remembered, though, that many of the verbs in the subjunctive have the same form as the indicative. Especially is this true of unreal conditions in past time; for example, —

Were we of open sense as the Greeks were, we *had found* [should have found] a poem here. — Carlyle.

# IMPERATIVE MOOD.

*Definition.*

**231.** The **imperative mood** is the form of the verb used in direct commands, entreaties, or requests.

*Usually second person.*

**232.** The imperative is naturally used mostly with the **second person**, since commands are directed to a person addressed.

(1) *Command.*

*Call up* the shades of Demosthenes and Cicero to vouch for your words; *point* to their immortal works. — J. Q. Adams.

*Honor* all men; *love* all men; *fear* none. — Channing.

(2) *Entreaty.*

> Oh, from these sterner aspects of thy face
> *Spare* me and mine, nor *let* us need the wrath
> Of the mad unchained elements.
> — Bryant.

(3) *Request.*

"*Hush*! mother," whispered Kit. "*Come* along with me." — Dickens

*Tell* me, how was it you thought of coming here? — Id.

*Sometimes with* first person *in the plural.*

But the imperative may be used with the plural of the first person. Since the first person plural person is not really I + I, but I + you, or I + they, etc., we may use the imperative with *we* in a command, request, etc., to *you* implied in it. This is scarcely ever found outside of poetry.

> *Part we* in friendship from your land,
> And, noble earl, receive my hand.
> — Scott.

Then *seek we* not their camp — for there
The silence dwells of my despair.
— Campbell.

*Break we* our watch up.
— Shakespeare.

Usually this is expressed by *let* with the objective: "*Let* us go."
And the same with the third person: "*Let* him be accursed."

### Exercises on the Moods.

(*a*) Tell the mood of each verb in these sentences, and what special
use it is of that mood: —

1. Wherever the standard of freedom and independence has
been or shall be unfurled, there will her heart and her prayers
be.

2.

Mark thou this difference, child of earth!
While each performs his part,
Not all the lip can speak is worth
The silence of the heart.

3. Oh, that I might be admitted to thy presence! that mine
were the supreme delight of knowing thy will!

4.

'Twere worth ten years of peaceful life,
One glance at their array!

5. Whatever inconvenience ensue, nothing is to be preferred
before justice.

6.

The vigorous sun would catch it up at eve
And use it for an anvil till he had filled
The shelves of heaven with burning thunderbolts.


7.

Meet is it changes should control
Our being, lest we rust in ease.


8.

Quoth she, "The Devil take the goose,
And God forget the stranger!"


9. Think not that I speak for your sakes.

10. "Now tread we a measure!" said young Lochinvar.

11. Were that a just return? Were that Roman magnanimity?

12. Well; how he may do his work, whether he do it right or wrong, or do it at all, is a point which no man in the world has taken the pains to think of.

13. He is, let him live where else he like, in what pomps and prosperities he like, no literary man.

14. Could we one day complete the immense figure which these flagrant points compose!

15. "Oh, then, my dear madam," cried he, "tell me where I may find my poor, ruined, but repentant child."

16.

That sheaf of darts, will it not fall unbound,
Except, disrobed of thy vain earthly vaunt,
Thou bring it to be blessed where saints and angels

haunt?

17.

Forget thyself to marble, till
With a sad leaden downward cast
Thou fix them on the earth as fast.

18.

He, as though an instrument,
Blew mimic hootings to the silent owls,
That they might answer him.

19.

From the moss violets and jonquils peep,
And dart their arrowy odor through the brain,
Till you might faint with that delicious pain.

20. That a man parade his doubt, and get to imagine that
debating and logic is the triumph and true work of what intellect he has; alas! this is as if you should overturn the tree.

21.

The fat earth feed thy branchy root
That under deeply strikes!
The northern morning o'er thee shoot,
High up in silver spikes!

22. Though abyss open under abyss, and opinion displace opinion, all are at last contained in the Eternal cause.

23. God send Rome one such other sight!

24. "Mr. Marshall," continued Old Morgan, "see that no one mentions the United States to the prisoner."

25. If there is only one woman in the nation who claims the right to vote, she ought to have it.

26. Though he were dumb, it would speak.

27. Meantime, whatever she did, — whether it were in display of her own matchless talents, or whether it were as one member of a general party, — nothing could exceed the amiable, kind, and unassuming deportment of Mrs. Siddons.

28. It makes a great difference to the force of any sentence whether there be a man behind it or no.

(*b*) Find sentences with five verbs in the indicative mood, five in the subjunctive, five in the imperative.

# TENSE.

**233.** *Tense* means *time*. The **tense** of a verb is the form or use indicating the time of an action or being.

*Tenses in English.*

Old English had only two tenses, — the present tense, which represented present and future time; and the past tense. We still use the present for the future in such expressions as, "I *go* away to-morrow;" "If he *comes*, tell him to wait."

But English of the present day not only has a tense for each of the natural time divisions, — present, past, and future, — but has other tenses to correspond with those of highly inflected languages, such as Latin and Greek.

The distinct inflections are found only in the present and past tenses, however: the others are compounds of verbal forms with various helping verbs, called **auxiliaries**; such as *be, have, shall, will*.

*The tenses in detail.*

**234.** Action or being may be represented as occurring in present, past, or future time, by means of the **present**, the **past**, and the **future tense**. It may also be represented as *finished* in present or past or future time by means of the present perfect, past perfect, and future perfect tenses.

Not only is this so: there are what are called **definite forms** of these tenses, showing more exactly the time of the action or being. These make the English speech even more exact than other languages, as will be shown later on, in the conjugations.

# PERSON AND NUMBER.

**235.** The English verb has never had full inflections for number and person, as the classical languages have.

When the older pronoun *thou* was in use, there was a form of the verb to correspond to it, or agree with it, as, "Thou walk*est*," present; "Thou walked*st*," past; also, in the third person singular, a form ending in *-eth*, as, "It is not in man that walk*eth*, to direct his steps."

But in ordinary English of the present day there is practically only one ending for person and number. This is the third person, singular number; as, "He walk*s*;" and this only in the present tense indicative. This is important in questions of agreement when we come to syntax.

# CONJUGATION.

*Definition.*

**236. Conjugation** is the regular arrangement of the forms of the verb in the various voices, moods, tenses, persons, and numbers.

In classical languages, **conjugation** means *joining together* the numerous endings to the stem of the verb; but in English, inflections are so few that conjugation means merely the exhibition of the forms and the different verb phrases that express the relations of voice, mood, tense, etc.

*Few forms.*

**237.** Verbs in modern English have only four or five forms; for example, *walk* has *walk, walks, walked, walking,* sometimes adding the old forms *walkest, walkedst, walketh.* Such verbs as *choose* have five, — *choose, chooses, chose, choosing, chosen* (old, *choosest, chooseth, chosest*).

The verb *be* has more forms, since it is composed of several different roots, — *am, are, is, were, been,* etc.

**238. INFLECTIONS OF THE VERB *BE* .**

239

# Indicative Mood.

| PRESENT TENSE. | | PAST TENSE. | |
| --- | --- | --- | --- |
| *Singular* | *Plural* | *Singular* | *Plural* |
| 1. I am | We are | 1. I was | We were |
| 2. You are (thou art) | You are | 2. You were (thou wast, wert) | You were |
| 3. [He] is | [They] are | 3. [He] was | [They were] |

# Subjunctive Mood.

| PRESENT TENSE. | | PAST TENSE. | |
|---|---|---|---|
| *Singular* | *Plural* | *Singular* | *Plural* |
| 1. I be | We be | 1. I were | We were |
| 2. You (thou) be | You be | 2. You were (thou wert) | You were |
| 3. [He] be | [They] be | 3. [He] were | [They] were |

# Imperative Mood.

*Singular and Plural*

Be.

*Remarks on the verb* be.

**239.** This conjugation is pieced out with three different roots: (1) *am, is;* (2) *was, were;* (3) *be.*

Instead of the plural *are,* Old English had *beoth* and *sind* or *sindon,* same as the German *sind. Are* is supposed to have come from the Norse language.

The old indicative third person plural *be* is sometimes found in literature, though it is usually a dialect form; for example, —

Where *be* the sentries who used to salute as the Royal chariots drove in and out? — Thackeray

Where *be* the gloomy shades, and desolate mountains? — Whittier

*Uses of* be.

**240.** The forms of the verb *be* have several uses: —

(1) *As principal verbs.*

The light that never *was* on sea and land. — Wordsworth.

(2) *As auxiliary verbs,* in four ways, —

(*a*) With verbal forms in *-ing* (imperfect participle) to form the definite tenses.

Broadswords *are maddening* in the rear, — Each broadsword bright *was brandishing* like beam of light. — Scott.

(*b*) With the past participle in *-ed, -en,* etc., to form the passive voice.

By solemn vision and bright silver dream,
His infancy *was nurtured*.
—Shelley.

(*c*) With past participle of intransitive verbs, being equivalent to the present perfect and past perfect tenses active; as,

When we *are gone*
From every object dear to mortal sight.
—Wordsworth

We drank tea, which *was* now *become* an occasional banquet.—Goldsmith.

(*d*) With the infinitive, to express intention, obligation, condition, etc.; thus,

It *was to have been called* the Order of Minerva.—Thackeray.

Ingenuity and cleverness *are to be rewarded* by State prizes.— *Id.*

If I *were to explain* the motion of a body falling to the ground.—Burke

**241.** INFLECTIONS OF THE VERB *CHOOSE.*

# Indicative Mood.

| PRESENT TENSE. | | PAST TENSE. | |
| --- | --- | --- | --- |
| *Singular.* | *Plural.* | *Singular.* | *Plural.* |
| 1. I choose | We choose | 1. I chose | We chose |
| 2. You choose | You choose | 2. You chose | You chose |
| 3. [He] chooses | [They] choose | 3. [He] chose | [They] chose |

# Subjunctive Mood.

|  | PRESENT TENSE. |  | PAST TENSE. |
| --- | --- | --- | --- |
| *Singular.* | *Plural.* | *Singular.* | *Plural.* |
| 1. I choose | We choose | 1. I chose | We chose |
| 2. You choose | You choose | 2. You chose | You chose |
| 3. [He] choose | [They] choose | 3. [He] chose | [They] chose |

# Imperative Mood.

PRESENT TENSE

*Singular and Plural*

Choose.

# FULL CONJUGATION OF THE VERB *CHOOSE*.

*Machinery of a verb in the voices, tenses, etc.*

**242.** In addition to the above *inflected* forms, there are many periphrastic or *compound* forms, made up of auxiliaries with the infinitives and participles. Some of these have been indicated in Sec. 240, (2).

The ordinary tenses yet to be spoken of are made up as follows: —

(1) *Future tense,* by using *shall* and *will* with the simple or root form of the verb; as, "I *shall be,*" "He *will choose.*"

(2) *Present perfect, past perfect, future perfect,* tenses, by placing *have, had,* and *shall* (or *will*) *have* before the past participle of any verb; as, "I *have gone*" (present perfect), "I *had gone*" (past perfect), "I *shall have gone*" (future perfect).

(3) The *definite form* of each tense, by using auxiliaries with the imperfect participle active; as, "I *am running,*" "They *had been running.*"

(4) The *passive forms,* by using the forms of the verb *be* before the past participle of verbs; as, "I *was chosen,*" "You *are chosen.*"

**243.** The following scheme will show how rich our language is in verb phrases to express every variety of meaning. Only the third person, singular number, of each tense, will be given:

# ACTIVE VOICE.

## Indicative Mood.

| | |
|---|---|
| *Present.* | He chooses. |
| *Present definite.* | He is choosing. |
| *Past.* | He chose. |
| *Past definite.* | He was choosing. |
| *Future.* | He will choose. |
| *Future definite.* | He will he choosing. |
| *Present perfect.* | He has chosen. |
| *Present perfect definite.* | He has been choosing. |
| *Past perfect.* | He had chosen. |
| *Past perfect definite.* | He had been choosing. |
| *Future perfect.* | He will have chosen. |
| *Future perfect definite.* | He will have been choosing. |

## Subjunctive Mood.

| | | |
|---|---|---|
| *Present.* | [If, though, lest, etc.] | he choose. |
| *Present definite.* | " | he be choosing. |
| *Past.* | " | he chose (or were to choose). |

| *Past definite.* | " | he were choosing (or were to be choosing). |
| *Present perfect.* | " | he have chosen. |
| *Present perfect definite.* | " | he have been choosing. |
| *Past perfect.* | " | Same as indicative. |
| *Past perfect definite.* | " | Same as indicative. |

## Imperative Mood.

| *Present.* | (2d per.) | Choose. |
| *Present definite.* | " | Be choosing. |

NOTE. — Since participles and infinitives are not really verbs, but verbals, they will be discussed later (Sec. 262).

# PASSIVE VOICE.

## Indicative Mood.

| | |
|---|---|
| *Present.* | He is chosen. |
| *Present definite.* | He is being chosen. |
| *Past.* | He was chosen. |
| *Past definite.* | He was being chosen. |
| *Future.* | He will be chosen. |
| *Future definite.* | None. |
| *Present perfect.* | He has been chosen. |
| *Present perfect definite.* | None. |
| *Past perfect.* | He had been chosen. |
| *Past perfect definite.* | None. |
| *Future perfect.* | He will have been chosen. |
| *Future perfect definite.* | None. |

## Subjunctive Mood.

| | | |
|---|---|---|
| *Present..* | [If, though, lest, etc.] | he be chosen. |
| *Present definite.* | " | None. |
| *Past.* | " | he were chosen (or were to be |

chosen).

| | | |
|---|---|---|
| *Past definite.* | " | he were being chosen. |
| *Present perfect.* | " | he have been chosen. |
| *Present perfect definite.* | " | None. |
| *Past Perfect.* | " | he had been chosen. |
| *Past perfect definite.* | " | None. |

## Imperative Mood.

| | | |
|---|---|---|
| *Present tense.* | (2d per.) | Be chosen. |

Also, in *affirmative sentences*, the indicative present and past tenses have emphatic forms made up of *do* and *did* with the infinitive or simple form; as, "He *does strike*," "He *did strike*."

[*Note to Teacher.*—This table is not to be learned now; if learned at all, it should be as practice work on strong and weak verb forms. Exercises should be given, however, to bring up sentences containing such of these conjugation forms as the pupil will find readily in literature.]

# VERBS CLASSIFIED ACCORDING TO FORM.

*Kinds.*

**244.** According to form, verbs are **strong** or **weak**.

*Definition.*

A **strong verb** forms its past tense by changing the vowel of the present tense form, but adds no ending; as, *run, ran; drive, drove.*

A **weak verb** always adds an ending to the present to form the past tense, and *may* or *may not* change the vowel: as, *beg, begged; lay, laid; sleep, slept; catch, caught.*

**245.** TABLE OF STRONG VERBS.

NOTE. Some of these also have weak forms, which are in parentheses

| Present Tense. | Past Tense. | Past Participle. |
|---|---|---|
| abide | abode | abode |
| arise | arose | arisen |
| awake | awoke (awaked) | awoke (awaked) |
| bear | bore | borne (active)born (passive) |
| begin | began | begun |
| behold | beheld | beheld |
| bid | bade, bid | bidden, bid |
| bind | bound | bound,[*adj.* bounden] |
| bite | bit | bitten, bit |
| blow | blew | blown |

| | | |
|---|---|---|
| break | broke | broken |
| chide | chid | chidden, chid |
| choose | chose | chosen |
| cleave | clove, clave (cleft) | cloven (cleft) |
| climb | [clomb] climbed | climbed |
| cling | clung | clung |
| come | came | come |
| crow | crew (crowed) | (crowed) |
| dig | dug | dug |
| do | did | done |
| draw | drew | drawn |
| drink | drank | drunk, drank[*adj.* drunken] |
| drive | drove | driven |
| eat | ate, eat | eaten, eat |
| fall | fell | fallen |
| fight | fought | fought |
| find | found | found |
| fling | flung | flung |
| fly | flew | flown |

| | | |
|---|---|---|
| forbear | forbore | forborne |
| forget | forgot | forgotten |
| forsake | forsook | forsaken |
| freeze | froze | frozen |
| get | got | got [gotten] |
| give | gave | given |
| go | went | gone |
| grind | ground | ground |
| grow | grew | grown |
| hang | hung (hanged) | hung (hanged) |
| hold | held | held |
| know | knew | known |
| lie | lay | lain |
| ride | rode | ridden |
| ring | rang | rung |
| run | ran | run |
| see | saw | seen |
| shake | shook | shaken |
| shear | shore (sheared) | shorn (sheared) |

| | | |
|---|---|---|
| shine | shone | shone |
| shoot | shot | shot |
| shrink | shrank or shrunk | shrunk |
| shrive | shrove | shriven |
| sing | sang or sung | sung |
| sink | sank or sunk | sunk [adj. sunken] |
| sit | sat [sate] | sat |
| slay | slew | slain |
| slide | slid | slidden, slid |
| sling | slung | slung |
| slink | slunk | slunk |
| smite | smote | smitten |
| speak | spoke | spoken |
| spin | spun | spun |
| spring | sprang, sprung | sprung |
| stand | stood | stood |
| stave | stove (staved) | (staved) |
| steal | stole | stolen |
| stick | stuck | stuck |

| | | |
|---|---|---|
| sting | stung | stung |
| stink | stunk, stank | stunk |
| stride | strode | stridden |
| strike | struck | struck, stricken |
| string | strung | strung |
| strive | strove | striven |
| swear | swore | sworn |
| swim | swam or swum | swum |
| swing | swung | swung |
| take | took | taken |
| tear | tore | torn |
| thrive | throve (thrived) | thriven (thrived) |
| throw | threw | thrown |
| tread | trod | trodden, trod |
| wear | wore | worn |
| weave | wove | woven |
| win | won | won |
| wind | wound | wound |
| wring | wrung | wrung |

write            wrote            written

# Remarks on Certain Verb Forms.

**246.** Several of the perfect participles are seldom used except as adjectives: as, "his *bounden* duty," "the *cloven* hoof," "a *drunken* wretch," "a *sunken* snag." *Stricken* is used mostly of diseases; as, "*stricken* with paralysis."

The verb **bear** (to bring forth) is peculiar in having one participle (*borne*) for the active, and another (*born*) for the passive. When it means *to carry* or to *endure, borne* is also a passive.

The form **clomb** is not used in prose, but is much used in vulgar English, and sometimes occurs in poetry; as, —

Thou hast *clomb* aloft. — Wordsworth

Or pine grove whither woodman never *clomb*. — Coleridge

The forms of **cleave** are really a mixture of two verbs, — one meaning *to adhere* or *cling*; the other, *to split*. The former used to be *cleave, cleaved, cleaved*; and the latter, *cleave, clave* or *clove, cloven*. But the latter took on the weak form *cleft* in the past tense and past participle, — as (from Shakespeare), "O Hamlet! thou hast *cleft* my heart in twain," — while *cleave* (to cling) sometimes has *clove*, as (from Holmes), "The old Latin tutor *clove* to Virgilius Maro." In this confusion of usage, only one set remains certain, — *cleave, cleft, cleft* (to split).

**Crew** is seldom found in present-day English.

Not a cock *crew*, nor a dog barked. — Irving.

Our cock, which always *crew* at eleven, now told us it was time for repose. — Goldsmith.

Historically, **drunk** is the one correct past participle of the verb *drink*. But *drunk* is very much used as an adjective, instead of *drunken* (meaning intoxicated); and, probably to avoid confusion with this, **drank** is a good deal used as a past participle: thus, —

We had each *drank* three times at the well. — B. Taylor.

This liquor *was* generally *drank* by Wood and Billings. — Thackeray.

Sometimes in literary English, especially in that of an earlier period, it is found that the verb **eat** has the past tense and past participle *eat* (ĕt), instead of *ate* and *eaten*; as, for example, —

It ate the food it ne'er had *eat*. — Coleridge.

How fairy Mab the junkets *eat*. — Milton.

> The island princes overbold
> Have *eat* our substance.
> — Tennyson.

This is also very much used in spoken and vulgar English.

The form **gotten** is little used, *got* being the preferred form of past participle as well as past tense. One example out of many is, —

We *had* all *got* safe on shore. — De Foe.

**Hung** and **hanged** both are used as the past tense and past participle of *hang*; but *hanged* is the preferred form when we speak of execution by hanging; as,

The butler *was hanged*. — *Bible*.

The verb **sat** is sometimes spelled *sate*; for example, —

Might we have *sate* and talked where gowans blow. — Wordsworth.

He *sate* him down, and seized a pen. — Byron.

"But I *sate* still and finished my plaiting." — Kingsley.

Usually **shear** is a weak verb. *Shorn* and *shore* are not commonly used: indeed, *shore* is rare, even in poetry.

> This heard Geraint, and grasping at his sword,
> *Shore* thro' the swarthy neck.
> — Tennyson.

*Shorn* is used sometimes as a participial adjective, as "a *shorn* lamb," but not much as a participle. We usually say, "The sheep were *sheared*" instead of "The sheep were *shorn*."

**Went** is borrowed as the past tense of *go* from the old verb *wend*, which is seldom used except in poetry; for example, —

> If, maiden, thou would'st *wend* with me
> To leave both tower and town.
> —Scott.

### Exercises.

(*a*) From the table (Sec. 245), make out lists of verbs having the same vowel changes as each of the following: —

- 1. Fall, fell, fallen.
- 2. Begin, began, begun.
- 3. Find, found, found.
- 4. Give, gave, given.
- 5. Drive, drove, driven.
- 6. Throw, threw, thrown.
- 7. Fling, flung, flung.
- 8. Break, broke, broken.
- 9. Shake, shook, shaken.
- 10. Freeze, froze, frozen.

(*b*) Find sentences using ten past-tense forms of strong verbs.

(*c*) Find sentences using ten past participles of strong verbs.

[*To the Teacher*, — These exercises should be continued for several lessons, for full drill on the forms.]

# DEFECTIVE STRONG VERBS.

**247.** There are several verbs which are lacking in one or more principal parts. They are as follows: —

| PRESENT. | PAST. | PRESENT. | PAST. |
|---|---|---|---|
| may | might | [ought] | ought |
| can | could | shall | should |
| [must] | must | will | would |

**248.** May is used as either indicative or subjunctive, as it has two meanings. It is indicative when it expresses *permission*, or, as it sometimes does, *ability*, like the word *can*: it is subjunctive when it expresses doubt as to the reality of an action, or when it expresses wish, purpose, etc.

*Indicative Use: Permission. Ability.*

If I *may* lightly employ the Miltonic figure, "far off his coming shines." — Winier.

> A stripling arm *might* sway
> A mass no host could raise.
> — Scott.

His superiority none *might* question. — Channing.

*Subjunctive use.*

In whatever manner the separate parts of a constitution *may* be arranged, there is one general principle, etc. — Paine.

(*See also Sec. 223.*)

> And from her fair and unpolluted flesh
> *May* violets spring!
> — Shakespeare.

**249. Can** is used in the indicative only. The *l* in *could* did not belong there originally, but came through analogy with *should* and *would*. *Could* may be subjunctive, as in Sec. 220.

**250. Must** is historically a past-tense form, from the obsolete verb *motan*, which survives in the sentence, "So *mote* it be." *Must* is present or past tense, according to the infinitive used.

All *must concede* to him a sublime power of action. — Channing

This, of course, *must have been* an ocular deception. — Hawthorne.

**251.** The same remarks apply to **ought**, which is historically the past tense of the verb *owe*. Like *must*, it is used only in the indicative mood; as,

The just imputations on our own faith *ought* first *to be removed....* Have we valuable territories and important posts...which *ought* long since *to have been surrendered*? — A. Hamilton.

It will be noticed that all the other defective verbs take the pure infinitive without *to*, while *ought* always has *to*.

# Shall and Will.

**252.** The principal trouble in the use of *shall* and *will* is the disposition, especially in the United States, to use *will* and *would*, to the neglect of *shall* and *should*, with pronouns of the first person; as, "I think I *will* go."

*Uses of* shall *and* should.

The following distinctions must be observed: —

(1) With the FIRST PERSON, shall and should are used, —

*Futurity and questions — first person.*

(*a*) In making simple statements or predictions about future time; as, —

The time will come full soon, I *shall* be gone. — L. C. Moulton.

(*b*) In questions asking for orders, or implying obligation or authority resting upon the subject; as, —

With respect to novels, what *shall* I say? — N. Webster.

How *shall* I describe the luster which at that moment burst upon my vision? — C. Brockden Brown.

*Second and third persons.*

(2) With the SECOND AND THIRD PERSONS, *shall* and *should* are used, —

(*a*) To express authority, in the form of command, promise, or confident prediction. The following are examples: —

Never mind, my lad, whilst I live thou *shalt* never want a friend to stand by thee. — Irving.

They *shall* have venison to eat, and corn to hoe. — Cooper.

The sea *shall* crush thee; yea, the ponderous wave up the loose beach *shall* grind and scoop thy grave. — Thaxter.

> She *should* not walk, he said, through the dust and heat of
> the noonday;
> Nay, she *should* ride like a queen, not plod along like a

peasant.

— Longfellow.

(*b*) In *indirect quotations*, to express the same idea that the original speaker put forth (i.e., future action); for example, —

He declares that he *shall* win the purse from you. — Bulwer.

She rejects his suit with scorn, but assures him that she *shall* make great use of her power over him. — Macaulay.

Fielding came up more and more bland and smiling, with the conviction that he *should* win in the end. — A. Larned.

Those who had too presumptuously concluded that they *should* pass without combat were something disconcerted. — Scott.

(*c*) With *direct questions* of the second person, when the answer expected would express simple futurity; thus, —

"*Should* you like to go to school at Canterbury?" — Dickens.

*First, second and third persons.*

(3) With ALL THREE PERSONS, —

(*a*) *Should* is used with the meaning of obligation, and is equivalent to *ought*.

I never was what I *should* be. — H. James, Jr.

Milton! thou *should'st* be living at this hour. — Wordsworth.

He *should* not flatter himself with the delusion that he can make or unmake the reputation of other men. — Winter.

(*b*) *Shall* and *should* are both used in *dependent clauses* of condition, time, purpose, etc.; for example, —

When thy mind
*Shall* be a mansion for all stately forms.
— Wordsworth.

Suppose this back-door gossip *should* be utterly blundering and untrue, would any one wonder? — Thackeray.

Jealous lest the sky *should* have a listener. — Byron.

If thou *should'st* ever come by chance or choice to Modena. — Rogers.

If I *should* be where I no more can hear thy voice. — Wordsworth.

That accents and looks so winning *should* disarm me of my resolution, was to be expected. — C. B. Brown.

**253. Will** and **would** are used as follows: —

*Authority as to future action — first person.*

(1) With the FIRST PERSON, *will* and *would* are used to express determination as to the future, or a promise; as, for example, —

I *will* go myself now, and *will* not return until all is finished. — Cable.

And promised...that I *would* do him justice, as the sole inventor. — Swift.

*Disguising a command.*

(2) With the SECOND PERSON, *will* is used to express command. This puts the order more mildly, as if it were merely expected action; as, —

Thou *wilt* take the skiff, Roland, and two of my people,... and fetch off certain plate and belongings. — Scott.

You *will* proceed to Manassas at as early a moment as practicable, and mark on the grounds the works, etc. — *War Records.*

*Mere futurity.*

(3) With both SECOND AND THIRD PERSONS, *will* and *would* are used to express simple futurity, action merely expected to occur; for example, —

All this *will* sound wild and chimerical. — Burke.

She *would* tell you that punishment is the reward of the wicked. — Landor.

When I am in town, *you'll* always have somebody to sit with you. To be sure, so you *will*. — Dickens.

(4) With FIRST, SECOND, AND THIRD PERSONS, *would* is used to express a *wish*,—the original meaning of the word *will*; for example,—

*Subject* I *omitted: often so.*

*Would* that a momentary emanation from thy glory would visit me!—C. B. Brown.

Thine was a dangerous gift, when thou wast born, The gift of Beauty. *Would* thou hadst it not.—Rogers

It shall be gold if thou *wilt*, but thou shalt answer to me for the use of it.—Scott.

What *wouldst* thou have a good great man obtain?—Coleridge.

(5) With the THIRD PERSON, *will* and *would* often denote an action as customary, without regard to future time; as,

They *will* go to Sunday schools, through storms their brothers are afraid of.... They *will* stand behind a table at a fair all day.—Holmes

On a slight suspicion, they *would* cut off the hands of numbers of the natives, for punishment or intimidation.—Bancroft.

In this stately chair *would* he sit, and this magnificent pipe *would* he smoke, shaking his right knee with a constant motion.—Irving.

# Conjugation of *Shall* and *Will* as Auxiliaries (with *Choose*).

**254.** To express simply expected action: —

| ACTIVE VOICE. | PASSIVE VOICE. |
|---|---|
| *Singular.* | *Singular.* |
| 1. I shall choose. | I shall be chosen. |
| 2. You will choose. | You will be chosen. |
| 3. [He] will choose. | [He] will be chosen. |
| *Plural.* | *Plural.* |
| 1. We shall choose. | We shall be chosen. |
| 2. You will choose. | You will be chosen. |
| 3. [They] will choose. | [They] will be chosen. |

To express determination, promise, etc.: —

| ACTIVE VOICE. | PASSIVE VOICE. |
|---|---|
| *Singular.* | *Singular.* |
| 1. I will choose. | I will be chosen. |
| 2. You shall choose. | You shall be chosen. |
| 3. [He] shall choose. | [He] shall be chosen. |
| *Plural.* | *Plural.* |

1. We will choose.

2. You shall choose.

3. [They] shall choose.

1. We will be chosen.

2. You shall be chosen.

3. [They] shall be chosen.

# Exercises on *Shall* and *Will*.

(*a*) From Secs. 252 and 253, write out a summary or outline of the various uses of *shall* and *will*.

(*b*) Examine the following sentences, and justify the use of *shall* and *will*, or correct them if wrongly used: —

    1. Thou art what I would be, yet only seem.

    2. We would be greatly mistaken if we thought so.

    3. Thou shalt have a suit, and that of the newest cut; the wardrobe keeper shall have orders to supply you.

    4. "I shall not run," answered Herbert stubbornly.

    5. He informed us, that in the course of another day's march we would reach the prairies on the banks of the Grand Canadian.

    6. What shall we do with him? This is the sphinx-like riddle which we must solve if we would not be eaten.

    7. Will not our national character be greatly injured? Will we not be classed with the robbers and destroyers of mankind?

    8. Lucy stood still, very anxious, and wondering whether she should see anything alive.

    9. I would be overpowered by the feeling of my disgrace.

    10. No, my son; whatever cash I send you is yours: you will spend it as you please, and I have nothing to say.

    11. But I will doubtless find some English person of whom to make inquiries.

    12. Without having attended to this, we will be at a loss to understand several passages in the classics.

    13. "I am a wayfarer," the stranger said, "and would like permission to remain with you a little while."

14. The beast made a sluggish movement, then, as if he would have more of the enchantment, stirred her slightly with his muzzle.

## WEAK VERBS.

**255.** Those weak verbs which add -d or -ed to form the past tense and past participle, and have no change of vowel, are so easily recognized as to need no special treatment. Some of them are already given as secondary forms of the strong verbs.

But the rest, which may be called **irregular weak verbs**, need some attention and explanation.

**256.** The irregular weak verbs are divided into two classes, —

*The two classes of irregular weak verbs.*

(1) Those which retain the -d or -t in the past tense, with some change of form for the past tense and past participle.

(2) Those which end in -d or -t, and have lost the ending which formerly was added to this.

The old ending to verbs of Class II. was -de or -te; as, —

This worthi man ful wel his wit *bisette* [used]. — Chaucer.

Of smale houndes *hadde* she, that sche *fedde* With rosted flessh, or mylk and wastel breed. — *Id.*

This ending has now dropped off, leaving some weak verbs with the same form throughout: as set, set, set; put, put, put.

## 257. Irregular Weak Verbs. — Class I.

| Present Tense. | Past Tense. | Past Participle. |
|---|---|---|
| bereave | bereft, bereave | bereft, bereaved |
| beseech | besought | besought |
| burn | burned, burnt | burnt |
| buy | bought | bought |

| | | |
|---|---|---|
| catch | caught | caught |
| creep | crept | crept |
| deal | dealt | dealt |
| dream | dreamt, dreamed | dreamt, dreamed |
| dwell | dwelt | dwelt |
| feel | felt | felt |
| flee | fled | fled |
| have | had | had (*once* haved) |
| hide | hid | hidden, hid |
| keep | kept | kept |
| kneel | knelt | knelt |
| lay | laid | laid |
| lean | leaned, leant | leaned, leant |
| leap | leaped, leapt | leaped, leapt |
| leave | left | left |
| lose | lost | lost |
| make | made (*once* maked) | made |
| mean | meant | meant |
| pay | paid | paid |

| | | |
|---|---|---|
| pen [inclose] | penned, pen | penned, pent |
| say | said | said |
| seek | sought | sought |
| sell | sold | sold |
| shoe | shod | shod |
| sleep | slept | slept |
| spell | spelled, spelt | spelt |
| spill | spilt | spilt |
| stay | staid, stayed | staid, stayed |
| sweep | swept | swept |
| teach | taught | taught |
| tell | told | told |
| think | thought | thought |
| weep | wept | wept |
| work | worked, wrought | worked, wrought |

### 258. Irregular Weak Verbs. — Class II.

| *Present Tense.* | *Past Tense.* | *Past Participle.* |
|---|---|---|
| bend | bent, bended | bent, bended |
| bleed | bled | bled |

| | | |
|---|---|---|
| breed | bred | bred |
| build | built | built |
| cast | cast | cast |
| cost | cost | cost |
| feed | fed | fed |
| gild | gilded, gilt | gilded, gilt |
| gird | girt, girded | girt, girded |
| hit | hit | hit |
| hurt | hurt | hurt |
| knit | knit, knitted | knit, knitted |
| lead | led | led |
| let | let | let |
| light | lighted, lit | lighted, lit |
| meet | met | met |
| put | put | put |
| quit | quit, quitted | quit, quitted |
| read | read | read |
| rend | rent | rent |
| rid | rid | rid |

| send | sent | sent |
|------|------|------|
| set | set | set |
| shed | shed | shed |
| shred | shred | shred |
| shut | shut | shut |
| slit | slit | slit |
| speed | sped | sped |
| spend | spent | spent |
| spit | spit [*obs.* spat] | spit [*obs.* spat] |
| split | split | split |
| spread | spread | spread |
| sweat | sweat | sweat |
| thrust | thrust | thrust |
| wed | wed, wedded | wed, wedded |
| wet | wet, wetted | wet, wetted |

*Tendency to phonetic spelling.*

**250.** There seems to be in Modern English a growing tendency toward phonetic spelling in the past tense and past participle of weak verbs. For example, *-ed*, after the verb *bless*, has the sound of *t*: hence the word is often written *blest*. So with *dipt, whipt, dropt, tost, crost, drest, prest,* etc. This is often seen in poetry, and is increasing in prose.

# Some Troublesome Verbs.

Lie *and* lay *in use and meaning.*

**260.** Some sets of verbs are often confused by young students, weak forms being substituted for correct, strong forms.

**Lie** and **lay** need close attention. These are the forms: —

| Present Tense. | Past Tense. | Pres. Participle. | Past Participle. |
| --- | --- | --- | --- |
| 1. Lie | lay | lying | lain |
| 2. Lay | laid | laying | laid |

The distinctions to be observed are as follows: —

(1) *Lie*, with its forms, is regularly *intransitive* as to use. As to meaning, *lie* means to rest, to recline, to place one's self in a recumbent position; as, "There *lies* the ruin."

(2) *Lay*, with its forms, is always *transitive* as to use. As to meaning, *lay* means to put, to place a person or thing in position; as, "Slowly and sadly we *laid* him down." Also *lay* may be used without any object expressed, but there is still a transitive meaning; as in the expressions, "to *lay* up for future use," "to *lay* on with the rod," "to *lay* about him lustily."

Sit *and* set.

**261. Sit** and **set** have principal parts as follows: —

| Present Tense. | Past Tense. | Pres. Participle. | Past Participle. |
| --- | --- | --- | --- |
| 1. Sit | sat | sitting | sat |
| 2. Set | set | setting | set |

Notice these points of difference between the two verbs: —

(1) *Sit*, with its forms, is always *intransitive* in use. In meaning, *sit* signifies (*a*) to place one's self on a seat, to rest; (*b*) to be adjusted, to fit; (*c*) to cover and warm eggs for hatching, as, "The hen *sits*."

(2) *Set*, with its forms, is always *transitive* in use when it has the following meanings: (*a*) to put or place a thing or person in position, as "He *set* down the book;" (*b*) to fix or establish, as, "He *sets* a good example."

*Set* is *intransitive* when it means (*a*) to go down, to decline, as, "The sun has *set*;" (*b*) to become fixed or rigid, as, "His eyes *set* in his head because of the disease;" (*c*) in certain idiomatic expressions, as, for example, "to *set* out," "to *set* up in business," "to *set* about a thing," "to *set* to work," "to *set* forward," "the tide *sets* in," "a strong wind *set* in," etc.

**Exercise.**

Examine the forms of *lie*, *lay*, *sit* and *set* in these sentences; give the meaning of each, and correct those used wrongly.

1. If the phenomena which lie before him will not suit his purpose, all history must be ransacked.

2. He sat with his eyes fixed partly on the ghost and partly on Hamlet, and with his mouth open.

3. The days when his favorite volume set him upon making wheelbarrows and chairs,... can never again be the realities they were.

4. To make the jacket sit yet more closely to the body, it was gathered at the middle by a broad leathern belt.

5. He had set up no unattainable standard of perfection.

6. For more than two hundred years his bones lay undistinguished.

7. The author laid the whole fault on the audience.

8. Dapple had to lay down on all fours before the lads could bestride him.

9.

And send'st him...to his gods where happy lies
His petty hope in some near port or bay,
And dashest him again to earth: — there let him lay.

10. Achilles is the swift-footed when he is sitting still.

11. It may be laid down as a general rule, that history begins in novel, and ends in essay.

12. I never took off my clothes, but laid down in them.

# VERBALS.

*Definition.*

**262. Verbals** are words that express action in a general way, without limiting the action to any time, or asserting it of any subject.

*Kinds.*

Verbals may be **participles**, **infinitives**, or **gerunds**.

# PARTICIPLES.

**263.** Participles are *adjectival* verbals; that is, they either belong to some substantive by expressing action in connection with it, or they express action, and directly modify a substantive, thus having a descriptive force. Notice these functions.

*Pure participle in function.*

1. At length, *wearied* by his cries and agitations, and not *knowing* how to put an end to them, he addressed the animal as if he had been a rational being. — Dwight.

Here *wearied* and *knowing* belong to the subject *he*, and express action in connection with it, but do not describe.

*Express action and also describe.*

2. Another name glided into her petition — it was that of the *wounded* Christian, whom fate had placed in the hands of bloodthirsty men, his *avowed* enemies. — Scott.

Here *wounded* and *avowed* are participles, but are used with the same adjectival force that *bloodthirsty* is (see Sec. 143, 4).

Participial adjectives have been discussed in Sec. 143 (4), but we give further examples for the sake of comparison and distinction.

*Fossil participles as adjectives.*

3. As *learned* a man may live in a cottage or a college commmon-room. — Thackeray

4. Not merely to the soldier are these campaigns *interesting* — Bayne.

5. How *charming* is divine philosophy! — Milton.

*Forms of the participle.*

**264.** Participles, in expressing action, may be **active** or **passive**, incomplete (or **imperfect**), complete (**perfect** or past), and **perfect definite**.

They cannot be divided into tenses (present, past, etc.), because they have no tense of their own, but derive their tense from the verb on which they depend; for example, —

1. He walked conscientiously through the services of the day, *fulfilling* every section the minutest, etc. — De Quincey.

*Fulfilling* has the form to denote continuance, but depends on the verb *walked*, which is past tense.

2.

Now the bright morning star, day's harbinger,
Comes *dancing* from the East.
— Milton.

*Dancing* here depends on a verb in the present tense.

### 265. PARTICIPLES OF THE VERB *CHOOSE*.

ACTIVE VOICE.

| | |
|---|---|
| *Imperfect.* | Choosing. |
| *Perfect.* | Having chosen. |
| *Perfect definite.* | Having been choosing. |

PASSIVE VOICE.

| | |
|---|---|
| *Imperfect.* | None |
| *Perfect.* | Chosen, being chosen, having been chosen. |
| *Perfect definite.* | None. |

**Exercise.**

Pick out the participles, and tell whether active or passive, imperfect, perfect, or perfect definite. If pure participles, tell to what word they belong; if adjectives, tell what words they modify.

1. The change is a large process, accomplished within a large and corresponding space, having, perhaps, some central or equatorial line, but lying, like that of our earth, between certain tropics, or limits widely separated.

2. I had fallen under medical advice the most misleading that it is possible to imagine.

3. These views, being adopted in a great measure from my mother, were naturally the same as my mother's.

4. Endowed with a great command over herself, she soon obtained an uncontrolled ascendency over her people.

5. No spectacle was more adapted to excite wonder.

6. Having fully supplied the demands of nature in this respect, I returned to reflection on my situation.

7. Three saplings, stripped of their branches and bound together at their ends, formed a kind of bedstead.

8. This all-pervading principle is at work in our system, — the creature warring against the creating power.

9. Perhaps I was too saucy and provoking.

10. Nothing of the kind having been done, and the principles of this unfortunate king having been distorted,... try clemency.

# INFINITIVES.

**266. Infinitives**, like participles, have no tense. When active, they have an indefinite, an imperfect, a perfect, and a perfect definite form; and when passive, an indefinite and a perfect form, to express action unconnected with a subject.

**267.** INFINITIVES OF THE VERB *CHOOSE*.

ACTIVE VOICE.

| | |
|---|---|
| *Indefinite.* | [To] choose. |
| *Imperfect.* | [To] be choosing. |
| *Perfect.* | [To] have chosen. |
| *Perfect definite.* | [To] have been choosing. |

PASSIVE VOICE.

| | |
|---|---|
| *Indefinite.* | [To] be chosen. |
| *Perfect.* | [To] have been chosen. |

To *with the infinitive.*

**268.** In Sec. 267 the word *to* is printed in brackets because it is not a necessary part of the infinitive.

It originally belonged only to an inflected form of the infinitive, expressing purpose; as in the Old English, "Ūt ēode se sǣdere his sǣd tō sāwenne" (Out went the sower his seed *to sow*).

*Cases when* to *is omitted.*

But later, when inflections became fewer, *to* was used before the infinitive generally, except in the following cases: —

(1) After the auxiliaries *shall, will* (with *should* and *would*).

(2) After the verbs *may (might), can (could), must*; also *let, make, do* (as, "I *do go*" etc.), *see, bid* (command), *feel, hear, watch, please*; sometimes *need* (as, "He *need* not *go*") and *dare* (to venture).

(3) After *had* in the idiomatic use; as, "You *had* better *go*" "He *had* rather *walk* than *ride*."

(4) In exclamations; as in the following examples: —

"He *find* pleasure in doing good!" cried Sir William. — Goldsmith.

I *urge* an address to his kinswoman! I *approach* her when in a base disguise! I *do* this! — Scott.

"She *ask* my pardon, poor woman!" cried Charles. — Macaulay.

**269.** *Shall* and *will* are not to be taken as separate verbs, but with the infinitive as one tense of a verb; as, "He *will choose*," "I *shall have chosen*," etc.

Also *do* may be considered an auxiliary in the interrogative, negative, and emphatic forms of the present and past, also in the imperative; as, —

What! *doth* she, too, as the credulous imagine, *learn* [*doth learn* is one verb, present tense] the love of the great stars? — Bulwer.

*Do* not *entertain* so weak an imagination — Burke.

She *did* not *weep* — she *did* not *break forth* into reproaches. — Irving.

**270.** The infinitive is sometimes active in form while it is passive in meaning, as in the expression, "a house *to let*." Examples are, —

She was a kind, liberal woman; rich rather more than needed where there were no opera boxes *to rent*. — De Quincey.

Tho' it seems my spurs are yet *to win*. — Tennyson.

But there was nothing *to do*. — Howells.

They shall have venison *to eat*, and corn *to hoe*. — Cooper.

Nolan himself saw that something was *to pay*. — E. E. Hale.

**271.** The various offices which the infinitive and the participle have in the sentence will be treated in Part II., under "Analysis," as we are now learning merely to recognize the forms.

# GERUNDS.

**272.** The gerund is like the participle in form, and like a noun in use.

The participle has been called an adjectival verbal; the gerund may be called a *noun verbal*. While the gerund expresses action, it has several attributes of a noun, — it may be governed as a noun; it may be the subject of a verb, or the object of a verb or a preposition; it is often preceded by the definite article; it is frequently modified by a possessive noun or pronoun.

*Distinguished from participle and verbal noun.*

**273.** It differs from the participle in being always used as a noun: it never belongs to or limits a noun.

It differs from the verbal noun in having the property of governing a noun (which the verbal noun has not) and of expressing action (the verbal noun merely names an action, Sec. II).

The following are examples of the uses of the gerund: —

(1) *Subject*: "The *taking* of means not to see another morning had all day absorbed every energy;" "Certainly *dueling* is bad, and has been put down."

(2) *Object*: (*a*) "Our culture therefore must not omit the *arming* of the man." (*b*) "Nobody cares for *planting* the poor fungus;" "I announce the good of *being interpenetrated* by the mind that made nature;" "The guilt of *having been cured* of the palsy by a Jewish maiden."

(3) *Governing and Governed*: "We are far from *having exhausted* the significance of the few symbols we use," also (2, *b*), above; "He could embellish the characters with new traits without *violating* probability;" "He could not help *holding* out his hand in return."

**Exercise.** — Find sentences containing five participles, five infinitives, and five gerunds.

# SUMMARY OF WORDS IN -*ING*

**274.** Words in **-ing** are of six kinds, according to use as well as meaning. They are as follows: —

(1) *Part of the verb*, making the definite tenses.

(2) *Pure participles*, which express action, but do not assert.

(3) *Participial adjectives*, which express action and also modify.

(4) *Pure adjectives*, which have lost all verbal force.

(5) *Gerunds*, which express action, may govern and be governed.

(6) *Verbal nouns,* which name an action or state, but cannot govern.

**Exercise.**

Tell to which of the above six classes each *-ing* word in the following sentences belongs: —

1. Here is need of apologies for shortcomings.

2. Then how pleasing is it, on your leaving the spot, to see the returning hope of the parents, when, after examining the nest, they find the nurslings untouched!

3. The crowning incident of my life was upon the bank of the Scioto Salt Creek, in which I had been unhorsed by the breaking of the saddle girths.

4. What a vast, brilliant, and wonderful store of learning!

5. He is one of the most charming masters of our language.

6. In explaining to a child the phenomena of nature, you must, by object lessons, give reality to your teaching.

7. I suppose I was dreaming about it. What is dreaming?

8. It is years since I heard the laughter ringing.

9. Intellect is not speaking and logicizing: it is seeing and ascertaining.

10. We now draw toward the end of that great martial drama which we have been briefly contemplating.

11. The second cause of failure was the burning of Moscow.

12. He spread his blessings all over the land.

13. The only means of ascending was by my hands.

14. A marble figure of Mary is stretched upon the tomb, round which is an iron railing, much corroded, bearing her national emblem.

15. The exertion left me in a state of languor and sinking.

16. Thackeray did not, like Sir Walter Scott, write twenty pages without stopping, but, dictating from his chair, he gave out sentence by sentence, slowly.

## HOW TO PARSE VERBS AND VERBALS.

# I. VERBS.

**275.** In parsing verbs, give the following points: —

(1) Class: (*a*) as to *form*, — strong or weak, giving principal parts; (*b*) as to *use*, — transitive or intransitive.

(2) Voice, — active or passive.

(3) Mood, — indicative, subjunctive, or imperative.

(4) Tense, — which of the tenses given in Sec. 234.

(5) Person and number, in determining which you must tell —

(6) What the subject is, for the form of the verb may not show the person and number.

*Caution.*

**276.** It has been intimated in Sec. 235, we must beware of the rule, "A verb agrees with its subject in person and number." Sometimes it does; usually it does not, if *agrees* means that the verb changes its form for the different persons and numbers. The verb *be* has more forms than other verbs, and may be said to *agree* with its subject in several of its forms. But unless the verb is present, and ends in *-s*, or is an old or poetic form ending in *-st* or *-eth*, it is best for the student not to state it as a general rule that "the verb agrees with its subject in person and number," but merely to *tell what the subject of the verb is*.

## II. VERB PHRASES.

**277.** Verb phrases are made up of a principal verb followed by an infinitive, and should always be analyzed as phrases, and not taken as single verbs. Especially frequent are those made up of *should*, *would*, *may*, *might*, *can*, *could*, *must*, followed by a pure infinitive without *to*. Take these examples: —

1. Lee *should* of himself *have replenished* his stock.

2. The government *might have been* strong and prosperous.

In such sentences as 1, call *should* a weak verb, intransitive, therefore active; indicative, past tense; has for its subject *Lee*. *Have replenished* is a perfect active infinitive.

In 2, call *might* a weak verb, intransitive, active, indicative (as it means could), past tense; has the subject *government*. *Have been* is a perfect active infinitive.

For fuller parsing of the infinitive, see Sec. 278(2).

# III. VERBALS.

**278.** (1) **Participle.** Tell (*a*) from what verb it is derived; (*b*) whether active or passive, imperfect, perfect, etc.; (*c*) to what word it belongs. If a participial adjective, give points (*a*) and (*b*), then parse it as an adjective.

(2) **Infinitive.** Tell (*a*) from what verb it is derived; (*b*) whether indefinite, perfect, definite, etc.

(3) **Gerund.** (*a*) From what verb derived; (*b*) its use (Sec. 273).

**Exercise.**

Parse the verbs, verbals, and verb phrases in the following sentences: —

1. Byron builds a structure that repeats certain elements in nature or humanity.

2. The birds were singing as if there were no aching hearts, no sin nor sorrow, in the world.

3. Let it rise! let it rise, till it meet the sun in his coming; let the earliest light of the morning gild it, and parting day linger and play on its summit.

4. You are gathered to your fathers, and live only to your country in her grateful remembrance.

5. Read this Declaration at the head of the army.

6.

Right graciously he smiled on us, as rolled from wing to wing,
Down all the line, a deafening shout, "God save our Lord the King!"

7. When he arose in the morning, he thought only of her, and wondered if she were yet awake.

8. He had lost the quiet of his thoughts, and his agitated soul reflected only broken and distorted images of things.

9.

> So, lest I be inclined
> To render ill for ill,
> Henceforth in me instill,
> O God, a sweet good will.

10. The sun appears to beat in vain at the casements.

11. Margaret had come into the workshop with her sewing, as usual.

12.

> Two things there are with memory will abide —
> Whatever else befall — while life flows by.

13. To the child it was not permitted to look beyond into the hazy lines that bounded his oasis of flowers.

14. With them, morning is not a new issuing of light, a new bursting forth of the sun; a new waking up of all that has life, from a sort of temporary death.

15. Whatever ground you sow or plant, see that it is in good condition.

16. However that be, it is certain that he had grown to delight in nothing else than this conversation.

17. The soul having been often born, or, as the Hindoos say, "traveling the path of existence through thousands of births," there is nothing of which she has not gained knowledge.

18. The ancients called it ecstasy or absence, — a getting-out of their bodies to think.

19. Such a boy could not whistle or dance.

20. He had rather stand charged with the imbecility of skepticism than with untruth.

21. He can behold with serenity the yawning gulf between the ambition of man and his power of performance.

22. He passed across the room to the washstand, leaving me upon the bed, where I afterward found he had replaced me on being awakened by hearing me leap frantically up and down on the floor.

23. In going for water, he seemed to be traveling over a desert plain to some far-off spring.

24. Hasheesh always brings an awakening of perception which magnifies the smallest sensation.

25. I have always talked to him as I would to a friend.

26. Over them multitudes of rosy children came leaping to throw garlands on my victorious road.

27. Oh, had we some bright little isle of our own!

28.

> Better it were, thou sayest, to consent;
> Feast while we may, and live ere life be spent.

29. And now wend we to yonder fountain, for the hour of rest is at hand.

## ADVERBS.

*Adverbs modify.*

**279.** The word *adverb* means *joined to a verb*. The adverb is the only word that can join to a verb to modify it.

*A verb.*

When **action** is expressed, an adverb is usually added to define the action in some way,—time, place, or manner: as, "He began *already* to be proud of being a Rugby boy [time];" "One of the young heroes scrambled up *behind* [place];" "He was absolute, but *wisely* and *bravely* ruling [manner]."

*An adjective or an adverb.*

But this does not mean that adverbs modify verbs *only*: many of them express degree, and limit **adjectives** or **adverbs**; as, "William's private life was *severely* pure;" "Principles of English law are put down *a little* confusedly."

*Sometimes a noun or pronoun.*

Sometimes an adverb may modify **a noun or pronoun**; for example, —

The young man reveres men of genius, because, to speak truly, they are *more* himself than he is. — Emerson.

Is it *only* poets, and men of leisure and cultivation, who live with nature? — *Id.*

To the *almost* terror of the persons present, Macaulay began with the senior wrangler of 1801-2-3-4, and so on. — Thackeray.

Nor was it *altogether* nothing. — Carlyle.

Sounds overflow the listener's brain So sweet that joy is *almost* pain. — Shelley.

The condition of Kate is *exactly* that of Coleridge's "Ancient Mariner." — De Quincey.

He was *incidentally* news dealer. — T. B. Aldrich.

NOTE. — These last differ from the words in Sec. 169, being adverbs naturally and fitly, while those in Sec. 169 are felt to be elliptical, and rather forced into the service of adjectives.

Also these adverbs modifying nouns are to be distinguished from those standing *after* a noun by ellipsis, but really modifying, not the noun, but some verb understood; thus, —

The gentle winds and waters [that are] near, Make music to the lonely ear. — Byron.

With bowering leaves [that grow] *o'erhead*, to which the eye Looked up half sweetly, and half awfully. — Leigh Hunt.

*A phrase.*

An adverb may modify a phrase which is equivalent to an adjective or an adverb, as shown in the sentences, —

They had begun to make their effort much *at the same time.* — Trollope.

I draw forth the fruit, all wet and glossy, maybe *nibbled by rabbits and hollowed out by crickets,* and perhaps *with a leaf or two cemented to it,* but still *with a rich bloom to it.* — Thoreau.

*A clause or sentence.*

It may also modify **a sentence**, emphasizing or qualifying the statement expressed; as, for example, —

And *certainly* no one ever entered upon office with so few resources of power in the past. — Lowell.

*Surely* happiness is reflective, like the light of heaven. — Irving.

We are offered six months' credit; and that, *perhaps,* has induced some of us to attend it. — Franklin.

*Definition.*

**280.** An **adverb**, then, is a modifying word, which may qualify an action word or a statement, and may add to the meaning of an adjective or adverb, or a word group used as such.

NOTE. — The expression *action word* is put instead of *verb,* because *any* verbal word may be limited by an adverb, not simply the forms used in predication.

**281.** Adverbs may be classified in two ways: (1) according to the meaning of the words; (2) according to their use in the sentence.

# ADVERBS CLASSIFIED ACCORDING TO MEANING.

**282.** Thus considered, there are six classes: —

(1) **Time**; as *now, to-day, ever, lately, before, hitherto,* etc.

(2) **Place.** These may be adverbs either of

- (*a*) PLACE WHERE; as *here,there,where,near,yonder, above,* etc.

- (*b*) PLACE TO WHICH; as *hither,thither,whither, whithersoever,* etc.

- (*c*) PLACE FROM WHICH; as *hence,thence,whence, whencesoever,* etc.

(3) **Manner**, telling *how* anything is done; as *well, slowly, better, bravely, beautifully.* Action is conceived or performed in so many ways, that these adverbs form a very large class.

(4) **Number**, telling *how many times: once, twice, singly, two by two,* etc.

(5) **Degree**, telling *how much*; as *little, slightly, too, partly, enough, greatly, much, very, just,* etc. (see also Sec. 283).

(6) **Assertion**, telling the speaker's belief or disbelief in a statement, or how far he believes it to be true; as *perhaps, maybe, surely, possibly, probably, not,* etc.

*Special remarks on adverbs of degree.*

**283. The** is an adverb of degree when it limits an adjective or an adverb, especially the comparative of these words; thus, —

But not *the* less the blare of the tumultuous organ wrought its own separate creations. — De Quincey.

*The* more they multiply, *the* more friends you will have; *the* more evidently they love liberty, *the* more perfect will be their obedience. — Burke.

**This** and **that** are very common as adverbs in spoken English, and not infrequently are found in literary English; for example, —

The master...was for *this* once of her opinion. — R. LOUIS STE-VENSON.

Death! To die! I owe *that* much To what, at least, I was. — Browning.

*This* long's the text. — Shakespeare.

[Sidenote *The status of such.*]

**Such** is frequently used as an equivalent of *so*: *such* precedes an adjective with its noun, while *so* precedes only the adjective usually.

Meekness,...which gained him *such* universal popularity. — Irving.

*Such* a glittering appearance that no ordinary man would have been able to close his eyes there. — Hawthorne.

An eye of *such* piercing brightness and *such* commanding power that it gave an air of inspiration. — Lecky.

So also in Grote, Emerson, Thackeray, Motley, White, and others.

*Pretty.*

**Pretty** has a wider adverbial use than it gets credit for.

I believe our astonishment is *pretty* equal. — Fielding.

Hard blows and hard money, the feel of both of which you know *pretty* well by now. — Kingsley.

The first of these generals is *pretty* generally recognized as the greatest military genius that ever lived. — Bayne.

A *pretty* large experience. — Thackeray.

*Pretty* is also used by Prescott, Franklin, De Quincey, Defoe, Dickens, Kingsley, Burke, Emerson, Aldrich, Holmes, and other writers.

Mighty.

The adverb mighty is very common in colloquial English; for example, —

"*Mighty* well, Deacon Gookin!" replied the solemn tones of the minister. — Hawthorne.

"Maybe you're wanting to get over? — anybody sick? Ye seem *mighty* anxious!" — H. B. Stowe.

It is only occasionally used in literary English; for example, —

You are *mighty* courteous. — Bulwer.

Beau Fielding, a *mighty* fine gentleman. — Thackeray.

"Peace, Neville," said the king, "thou think'st thyself *mighty* wise, and art but a fool." — Scott.

I perceived his sisters *mighty* busy. — Goldsmith.

*Notice meanings.*

**284.** Again, the meaning of words must be noticed rather than their form; for many words given above may be moved from one class to another at will: as these examples, — "He walked too *far* [place];" "That were *far* better [degree];" "He spoke *positively* [manner];" "That is *positively* untrue [assertion];" "I have seen you *before* [time];" "The house, and its lawn *before* [place]."

# ADVERBS CLASSIFIED ACCORDING TO USE.

*Simple.*

**285.** All adverbs which have no function in the sentence except to modify are called **simple adverbs**. Such are most of those given already in Sec. 282.

*Interrogative.*

**286.** Some adverbs, besides modifying, have the additional function of asking a question.

*Direct questions.*

These may introduce **direct** questions of —

(1) **Time.**

*When* did this humane custom begin? — H. Clay.

(2) **Place.**

*Where* will you have the scene? — Longfellow

(3) **Manner.**

And *how* looks it now? — Hawthorne.

(4) **Degree.**

"*How* long have you had this whip?" asked he. — Bulwer.

(5) **Reason.**

*Why* that wild stare and wilder cry? — Whittier

Now *wherefore* stopp'st thou me? — Coleridge

*Indirect questions.*

Or they may introduce indirect questions of —

(1) **Time.**

I do not remember *when* I was taught to read. — D. Webster.

(2) **Place.**

I will not ask *where* thou liest low. — Byron

(3) **Manner.**

Who set you to cast about what you should say to the select souls, or *how* to say anything to such? — Emerson.

(4) **Degree.**

> Being too full of sleep to understand
> *How* far the unknown transcends the what we know.
> — Longfellow

(5) **Reason.**

I hearkened, I know not *why*. — Poe.

**287.** There is a class of words usually classed as **conjunctive adverbs**, as they are said to have the office of conjunctions in joining clauses, while having the office of adverbs in modifying; for example, —

*When* last I saw thy young blue eyes, they smiled. — Byron.

But in reality, *when* does not express time and modify, but the whole clause, *when...eyes*; and *when* has simply the use of a conjunction, not an adverb. For further discussion, see Sec. 299 under "Subordinate Conjunctions."

**Exercise.** — Bring up sentences containing twenty adverbs, representing four classes.

# COMPARISON OF ADVERBS.

**288.** Many adverbs are compared, and, when compared, have the same inflection as adjectives.

The following, irregularly compared, are often used as adjectives: —

| Positive. | Comparative. | Superlative. |
|---|---|---|
| well | better | best |
| ill or badly | worse | worst |
| much | more | most |
| little | less | least |
| nigh or near | nearer | nearest or next |
| far | farther, further | farthest, furthest |
| late | later | latest, last |
| (rathe, *obs.*) | rather | |

**289.** Most monosyllabic adverbs add *-er* and *-est* to form the comparative and superlative, just as adjectives do; as, *high, higher, highest; soon, sooner, soonest.*

Adverbs in *-ly* usually have *more* and *most* instead of the inflected form, only occasionally having *-er* and *-est.*

Its strings *boldlier* swept. — Coleridge.

None can deem *harshlier* of me than I deem. — Byron.

Only that we may *wiselier* see. — Emerson.

Then must she keep it *safelier*. — Tennyson.

I should *freelier* rejoice in that absence. — Shakespeare.

*Form* vs. *use.*

**290.** The fact that a word ends in *-ly* does not make it an adverb. Many adjectives have the same ending, and must be distinguished by their use in the sentence.

**Exercise.**

Tell what each word in *ly* modifies, then whether it is an adjective or an adverb.

1. It seems certain that the Normans were more cleanly in their habits, more courtly in their manners.

2. It is true he was rarely heard to speak.

3. He would inhale the smoke slowly and tranquilly.

4. The perfectly heavenly law might be made law on earth.

5. The king winced when he saw his homely little bride.

6.

> With his proud, quick-flashing eye,
> And his mien of kingly state.

7.

> And all about, a lovely sky of blue
> Clearly was felt, or down the leaves laughed through.

8. He is inexpressibly mean, curiously jolly, kindly and good-natured in secret.

**291.** Again, many words without *-ly* have the same form, whether adverbs or adjectives.

The reason is, that in Old and Middle English, adverbs derived from adjectives had the ending *-e* as a distinguishing mark; as, —

If men smoot it with a yerde *smerte* [If men smote it with a rod smartly]. — Chaucer.

This *e* dropping off left both words having the same form.

Weeds were sure to grow *quicker* in his fields. — Irving.

O *sweet* and *far* from cliff and scar The horns of Elfland faintly blowing. — Tennyson.

But he must do his errand *right.* — Drake

*Long* she looked in his tiny face. — *Id.*

Not *near* so black as he was painted. — Thackeray.

In some cases adverbs with -*ly* are used side by side with those without -*ly*, but with a different meaning. Such are *most, mostly; near, nearly; even, evenly; hard, hardly;* etc.

*Special use of* there.

**292.** Frequently the word **there**, instead of being used adverbially, merely introduces a sentence, and inverts the usual order of subject and predicate.

This is such a fixed idiom that the sentence, if it has the verb *be*, seems awkward or affected without this "*there* introductory." Compare these: —

1. *There* are eyes, to be sure, that give no more admission into the man than blueberries. — Emerson.

2. Time was when field and watery cove With modulated echoes rang. — Wordsworth.

# HOW TO PARSE ADVERBS.

**293. In parsing** adverbs, give —

(1) The class, according to meaning and also use.

(2) Degree of comparison, if the word is compared.

(3) What word or word group it modifies.

**Exercise.**

Parse all the adverbs in the following sentences: —

1. Now the earth is so full that a drop overfills it.

2. The higher we rise in the scale of being, the more certainly we quit the region of the brilliant eccentricities and dazzling contrasts which belong to a vulgar greatness.

3.

> We sit in the warm shade and feel right well
> How the sap creeps up and blossoms swell.

4. Meanwhile the Protestants believed somewhat doubtfully that he was theirs.

5. Whence else could arise the bruises which I had received, but from my fall?

6. We somehow greedily gobble down all stories in which the characters of our friends are chopped up.

7. How carefully that blessed day is marked in their little calendars!

8. But a few steps farther on, at the regular wine-shop, the Madonna is in great glory.

9. The foolish and the dead alone never change their opinion.

10. It is the Cross that is first seen, and always, burning in the center of the temple.

11. For the impracticable, however theoretically enticing, is always politically unwise.

12. Whence come you? and whither are you bound?

13. How comes it that the evil which men say spreads so widely and lasts so long, whilst our good kind words don't seem somehow to take root and blossom?

14. At these carousals Alexander drank deep.

15. Perhaps he has been getting up a little architecture on the road from Florence.

16. It is left you to find out why your ears are boxed.

17. Thither we went, and sate down on the steps of a house.

18. He could never fix which side of the garden walk would suit him best, but continually shifted.

19. But now the wind rose again, and the stern drifted in toward the bank.

20. He caught the scent of wild thyme in the air, and found room to wonder how it could have got there.

21. They were soon launched on the princely bosom of the Thames, upon which the sun now shone forth.

22. Why should we suppose that conscientious motives, feeble as they are constantly found to be in a good cause, should be omnipotent for evil?

24. It was pretty bad after that, and but for Polly's outdoor exercise, she would undoubtedly have succumbed.

## CONJUNCTIONS.

**294.** Unlike adverbs, conjunctions do not modify: they are used solely for the purpose of connecting.

Examples of the use of conjunctions:—

*They connect* words.

(1) *Connecting words*: "It is the very necessity *and* condition of existence;" "What a simple *but* exquisite illustration!"

Word groups: *Phrases.*

*Clauses.*

(2) *Connecting word groups*: "Hitherto the two systems have existed in different States, *but* side by side within the American Union;" "This has happened *because* the Union is a confederation of States."

*Sentences.*

(3) *Connecting sentences*: "Unanimity in this case can mean only a very large majority. *But* even unanimity itself is far from indicating the voice of God."

*Paragraphs.*

(4) *Connecting sentence groups*: Paragraphs would be too long to quote here, but the student will readily find them, in which the writer connects the divisions of narration or argument by such words as *but, however, hence, nor, then, therefore,* etc.

*Definition.*

**295.** A **conjunction** is a linking word, connecting words, word groups, sentences, or sentence groups.

*Classes of conjunctions.*

**296.** Conjunctions have two principal divisions: —

(1) **Coördinate**, joining words, word groups, etc., of the *same rank.*

(2) **Subordinate**, joining a subordinate or dependent clause to a principal or independent clause.

# COÖRDINATE CONJUNCTIONS.

**297.** Coördinate conjunctions are of four kinds:

(1) COPULATIVE, coupling or uniting words and expressions in the same line of thought; as *and, also, as well as, moreover,* etc.

(2) ADVERSATIVE, connecting words and expressions that are opposite in thought; as *but, yet, still, however, while, only,* etc.

(3) CAUSAL, introducing a reason or cause. The chief ones are, *for, therefore, hence, then.*

(4) ALTERNATIVE, expressing a choice, usually between two things. They are *or, either, else, nor, neither, whether.*

*Correlatives.*

**298.** Some of these go in pairs, answering to each other in the same sentence; as, *both...and; not only...but* (or *but also*); *either...or; whether...or; neither...nor; whether...or whether.*

Some go in threes; as, *not only...but... and; either...or...or; neither...nor... nor.*

Further examples of the use of coördinate conjunctions: —

*Copulative.*

Your letter, *likewise,* had its weight; the bread was spent, the butter *too;* the window being open, *as well as* the room door.

*Adversative.*

The assertion, *however,* serves but to show their ignorance. "Can this be so?" said Goodman Brown. "*Howbeit,* I have nothing to do with the governor and council."

*Nevertheless,* in this mansion of gloom I now proposed to myself a sojourn of some weeks.

*Alternative.*

While the earth bears a plant, *or* the sea rolls its waves.

*Nor* mark'd they less, where in the air
A thousand streamers flaunted fair.

*Causal.*

*Therefore* the poet is not any permissive potentate, but is emperor in his own right. *For* it is the rule of the universe that corn shall serve man, and not man corn.

Examples of the use of correlatives: —

He began to doubt whether *both* he *and* the world around him were not bewitched. — Irving.

He is *not only* bold and vociferous, *but* possesses a considerable talent for mimicry, *and* seems to enjoy great satisfaction in mocking and teasing other birds. — Wilson.

It is...the same *whether* I move my hand along the surface of a body, *or whether* such a body is moved along my hand. — Burke.

*Neither* the place in which he found himself, *nor* the exclusive attention that he attracted, disturbed the self-possession of the young Mohican. — Cooper.

*Neither* was there any phantom memorial of life, *nor* wing of bird, *nor* echo, *nor* green leaf, *nor* creeping thing, that moved or stirred upon the soundless waste. — De Quincey.

# SUBORDINATE CONJUNCTIONS.

**299.** Subordinate conjunctions are of the following kinds: —

(1) PLACE: *where, wherever, whither, whereto, whithersoever, whence,* etc.

(2) TIME: *when, before, after, since, as, until, whenever, while, ere,* etc.

(3) MANNER: *how, as, however, howsoever.*

(4) CAUSE or REASON: *because, since, as, now, whereas, that, seeing,* etc.

(5) COMPARISON: *than* and *as.*

(6) PURPOSE: *that, so, so that, in order that, lest, so...as.*

(7) RESULT: *that, so that,* especially *that* after *so.*

(8) CONDITION or CONCESSION: *if, unless, so, except, though, although; even if, provided, provided that, in case, on condition that,* etc.

(9) SUBSTANTIVE: *that, whether,* sometimes *if,* are used frequently to introduce noun clauses used as *subject, object, in apposition,* etc.

Examples of the use of subordinate conjunctions: —

*Place.*

Where the treasure is, there will the heart be also. — *Bible.*

To lead from eighteen to twenty millions of men *whithersoever* they will. — J. Quincy.

An artist will delight in excellence *wherever* he meets it. — Allston.

*Time.*

I promise to devote myself to your happiness *whenever* you shall ask it of me. — Paulding.

It is sixteen years *since* I saw the Queen of France. — Burke.

*Manner.*

Let the world go *how* it will. — Carlyle

Events proceed, not *as* they were expected or intended, but *as* they are impelled by the irresistible laws. — Ames.

*Cause, reason.*

I see no reason *why* I should not have the same thought. — Emerson.

> Then Denmark blest our chief,
> *That* he gave her wounds repose.
> — Campbell.

> *Now* he is dead, his martyrdom will reap
> Late harvests of the palms he should have had in life.
> — H. H. Jackson.

Sparing neither whip nor spur, *seeing that* he carried the vindication of his patron's fame in his saddlebags. — Irving.

*Comparison.*

As a soldier, he was more solicitous to avoid mistakes *than* to perform exploits that are brilliant. — Ames.

All the subsequent experience of our race had gone over him with as little permanent effect *as* [*as* follows the semi-adverbs *as* and *so* in expressing comparison] the passing breeze. — Hawthorne.

*Purpose.*

We wish for a thousand heads, a thousand bodies, *that* we might celebrate its immense beauty. — Emerson.

*Result.*

> So many thoughts moved to and fro,
> *That* vain it were her eyes to close.
> — Coleridge.

I was again covered with water, but not so long *but* I held it out. — Defoe.

*Condition.*

A ridicule which is of no import *unless* the scholar heed it. — Emerson.

> There flowers or weeds at will may grow,
> *So* I behold them not.
> — Byron.

*Concession.*

> What *though* the radiance which was once so bright
> Be now forever taken from my sight.
> — Wordsworth.

*Substantive.*

It seems a pity *that* we can only spend it once. — Emerson.

We do not believe *that* he left any worthy man his foe who had ever been his friend. — Ames.

Let us see *whether* the greatest, the wisest, the purest-hearted of all ages are agreed in any wise on this point. — Ruskin.

Who can tell *if* Washington be a great man or no? — Emerson.

**300.** As will have been noticed, some words — for example, *since, while, as, that,* etc. — may belong to several classes of conjunctions, according to their meaning and connection in the sentence.

**Exercises.**

(*a*) Bring up sentences containing five examples of coördinate conjunctions.

(*b*) Bring up sentences containing three examples of correlatives.

(*c*) Bring up sentences containing ten subordinate conjunctions.

(*d*) Tell whether the italicized words in the following sentences are conjunctions or adverbs; classify them if conjunctions: —

1. *Yet* these were often exhibited throughout our city.

2. No one had *yet* caught his character.

3. *After* he was gone, the lady called her servant.

4. And they lived happily forever *after*.

5. They, *however*, hold a subordinate rank.

6. *However* ambitious a woman may be to command admiration abroad, her real merit is known at home.

7. *Whence* else could arise the bruises which I had received?

8. He was brought up for the church, *whence* he was occasionally called the Dominie.

9. And *then* recovering, she faintly pressed her hand.

10. In what point of view, *then*, is war not to be regarded with horror?

11. The moth fly, *as* he shot in air, Crept under the leaf, and hid her there.

12. Besides, *as* the rulers of a nation are *as* liable *as* other people to be governed by passion and prejudice, there is little prospect of justice in permitting war.

13. *While* a faction is a minority, it will remain harmless.

14. *While* patriotism glowed in his heart, wisdom blended in his speech her authority with her charms.

15. *Hence* it is highly important that the custom of war should be abolished.

16. The raft and the money had been thrown near her, none of the lashings having given way; *only* what is the use of a guinea amongst tangle and sea gulls?

17. *Only* let his thoughts be of equal scope, and the frame will suit the picture.

# SPECIAL REMARKS.

As if.

**301.** *As if* is often used as one conjunction of manner, but really there is an ellipsis between the two words; thus, —

> But thy soft murmuring
> Sounds sweet *as if* a sister's voice reproved.
> — Byron.

If analyzed, the expression would be, "sounds sweet *as* [the sound would be] *if* a sister's voice reproved;" *as*, in this case, expressing degree if taken separately.

But the ellipsis seems to be lost sight of frequently in writing, as is shown by the use of *as though*.

As though.

**302.** In Emerson's sentence, "We meet, and part *as though* we parted not," it cannot be said that there is an ellipsis: it cannot mean "we part *as* [we should part] *though*" etc.

Consequently, *as if* and *as though* may be taken as double conjunctions expressing manner. *As though* seems to be in as wide use as the conjunction *as if*; for example, —

Do you know a farmer who acts and lives *as though* he believed one word of this? — H. Greeley.

His voice ... sounded *as though* it came out of a barrel. — Irving.

> Blinded alike from sunshine and from rain,
> *As though* a rose should shut, and be a bud again.
> — Keats

Examples might be quoted from almost all authors.

As *for* as if.

**303.** In poetry, *as* is often equivalent to *as if.*

> And their orbs grew strangely dreary,
> Clouded, even *as* they would weep.
> —Emily Bronte.

> So silently we seemed to speak,
> So slowly moved about,
> *As* we had lent her half our powers
> To eke her living out.
> —Hood.

### HOW TO PARSE CONJUNCTIONS.

**304.** In parsing conjunctions, tell—

(1) To what class and subclass they belong.

(2) What words, word groups, etc., they connect.

*Caution.*

In classifying them, particular attention must be paid to the *meaning* of the word. Some conjunctions, such as *nor, and, because, when*, etc., are regularly of one particular class; others belong to several classes. For example, compare the sentences,—

1. It continued raining, *so* that I could not stir abroad.—Defoe

2. There will be an agreement in whatever variety of actions, *so* they be each honest and natural in their hour.—Emerson

3. It was too dark to put an arrow into the creature's eye; *so* they paddled on.—Kingsley

In sentence 1, *so that* expresses result, and its clause depends on the other, hence it is a subordinate conjunction of result; in 2, *so* means provided,—is subordinate of condition; in 3, *so* means therefore, and its clause is independent, hence it is a coördinate conjunction of reason.

**Exercise.**

Parse all the conjunctions in these sentences: —

1. When the gods come among men, they are not known.

2. If he could solve the riddle, the Sphinx was slain.

3. A lady with whom I was riding in the forest said to me that the woods always seemed to wait, as if the genii who inhabit them suspended their deeds until the wayfarer had passed.

4. The mountain of granite blooms into an eternal flower, with the lightness and delicate finish as well as the aërial proportions and perspective of vegetable scenery.

5. At sea, or in the forest, or in the snow, he sleeps as warm, dines with as good an appetite, and associates as happily, as beside his own chimneys.

6. Our admiration of the antique is not admiration of the old, but of the natural.

7. "Doctor," said his wife to Martin Luther, "how is it that whilst subject to papacy we prayed so often and with such fervor, whilst now we pray with the utmost coldness, and very seldom?"

8. All the postulates of elfin annals, — that the fairies do not like to be named; that their gifts are capricious and not to be trusted; and the like, — I find them true in Concord, however they might be in Cornwall or Bretagne.

9. He is the compend of time; he is also the correlative of nature.

10. He dismisses without notice his thought, because it is his.

11. The eye was placed where one ray should fall, that it might testify of that particular ray.

12. It may be safely trusted, so it be faithfully imparted.

13. He knows how to speak to his contemporaries.

14. Goodness must have some edge to it, — else it is none.

15. I hope it is somewhat better than whim at last.

16. Now you have the whip in your hand, won't you lay on?

17. I scowl as I dip my pen into the inkstand.

18. I speak, therefore, of good novels only.

19. Let her loose in the library as you do a fawn in a field.

20. And whether consciously or not, you must be, in many a heart, enthroned.

21. It is clear, however, the whole conditions are changed.

22. I never rested until I had a copy of the book.

23. For, though there may be little resemblance otherwise, in this they agree, that both were wayward.

24. Still, she might have the family countenance; and Kate thought he looked with a suspicious scrutiny into her face as he inquired for the young don.

25. He follows his genius whithersoever it may lead him.

26. The manuscript indeed speaks of many more, whose names I omit, seeing that it behooves me to hasten.

27. God had marked this woman's sin with a scarlet letter, which had such efficacy that no human sympathy could reach her, save it were sinful like herself.

28. I rejoice to stand here no longer, to be looked at as though I had seven heads and ten horns.

29. He should neither praise nor blame nor defend his equals.

30. There was no iron to be seen, nor did they appear acquainted with its properties; for they unguardedly took a drawn sword by the edge, when it was presented to them.

## PREPOSITIONS..

**305.** The word *preposition* implies *place before*: hence it would seem that a preposition is always *before* its object. It may be so in the majority of cases, but in a considerable proportion of instances the preposition is *after* its object.

This occurs in such cases as the following: —

Preposition not before its object.

(1) *After a relative pronoun*, a very common occurrence; thus, —

The most dismal Christmas fun *which* these eyes ever looked *on*. — Thackeray.

An ancient nation *which* they know nothing *of*. — Emerson.

A foe, *whom* a champion has fought *with* to-day. — Scott.

Some little toys *that* girls are fond *of*. — Swift.

"It's the man *that* I spoke to you *about*" said Mr. Pickwick. — Dickens.

(2) *After an interrogative adverb, adjective, or pronoun*, also frequently found: —

*What* God doth the wizard pray *to*? — Hawthorne.

*What* is the little one thinking *about*? — J. G. Holland.

*Where* the Devil did it come *from*, I wonder? — Dickens.

(3) *With an infinitive*, in such expressions as these: —

A proper *quarrel* for a Crusader to do battle *in*. — Scott.

"You know, General, it was *nothing* to joke *about*." — Cable

Had no harsh *treatment* to reproach herself *with*. — Boyesen

A *loss of vitality* scarcely to be accounted *for*. — Holmes.

Places for *horses* to be hitched *to*. — Id.

(4) *After a noun*, — the case in which the preposition is expected to be, and regularly is, before its object; as, —

> And unseen mermaids' pearly song
> Comes bubbling up, the weeds *among*.
> — Beddoes.

Forever panting and forever young,
All breathing human passion far *above*.
— Keats.

**306.** Since the object of a preposition is most often a noun, the statement is made that the preposition usually precedes its object; as in the following sentence, "Roused *by* the shock, he started *from* his trance."

Here the words *by* and *from* are connectives; but they do more than connect. *By* shows the relation in thought between *roused* and *shock*, expressing means or agency; *from* shows the relation in thought between *started* and *trance*, and expresses separation. Both introduce phrases.

*Definition.*

**307.** A **preposition** is a word joined to a noun or its equivalent to make up a qualifying or an adverbial phrase, and to show the relation between its object and the word modified.

*Objects, nouns and the following.*

**308.** Besides nouns, prepositions may have as objects —

(1) *Pronouns*: "Upon *them* with the lance;" "With *whom* I traverse earth."

(2) *Adjectives*: "On *high* the winds lift up their voices."

(3) *Adverbs*: "If I live wholly from *within*;" "Had it not been for the sea from *aft*."

(4) *Phrases*: "Everything came to her from *on high*;" "From *of old* they had been zealous worshipers."

(5) *Infinitives*: "The queen now scarce spoke to him save *to convey* some necessary command for her service."

(6) *Gerunds*: "They shrink from *inflicting* what they threaten;" "He is not content with *shining* on great occasions."

(7) *Clauses*:

"Each soldier eye shall brightly turn
To *where thy sky-born glories burn.*"


*Object usually objective case, if noun or pronoun.*

**309.** The object of a preposition, if a noun or pronoun, is usually in the objective case. In pronouns, this is shown by the form of the word, as in Sec. 308 (1).

*Often possessive.*

In the double-possessive idiom, however, the object is in the possessive case after *of;* for example, —

There was also a book *of Defoe's,...* and another *of Mather's.* — Franklin.

See also numerous examples in Secs. 68 and 87.

*Sometimes nominative.*

And the prepositions *but* and *save* are found with the nominative form of the pronoun following; as, —

Nobody knows *but* my mate and *I*
Where our nest and our nestlings lie.
— BRYANT.

# USES OF PREPOSITIONS.

*Inseparable.*

**310.** Prepositions are used in three ways: —

(1) *Compounded with verbs, adverbs,* or *conjunctions;* as, for example, with verbs, *with*draw, *under*stand, *over*look, *over*take, *over*flow, *un*dergo, *out*stay, *out*number, *over*run, *over*grow, etc.; with adverbs, there*at*, there*in*, there*from*, there*by*, there*with*, etc.; with conjunctions, where*at*, where*in*, where*on*, where*through*, where*upon*, etc.

*Separable.*

(2) *Following a verb,* and being really a part of the verb. This use needs to be watched closely, to see whether the preposition belongs to the verb or has a separate prepositional function. For example, in the sentences, (*a*) "He broke a pane *from* the window," (*b*) "He broke *into* the bank," in (*a*), the verb *broke* is a predicate, modified by the phrase introduced by *from*; in (*b*), the predicate is not *broke*, modified by *into the bank*, but *broke into* — the object, *bank*.

Study carefully the following prepositions with verbs: —

Considering the space they *took up*. — Swift.

I loved, *laughed at*, and pitied him. — Goldsmith.

The sun *breaks through* the darkest clouds. — Shakespeare.

They will *root up* the whole ground. — Swift.

A friend *prevailed upon* one of the interpreters. — Addison

My uncle *approved of* it. — Franklin.

The robber who *broke into* them. — Landor.

This period is not obscurely *hinted at*. — Lamb.

The judge *winked at* the iniquity of the decision. — *Id*.

The pupils' voices, *conning over* their lessons. — Irving.

To *help out* his maintenance. — *Id*.

With such pomp is Merry Christmas *ushered in*. — Longfellow.

*Ordinary use as connective, relation words.*

(3) As *relation words*, introducing phrases,—the most common use, in which the words have their own proper function.

*Usefulness of prepositions.*

**311.** Prepositions are the subtlest and most useful words in the language for compressing a clear meaning into few words. Each preposition has its proper and general meaning, which, by frequent and exacting use, has expanded and divided into a variety of meanings more or less close to the original one.

Take, for example, the word *over*. It expresses place, with motion, as, "The bird flew *over* the house;" or rest, as, "Silence broods *over* the earth." It may also convey the meaning of *about, concerning*; as, "They quarreled *over* the booty." Or it may express time: "Stay *over* night."

The language is made richer and more flexible by there being several meanings to each of many prepositions, as well as by some of them having the same meaning as others.

# CLASSES OF PREPOSITIONS.

**312.** It would be useless to attempt to classify all the prepositions, since they are so various in meaning.

The largest groups are those of **place**, **time**, and **exclusion**.

# PREPOSITIONS OF PLACE.

**313.** The following are the most common to indicate **place**: —

(1) PLACE WHERE: *abaft, about, above, across, amid (amidst), among (amongst), at, athwart, below, beneath, beside, between (betwixt), beyond, in, on, over, under (underneath), upon, round* or *around, without*.

(2) PLACE WHITHER: *into, unto, up, through, throughout, to, towards*.

(3) PLACE WHENCE: *down, from (away from, down from, from out,* etc.), *off, out of*.

**Abaft** is exclusively a sea term, meaning *back of*.

**Among** (or **amongst**) and **between** (or **betwixt**) have a difference in meaning, and usually a difference in use. *Among* originally meant in the crowd (*on gemong*), referring to several objects; *between* and *betwixt* were originally made up of the preposition *be* (meaning *by*) and *twēon* or *twēonum* (modern *twain*), *by two*, and *be* with *twīh* (or *twuh*), having the same meaning, *by two* objects.

As to modern use, see "Syntax" (Sec. 459).

# PREPOSITIONS OF TIME.

**314.** They are *after, during, pending, till* or *until*; also many of the prepositions of place express **time** when put before words indicating time, such as *at, between, by, about, on, within*, etc.

These are all familiar, and need no special remark.

# EXCLUSION OR SEPARATION.

**315.** The chief ones are *besides, but, except, save, without.* The participle *excepting* is also used as a preposition.

# MISCELLANEOUS PREPOSITIONS.

**316. Against** implies opposition, sometimes place where. In colloquial English it is sometimes used to express time, now and then also in literary English; for example, —

She contrived to fit up the baby's cradle for me *against* night. — Swift

**About**, and the participial prepositions **concerning, respecting, regarding,** mean *with reference to.*

*Phrase prepositions.*

**317.** Many phrases are used as single prepositions: *by means of, by virtue of, by help of, by dint of, by force of; out of, on account of, by way of, for the sake of; in consideration of, in spite of, in defiance of, instead of, in view of, in place of; with respect to, with regard to, according to, agreeably to;* and some others.

**318.** Besides all these, there are some prepositions that have so many meanings that they require separate and careful treatment: *on* (*upon*), *at, by, for, from, of, to, with.*

No attempt will be made to give *all* the meanings that each one in this list has: the purpose is to stimulate observation, and to show how useful prepositions really are.

# At.

**319.** The general meaning of **at** is *near, close to,* after a verb or expression implying position; and *towards* after a verb or expression indicating motion. It defines position approximately, while *in* is exact, meaning *within*.

Its principal uses are as follows: —

(1) *Place where.*

They who heard it listened with a curling horror *at* the heart. — J. F. Cooper.

There had been a strike *at* the neighboring manufacturing village, and there was to be a public meeting, *at* which he was besought to be present. — T. W. Higginson.

(2) *Time,* more exact, meaning the point of time at which.

He wished to attack *at* daybreak. — Parkman.

They buried him darkly, *at* dead of night. — Wolfe

(3) *Direction.*

The mother stood looking wildly down *at* the unseemly object. — Cooper.

You are next invited...to grasp *at* the opportunity, and take for your subject, "Health." — Higginson.

Here belong such expressions as *laugh at, look at, wink at, gaze at, stare at, peep at, scowl at, sneer at, frown at,* etc.

We *laugh at* the elixir that promises to prolong life to a thousand years. — Johnson.

"You never mean to say," pursued Dot, sitting on the floor and *shaking* her head *at* him. — Dickens.

(4) *Source* or *cause,* meaning *because of, by reason of.*

I felt my heart chill *at* the dismal sound. — T. W. Knox.

Delighted *at* this outburst against the Spaniards. — Parkman.

(5) Then the idiomatic phrases *at last, at length, at any rate, at the best, at the worst, at least, at most, at first, at once, at all, at one, at naught, at random*, etc.; and phrases signifying state or condition of being, as, *at work, at play, at peace, at war, at rest*, etc.

**Exercise.** — Find sentences with three different uses of *at*.

# By.

**320.** Like *at*, **by** means *near* or *close to*, but has several other meanings more or less connected with this, —

(1) The general meaning of *place*.

Richard was standing *by* the window. — Aldrich.

Provided always the coach had not shed a wheel *by* the roadside. — *Id.*

(2) *Time.*

But *by* this time the bell of Old Alloway began tolling. — B. Taylor

The angel came *by* night. — R. H. Stoddard.

(3) *Agency* or *means.*

Menippus knew which were the kings *by* their howling louder. — M. D. Conway.

At St. Helena, the first port made *by* the ship, he stopped. — Parton.

(4) *Measure of excess*, expressing the degree of difference.

At that time [the earth] was richer, *by* many a million of acres. — De Quincey.

He was taller *by* almost the breadth of my nail. — Swift.

(5) It is also used in *oaths and adjurations.*

*By* my faith, that is a very plump hand for a man of eighty-four! — Parton.

They implore us *by* the long trials of struggling humanity; *by* the blessed memory of the departed; *by* the wrecks of time; *by* the ruins of nations. — Everett.

**Exercise.** — Find sentences with three different meanings of *by*.

# For.

**321.** The chief meanings of **for** are as follows: —

(1) *Motion towards* a place, or a tendency or action toward the attainment of any object.

Pioneers who were opening the way *for* the march of the nation. — Cooper.

She saw the boat headed *for* her. — Warner.

(2) *In favor of, for the benefit of, in behalf of,* a person or thing.

He and they were *for* immediate attack. — Parkman

The people were then against us; they are now *for* us. — W. L. Garrison.

(3) *Duration of time,* or *extent of space.*

*For* a long time the disreputable element outshone the virtuous. — H. H. Bancroft.

He could overlook all the country *for* many a mile of rich woodland. — Irving.

(4) *Substitution* or *exchange.*

There are gains *for* all our losses. — Stoddard.

Thus did the Spaniards make bloody atonement *for* the butchery of Fort Caroline. — Parkman.

(5) *Reference,* meaning *with regard to, as to, respecting,* etc.

*For* the rest, the Colonna motto would fit you best. — Emerson.

*For* him, poor fellow, he repented of his folly. — E. E. Hale

This is very common with *as* — *as for* me, etc.

(6) Like *as,* meaning *in the character of, as being,* etc.

"Nay, if your worship can accomplish that," answered Master Brackett, "I shall own you *for* a man of skill indeed!" — Hawthorne.

Wavering whether he should put his son to death *for* an unnatural monster. — Lamb.

(7) *Concession*, meaning *although*, *considering that* etc.

"*For* a fool," said the Lady of Lochleven, "thou hast counseled wisely." — Scott

By my faith, that is a very plump hand *for* a man of eighty-four! — Parton.

(8) Meaning *notwithstanding*, or *in spite of*.

But the Colonel, *for* all his title, had a forest of poor relations. — Holmes.

> Still, *for* all slips of hers,
> One of Eve's family.
> — Hood.


(9) *Motive, cause, reason, incitement to action.*

The twilight being...hardly more wholesome *for* its glittering mists of midge companies. — Ruskin.

An Arab woman, but a few sunsets since, ate her child, *for* famine. — *Id.*

Here Satouriona forgot his dignity, and leaped *for* joy. — Parkman.

(10) *For* with its object preceding the infinitive, and having the same meaning as a noun clause, as shown by this sentence: —

It is by no means necessary *that he should devote his whole school existence to physical science*; nay, more, it is not necessary for *him to give up more than a moderate share of his time to such studies.* — Huxley.

**Exercise.** — Find sentences with five meanings of *for*.

# From.

**322.** The general idea in **from** is separation or source. It may be with regard to —

(1) *Place.*

Like boys escaped *from* school. — H. H. Bancroft

Thus they drifted *from* snow-clad ranges to burning plain. — *Id.*

(2) *Origin.*

Coming *from* a race of day-dreamers, Ayrault had inherited the faculty of dreaming also by night. — Higginson.

> *From* harmony, *from* heavenly harmony
> This universal frame began.
> — Dryden.

(3) *Time.*

A distrustful, if not a desperate man, did he become *from* the night of that fearful dream — Hawthorne.

(4) *Motive, cause,* or *reason.*

It was *from* no fault of Nolan's. — Hale.

The young cavaliers, *from* a desire of seeming valiant, ceased to be merciful. — Bancroft.

**Exercise.** — Find sentences with three meanings of *from.*

# Of.

**323.** The original meaning of **of** was separation or source, like *from*. The various uses are shown in the following examples: —

# I. The *From* Relation.

(1) *Origin or source.*

The king holds his authority *of* the people. — Milton.

Thomas à Becket was born *of* reputable parents in the city of London. — Hume.

(2) *Separation*: (*a*) After certain verbs, such as *ease, demand, rob, divest, free, clear, purge, disarm, deprive, relieve, cure, rid, beg, ask*, etc.

Two old Indians cleared the spot *of* brambles, weeds, and grass. — Parkman.

Asked no odds *of*, acquitted them *of*, etc. — Aldrich.

(*b*) After some adjectives, — *clear of, free of, wide of, bare of*, etc.; especially adjectives and adverbs of direction, as *north of, south of*, etc.

The hills were bare *of* trees. — Bayard Taylor.

Back *of* that tree, he had raised a little Gothic chapel. —Gavarre.

(*c*) After nouns expressing lack, deprivation, etc.

A singular want *of* all human relation. — Higginson.

(*d*) With words expressing distance.

Until he had come within a staff's length *of* the old dame. — Hawthorne

Within a few yards *of* the young man's hiding place. — *Id.*

(3) *With expressions of material*, especially *out of.*

White shirt with diamond studs, or breastpin *of* native gold. — Bancroft.

Sandals, bound with thongs *of* boar's hide. — Scott

Who formed, *out of* the most unpromising materials, the finest army that Europe had yet seen. — Macaulay

(4) *Expressing cause, reason, motive.*

The author died *of* a fit of apoplexy. — Boswell.

More than one altar was richer *of* his vows. — Lew Wallace.

"Good for him!" cried Nolan. "I am glad *of* that." — E. E. Hale.

(5) *Expressing agency.*

You cannot make a boy know, *of* his own knowledge, that Cromwell once ruled England. — Huxley.

He is away *of* his own free will. — Dickens

**II. Other Relations expressed by *Of* .**

(6) *Partitive*, expressing a part of a number or quantity.

*Of* the Forty, there were only twenty-one members present. — Parton.

He washed out some *of* the dirt, separating thereby as much of the dust as a ten-cent piece would hold. — Bancroft.

*See also Sec. 309.*

(7) *Possessive*, standing, with its object, for the possessive, or being used with the possessive case to form the double possessive.

Not even woman's love, and the dignity *of* a queen, could give shelter from his contumely. — W. E. Channing.

And the mighty secret *of* the Sierra stood revealed. — Bancroft.

(8) *Appositional*, which may be in the case of —

(*a*) Nouns.

Such a book as that *of* Job. — Froude.

The fair city *of* Mexico. — Prescott.

The nation *of* Lilliput. — Swift.

(*b*) Noun and gerund, being equivalent to an infinitive.

In the vain hope *of* appeasing the savages. — Cooper.

Few people take the trouble *of* finding out what democracy really is. — Lowell.

(*c*) Two nouns, when the first is descriptive of the second.

This crampfish *of* a Socrates has so bewitched him. — Emerson

A sorry antediluvian makeshift *of* a building you may think it. — Lamb.

An inexhaustible bottle *of* a shop. — Aldrich.

(9) *Of time.* Besides the phrases *of old, of late, of a sudden,* etc., *of* is used in the sense of *during.*

I used often to linger *of* a morning by the high gate. — Aldrich

I delighted to loll over the quarter railing *of* a calm day. — Irving.

(10) *Of reference,* equal to *about, concerning, with regard to.*

The Turk lay dreaming *of* the hour. — Halleck.

Boasted *of* his prowess as a scalp hunter and duelist. — Bancroft.

Sank into reverie *of* home and boyhood scenes. — *Id.*

*Idiomatic use with verbs.*

*Of* is also used as an appendage of certain verbs, such as *admit, accept, allow, approve, disapprove, permit,* without adding to their meaning. It also accompanies the verbs *tire, complain, repent, consist, avail* (one's self), and others.

**Exercise.** — Find sentences with six uses of *of.*

# On, Upon.

**324.** The general meaning of **on** is position or direction. *On* and *upon* are interchangeable in almost all of their applications, as shown by the sentences below: —

(1) *Place*: (*a*) Where.

Cannon were heard close *on* the left. — Parkman.

> The Earl of Huntley ranged his host
> *Upon* their native strand.
> — Mrs. Sigourney.

(*b*) With motion.

It was the battery at Samos firing *on* the boats. — Parkman.

Thou didst look down *upon* the naked earth. — Bryant.

(2) *Time.*

The demonstration of joy or sorrow *on* reading their letters. — Bancroft.

*On* Monday evening he sent forward the Indians. — Parkman.

**Upon** is seldom used to express time.

(3) *Reference*, equal to *about*, *concerning*, etc.

I think that one abstains from writing *on* the immortality of the soul. — Emerson.

He pronounced a very flattering opinion *upon* my brother's promise of excellence. — De Quincey.

(4) *In adjurations.*

*On* my life, you are eighteen, and not a day more. — Aldrich.

*Upon* my reputation and credit. — Shakespeare

(5) *Idiomatic phrases*: *on fire, on board, on high, on the wing, on the alert, on a sudden, on view, on trial*, etc.

**Exercise.** — Find sentences with three uses of *on* or *upon*.

# To.

**325.** Some uses of to are the following: —

(1) *Expressing motion*: (*a*) To a place.

Come *to* the bridal chamber, Death! — Halleck.

Rip had scrambled *to* one of the highest peaks. — Irving.

(*b*) Referring to time.

Full of schemes and speculations *to* the last. — Parton.

Revolutions, whose influence is felt *to* this hour. — Parkman.

(2) *Expressing result.*

He usually gave his draft to an aid...to be written over, — often *to* the loss of vigor. — Benton

*To* our great delight, Ben Lomond was unshrouded. — B. Taylor

(3) *Expressing comparison.*

> But when, unmasked, gay Comedy appears,
> 'Tis ten *to* one you find the girl in tears.
> — Aldrich

They are arrant rogues: Cacus was nothing *to* them. — Bulwer.

Bolingbroke and the wicked Lord Littleton were saints *to* him. — Webster

(4) *Expressing concern, interest.*

*To* the few, it may be genuine poetry. — Bryant.

His brother had died, had ceased to be, *to* him. — Hale.

Little mattered *to* them occasional privations — Bancroft.

(5) *Equivalent to* according to.

Nor, *to* my taste, does the mere music...of your style fall far below the highest efforts of poetry. — Lang.

We cook the dish *to* our own appetite. — Goldsmith.

(6) *With the infinitive* (see Sec. 268).

**Exercise**. — Find sentences containing three uses of *to*.

# With.

**326. With** expresses the idea of accompaniment, and hardly any of its applications vary from this general signification.

In Old English, *mid* meant *in company with*, while *wið* meant *against*: both meanings are included in the modern *with*.

The following meanings are expressed by *with*: —

(1) *Personal accompaniment.*

The advance, *with* Heyward at its head, had already reached the defile. — Cooper.

For many weeks I had walked *with* this poor friendless girl. — De Quincey.

(2) *Instrumentality.*

*With* my crossbow I shot the albatross. — Coleridge.

Either *with* the swingle-bar, or *with* the haunch of our near leader, we had struck the off-wheel of the little gig. — De Quincey.

(3) *Cause, reason, motive.*

He was wild *with* delight about Texas. — Hale.

She seemed pleased *with* the accident. — Howells.

(4) *Estimation, opinion.*

How can a writer's verses be numerous if *with* him, as *with* you, "poetry is not a pursuit, but a pleasure"? — Lang.

It seemed a supreme moment *with* him. — Howells.

(5) *Opposition.*

After battling *with* terrific hurricanes and typhoons on every known sea. — Aldrich.

The quarrel of the sentimentalists is not *with* life, but *with* you. — Lang.

(6) *The equivalent of* notwithstanding, in spite of.

*With* all his sensibility, he gave millions to the sword. — Channing.

Messala, *with* all his boldness, felt it unsafe to trifle further. — Wallace

(7) *Time.*

He expired *with* these words. — Scott.

*With* each new mind a new secret of nature transpires. — Emerson.

**Exercise**. — Find sentences with four uses of *with*.

# HOW TO PARSE PREPOSITIONS.

**327.** Since a preposition introduces a phrase and shows the relation between two things, it is necessary, first of all, to find the object of the preposition, and then to find what word the prepositional phrase limits. Take this sentence: —

The rule adopted on board the ships on which I have met "the man without a country" was, I think, transmitted from the beginning. — E. E. Hale.

The phrases are (1) *on board the ships*, (2) *on which*, (3) *without a country*, (4) *from the beginning*. The object of *on board* is *ships*; of *on*, *which*; of *without, country*; of *from, beginning*.

In (1), the phrase answers the question *where*, and has the office of an adverb in telling *where* the rule is adopted; hence we say, *on board* shows the relation between *ships* and the participle *adopted*.

In (2), *on which* modifies the verb *have met* by telling where: hence *on* shows the relation between *which* (standing for *ships*) and the verb *have met*.

In (3), *without a country* modifies *man*, telling what man, or the verb *was* understood: hence *without* shows the relation between *country* and *man*, or *was*. And so on.

The **parsing** of prepositions means merely telling between what words or word groups they show relation.

### Exercises.

(*a*) Parse the prepositions in these paragraphs: —

1. I remember, before the dwarf left the queen, he followed us one day into those gardens. I must needs show my wit by a silly illusion between him and the trees, which happens to hold in their language as it does in ours. Whereupon, the malicious rogue, watching his opportunity when I was walking under one of them, shook it directly over my head, by which a dozen apples, each of them near as large as a Bristol barrel, came tumbling about my ears; one of them hit me on the back as I chanced to stoop, and knocked me down flat

on my face; but I received no other hurt, and the dwarf was pardoned at my desire, because I had given the provocation. —Swift

2. Be that as it will, I found myself suddenly awakened with a violent pull upon the ring, which was fastened at the top of my box for the conveniency of carriage. I felt my box raised very high in the air, and then borne forward with prodigious speed. The first jolt had like to have shaken me out of my hammock. I called out several times, but all to no purpose. I looked towards my windows, and could see nothing but the clouds and the sky. I heard a noise just over my head, like the clapping of wings, and then began to perceive the woeful condition I was in; that some eagle had got the ring of my box in his beak, with an intent to let it fall on a rock: for the sagacity and smell of this bird enabled him to discover his quarry at a great distance, though better concealed than I could be within a two-inch board. — *Id.*

(*b*) Give the exact meaning of each italicized preposition in the following sentences: —

1. The guns were cleared *of* their lumber.

2. They then left *for* a cruise up the Indian Ocean.

3. I speak these things *from* a love of justice.

4. *To* our general surprise, we met the defaulter here.

5. There was no one except a little sunbeam *of* a sister.

6. The great gathering in the main street was *on* Sundays, when, after a restful morning, though unbroken *by* the peal of church bells, the miners gathered *from* hills and ravines *for* miles around *for* marketing.

7. The troops waited in their boats *by* the edge of a strand.

8. His breeches were *of* black silk, and his hat was garnished *with* white and sable plumes.

9. A suppressed but still distinct murmur of approbation ran through the crowd *at* this generous proposition.

10. They were shriveled and colorless *with* the cold.

11. On every solemn occasion he was the striking figure, even *to* the eclipsing of the involuntary object of the ceremony.

12. *On* all subjects known to man, he favored the world with his opinions.

13. Our horses ran *on* a sandy margin of the road.

14. The hero of the poem is *of* a strange land and a strange parentage.

15. He locked his door *from* mere force of habit.

16. The lady was remarkable *for* energy and talent.

17. Roland was acknowledged *for* the successor and heir.

18. *For* my part, I like to see the passing, in town.

19. A half-dollar was the smallest coin that could be tendered *for* any service.

20. The mother sank and fell, grasping *at* the child.

21. The savage army was in war-paint, plumed *for* battle.

22. He had lived in Paris *for* the last fifty years.

23. The hill stretched *for* an immeasurable distance.

24.

> The baron of Smaylho'me rose *with* day,
> He spurred his courser on,
> Without stop or stay, down the rocky way
> That leads *to* Brotherstone.

25. *With* all his learning, Carteret was far from being a pedant.

26. An immense mountain covered with a shining green turf is nothing, in this respect, *to* one dark and gloomy.

27. Wilt thou die *for* very weakness?

28. The name of Free Joe strikes humorously *upon* the ear of memory.

29. The shout I heard was *upon* the arrival of this engine.

30. He will raise the price, not merely *by* the amount of the tax.

## WORDS THAT NEED WATCHING.

**328.** If the student has now learned fully that words must be studied in grammar according to their function or use, and not according to form, he will be able to handle some words that are used as several parts of speech. A few are discussed below,—a summary of their treatment in various places as studied heretofore.

**THAT**.

**329. That** may be used as follows:

(1) *As a demonstrative adjective.*

*That* night was a memorable one. — Stockton.

(2) *As an adjective pronoun.*

*That* was a dreadful mistake. — Webster.

(3) *As a relative pronoun.*

> And now it is like an angel's song,
> *That* makes the heavens be mute.
> — Coleridge.

(4) *As an adverb of degree.*

*That* far I hold that the Scriptures teach. — Beecher.

(5) *As a conjunction*: (*a*) Of purpose.

Has bounteously lengthened out your lives, *that* you might behold this joyous day. — Webster.

(*b*) Of result.

Gates of iron so massy *that* no man could without the help of engines open or shut them. — Johnson.

(*c*) Substantive conjunction.

We wish *that* labor may look up here, and be proud in the midst of its toil. — Webster.

# WHAT.

**330.** (1) *Relative pronoun.*

That is *what* I understand by scientific education. — Huxley.

(*a*) Indefinite relative.

> Those shadowy recollections,
> Which be they *what* they may,
> Are yet the fountain light of all our day.
> — Wordsworth.

(2) *Interrogative pronoun*: (*a*) Direct question.

*What* would be an English merchant's character after a few such transactions? — Thackeray.

(*b*) Indirect question.

I have not allowed myself to look beyond the Union, to see *what* might be hidden. — Webster.

(3) *Indefinite pronoun:* The saying, "I'll tell you *what*."

(4) *Relative adjective.*

But woe to *what* thing or person stood in the way. — Emerson.

(*a*) Indefinite relative adjective.

To say *what* good of fashion we can, it rests on reality. — Id.

(5) *Interrogative adjective*: (*a*) Direct question.

*What* right have you to infer that this condition was caused by the action of heat? — Agassiz.

(*b*) Indirect question.

At *what* rate these materials would be distributed,...it is impossible to determine. — Id.

(6) *Exclamatory adjective.*

Saint Mary! *what* a scene is here! — Scott.

(7) *Adverb of degree.*

If he has [been in America], he knows *what* good people are to be found there. — Thackeray.

(8) *Conjunction*, nearly equivalent to *partly... partly*, or *not only...but*.

*What* with the Maltese goats, who go tinkling by to their pasturage; *what* with the vocal seller of bread in the early morning;...these sounds are only to be heard...in Pera. — S.S. Cox.

(9) *As an exclamation.*

*What*, silent still, and silent all! — Byron.

*What*, Adam Woodcock at court! — Scott.

# BUT.

**331.** (1) *Coördinate conjunction*: (*a*) Adversative.

His very attack was never the inspiration of courage, *but* the result of calculation. — Emerson.

(*b*) Copulative, after *not only*.

Then arose not only tears, *but* piercing cries, on all sides. — Carlyle.

(2) *Subordinate conjunction*: (*a*) Result, equivalent to *that ... not*.

Nor is Nature so hard *but* she gives me this joy several times. — Emerson.

(*b*) Substantive, meaning *otherwise ... than*.

Who knows *but*, like the dog, it will at length be no longer traceable to its wild original — Thoreau.

(3) *Preposition*, meaning *except*.

Now there was nothing to be seen *but* fires in every direction. — Lamb.

(4) *Relative pronoun*, after a negative, stands for *that ... not*, or *who ... not*.

There is not a man in them *but* is impelled withal, at all moments, towards order. — Carlyle.

(5) *Adverb*, meaning *only*.

The whole twenty years had been to him *but* as one night. — Irving.

To lead *but* one measure. — Scott.

# AS.

**332.** (1) *Subordinate conjunction*: (*a*) Of time.

Rip beheld a precise counterpart of himself *as* he went up the mountain. — Irving.

(*b*) Of manner.

> *As* orphans yearn on to their mothers,
> He yearned to our patriot bands.
> — Mrs Browning.

(*c*) Of degree.

> His wan eyes
> Gaze on the empty scene *as* vacantly
> *As* ocean's moon looks on the moon in heaven.
> — Shelley.

(*d*) Of reason.

I shall see but little of it, *as* I could neither bear walking nor riding in a carriage. — Franklin.

(*e*) Introducing an appositive word.

Reverenced *as* one of the patriarchs of the village. — Irving.

Doing duty *as* a guard. — Hawthorne.

(2) *Relative pronoun*, after *such*, sometimes *same*.

And was there such a resemblance *as* the crowd had testified? — Hawthorne.

# LIKE.

*Modifier of a noun or pronoun.*

**333.** (1) *An adjective.*

The aforesaid general had been exceedingly *like* the majestic image. — Hawthorne.

They look, indeed, *liker* a lion's mane than a Christian man's locks.-SCOTT.

No Emperor, this, *like* him awhile ago. — Aldrich.

There is no statue *like* this living man. — Emerson.

That face, *like* summer ocean's. — Halleck.

In each case, *like* clearly modifies a noun or pronoun, and is followed by a dative-objective.

*Introduces a clause, but its verb is omitted.*

(2) *A subordinate conjunction* of manner. This follows a verb or a verbal, but the verb of the clause introduced by *like* is *regularly omitted*. Note the difference between these two uses. In Old English *gelic* (like) was followed by the dative, and was clearly an adjective. In this second use, *like* introduces a shortened clause modifying a verb or a verbal, as shown in the following sentences: —

Goodman Brown came into the street of Salem village, staring *like* a bewildered man. — Hawthorne.

Give Ruskin space enough, and he grows frantic and beats the air *like* Carlyle. — Higginson.

They conducted themselves much *like* the crew of a man-of-war. — Parkman.

[The sound] rang in his ears *like* the iron hoofs of the steeds of Time. — Longfellow.

Stirring it vigorously, *like* a cook beating eggs. — Aldrich.

If the verb is expressed, *like* drops out, and *as* or *as if* takes its place.

The sturdy English moralist may talk of a Scotch supper *as* he pleases. — Cass.

Mankind for the first seventy thousand ages ate their meat raw, just *as* they do in Abyssinia to this day. — Lamb.

I do with my friends *as* I do with my books. — Emerson.

NOTE. — Very rarely *like* is found with a verb following, but this is not considered good usage: for example, —

A timid, nervous child, *like* Martin *was*. — Mayhew.

Through which they put their heads, *like* the Gauchos *do* through their cloaks. — Darwin.

> *Like* an arrow shot
> From a well-experienced archer *hits* the mark.
> — Shakespeare.

## INTERJECTIONS.

*Definition.*

**334. Interjections** are exclamations used to express emotion, and are not parts of speech in the same sense as the words we have discussed; that is, entering into the structure of a sentence.

Some of these are imitative sounds; as, tut! buzz! etc.

*Humph*! attempts to express a contemptuous nasal utterance that no letters of our language can really spell.

*Not all exclamatory words are interjections.*

Other interjections are *oh*! *ah*! *alas*! *pshaw*! *hurrah*! etc. But it is to be remembered that almost any word may be used as an exclamation, but it still retains its identity as noun, pronoun, verb, etc.: for example, "Books! lighthouses built on the sea of time [noun];" "Halt! the dust-brown ranks stood fast [verb]," "Up! for shame! [adverb]," "Impossible! it cannot be [adjective]."

# PART II.

*ANALYSIS OF SENTENCES.*

## CLASSIFICATION ACCORDING TO FORM.

*What analysis is..*

**335.** All discourse is made up of sentences: consequently the sentence is the unit with which we must begin. And in order to get a clear and practical idea of the structure of sentences, it is necessary to become expert in **analysis**; that is, in separating them into their component parts.

A general idea of analysis was needed in our study of the parts of speech, — in determining case, subject and predicate, clauses introduced by conjunctions, etc.

*Value of analysis.*

A more thorough and accurate acquaintance with the subject is necessary for two reasons, — not only for a correct understanding of the principles of syntax, but for the study of punctuation and other topics treated in rhetoric.

*Definition.*

**336.** A **sentence** is the expression of a thought in words.

*Kinds of sentences as to form.*

**337.** According to the way in which a thought is put before a listener or reader, sentences may be of three kinds: —

(1) **Declarative**, which puts the thought in the form of a declaration or assertion. This is the most common one.

(2) **Interrogative**, which puts the thought in a question.

(3) **Imperative**, which expresses command, entreaty, or request.

Any one of these may be put in the form of an exclamation, but the sentence would still be declarative, interrogative, or imperative; hence, *according to form*, there are only the three kinds of sentences already named.

Examples of these three kinds are, declarative, "Old year, you must not die!" interrogative, "Hath he not always treasures, always friends?" imperative, "Come to the bridal chamber, Death!"

# CLASSIFICATION ACCORDING TO NUMBER OF STATEMENTS.

## SIMPLE SENTENCES.

*Division according to number of statements.*

**338.** But the division of sentences most necessary to analysis is the division, not according to the form in which a thought is put, but according to how many statements there are.

The one we shall consider first is the **simple sentence.**

*Definition.*

**339.** A **simple sentence** is one which contains a single statement, question, or command: for example, "The quality of mercy is not strained;" "What wouldst thou do, old man?" "Be thou familiar, but by no means vulgar."

**340.** Every sentence must contain two parts,—a **subject** and a **predicate**.

*Definition: Predicate.*

The **predicate** of a sentence is a verb or verb phrase which says something about the subject.

In order to get a correct definition of the subject, let us examine two specimen sentences:—

1. But now all is to be changed.

2. A rare old plant is the ivy green.

In the first sentence we find the subject by placing the word *what* before the predicate,—*What* is to be changed? Answer, *all*. Consequently, we say *all* is the subject of the sentence.

But if we try this with the second sentence, we have some trouble,—*What* is the ivy green? Answer, *a rare old plant*. But we cannot help seeing that an assertion is made, not of *a rare old plant*, but about *the ivy green*; and the real subject is the latter. Sentences are frequently in this inverted order, especially in poetry; and our definition must be the following, to suit all cases: —

*Subject.*

The **subject** is that which answers the question *who* or *what* placed before the predicate, and which at the same time names that of which the predicate says something.

*The subject in interrogative and imperative simple sentences.*

**341.** In the interrogative sentence, the subject is frequently after the verb. Either the verb is the first word of the sentence, or an interrogative pronoun, adjective, or adverb that asks about the subject. In analyzing such sentences, *always reduce them to the order of a statement.* Thus, —

(1) "When should this scientific education be commenced?"

(2) "This scientific education should be commenced when?"

(3) "What wouldst thou have a good great man obtain?"

(4) "Thou wouldst have a good great man obtain what?"

In the imperative sentence, the subject (*you, thou,* or *ye*) is in most cases omitted, and is to be supplied; as, "[You] behold her single in the field."

**Exercise.**

Name the subject and the predicate in each of the following sentences: —

1.

The shadow of the dome of pleasure
Floated midway on the waves.

2. Hence originated their contempt for terrestrial distinctions.

3. Nowhere else on the Mount of Olives is there a view like this.

4. In the sands of Africa and Arabia the camel is a sacred and precious gift.

5. The last of all the Bards was he.

6. Slavery they can have anywhere.

7. Listen, on the other hand, to an ignorant man.

8. What must have been the emotions of the Spaniards!

9. Such was not the effect produced on the sanguine spirit of the general.

10. What a contrast did these children of southern Europe present to the Anglo-Saxon races!

# ELEMENTS OF THE SIMPLE SENTENCE.

**342.** All the **elements** of the simple sentence are as follows: —

(1) The subject.

(2) The predicate.

(3) The object.

(4) The complements.

(5) Modifiers.

(6) Independent elements.

The subject and predicate have been discussed.

**343.** The object may be of two kinds: —

*Definitions. Direct Object.*

(1) The DIRECT OBJECT is that word or expression which answers the question *who* or *what* placed after the verb; or the direct object names that toward which the action of the predicate is directed.

It must be remembered that any verbal may have an object; but for the present we speak of the object of the verb, and by *object* we mean the *direct* object.

*Indirect object.*

(2) The INDIRECT OBJECT is a noun or its equivalent used as the modifier of a verb or verbal to name the person or thing for whose benefit an action is performed.

Examples of direct and indirect objects are, direct, "She seldom saw her *course* at a glance;" indirect, "I give *thee* this to wear at the collar."

*Complement*:

**344.** A **complement** is a word added to a verb of incomplete predication to complete its meaning.

Notice that a verb of incomplete predication may be of two kinds, — transitive and intransitive.

*Of a transitive verb.*

The *transitive verb* often requires, in addition to the object, a word to define fully the action that is exerted upon the object; for example, "Ye call me chief." Here the verb *call* has an object *me* (if we leave out *chief*), and means summoned; but *chief* belongs to the verb, and *me* here is not the object simply of *call*, but of *call chief*, just as if to say, "Ye *honor me*." This word completing a transitive verb is sometimes called a *factitive object*, or *second object*, but it is a true complement.

The fact that this is a complement can be more clearly seen when the verb is in the passive. See sentence 19, in exercise following Sec. 364.

*Complement of an intransitive verb.*

An *intransitive verb*, especially the forms of *be, seem, appear, taste, feel, become*, etc., must often have a word to complete the meaning: as, for instance, "Brow and head were *round, and of massive weight;*" "The good man, he was now getting *old*, above sixty;" "Nothing could be *more copious* than his talk;" "But in general he seemed *deficient in laughter*."

All these complete intransitive verbs. The following are examples of complements of transitive verbs: "Hope deferred maketh the heart *sick;*" "He was termed *Thomas*, or, more familiarly, *Thom of the Gills;*" "A plentiful fortune is reckoned *necessary*, in the popular judgment, to the completion of this man of the world."

**345.** The **modifiers** and **independent elements** will be discussed in detail in Secs. 351, 352, 355.

*Phrases.*

**346.** A phrase is a group of words, not containing a verb, but used as a single modifier.

As to *form*, phrases are of three kinds:—

*Three kinds.*

(1) PREPOSITIONAL, introduced by a preposition: for example, "Such a convulsion is the struggle *of gradual suffocation*, as *in drow-*

*ning*; and, *in the original Opium Confessions*, I mentioned a case *of that nature."*

(2) PARTICIPIAL, consisting of a participle and the words dependent on it. The following are examples: "Then *retreating into the warm house*, and *barring the door*, she sat down to undress the two youngest children."

(3) INFINITIVE, consisting of an infinitive and the words dependent upon it; as in the sentence, "She left her home forever in order *to present herself at the Dauphin's court."*

# Things used as Subject.

**347.** The subject of a simple sentence may be —

(1) *Noun*: "There seems to be no *interval* between greatness and meanness." Also an expression used as a noun; as, "A cheery, '*Ay, ay, sir*!' rang out in response."

(2) *Pronoun*: "*We* are fortified by every heroic anecdote."

(3) *Infinitive phrase*: "*To enumerate and analyze these relations* is to teach the science of method."

(4) *Gerund*: "There will be *sleeping* enough in the grave;" "What signifies *wishing* and *hoping* for better things?"

(5) *Adjective used as noun*: "*The good* are befriended even by weakness and defect;" "*The dead* are there."

(6) *Adverb*: "*Then* is the moment for the humming bird to secure the insects."

**348.** The subject is often found *after the verb* —

(1) *By simple inversion*: as, "Therein has been, and ever will be, my *deficiency*, — the talent of starting the game;" "Never, from their lips, was heard one *syllable* to justify," etc.

(2) *In interrogative sentences*, for which see Sec. 341.

(3) *After* "it *introductory*:" "It ought not to need *to print* in a reading room a caution not to read aloud."

In this sentence, *it* stands in the position of a grammatical subject; but the real or logical subject is *to print*, etc. *It* merely serves to throw the subject after a verb.

*Disguised infinitive subject.*

There is one kind of expression that is really an infinitive, though disguised as a prepositional phrase: "It is hard *for honest men to separate* their country from their party, or their religion from their sect."

The *for* did not belong there originally, but obscures the real subject, — the infinitive phrase. Compare Chaucer: "No wonder is a lewed man to ruste" (No wonder [it] is [for] a common man to rust).

(4) *After* "there *introductory*," which has the same office as *it* in reversing the order (see Sec. 292): "There was a *description* of the destructive operations of time;" "There are *asking eyes, asserting eyes, prowling eyes.*"

# Things used as Direct Object.

**349.** The words used as direct object are mainly the same as those used for subject, but they will be given in detail here, for the sake of presenting examples: —

(1) *Noun*: "Each man has his own *vocation*." Also expressions used as nouns: for example, "'*By God, and by Saint George!*' said the King."

(2) *Pronoun*: "Memory greets *them* with the ghost of a smile."

(3) *Infinitive*: "We like *to see* everything do its office."

(4) *Gerund*: "She heard that *sobbing* of litanies, or the *thundering* of organs."

(5) *Adjective used as a noun*: "For seventy leagues through the mighty cathedral, I saw *the quick* and *the dead*."

# Things used as Complement.

*Complement: Of an intransitive verb.*

**350.** As complement of an *intransitive* verb, —

(1) *Noun*: "She had been an ardent *patriot*."

(2) *Pronoun*: "*Who* is she in bloody coronation robes from Rheims?" "This is *she*, the shepherd girl."

(3) *Adjective*: "Innocence is ever *simple* and *credulous*."

(4) *Infinitive*: "To enumerate and analyze these relations is *to teach* the science of method."

(5) *Gerund*: "Life is a *pitching* of this penny, — heads or tails;" "Serving others is *serving* us."

(6) *A prepositional phrase*: "His frame is *on a larger scale;*" "The marks were *of a kind* not to be mistaken."

It will be noticed that all these complements have a double office, — completing the predicate, and explaining or modifying the subject.

*Of a transitive verb.*

As complement of a *transitive* verb, —

(1) *Noun*: "I will not call you *cowards*."

(2) *Adjective*: "Manners make beauty *superfluous* and *ugly;*" "Their tempers, doubtless, are rendered *pliant* and *malleable* in the fiery furnace of domestic tribulation." In this last sentence, the object is made the subject by being passive, and the words italicized are still complements. Like all the complements in this list, they are adjuncts of the object, and, at the same time, complements of the predicate.

(3) *Infinitive*, or *infinitive phrase*: "That cry which made me *look a thousand ways;*" "I hear the echoes *throng*."

(4) *Participle*, or *participial phrase*: "I can imagine him *pushing firmly on, trusting the hearts of his countrymen*."

(5) *Prepositional phrase:* "My antagonist would render my poniard and my speed *of no use* to me."

# Modifiers.

# I. Modifiers of Subject, Object, or Complement.

**351.** Since the subject and object are either nouns or some equivalent of a noun, the words modifying them must be adjectives or some equivalent of an adjective; and whenever the complement is a noun, or the equivalent of the noun, it is modified by the same words and word groups that modify the subject and the object.

These **modifiers** are as follows: —

(1) *A possessive*: "*My* memory assures me of this;" "She asked her *father's* permission."

(2) *A word in apposition*: "Theodore Wieland, the *prisoner* at the bar, was now called upon for his defense;" "Him, this young *idolater*, I have seasoned for thee."

(3) *An adjective*: "*Great* geniuses have the *shortest* biographies;" "Her father was a prince in Lebanon, — *proud, unforgiving, austere.*"

(4) *Prepositional phrase*: "Are the opinions *of a man on right and wrong on fate and causation*, at the mercy of a broken sleep or an indigestion?" "The poet needs a ground *in popular tradition* to work on."

(5) *Infinitive phrase*: "The way *to know him* is to compare him, not with nature, but with other men;" "She has a new and unattempted problem *to solve*;" "The simplest utterances are worthiest *to be written.*"

(6) *Participial phrase*: "Another reading, *given at the request of a Dutch lady*, was the scene from King John;" "This was the hour *already appointed for the baptism* of the new Christian daughter."

**Exercise.** — In each sentence in Sec. 351, tell whether the subject, object, or complement is modified.

# II. Modifiers of the Predicate.

**352.** Since the predicate is always a verb, the word modifying it must be an adverb or its equivalent: —

(1) *Adverb*: "*Slowly* and *sadly* we laid him down."

(2) *Prepositional phrase*: "The little carriage is creeping on *at one mile an hour;*" "*In the twinkling of an eye,* our horses had carried us *to the termination of the umbrageous isle.*"

In such a sentence as, "He died like a God," the word group *like a God* is often taken as a phrase; but it is really a contracted clause, the verb being omitted.

*Tells how.*

(3) *Participial phrase:* "She comes down from heaven to his help, *interpreting for him the most difficult truths,* and *leading him from star to star.*"

(4) *Infinitive phrase:* "No imprudent, no sociable angel, ever dropped an early syllable *to answer his longing.*"

(For participial and infinitive phrases, see further Secs. 357-363.)

(5) *Indirect object:* "I gave *every man* a trumpet;" "Give *them* not only noble teachings, but noble teachers."

These are equivalent to the phrases *to every man* and *to them,* and modify the predicate in the same way.

*Retained with passive; or*

When the verb is changed from active to passive, the indirect object is retained, as in these sentences: "It is left *you* to find out the reason why;" "All such knowledge should be given *her.*"

*subject of passive verb and direct object retained.*

Or sometimes the indirect object of the active voice becomes the subject of the passive, and the direct object is retained: for example, "She is to be taught *to extend the limits of her sympathy;*" "I was shown an immense *sarcophagus.*"

(6) *Adverbial objective.* These answer the question *when,* or *how long, how far,* etc., and are consequently equivalent to adverbs in modifying a predicate: "We were now running *thirteen miles an hour;*" "*One way* lies hope;" "*Four hours* before midnight we approached a mighty minster."

**Exercises.**

(*a*) Pick out subject, predicate, and (direct) object: —

1. This, and other measures of precaution, I took.

2. The pursuing the inquiry under the light of an end or final cause, gives wonderful animation, a sort of personality to the whole writing.

3. Why does the horizon hold me fast, with my joy and grief, in this center?

4. His books have no melody, no emotion, no humor, no relief to the dead prosaic level.

5. On the voyage to Egypt, he liked, after dinner, to fix on three or four persons to support a proposition, and as many to oppose it.

6. Fashion does not often caress the great, but the children of the great.

7. No rent roll can dignify skulking and dissimulation.

8. They do not wish to be lovely, but to be loved.

(*b*) Pick out the subject, predicate, and complement:

• 1. Evil, according to old philosophers, is good in the making.

• 2. But anger drives a man to say anything.

• 3. The teachings of the High Spirit are abstemious, and, in regard to particulars, negative.

• 4. Spanish diet and youth leave the digestion undisordered and the slumbers light.

- 5. Yet they made themselves sycophantic servants of the King of Spain.

- 6. A merciless oppressor hast thou been.

- 7. To the men of this world, to the animal strength and spirits, the man of ideas appears out of his reason.

- 8. I felt myself, for the first time, burthened with the anxieties of a man, and a member of the world.

(c) Pick out the direct and the indirect object in each: —

- 1. Not the less I owe thee justice.

- 2. Unhorse me, then, this imperial rider.

- 3. She told the first lieutenant part of the truth.

- 4. I promised her protection against all ghosts.

- 5. I gave him an address to my friend, the attorney.

- 6. Paint me, then, a room seventeen feet by twelve.

(d) Pick out the words and phrases in apposition: —

- 1. To suffer and to do, that was thy portion in life.

- 2. A river formed the boundary, — the river Meuse.

- 3. In one feature, Lamb resembles Sir Walter Scott; viz., in the dramatic character of his mind and taste.

- 4. This view was luminously expounded by Archbishop Whately, the present Archbishop of Dublin.

- 5. Yes, at length the warrior lady, the blooming cornet, this nun so martial, this dragoon so lovely, must visit again the home of her childhood.

(e) Pick out the modifiers of the predicate: —

- 1. It moves from one flower to another like a gleam of light, upwards, downwards, to the right and to the left.

- 2.

- And hark! like the roar of the billows on the shore,
  The cry of battle rises along their changing line.


- 3. Their intention was to have a gay, happy dinner, after their long confinement to a ship, at the chief hotel.
- 4. That night, in little peaceful Easedale, six children sat by a peat fire, expecting the return of their parents.

# Compound Subject, Compound Predicate, etc.

*Not compound sentences.*

**353.** Frequently in a simple sentence the writer uses two or more predicates to the same subject, two or more subjects of the same predicate, several modifiers, complements, etc.; but it is to be noticed that, in all such sentences as we quote below, the writers of them purposely combined them *in single statements,* and they are not to be expanded into compound sentences. In a compound sentence the object is to make two or more full statements.

Examples of compound subjects are, "By degrees Rip's *awe* and *apprehension* subsided;" "The *name of the child, the air of the mother,* the *tone of her voice,* — all awakened a train of recollections in his mind."

Sentences with compound predicates are, "The company *broke up,* and *returned* to the more important concerns of the election;" "He *shook* his head, *shouldered* the rusty firelock, and, with a heart full of trouble and anxiety, *turned* his steps homeward."

Sentences with compound objects of the same verb are, "He caught his *daughter* and her *child* in his arms;" "*Voyages* and *travels* I would also have."

And so with complements, modifiers, etc.

# Logical Subject and Logical Predicate.

**354.** The **logical subject** is the simple or grammatical subject, together with all its modifiers.

The **logical predicate** is the simple or grammatical predicate (that is, the verb), together with its modifiers, and its object or complement.

*Larger view of a sentence.*

It is often a help to the student to find the logical subject and predicate first, then the grammatical subject and predicate. For example, in the sentence, "The situation here contemplated exposes a dreadful ulcer, lurking far down in the depths of human nature," the logical subject is *the situation here contemplated*, and the rest is the logical predicate. Of this, the simple subject is *situation*; the predicate, *exposes*; the object, *ulcer*, etc.

# Independent Elements of the Sentence.

**355.** The following words and expressions are grammatically **independent** of the rest of the sentence; that is, they are not a necessary part, do not enter into its structure: —

(1) *Person or thing addressed*: "But you know them, *Bishop;*" "*Ye crags and peaks*, I'm with you once again."

(2) *Exclamatory expressions*: "But the *lady* —! Oh, *heavens*! will that spectacle ever depart from my dreams?"

*Caution.*

The exclamatory expression, however, may be the person or thing addressed, same as (1), above: thus, "Ah, *young sir*! what are you about?" Or it may be an imperative, forming a sentence: "Oh, *hurry, hurry*, my brave young man!"

(3) *Infinitive phrase* thrown in loosely: "*To make a long story short*, the company broke up;" "*Truth to say*, he was a conscientious man."

(4) *Prepositional phrase* not modifying: "Within the railing sat, *to the best of my remembrance*, six quill-driving gentlemen;" "*At all events*, the great man of the prophecy had not yet appeared."

(5) *Participial phrase:* "But, *generally speaking*, he closed his literary toils at dinner;" "*Considering the burnish of her French tastes*, her noticing even this is creditable."

(6) *Single words*: as, "Oh, *yes*! everybody knew them;" "*No*, let him perish;" "*Well*, he somehow lived along;" "*Why*, grandma, how you're winking!" "*Now*, this story runs thus."

*Another caution.*

There are some adverbs, such as *perhaps, truly, really, undoubtedly, besides*, etc., and some conjunctions, such as *however, then, moreover, therefore, nevertheless*, etc., that have an office in the sentence, and should not be confused with the words spoken of above. The words *well, now, why*, and so on, are independent when they merely arrest the attention without being necessary.

## PREPOSITIONAL PHRASES.

**356.** In their use, prepositional phrases may be,

(1) *Adjectival*, modifying a noun, pronoun, or word used as a noun: for example, "He took the road *to King Richard's pavilion;*" "I bring reports *on that subject* from Ascalon."

(2) *Adverbial*, limiting in the same way an adverb limits: as, "All nature around him slept *in calm moonshine* or *in deep shadow;*" "Far *from the madding crowd's ignoble strife.*"

(3) *Independent*, not dependent on any word in the sentence (for examples, see Sec. 355, 4).

# PARTICIPLES AND PARTICIPIAL PHRASES.

**357.** It will be helpful to sum up here the results of our study of participles and participial phrases, and to set down all the uses which are of importance in analysis: —

(1) *The adjectival use*, already noticed, as follows: —

- (*a*) As a complement of a transitive verb, and at the same time a modifier of the object (for an example, see Sec. 350, 4).

- (*b*) As a modifier of subject, object, or complement (see Sec. 351, 6).

(2) *The adverbial use*, modifying the predicate, instances of which were seen in Sec. 352, 3. In these the participial phrases connect closely with the verb, and there is no difficulty in seeing that they modify.

*These need close watching.*

There are other participial phrases which are used adverbially, but require somewhat closer attention; thus, "The letter of introduction, *containing no matters of business*, was speedily run through."

In this sentence, the expression *containing no matters of business* does not describe *letter*, but it is equivalent to *because it contained no matters of business*, and hence is adverbial, modifying *was speedily run through*.

Notice these additional examples: —

*Being a great collector of everything relating to Milton* [reason, "Because I was," etc.], I had naturally possessed myself of Richardson the painter's thick octavo volumes.

Neither the one nor the other writer was valued by the public, *both having* [since they had] *a long warfare to accomplish of contumely and ridicule.*

Wilt thou, therefore, *being now wiser* [as thou art] *in thy thoughts*, suffer God to give by seeming to refuse?

(3) *Wholly independent* in meaning and grammar. See Sec. 355, (5), and these additional examples: —

*Assuming the specific heat to be the same as that of water*, the entire mass of the sun would cool down to 15,000° Fahrenheit in five thousand years.

*This case excepted*, the French have the keenest possible sense of everything odious and ludicrous in posing.

# INFINITIVES AND INFINITIVE PHRASES.

**358.** The various uses of the infinitive give considerable trouble, and they will be presented here in full, or as nearly so as the student will require.

**I. The verbal use.** (1) Completing an incomplete verb, but having no other office than a verbal one.

> • (*a*) With *may (might),can (could),should,would,seem, ought*, etc.: "My weekly bill used invariably *to be* about fifty shillings;" "There, my dear, he should not *have known* them at all;" "He would *instruct* her in the white man's religion, and *teach* her how to be happy and good."

> • (*b*) With the forms of *be*, being equivalent to a future with obligation, necessity, etc.: as in the sentences, "Ingenuity and cleverness are *to be rewarded* by State prizes;" "'The Fair Penitent' was *to be acted* that evening."

> • (*c*) With the definite forms of *go*, equivalent to a future: "I was going *to repeat* my remonstrances;" "I am not going *to dissert* on Hood's humor."

(2) Completing an incomplete transitive verb, but also belonging to a subject or an object (see Sec. 344 for explanation of the complements of transitive verbs): "I am constrained every moment *to acknowledge* a higher origin for events" (retained with passive); "Do they not cause the heart *to beat*, and the eyes *to fill*?"

**359. II. The substantive use**, already examined; but see the following examples for further illustration: —

(1) *As the subject:* "*To have* the wall there, was to have the foe's life at their mercy;" "*To teach* is to learn."

(2) *As the object*: "I like *to hear* them tell their old stories;" "I don't wish *to detract* from any gentleman's reputation."

(3) *As complement:* See examples under (1), above.

(4) *In apposition*, explanatory of a noun preceding: as, "She forwarded to the English leaders a touching invitation *to unite* with the French;" "He insisted on his right *to forget* her."

**360. III. The adjectival use**, modifying a noun that may be a subject, object, complement, etc.: for example, "But there was no time *to be lost*;" "And now Amyas had time *to ask* Ayacanora the meaning of this;" "I have such a desire *to be* well with my public" (see also Sec. 351, 5).

**361. IV. The adverbial use**, which may be to express—

(1) *Purpose:* "The governor, Don Guzman, sailed to the eastward only yesterday *to look* for you;" "Isn't it enough to bring us to death, *to please* that poor young gentleman's fancy?"

(2) *Result:* "Don Guzman returns to the river mouth *to find* the ship a blackened wreck;" "What heart could be so hard as *not to take* pity on the poor wild thing?"

(3) *Reason:* "I am quite sorry *to part* with them;" "Are you mad, *to betray* yourself by your own cries?" "Marry, hang the idiot, *to bring me* such stuff!"

(4) *Degree:* "We have won gold enough *to serve* us the rest of our lives;" "But the poor lady was too sad *to talk* except to the boys now and again."

(5) *Condition:* "You would fancy, *to hear* McOrator after dinner, the Scotch fighting all the battles;" "*To say* what good of fashion we can, it rests on reality" (the last is not a simple sentence, but it furnishes a good example of this use of the infinitive).

**362.** The fact that the infinitives in Sec. 361 are used adverbially, is evident from the meaning of the sentences.

Whether each sentence containing an adverbial infinitive has the meaning of purpose, result, etc., may be found out by turning the infinitive into an equivalent clause, such as those studied under subordinate conjunctions.

To test this, notice the following:—

In (1), *to look* means *that he might look*; *to please* is equivalent to *that he may please*,—both purpose clauses.

In (2), *to find* shows the result of the return; *not to take pity* is equivalent to *that it would not take pity*.

In (3), *to part* means *because I part*, etc.; and *to betray* and *to bring* express the reason, equivalent to *that you betray*, etc.

In (4), *to serve* and *to talk* are equivalent to [*as much gold*] *as will serve us*; and "too sad *to talk*" also shows degree.

In (5), *to hear* means *if you should hear*, and *to say* is equivalent to *if we say*, — both expressing condition.

**363. V. The independent use**, which is of two kinds, —

(1) Thrown loosely into the sentence; as in Sec. 355, (3).

(2) *Exclamatory:* "I a philosopher! I *advance* pretensions;" "'He *to die*!' resumed the bishop." (See also Sec. 268, 4.)

# OUTLINE OF ANALYSIS.

**364.** In analyzing simple sentences, give —

(1) The predicate. If it is an incomplete verb, give the complement (Secs. 344 and 350) and its modifiers (Sec. 351).

(2) The object of the verb (Sec. 349).

(3) Modifiers of the object (Sec. 351).

(4) Modifiers of the predicate (Sec. 352).

(5) The subject (Sec. 347).

(6) Modifiers of the subject (Sec. 351).

(7) Independent elements (Sec. 355).

This is not the same order that the parts of the sentence usually have; but it is believed that the student will proceed more easily by finding the predicate with its modifiers, object, etc., and then finding the subject by placing the question *who* or *what* before it.

### Exercise in Analyzing Simple Sentences.

Analyze the following according to the directions given: —

1. Our life is March weather, savage and serene in one hour.

2. I will try to keep the balance true.

3. The questions of Whence? What? and Whither? and the solution of these, must be in a life, not in a book.

4. The ward meetings on election days are not softened by any misgiving of the value of these ballotings.

5. Our English Bible is a wonderful specimen of the strength and music of the English language.

6. Through the years and the centuries, through evil agents, through toys and atoms, a great and beneficent tendency irresistibly streams.

7. To be hurried away by every event, is to have no political system at all.

8. This mysticism the ancients called ecstasy, — a getting-out of their bodies to think.

9. He risked everything, and spared nothing, neither ammunition, nor money, nor troops, nor generals, nor himself.

10. We are always in peril, always in a bad plight, just on the edge of destruction, and only to be saved by invention and courage.

11. His opinion is always original, and to the purpose.

12. To these gifts of nature, Napoleon added the advantage of having been born to a private and humble fortune.

13.

> The water, like a witch's oils,
> Burnt green and blue and white.

14. We one day descried some shapeless object floating at a distance.

15.

> Old Adam, the carrion crow,
> The old crow of Cairo;
> He sat in the shower, and let it flow
> Under his tail and over his crest.

16. It costs no more for a wise soul to convey his quality to other men.

17. It is easy to sugar to be sweet.

18. At times the black volume of clouds overhead seemed rent asunder by flashes of lightning.

19. The whole figure and air, good and amiable otherwise, might be called flabby and irresolute.

20. I have heard Coleridge talk, with eager energy, two stricken hours, and communicate no meaning whatsoever to any individual.

21. The word *conscience* has become almost confined, in popular use, to the moral sphere.

22. You may ramble a whole day together, and every moment discover something new.

23. She had grown up amidst the liberal culture of Henry's court a bold horsewoman, a good shot, a graceful dancer, a skilled musician, an accomplished scholar.

24. Her aims were simple and obvious, — to preserve her throne, to keep England out of war, to restore civil and religious order.

25.

> Fair name might he have handed down,
> Effacing many a stain of former crime.

26. Of the same grandeur, in less heroic and poetic form, was the patriotism of Peel in recent history.

27. Oxford, ancient mother! hoary with ancestral honors, time-honored, and, haply, time-shattered power — I owe thee nothing!

28. The villain, I hate him and myself, to be a reproach to such goodness.

29. I dare this, upon my own ground, and in my own garden, to bid you leave the place now and forever.

30. Upon this shore stood, ready to receive her, in front of all this mighty crowd, the prime minister of Spain, the same Condé Olivarez.

31. Great was their surprise to see a young officer in uniform stretched within the bushes upon the ground.

32. She had made a two days' march, baggage far in the rear, and no provisions but wild berries.

33. This amiable relative, an elderly man, had but one foible, or perhaps one virtue, in this world.

34. Now, it would not have been filial or ladylike.

35. Supposing this computation to be correct, it must have been in the latitude of Boston, the present capital of New England.

36. The cry, "A strange vessel close aboard the frigate!" having already flown down the hatches, the ship was in an uproar.

37.

> But yield, proud foe, thy fleet
> With the crews at England's feet.

38. Few in number, and that number rapidly perishing away through sickness and hardships; surrounded by a howling wilderness and savage tribes; exposed to the rigors of an almost arctic winter, — their minds were filled with doleful forebodings.

39. List to the mournful tradition still sung by the pines of the forest.

40.

> In the Acadian land, on the shores of the Basin of Minas,
> Distant, secluded, still, the little village of Grand-Pré
> Lay in the fruitful valley.

41. Must we in all things look for the how, and the why, and the wherefore?

# CONTRACTED SENTENCES.

*Words left out after* than *or* as.

**365.** Some sentences look like simple ones in form, but have an essential part omitted that is so readily supplied by the mind as not to need expressing. Such are the following:—

"There is no country more worthy of our study than England [is worthy of our study]."

"The distinctions between them do not seem to be so marked as [they are marked] in the cities."

To show that these words are really omitted, compare with them the two following:—

"The nobility and gentry are more popular among the inferior orders than *they are* in any other country."

"This is not so universally the case at present as *it was* formerly."

*Sentences with* like.

**366.** As shown in Part I. (Sec. 333). the expressions *of manner* introduced by *like*, though often treated as phrases, are really contracted clauses; but, if they were expanded, *as* would be the connective instead of *like*; thus,—

"They'll shine o'er her sleep, like [as] a smile from the west [would shine].
From her own loved island of sorrow."

This must, however, be carefully discriminated from cases where *like* is an adjective complement; as,—

"She is *like* some tender tree, the pride and beauty of the grove;" "The ruby seemed *like* a spark of fire burning upon her white bosom."

Such contracted sentences form a connecting link between our study of simple and complex sentences.

# COMPLEX SENTENCES.

*The simple sentence the basis.*

**367.** Our investigations have now included all the machinery of the simple sentence, which is the *unit of speech*.

Our further study will be in sentences which are combinations of simple sentences, made merely for convenience and smoothness, to avoid the tiresome repetition of short ones of monotonous similarity.

Next to the simple sentence stands the complex sentence. The basis of it is two or more simple sentences, which are so united that one member is the main one, — the backbone, — the other members subordinate to it, or dependent on it; as in this sentence, —

"When such a spirit breaks forth into complaint, we are aware how great must be the suffering that extorts the murmur."

The relation of the parts is as follows: —

> **we are aware** _____ \_\_\_\_\_ | | \_\_| *when such a spirit breaks* | *forth into complaint,* | *how great must be the suffering* | that extorts the murmur.

This arrangement shows to the eye the picture that the sentence forms in the mind, — how the first clause is held in suspense by the mind till the second, **we are aware**, is taken in; then we recognize this as the main statement; and the next one, *how great ... suffering*, drops into its place as subordinate to *we are aware*; and the last, *that ... murmur*, logically depends on *suffering*.

Hence the following definition: —

*Definition.*

**368.** A **complex sentence** is one containing one main or independent clause (also called the principal proposition or clause), and *one or more* subordinate or dependent clauses.

**369.** The **elements** of a complex sentence are the same as those of the simple sentence; that is, each clause has its subject, predicate, object, complements, modifiers, etc.

But there is this difference: whereas the simple sentence always has a word or a phrase for subject, object, complement, and modifier, the complex sentence has *statements* or *clauses* for these places.

# CLAUSES.

*Definition.*

**370.** A clause is a division of a sentence, containing a verb with its subject.

Hence the term *clause* may refer to the main division of the complex sentence, or it may be applied to the others, — the dependent or subordinate clauses.

*Independent clause.*

**371.** A **principal, main**, or **independent clause** is one making a statement without the help of any other clause.

*Dependent clause.*

A **subordinate** or **dependent clause** is one which makes a statement depending upon or modifying some word in the principal clause.

*Kinds.*

**372.** As to their office in the sentence, clauses are divided into NOUN, ADJECTIVE, and ADVERB clauses, according as they are equivalent in use to nouns, adjectives, or adverbs.

## Noun Clauses.

**373.** Noun clauses have the following uses: —

(1) *Subject*: "*That such men should give prejudiced views of America* is not a matter of surprise."

(2) *Object of a verb, verbal, or the equivalent of a verb*: (*a*) "I confess *these stories, for a time, put an end to my fancies*;" (*b*) "I am aware [I know] *that a skillful illustrator of the immortal bard would have swelled the materials.*"

Just as the object noun, pronoun, infinitive, etc., is retained after a passive verb (Sec. 352, 5), so the object clause is retained, and should not be called an adjunct of the subject; for example, "We are persuaded *that a thread runs through all things*;" "I was told *that the house had not been shut, night or day, for a hundred years.*"

(3) *Complement*: "The terms of admission to this spectacle are, *that he have a certain solid and intelligible way of living.*"

(4) *Apposition.* (*a*) Ordinary apposition, explanatory of some noun or its equivalent: "Cecil's saying of Sir Walter Raleigh, '*I know that he can toil terribly,*' is an electric touch."

(*b*) After "it *introductory*" (logically this is a subject clause, but it is often treated as in apposition with *it*): "*It* was the opinion of some, *that this might be the wild huntsman famous in German legend.*"

(5) *Object of a preposition*: "At length he reached to *where the ravine had opened through the cliffs.*"

Notice that frequently only the introductory word is the object of the preposition, and the whole clause is not; thus, "The rocks presented a high impenetrable wall, *over which* the torrent came tumbling."

**374.** Here are to be noticed certain sentences seemingly complex, with a noun clause in apposition with *it*; but logically they are nothing but simple sentences. But since they are *complex in form*, attention is called to them here; for example, —

"Alas! it is we ourselves that are getting buried alive under this avalanche of earthly impertinences."

To divide this into two clauses — (*a*) *It is we ourselves*, (*b*) *that are ... impertinences* — would be grammatical; but logically the sentence is, *We ourselves are getting ... impertinences*, and *it is ... that* is merely a framework used to effect emphasis. The sentence shows how *it* may lose its pronominal force.

Other examples of this construction are, —

"It is on the understanding, and not on the sentiment, of a nation, that all safe legislation must be based."

"Then it is that deliberative Eloquence lays aside the plain attire of her daily occupation."

### Exercise.

Tell how each noun clause is used in these sentences: —

1. I felt that I breathed an atmosphere of sorrow.

2. But the fact is, I was napping.

3. Shaking off from my spirit what must have been a dream, I scanned more narrowly the aspect of the building.

4. Except by what he could see for himself, he could know nothing.

5. Whatever he looks upon discloses a second sense.

6. It will not be pretended that a success in either of these kinds is quite coincident with what is best and inmost in his mind.

7. The reply of Socrates, to him who asked whether he should choose a wife, still remains reasonable, that, whether he should choose one or not, he would repent it.

8. What history it had, how it changed from shape to shape, no man will ever know.

9. Such a man is what we call an original man.

10. Our current hypothesis about Mohammed, that he was a scheming impostor, a falsehood incarnate, that his religion is a mere mass of quackery and fatuity, begins really to be no longer tenable to any one.

# Adjective Clauses.

**375.** As the office of an adjective is to modify, the only use of an adjective clause is to limit or describe some noun, or equivalent of a noun: consequently the adjective may modify *any* noun, or equivalent of a noun, in the sentence.

The adjective clause may be introduced by the relative pronouns *who, which, that, but, as*; sometimes by the conjunctions *when, where, whither, whence, wherein, whereby,* etc.

Frequently there is no connecting word, a relative pronoun being understood.

*Examples of adjective clauses.*

**376.** Adjective clauses may modify —

(1) *The subject*: "The themes *it offers for contemplation* are too vast for their capacities;" "Those *who see the Englishman only in town*, are apt to form an unfavorable opinion of his social character."

(2) *The object*: "From this piazza Ichabod entered the hall, *which formed the center of the mansion.*"

(3) *The complement*: "The animal he bestrode was a broken-down plow-horse, *that had outlived almost everything but his usefulness*;" "It was such an apparition *as is seldom to be met with in broad daylight.*"

(4) *Other words*: "He rode with short stirrups, *which brought his knees nearly up to the pommel of the saddle*;" "No whit anticipating the oblivion *which awaited their names and feats*, the champions advanced through the lists;" "Charity covereth a multitude of sins, in another sense than that *in which it is said to do so in Scripture.*"

**Exercise.**

Pick out the adjective clauses, and tell what each one modifies; i.e., whether subject, object, etc.

1. There were passages that reminded me perhaps too much of Massillon.

2. I walked home with Calhoun, who said that the principles which I had avowed were just and noble.

3. Other men are lenses through which we read our own minds.

4. In one of those celestial days when heaven and earth meet and adorn each other, it seems a pity that we can only spend it once.

5. One of the maidens presented a silver cup, containing a rich mixture of wine and spice, which Rowena tasted.

6. No man is reason or illumination, or that essence we were looking for.

7. In the moment when he ceases to help us as a cause, he begins to help us more as an effect.

8. Socrates took away all ignominy from the place, which could not be a prison whilst he was there.

9. This is perhaps the reason why we so seldom hear ghosts except in our long-established Dutch settlements.

10. From the moment you lose sight of the land you have left, all is vacancy.

11. Nature waited tranquilly for the hour to be struck when man should arrive.

**Adverbial Clauses**.

**377.** The adverb clause takes the place of an adverb in modifying a verb, a verbal, an adjective, or an adverb. The student has met with many adverb clauses in his study of the subjunctive mood and of subordinate conjunctions; but they require careful study, and will be given in detail, with examples.

**378.** Adverb clauses are of the following kinds:

(1) TIME: "*As we go*, the milestones are grave-stones;" "He had gone but a little way *before he espied a foul fiend coming*;" "*When he was come up to Christian*, he beheld him with a disdainful countenance."

(2) PLACE: *"Wherever the sentiment of right comes in,* it takes precedence of everything else;" "He went several times to England, *where he does not seem to have attracted any attention."*

(3) REASON, or CAUSE: "His English editor lays no stress on his discoveries, *since he was too great to care to be original;"* "I give you joy *that truth is altogether wholesome."*

(4) MANNER: "The knowledge of the past is valuable only *as it leads us to form just calculations with respect to the future;"* "After leaving the whole party under the table, he goes away *as if nothing had happened."*

(5) DEGREE, or COMPARISON: "They all become wiser *than they were;"* "The right conclusion is, that we should try, so far *as we can,* to make up our shortcomings;" "Master Simon was in as chirping a humor *as a grasshopper filled with dew* [is];" *"The broader their education is,* the wider is the horizon of their thought." The first clause in the last sentence is dependent, expressing the degree in which the horizon, etc., is wider.

(6) PURPOSE: "Nature took us in hand, shaping our actions, *so that we might not be ended untimely by too gross disobedience."*

(7) RESULT, or CONSEQUENCE: "He wrote on the scale of the mind itself, *so that all things have symmetry in his tablet;"* "The window was so far superior to every other in the church, *that the vanquished artist killed himself from mortification."*

(8) CONDITION: *"If we tire of the saints,* Shakespeare is our city of refuge;" "Who cares for that, *so thou gain aught wider and nobler?"* "You can die grandly, and as goddesses would die *were goddesses mortal."*

(9) CONCESSION, introduced by indefinite relatives, adverbs, and adverbial conjunctions, — *whoever, whatever, however,* etc.: "But still, *however good she may be as a witness,* Joanna is better;" *"Whatever there may remain of illiberal in discussion,* there is always something illiberal in the severer aspects of study."

These mean *no matter how good, no matter what remains,* etc.

**Exercise.**

Pick out the adverbial clauses in the following sentences; tell what kind each is, and what it modifies: —

1. As I was clearing away the weeds from this epitaph, the little sexton drew me on one side with a mysterious air, and informed me in a low voice that once upon a time, on a dark wintry night, when the wind was unruly, howling and whistling, banging about doors and windows, and twirling weathercocks, so that the living were frightened out of their beds, and even the dead could not sleep quietly in their graves, the ghost of honest Preston was attracted by the well-known call of "waiter," and made its sudden appearance just as the parish clerk was singing a stave from the "mirrie garland of Captain Death."

2. If the children gathered about her, as they sometimes did, Pearl would grow positively terrible in her puny wrath, snatching up stones to fling at them, with shrill, incoherent exclamations, that made her mother tremble because they had so much the sound of a witch's anathemas.

3. The spell of life went forth from her ever-creative spirit, and communicated itself to a thousand objects, as a torch kindles a flame wherever it may be applied.

# ANALYZING COMPLEX SENTENCES.

**379.** These suggestions will be found helpful: —

(1) See that the sentence and all its parts are placed in the natural order of subject, predicate, object, and modifiers.

(2) First take the sentence *as a whole*; find the principal subject and principal predicate; then treat noun clauses as nouns, adjective clauses as adjectives modifying certain words, and adverb clauses as single modifying adverbs.

(3) Analyze each clause as a simple sentence. For example, in the sentence, "Cannot we conceive that Odin was a reality?" *we* is the principal subject; *cannot conceive* is the principal predicate; its object is *that Odin was a reality*, of which clause *Odin* is the subject, etc.

**380.** It is sometimes of great advantage to map out a sentence after analyzing it, so as to picture the parts and their relations. To take a sentence: —

"I cannot help thinking that the fault is in themselves, and that if the church and the cataract were in the habit of giving away their thoughts with that rash generosity which characterizes tourists, they might perhaps say of their visitors, 'Well, if you are those men of whom we have heard so much, we are a little disappointed, to tell the truth.'"

This may be represented as follows: —

**I cannot help thinking** _____ |
_____ | | | (*a*) THAT THE FAULT IS IN
THEMSELVES, AND | | (*b*) [THAT] THEY MIGHT
(PERHAPS) SAY OF THEIR VISITORS |
_____ | | |
_____ |_____
_____ | | | | | (*a*) We are (a little) disappointed | | O|
_____ | O| b|
_____ | | b| j| M| | j| e| o| (*b*) If you
are those men | e| c| d| ___ | c| t| i|
_____ | | t| | f| M| | | | i| o| Of

whom we have heard so much. | | | e| d. | | \ r\ \ | |

_____ |

| M | | o | (a) If the church and ... that rash generosity | d |
_____ | i | | | f |

_____ | | i | |

| e | | (b) Which characterizes tourists. | r | | \ \ \

# OUTLINE

**381.** (1) Find the principal clause.

(2) Analyze it according to Sec. 364.

(3) Analyze the dependent clauses according to Sec. 364. This of course includes dependent clauses that depend on other dependent clauses, as seen in the "map" (Sec. 380).

**Exercises.**

(*a*) Analyze the following complex sentences: —

1. Take the place and attitude which belong to you.

2. That mood into which a friend brings us is his dominion over us.

3. True art is only possible on the condition that every talent has its apotheosis somewhere.

4. The deep eyes, of a light hazel, were as full of sorrow as of inspiration.

5. She is the only church that has been loyal to the heart and soul of man, that has clung to her faith in the imagination.

6. She has never lost sight of the truth that the product human nature is composed of the sum of flesh and spirit.

7. But now that she has become an establishment, she begins to perceive that she made a blunder in trusting herself to the intellect alone.

8. Before long his talk would wander into all the universe, where it was uncertain what game you would catch, or whether any.

9. The night proved unusually dark, so that the two principals had to tie white handkerchiefs round their elbows in order to descry each other.

10. Whether she would ever awake seemed to depend upon an accident.

11. Here lay two great roads, not so much for travelers that were few, as for armies that were too many by half.

12. It was haunted to that degree by fairies, that the parish priest was obliged to read mass there once a year.

13. More than one military plan was entered upon which she did not approve.

14. As surely as the wolf retires before cities, does the fairy sequester herself from the haunts of the licensed victualer.

15. M. Michelet is anxious to keep us in mind that this bishop was but an agent of the English.

16. Next came a wretched Dominican, that pressed her with an objection, which, if applied to the Bible, would tax every miracle with unsoundness.

17. The reader ought to be reminded that Joanna D'Arc was subject to an unusually unfair trial.

18. Now, had she really testified this willingness on the scaffold, it would have argued nothing at all but the weakness of a genial nature.

19. And those will often pity that weakness most, who would yield to it least.

20. Whether she said the word is uncertain.

21. This is she, the shepherd girl, counselor that had none for herself, whom I choose, bishop, for yours.

22. Had *they* been better chemists, had *we* been worse, the mixed result, namely, that, dying for *them*, the flower should revive for *us*, could not have been effected.

23. I like that representation they have of the tree.

24. He was what our country people call *an old one*.

25. He thought not any evil happened to men of such magnitude as false opinion.

26. These things we are forced to say, if we must consider the effort of Plato to dispose of Nature, — which will not be disposed of.

27. He showed one who was afraid to go on foot to Olympia, that it was no more than his daily walk, if continuously extended, would easily reach.

28. What can we see or acquire but what we are?

29. Our eyes are holden that we cannot see things that stare us in the face, until the hour arrives when the mind is ripened.

30. There is good reason why we should prize this liberation.

(b) First analyze, then map out as in Sec. 380, the following complex sentences: —

1. The way to speak and write what shall not go out of fashion, is to speak and write sincerely.

2. The writer who takes his subject from his ear, and not from his heart, should know that he has lost as much as he has gained.

3. "No book," said Bentley, "was ever written down by any but itself."

4. That which we do not believe, we cannot adequately say, though we may repeat the words never so often.

5. We say so because we feel that what we love is not in your will, but above it.

6. It makes no difference how many friends I have, and what content I can find in conversing with each, if there be one to whom I am not equal.

7. In every troop of boys that whoop and run in each yard and square, a new-comer is as well and accurately weighed in the course of a few days, and stamped with his right number, as if he had undergone a formal trial of his strength, speed, and temper.

# COMPOUND SENTENCES.

*How formed.*

**382.** The **compound sentence** is a combination of two or more simple or complex sentences. While the complex sentence has only *one* main clause, the compound has *two or more* independent clauses making statements, questions, or commands. Hence the definition, —

*Definition.*

**383.** A **compound sentence** is one which contains two or more independent clauses.

This leaves room for any number of subordinate clauses in a compound sentence: the requirement is simply that it have at least two independent clauses.

Examples of compound sentences: —

*Examples.*

(1) *Simple sentences united:* "He is a palace of sweet sounds and sights; he dilates; he is twice a man; he walks with arms akimbo; he soliloquizes."

(2) *Simple with complex:* "The trees of the forest, the waving grass, and the peeping flowers have grown intelligent; and he almost fears to trust them with the secret which they seem to invite."

(3) *Complex with complex:* "The power which resides in him is new in nature, and none but he knows what that is which he can do, nor does he know until he has tried."

**384.** From this it is evident that nothing new is added to the work of analysis already done.

The same analysis of simple sentences is repeated in (1) and (2) above, and what was done in complex sentences is repeated in (2) and (3).

The division into members will be easier, for the coördinate independent statements are readily taken apart with the subordinate clauses attached, if there are any.

Thus in (1), the semicolons cut apart the independent members, which are simple statements; in (2), the semicolon separates the first, a simple member, from the second, a complex member; in (3), *and* connects the first and second complex members, and *nor* the second and third complex members.

*Connectives.*

**385.** The coördinate conjunctions *and, nor, or but*, etc., introduce independent clauses (see Sec. 297).

But the conjunction is often omitted in copulative and adversative clauses, as in Sec. 383 (1). Another example is, "Only the star dazzles; the planet has a faint, moon-like ray" (adversative).

*Study the thought.*

**386.** The one point that will give trouble is the variable use of some connectives; as *but, for, yet, while* (*whilst*), *however, whereas*, etc. Some of these are now conjunctions, now adverbs or prepositions; others sometimes coördinate, sometimes subordinate conjunctions.

The student must watch *the logical connection* of the members of the sentence, and not the form of the connective.

**Exercise.**

Of the following illustrative sentences, tell which are compound, and which complex: —

1. Speak your latent conviction, and it shall be the universal sense; for the inmost in due time becomes the outmost.

2. I no longer wish to meet a good I do not earn, for example, to find a pot of buried gold.

3. Your goodness must have some edge to it — else it is none.

4. Man does not stand in awe of man, nor is his genius admonished to stay at home, but it goes abroad to beg a cup of water of the urns of other men.

5. A man cannot speak but he judges himself.

6. In your metaphysics you have denied personality to the Deity, yet when the devout motions of the soul come, yield to them heart and life.

7. I thought that it was a Sunday morning in May; that it was Easter Sunday, and as yet very early in the morning.

8. We denote the primary wisdom as intuition, whilst all later teachings are tuitions.

9. Whilst the world is thus dual, so is every one of its parts.

10. They measure the esteem of each other by what each has, and not by what each is.

11. For everything you have missed, you have gained something else; and for everything you gain, you lose something.

12. I sometimes seemed to have lived for seventy or one hundred years in one night; nay, I sometimes had feelings representative of a millennium, passed in that time, or, however, of a duration far beyond the limits of experience.

13. However some may think him wanting in zeal, the most fanatical can find no taint of apostasy in any measure of his.

14. In this manner, from a happy yet often pensive child, he grew up to be a mild, quiet, unobtrusive boy, and sunbrowned with labor in the fields, but with more intelligence than is seen in many lads from the schools.

# OUTLINE FOR ANALYZING COMPOUND SENTENCES.

**387.** (i) Separate it into its main members. (2) Analyze each complex member as in Sec. 381. (3) Analyze each simple member as in Sec. 364.

**Exercise.**

Analyze the following compound sentences: —

1. The gain is apparent; the tax is certain.

2. If I feel overshadowed and outdone by great neighbors, I can yet love; I can still receive; and he that loveth maketh his own the grandeur that he loves.

3. Love, and thou shalt be loved.

4. All loss, all pain, is particular; the universe remains to the heart unhurt.

5. Place yourself in the middle of the stream of power and wisdom which animates all whom it floats, and you are without effort impelled to truth.

6. He teaches who gives, and he learns who receives.

7. Whatever he knows and thinks, whatever in his apprehension is worth doing, that let him communicate, or men will never know and honor him aright.

8. Stand aside; give those merits room; let them mount and expand.

9. We see the noble afar off, and they repel us; why should we intrude?

10. We go to Europe, or we pursue persons, or we read books, in the instinctive faith that these will call it out and reveal us to ourselves.

11. A gay and pleasant sound is the whetting of the scythe in the mornings of June, yet what is more lonesome and sad

than the sound of a whetstone or mower's rifle when it is too late in the season to make hay?

12. "Strike," says the smith, "the iron is white;" "keep the rake," says the haymaker, "as nigh the scythe as you can, and the cart as nigh the rake."

13. Trust men, and they will be true to you; treat them greatly, and they will show themselves great, though they make an exception in your favor to all their rules of trade.

14. On the most profitable lie the course of events presently lays a destructive tax; whilst frankness invites frankness, puts the parties on a convenient footing, and makes their business a friendship.

15. The sturdiest offender of your peace and of the neighborhood, if you rip up his claims, is as thin and timid as any; and the peace of society is often kept, because, as children, one is afraid, and the other dares not.

16. They will shuffle and crow, crook and hide, feign to confess here, only that they may brag and conquer there, and not a thought has enriched either party, and not an emotion of bravery, modesty, or hope.

17. The magic they used was the ideal tendencies, which always make the Actual ridiculous; but the tough world had its revenge the moment they put their horses of the sun to plow in its furrow.

18. Come into port greatly, or sail with God the seas.

19. When you have chosen your part, abide by it, and do not weakly try to reconcile yourself with the world.

20. Times of heroism are generally times of terror, but the day never shines in which this element may not work.

21. Life is a train of moods like a string of beads, and as we pass through them they prove to be many-colored lenses which paint the world their own hue, and each shows only what lies at its focus.

22. We see young men who owe us a new world, so readily and lavishly they promise, but they never acquit the debt; they die young, and dodge the account; or, if they live, they lose themselves in the crowd.

23. So does culture with us; it ends in headache.

24. Do not craze yourself with thinking, but go about your business anywhere.

25. Thus journeys the mighty Ideal before us; it never was known to fall into the rear.

# PART III.

# *SYNTAX.*

## INTRODUCTORY.

*By way of introduction.*

**388.** Syntax is from a Greek word meaning *order* or *arrangement*.

Syntax deals with the relation of words to each other as component parts of a sentence, and with their proper arrangement to express clearly the intended meaning.

*Ground covered by syntax.*

**380.** Following the Latin method, writers on English grammar usually divide syntax into the two general heads, — **agreement** and **government**.

**Agreement** is concerned with the following relations of words: words in apposition, verb and subject, pronoun and antecedent, adjective and noun.

**Government** has to do with verbs and prepositions, both of which are said to govern words by having them in the objective case.

**390.** Considering the scarcity of inflections in English, it is clear that if we merely follow the Latin treatment, the department of syntax will be a small affair. But there is a good deal else to watch in addition to the few forms; for there is an important and marked difference between Latin and English syntax. It is this: —

Latin syntax depends upon fixed rules governing the use of inflected forms: hence the *position* of words in a sentence is of little grammatical importance.

*Essential point in English syntax.*

English syntax follows the Latin to a limited extent; but its leading characteristic is, that English syntax is founded upon *the meaning* and *the logical connection* of words rather than upon their form: consequently it is quite as necessary to place words properly, and to think clearly of the meaning of words, as to study inflected forms.

For example, the sentence, "The savage here the settler slew," is ambiguous. *Savage* may be the subject, following the regular order of subject; or *settler* may be the subject, the order being inverted. In Latin, distinct forms would be used, and it would not matter which one stood first.

*Why study syntax?*

**391.** There is, then, a double reason for not omitting syntax as a department of grammar, —

*First*, To study the rules regarding the use of inflected forms, some of which conform to classical grammar, while some are idiomatic (peculiar to our own language).

*Second*, To find out the *logical methods* which control us in the arrangement of words; and particularly when the grammatical and the logical conception of a sentence do not agree, or when they exist side by side in good usage.

As an illustration of the last remark, take the sentence, "Besides these famous books of Scott's and Johnson's, there is a copious 'Life' by Sheridan." In this there is a possessive form, and added to it the preposition *of*, also expressing a possessive relation. This is not logical; it is not consistent with the general rules of grammar: but none the less it is good English.

Also in the sentence, "None remained but he," grammatical rules would require *him* instead of *he* after the preposition; yet the expression is sustained by good authority.

*Some rules not rigid.*

**392.** In some cases, authorities — that is, standard writers — differ as to which of two constructions should be used, or the same writer will use both indifferently. Instances will be found in treating of the pronoun or noun with a gerund, pronoun and antecedent, sometimes verb and subject, etc.

When usage varies as to a given construction, both forms will be given in the following pages.

*The basis of syntax.*

**393.** Our treatment of syntax will be an endeavor to record the best usage of the present time on important points; and nothing but important points will be considered, for it is easy to confuse a student with too many obtrusive *don'ts.*

The constructions presented as general will be justified by quotations from *modern writers of English* who are regarded as "standard;" that is, writers whose style is generally acknowledged as superior, and whose judgment, therefore, will be accepted by those in quest of authoritative opinion.

Reference will also be made to spoken English when its constructions differ from those of the literary language, and to vulgar English when it preserves forms which were once, but are not now, good English.

It may be suggested to the student that the only way to acquire correctness is to watch good usage *everywhere*, and imitate it.

## NOUNS.

**394.** Nouns have no distinct forms for the nominative and objective cases: hence no mistake can be made in using them. But some remarks are required concerning the use of the possessive case.

*Use of the possessive. Joint possession.*

**395.** When two or more possessives modify the same noun, or indicate joint ownership or possession, the possessive sign is added to the last noun only; for example, —

Live your *king and country's* best support. — Rowe.

Woman, *sense and nature's* easy fool. — Byron.

*Oliver and Boyd's* printing office. — Mcculloch.

*Adam and Eve's* morning hymn. — Milton.

In *Beaumont and Fletcher's* "Sea Voyage," Juletta tells, etc. — Emerson.

*Separate possession.*

**396.** When two or more possessives stand before the same noun, but imply separate possession or ownership, the possessive sign is used with each noun; as, —

He lands us on a grassy stage, Safe from the *storm's* and *prelate's* rage. — Marvell

Where were the sons of Peers and Members of Parliament in *Anne's* and *George's* time? — Thackeray.

*Levi's* station in life was the receipt of custom; and *Peter's*, the shore of Galilee; and *Paul's*, the antechamber of the High Priest. — Ruskin.

Swift did not keep *Stella's* letters. He kept *Bolingbroke's,* and *Pope's*, and *Harley's*, and *Peterborough's*. — Thackeray.

An actor in one of *Morton's* or *Kotzebue's* plays. — Macaulay.

Putting *Mr. Mill's* and *Mr. Bentham's* principles together. — *Id.*

**397.** The possessive preceding the gerund will be considered under the possessive of pronouns (Sec. 408).

# PRONOUNS.

# PERSONAL PRONOUNS.

# I. NOMINATIVE AND OBJECTIVE FORMS.

**398.** Since most of the personal pronouns, together with the relative *who*, have separate forms for nominative and objective use, there are two general rules that require attention.

*General rules.*

(1) The *nominative use* is usually marked by the nominative form of the pronoun.

(2) The *objective use* is usually marked by the objective form of the pronoun.

These simple rules are sometimes violated in spoken and in literary English. Some of the violations are universally condemned; others are generally, if not universally, sanctioned.

*Objective for the nominative.*

**399.** The objective is sometimes found instead of the nominative in the following instances: —

(1) By a common vulgarism of ignorance or carelessness, no notice is taken of the proper form to be used as subject; as, —

He and *me* once went in the dead of winter in a one-hoss shay out to Boonville. — Whitcher, *Bedott Papers.*

It seems strange to me that *them* that preach up the doctrine don't admire one who carrys it out. — *Josiah Allens Wife.*

(2) By faulty analysis of the sentence, the true relation of the words is misunderstood; for example, "*Whom* think ye that I am?" (In this, *whom* is the complement after the verb *am*, and should be the nominative form, *who*.) "The young Harper, *whom* they agree was rather nice-looking" (*whom* is the subject of the verb *was*).

Especially is this fault to be noticed after an ellipsis with *than* or *as*, the real thought being forgotten; thus, —

But the consolation coming from devotion did not go far with such a one as *her*. — Trollope.

This should be "as *she*," because the full expression would be "such a one as *she is*."

**400.** Still, the last expression has the support of many good writers, as shown in the following examples: —

She was neither better bred nor wiser than you or *me*. — Thackeray.

No mightier than thyself or *me*. — Shakespeare.

Lin'd with Giants deadlier than '*em* all. — Pope.

But he must be a stronger than *thee*. — Southey.

Not to render up my soul to such as *thee*. — Byron.

I shall not learn my duty from such as *thee*. — Fielding.

*A safe rule.*

It will be safer for the student to follow the general rule, as illustrated in the following sentences: —

If so, they are yet holier than *we*. — Ruskin.

Who would suppose it is the game of such as *he*? — Dickens.

> Do we see
> The robber and the murd'rer weak as *we*?
> — Milton.


I have no other saint than *thou* to pray to. — Longfellow.

"*Than* whom."

**401.** One exception is to be noted. The expression **than whom** seems to be used universally instead of "than *who*." There is no special reason for this, but such is the fact; for example, —

One I remember especially, — one *than whom* I never met a bandit more gallant. — Thackeray.

The camp of Richard of England, *than whom* none knows better how to do honor to a noble foe. — Scott.

She had a companion who had been ever agreeable, and her esta-te a steward *than whom* no one living was supposed to be more competent. — Parton.

"*It was* he" *or* "*It was* him"?

**402.** And there is one question about which grammarians are not agreed, namely, whether the nominative or the objective form should be used in the predicate after *was, is, are,* and the other forms of the verb *be.*

It may be stated with assurance that the literary language *prefers the nominative* in this instance, as, —

For there was little doubt that it was *he.* — Kingsley.

But still it is not *she.* — Macaulay.

> And it was *he*
> That made the ship to go.
> — Coleridge.

In spoken English, on the other hand, both in England and Ame-rica, the objective form is regularly found, unless a special, careful effort is made to adopt the standard usage. The following are exa-mples of spoken English from conversations: —

"Rose Satterne, the mayor's daughter?" — "That's *her.*" — Kingsley.

"Who's there?" — "*Me*, Patrick the Porter." — Winthrop.

"If there is any one embarrassed, it will not be *me.*" — Wm. Black.

The usage is too common to need further examples.

**Exercise.**

Correct the italicized pronouns in the following sentences, giving reasons from the analysis of the sentence: —

1. *Whom* they were I really cannot specify.

2. Truth is mightier than *us* all.

3. If there ever was a rogue in the world, it is *me.*

4. They were the very two individuals *whom* we thought were far away.

5. "Seems to me as if *them* as writes must hev a kinder gift fur it, now."

6. The sign of the Good Samaritan is written on the face of *whomsoever* opens to the stranger.

7. It is not *me* you are in love with.

8. You know *whom* it is that you thus charge.

9. The same affinity will exert its influence on *whomsoever* is as noble as these men and women.

10. It was *him* that Horace Walpole called a man who never made a bad figure but as an author.

11. We shall soon see which is the fittest object of scorn, you or *me*.

Me *in exclamations.*

**403.** It is to be remembered that the objective form is used in exclamations which turn the attention upon a person; as, —

Unhappy *me!* That I cannot risk my own worthless life. — Kingsley

Alas! miserable *me*! Alas! unhappy Señors! — *Id.*

Ay *me*! I fondly dream — had ye been there. — Milton.

Nominative for the objective.

**404.** The rule for the objective form is wrongly departed from —

(1) When the object is far removed from the verb, verbal, or preposition which governs it; as, "*He* that can doubt whether he be anything or no, I speak not to" (*he* should be *him*, the object of *to*); "I saw men very like him at each of the places mentioned, but not *he*" (*he* should be *him*, object of *saw*).

(2) In the case of certain pairs of pronouns, used after verbs, verbals, and prepositions, as this from Shakespeare, "All debts are cleared between you and I" (for *you* and *me*); or this, "Let *thou* and *I* the battle try" (for *thee* and *me*, or *us*).

(3) By forgetting the construction, in the case of words used in apposition with the object; as, "Ask the murderer, *he* who has steeped his hands in the blood of another" (instead of "*him* who," the word being in apposition with *murderer*).

*Exception 1, who interrogative.*

**405.** The interrogative pronoun **who** may be said to have no objective form in spoken English. We regularly say, "*Who* did you see?" or, "*Who* were they talking to?" etc. The more formal "To *whom* were they talking?" sounds stilted in conversation, and is usually avoided.

In literary English the objective form *whom* is *preferred* for objective use; as, —

Knows he now to *whom* he lies under obligation? — Scott.

What doth she look on? *Whom* doth she behold? — Wordsworth.

Yet the nominative form is found quite frequently to divide the work of the objective use; for example, —

My son is going to be married to I don't know *who*. — Goldsmith.

*Who* have we here? — *Id.*

*Who* should I meet the other day but my old friend. — Steele.

He hath given away half his fortune to the Lord knows *who*. — Kingsley.

*Who* have we got here? — Smollett.

*Who* should we find there but Eustache? — Marrvat.

*Who* the devil is he talking to? — Sheridan.

*Exception 2, but he, etc.*

**406.** It is a well-established usage to put the nominative form, as well as the objective, after the preposition *but* (sometimes *save*); as, —

All were knocked down but *us* two. — Kingsley.

Thy shores are empires, changed in all save *thee.* — Byron.

Rich are the sea gods: — who gives gifts but *they?* — Emerson.

The Chieftains then
Returned rejoicing, all but *he*.
—Southey


No man strikes him but *I*.—Kingsley.

None, save *thou* and thine, I've sworn,
Shall be left upon the morn.
—Byron.


**Exercise.**

Correct the italicized pronouns in the following, giving reasons from the analysis of the quotation:—

1. *Thou*, Nature, partial Nature, I arraign.

2. Let you and *I* look at these, for they say there are none such in the world.

3. "Nonsense!" said Amyas, "we could kill every soul of them in half an hour, and they know that as well as *me*."

4. Markland, *who*, with Jortin and Thirlby, Johnson calls three contemporaries of great eminence.

5. They are coming for a visit to *she* and *I*.

6.

They crowned him long ago;
But *who* they got to put it on
Nobody seems to know.


7. I experienced little difficulty in distinguishing among the pedestrians *they* who had business with St. Bartholomew.

8. The great difference lies between the laborer who moves to Yorkshire and *he* who moves to Canada.

9. Besides my father and Uncle Haddock—*he* of the silver plates.

10.

> *Ye* against whose familiar names not yet
> The fatal asterisk of death is set,
> *Ye* I salute.

11. It can't be worth much to *they* that hasn't larning.

12. To send me away for a whole year—*I* who had never crept from under the parental wing—was a startling idea.

# II. POSSESSIVE FORMS.

*As antecedent of a relative.*

**407.** The possessive forms of personal pronouns and also of nouns are sometimes found as antecedents of relatives. This usage is not frequent. The antecedent is usually nominative or objective, as the use of the possessive is less likely to be clear.

We should augur ill of any *gentleman's* property to whom this happened every other day in his drawing room. — Ruskin.

For *their* sakes whose distance disabled them from knowing me. — C. B. Brown.

Now by *His* name that I most reverence in Heaven, and by *hers* whom I most worship on earth. — Scott.

He saw her smile and slip money into the *man's* hand who was ordered to ride behind the coach. — Thackeray.

He doubted whether *his* signature whose expectations were so much more bounded would avail. — De Quincey.

> For boys with hearts as bold
> As *his* who kept the bridge so well.
> — Macaulay.

*Preceding a gerund, — possessive, or objective?*

**408.** Another point on which there is some variance in usage is such a construction as this: "We heard of *Brown* studying law," or "We heard of *Brown's* studying law."

That is, should the possessive case of a noun or pronoun always be used with the gerund to indicate the active agent? Closely scrutinizing these two sentences quoted, we might find a difference between them: saying that in the first one *studying* is a participle, and the meaning is, *We heard of Brown,* [who was] *studying law*; and that in the second, *studying* is a gerund, object of *heard of,* and modified by the possessive case as any other substantive would be.

*Why both are found.*

But in common use there is no such distinction. Both types of sentences are found; both are gerunds; sometimes the gerund has the possessive form before it, sometimes it has the objective. The use of the objective is older, and in keeping with the old way of regarding the *person* as the chief object before the mind: the possessive use is more modern, in keeping with the disposition to proceed from the material thing to the *abstract idea*, and to make the action substantive the chief idea before the mind.

In the examples quoted, it will be noticed that the possessive of the pronoun is more common than that of the noun.

*Objective.*

The last incident which I recollect, was my learned and worthy *patron* falling from a chair. — Scott.

He spoke of *some one* coming to drink tea with him, and asked why it was not made. — Thackeray.

The old sexton even expressed a doubt as to *Shakespeare* having been born in her house. — Irving.

The fact of the *Romans* not burying their dead within the city walls proper is a strong reason, etc. — Brewer.

I remember *Wordsworth* once laughingly reporting to me a little personal anecdote. — De Quincey.

Here I state them only in brief, to prevent the *reader* casting about in alarm for my ultimate meaning. — Ruskin.

We think with far less pleasure of *Cato* tearing out his entrails than of *Russell* saying, as he turned away from his wife, that the bitterness of death was past. — Macaulay.

There is actually a kind of sacredness in the fact of such a *man* being sent into this earth. — Carlyle.

*Possessive.*

There is no use for any *man's* taking up his abode in a house built of glass. — Carlyle.

As to *his* having good grounds on which to rest an action for life. — Dickens.

The case was made known to me by a *man's* holding out the little creature dead. — De Quincey.

There may be reason for a *savage's* preferring many kinds of food which the civilized man rejects. — Thoreau.

It informs me of the previous circumstances of *my* laying aside my clothes. — C. Brockden Brown.

The two strangers gave me an account of *their* once having been themselves in a somewhat similar condition. — Audubon.

There was a chance of *their* being sent to a new school, where there were examinations. — Ruskin

This can only be by *his* preferring truth to his past apprehension of truth. — Emerson

### III. PERSONAL PRONOUNS AND THEIR ANTECEDENTS.

**409.** The pronouns of the third person usually refer back to some preceding noun or pronoun, and ought to agree with them in person, number, and gender.

*Watch for the real antecedent.*

There are two constructions in which the student will need to watch the pronoun, — when the antecedent, in one person, is followed by a phrase containing a pronoun of a different person; and when the antecedent is of such a form that the pronoun following cannot indicate exactly the gender. Examples of these constructions are, —

*Those* of us who can only maintain *themselves* by continuing in some business or salaried office. — Ruskin.

Suppose the life and fortune of *every one* of us would depend on *his* winning or losing a game of chess. — Huxley.

If *any one* did not know it, it was *his* own fault. — Cable.

*Everybody* had *his* own life to think of. — Defoe.

**410.** In such a case as the last three sentences, — when the antecedent includes both masculine and feminine, or is a distributive word, taking in each of many persons,—the preferred method is to put the pronoun following in the masculine singular; if the antecedent is neuter, preceded by a distributive, the pronoun will be neuter singular.

The following are additional examples:—

The next *correspondent* wants you to mark out a whole course of life for *him*.—Holmes.

Every *city* threw open *its* gates.—De Quincey.

Every *person* who turns this page has *his* own little diary.—Thackeray.

> The pale realms of shade, where *each* shall take
> *His* chamber in the silent halls of death.
> —Bryant.

*Avoided: By using both pronouns.*

Sometimes this is avoided by using both the masculine and the feminine pronoun; for example,—

Not the feeblest *grandame*, not a mowing *idiot*, but uses what spark of perception and faculty is left, to chuckle and triumph in *his or her* opinion.—Emerson.

It is a game which has been played for untold ages, every *man* and *woman* of us being one of the two players in a game of *his or her* own.—Huxley.

*By using the plural pronoun.*

**411.** Another way of referring to an antecedent which is a distributive pronoun or a noun modified by a distributive adjective, is to use the plural of the pronoun following. This is not considered the best usage, the logical analysis requiring the singular pronoun in each case; but the construction is frequently found *when the antecedent includes or implies both genders*. The masculine does not really represent a feminine antecedent, and the expression *his or her* is avoided as being cumbrous.

Notice the following examples of the plural: —

*Neither* of the sisters *were* very much deceived. — Thackeray.

*Every one* must judge of *their* own feelings. — Byron.

Had the doctor been contented to take my dining tables, as *anybody* in *their* senses would have done. — Austen.

If the part deserve any comment, every considering *Christian* will make it *themselves* as they go. — Defoe.

*Every person's* happiness depends in part upon the respect *they* meet in the world. — Paley.

*Every nation* have *their* refinements — Sterne.

*Neither* gave vent to *their* feelings in words. — Scott.

*Each* of the nations acted according to *their* national custom. — Palgrave.

The sun, which pleases *everybody* with it and with *themselves*. — Ruskin.

Urging *every one* within reach of your influence to be neat, and giving *them* means of being so. — *Id.*

*Everybody* will become of use in *their* own fittest way. — *Id.*

*Everybody* said *they* thought it was the newest thing there. — Wendell Phillips.

Struggling for life, *each* almost bursting *their* sinews to force the other off. — Paulding.

*Whosoever* hath any gold, let *them* break it off. — *Bible.*

*Nobody* knows what it is to lose a friend, till *they* have lost him. — Fielding.

Where she was gone, or what was become of her, *no one* could take upon *them* to say. — Sheridan.

I do not mean that I think *any one* to blame for taking due care of *their* health. — Addison.

**Exercise.** — In the above sentences, *unless both genders are implied*, change the pronoun to agree with its antecedent.

# RELATIVE PRONOUNS.

# I. RESTRICTIVE AND UNRESTRICTIVE RE-LATIVES.

*What these terms mean.*

**412.** As to their conjunctive use, the definite relatives **who**, **which**, and **that** may be **coördinating** or **restrictive**.

A relative, when coördinating, or unrestrictive, is equivalent to a conjunction (*and*, *but*, *because*, etc.) and a personal pronoun. It adds a new statement to what precedes, that being considered already clear; as, "I gave it to the beggar, *who* went away." This means, "I gave it to the beggar [we know which one], *and he* went away."

A relative, when restrictive, introduces a clause to limit and make clear some preceding word. The clause is restricted to the antecedent, and does not add a new statement; it merely couples a thought necessary to define the antecedent: as, "I gave it to a beggar *who* stood at the gate." It defines *beggar*.

**413.** It is sometimes contended that **who** and **which** should always be coördinating, and **that** always restrictive; but, according to the practice of every modern writer, the usage must be stated as follows: —

*A loose rule the only one to be formulated.*

**Who** and **which** are either coördinating or restrictive, the taste of the writer and regard for euphony being the guide.

**That** is in most cases restrictive, the coördinating use not being often found among careful writers.

**Exercise.**

In the following examples, tell whether *who*, *which*, and *that* are restrictive or not, in each instance: —

Who.

1. "Here he is now!" cried those who stood near Ernest. — Hawthorne.

2. He could overhear the remarks of various individuals, who were comparing the features with the face on the mountain side. — *Id.*

3. The particular recording angel who heard it pretended not to understand, or it might have gone hard with the tutor. — Holmes.

4. Yet how many are there who up, down, and over England are saying, etc. — H. W. Beecher

5. A grizzly-looking man appeared, whom we took to be sixty or seventy years old. — Thoreau.

Which.

6. The volume which I am just about terminating is almost as much English history as Dutch. — Motley.

7. On hearing their plan, which was to go over the Cordilleras, she agreed to join the party. — De Quincey.

8. Even the wild story of the incident which had immediately occasioned the explosion of this madness fell in with the universal prostration of mind. — *Id.*

9. Their colloquies are all gone to the fire except this first, which Mr. Hare has printed. — Carlyle.

10. There is a particular science which takes these matters in hand, and it is called logic. — Newman.

That.

11. So different from the wild, hard-mouthed horses at Westport, that were often vicious. — De Quincey.

12. He was often tempted to pluck the flowers that rose everywhere about him in the greatest variety. — Addison.

13. He felt a gale of perfumes breathing upon him, that grew stronger and sweeter in proportion as he advanced. — *Id.*

14. With narrow shoulders, long arms and legs, hands that dangled a mile out of his sleeves. — Irving.

# II. RELATIVE AND ANTECEDENT.

*The rule.*

**414.** The general rule is, that the relative pronoun agrees with its antecedent in person and number.

*In what sense true.*

This cannot be true as to the form of the pronoun, as that does not vary for person or number. We say *I, you, he, they*, etc., *who; these* or *that which*, etc. However, the relative *carries over* the agreement from the antecedent before to the verb following, so far as the verb has forms to show its agreement with a substantive. For example, in the sentence, "He that writes to himself writes to an eternal public," *that* is invariable as to person and number, but, because of its antecedent, it makes the verb third person singular.

Notice the agreement in the following sentences: —

There is not *one* of the company, but *myself*, who rarely *speak* at all, but *speaks* of him as that sort, etc. — Addison.

O *Time!* who *know'st* a lenient hand to lay Softest on sorrow's wound. — Bowles.

Let us be of good cheer, remembering that the misfortunes hardest to bear are *those* which never *come*. — Lowell.

*A disputed point.*

**415.** This prepares the way for the consideration of one of the vexed questions, — whether we should say, "one of the finest books that *has* been published," or, "one of the finest books that *have* been published."

One of ... [*plural*] that who, *or* which ... [*singular or plural.*]

Both constructions are frequently found, the reason being a difference of opinion as to the antecedent. Some consider it to be *one* [book] *of the finest books*, with *one* as the principal word, the true antecedent; others regard *books* as the antecedent, and write the verb in the plural. The latter is rather more frequent, but the former has good authority.

The following quotations show both sides: —

*Plural.*

He was one of the very few commanders who *appear* to have shown equal skill in directing a campaign, in winning a battle, and in improving a victory. — Lecky.

He was one of the most distinguished scientists who *have* ever lived. — J. T. Morse, Jr., *Franklin.*

It is one of those periods which *shine* with an unnatural and delusive splendor. — Macaulay.

A very little encouragement brought back one of those overflows which *make* one more ashamed, etc. — Holmes.

I am one of those who *believe* that the real will never find an irremovable basis till it rests on the ideal. — Lowell.

French literature of the eighteenth century, one of the most powerful agencies that *have* ever existed. — M. Arnold.

What man's life is not overtaken by one or more of those tornadoes that *send* us out of our course? — Thackeray.

He is one of those that *deserve* very well. — Addison.

*Singular.*

The fiery youth ... struck down one of those who *was* pressing hardest. — Scott.

He appeared to me one of the noblest creatures that ever *was*, when he derided the shams of society. — Howells.

A rare Roundabout performance, — one of the very best that *has* ever appeared in this series. — Thackeray.

Valancourt was the hero of one of the most famous romances which ever *was* published in this country. — *Id.*

It is one of the errors which *has* been diligently propagated by designing writers. — Irving.

"I am going to breakfast with one of these fellows who *is* at the Piazza Hotel." — Dickens.

The "Economy of the Animal Kingdom" is one of those books which *is* an honor to the human race. — Emerson.

Tom Puzzle is one of the most eminent immethodical disputants of any that *has* fallen under my observation. — Addison.

The richly canopied monument of one of the most earnest souls that ever gave *itself* to the arts. — Ruskin.

# III. OMISSION OF THE RELATIVE.

**416.** Although the omission of the relative is common when it would be the object of the verb or preposition *expressed*, there is an omission which is not frequently found in careful writers; that is, when the relative word is a pronoun, object of a preposition *understood*, or is equivalent to the conjunction *when, where, whence,* and such like: as, "He returned by the same route [by which] he came;" "India is the place [in which, or where] he died." Notice these sentences: —

In the posture I lay, I could see nothing except the sky. — Swift.

This is he that should marshal us the way we were going. — Emerson.

> But I by backward steps would move;
> And, when this dust falls to the urn,
> In that same state I came, return.
> — Vaughan.

> Welcome the hour my aged limbs
> Are laid with thee to rest.
> — Burns.

The night was concluded in the manner we began the morning. — Goldsmith.

The same day I went aboard we set sail. — Defoe.

The vulgar historian of a Cromwell fancies that he had determined on being Protector of England, at the time he was plowing the marsh lands of Cambridgeshire. — Carlyle.

To pass under the canvas in the manner he had entered required time and attention. — Scott.

**Exercise.** — In the above sentences, insert the omitted conjunction or phrase, and see if the sentence is made clearer.

# IV. THE RELATIVE *AS* AFTER *SAME*.

**417.** It is very rarely that we find such sentences as, —

He considered...me as his apprentice, and accordingly expected the same service from me *as* he would from another. — Franklin.

This has the same effect in natural faults *as* maiming and mutilation produce from accidents. — Burke.

*The regular construction.*

*Caution.*

The usual way is to use the relative *as* after *same* if no verb follows *as*; but, if *same* is followed by a complete clause, *as* is not used, but we find the relative *who, which,* or *that*. Remember this applies only to *as* when used as a relative.

Examples of the use of *as* in a contracted clause: —

Looking to the same end *as* Turner, and working in the same spirit, he, with Turner, was a discoverer, etc. — R. W. Church.

They believe the same of all the works of art, *as* of knives, boats, looking-glasses. — Addison.

Examples of relatives following *same* in full clauses: —

Who.

This is the very same rogue *who* sold us the spectacles. — Goldsmith.

The same person *who* had clapped his thrilling hands at the first representation of the Tempest. — Macaulay.

That.

I rubbed on some of the same ointment *that* was given me at my first arrival. — Swift.

Which.

> For the same sound is in my ears
> *Which* in those days I heard.
> — Wordsworth.

With the same minuteness *which* her predecessor had exhibited, she passed the lamp over her face and person. — Scott.

# V. MISUSE OF RELATIVE PRONOUNS.

*Anacoluthic use of* which.

**418.** There is now and then found in the pages of literature a construction which imitates the Latin, but which is usually carefully avoided. It is a use of the relative *which* so as to make an anacoluthon, or lack of proper connection between the clauses; for example, —

*Which*, if I had resolved to go on with, I might as well have staid at home. — Defoe

*Which* if he attempted to do, Mr. Billings vowed that he would follow him to Jerusalem. — Thackeray.

We know not the incantation of the heart that would wake them; — *which* if they once heard, they would start up to meet us in the power of long ago. — Ruskin.

He delivered the letter, *which* when Mr. Thornhill had read, he said that all submission was now too late. — Goldsmith.

> But still the house affairs would draw her thence;
> *Which* ever as she could with haste dispatch,
> She'd come again.
> — Shakespeare.


As the sentences stand, *which* really has no office in the sentence: it should be changed to a demonstrative or a personal pronoun, and this be placed in the proper clause.

**Exercise.** — Rewrite the above five sentences so as to make the proper grammatical connection in each.

*And who, and which, etc.*

**419.** There is another kind of expression which slips into the lines of even standard authors, but which is always regarded as an oversight and a blemish.

The following sentence affords an example: "The rich are now engaged in distributing what remains among the poorer sort, *and who* are now thrown upon their compassion." The trouble is that such conjunctions as *and*, *but*, *or*, etc., should connect expressions of the same kind: *and who* makes us look for a preceding *who*, but none is expressed. There are three ways to remedy the sentence quoted: thus, (1) "Among those *who* are poor, *and who* are now," etc.; (2) "Among the poorer sort, *who* are now thrown," etc.; (3) "Among the poorer sort, now thrown upon their," etc. That is, —

*Direction for rewriting.*

Express both relatives, or omit the conjunction, or leave out both connective and relative.

**Exercise.**

Rewrite the following examples according to the direction just given: —

And who.

1. Hester bestowed all her means on wretches less miserable than herself, and who not unfrequently insulted the hand that fed them. — Hawthorne.

2. With an albatross perched on his shoulder, and who might be introduced to the congregation as the immediate organ of his conversion. — De Quincey.

3. After this came Elizabeth herself, then in the full glow of what in a sovereign was called beauty, and who would in the lowest walk of life have been truly judged to possess a noble figure. — Scott.

4. This was a gentleman, once a great favorite of M. le Conte, and in whom I myself was not a little interested. — Thackeray.

But who.

5. Yonder woman was the wife of a certain learned man, English by name, but who had long dwelt in Amsterdam. — Hawthorne.

6. Dr. Ferguson considered him as a man of a powerful capacity, but whose mind was thrown off its just bias. — Scott.

Or who.

7. "What knight so craven, then," exclaims the chivalrous Venetian, "that he would not have been more than a match for the stoutest adversary; or who would not have lost his life a thousand times sooner than return dishonored by the lady of his love?" — Prescott.

And which.

8. There are peculiar quavers still to be heard in that church, and which may even be heard a mile off. — Irving.

9. The old British tongue was replaced by a debased Latin, like that spoken in the towns, and in which inscriptions are found in the western counties. — Pearson.

10. I shall have complete copies, one of signal interest, and which has never been described. — Motley.

But which.

11. "A mockery, indeed, but in which the soul trifled with itself!" — Hawthorne.

12. I saw upon the left a scene far different, but which yet the power of dreams had reconciled into harmony. — De Quincey.

Or which.

13. He accounted the fair-spoken courtesy, which the Scotch had learned, either from imitation of their frequent allies, the French, or which might have arisen from their own proud and reserved character, as a false and astucious mark, etc. — Scott.

That ... and which, *etc.*

**420.** Akin to the above is another fault, which is likewise a variation from the best usage. Two different relatives are sometimes found referring back to the same antecedent in one sentence; whereas the better practice is to choose one relative, and repeat this for any further reference.

**Exercise.**

Rewrite the following quotations by repeating one relative instead of using two for the same antecedent: —

That ... who.

1. Still in the confidence of children that tread without fear every chamber in their father's house, and to whom no door is closed. — De Quincey.

2. Those renowned men that were our ancestors as much as yours, and whose examples and principles we inherit. — Beecher.

3. The Tree Igdrasil, that has its roots down in the kingdoms of Hela and Death, and whose boughs overspread the highest heaven! — Carlyle.

That ... which.

4. Christianity is a religion that reveals men as the object of God's infinite love, and which commends him to the unbounded love of his brethren. — W. E. Channing.

5. He flung into literature, in his Mephistopheles, the first organic figure that has been added for some ages, and which will remain as long as the Prometheus. — Emerson.

6. Gutenburg might also have struck out an idea that surely did not require any extraordinary ingenuity, and which left the most important difficulties to be surmounted. — Hallam.

7. Do me the justice to tell me what I have a title to be acquainted with, and which I am certain to know more truly from you than from others. — Scott.

8. He will do this amiable little service out of what one may say old civilization has established in place of goodness of heart, but which is perhaps not so different from it. — Howells.

9. In my native town of Salem, at the head of what, half a century ago, was a bustling wharf, — but which is now burdened with decayed wooden warehouses. — Hawthorne.

10. His recollection of what he considered as extreme presumption in the Knight of the Leopard, even when he stood high in the roles of chivalry, but which, in his present condition, appeared an insult sufficient to drive the fiery monarch into a frenzy of passion. — Scott

That which ... what.

11. He, now without any effort but that which he derived from the sill, and what little his feet could secure the irregular crevices, was hung in air. — W. G. Simms.

Such as ... which.

12. It rose into a thrilling passion, such as my heart had always dimly craved and hungered after, but which now first interpreted itself to my ear. — De Quincey.

13. I recommend some honest manual calling, such as they have very probably been bred to, and which will at least give them a chance of becoming President. — Holmes.

Such as ... whom.

14. I grudge the dollar, the dime, the cent, I give to such men as do not belong to me, and to whom I do not belong. — Emerson.

Which ... that ... that.

15. That evil influence which carried me first away from my father's house, that hurried me into the wild and undigested notion of making my fortune, and that impressed these conceits so forcibly upon me. — Defoe.

# ADJECTIVE PRONOUNS.

Each other, one another.

**421.** The student is sometimes troubled whether to use **each other** or **one another** in expressing reciprocal relation or action. Whether either one refers to a certain number of persons or objects, whether or not the two are equivalent, may be gathered from a study of the following sentences: —

They [Ernest and the poet] led *one another*, as it were, into the high pavilion of their thoughts. — Hawthorne.

Men take *each other's* measure when they meet for the first time. — Emerson.

You ruffian! do you fancy I forget that we were fond of *each other*? — Thackeray.

England was then divided between kings and Druids, always at war with *one another*, carrying off *each other's* cattle and wives. — Brewer

The topics follow *each other* in the happiest order. — Macaulay.

The Peers at a conference begin to pommel *each other.* — Id.

We call ourselves a rich nation, and we are filthy and foolish enough to thumb *each other's* books out of circulating libraries. — Ruskin.

The real hardships of life are now coming fast upon us; let us not increase them by dissension among *each other.* — Goldsmith.

In a moment we were all shaking hands with *one another.* — Dickens.

The unjust purchaser forces the two to bid against *each other.* — Ruskin.

*Distributives* either *and* neither.

**422.** By their original meaning, **either** and **neither** refer to only two persons or objects; as, for example, —

Some one must be poor, and in want of his gold — or his corn. Assume that no one is in want of *either*. — Ruskin

Their [Ernest's and the poet's] minds accorded into one strain, and made delightful music which *neither* could have claimed as all his own. — Hawthorne.

*Use of* any.

Sometimes these are made to refer to several objects, in which case any should be used instead; as, —

Was it the winter's storm? was it hard labor and spare meals? was it disease? was it the tomahawk? Is it possible that *neither* of these causes, that not all combined, were able to blast this bud of hope? — Everett.

Once I took such delight in Montaigne ...; before that, in Shakespeare; then in Plutarch; then in Plotinus; at one time in Bacon; afterwards in Goethe; even in Bettine; but now I turn the pages of *either* of them languidly, whilst I still cherish their genius. — Emerson.

Any *usually plural*.

**423.** The adjective pronoun **any** is nearly always regarded as plural, as shown in the following sentences: —

If *any* of you *have* been accustomed to look upon these hours as mere visionary hours, I beseech you, etc. — Beecher

Whenever, during his stay at Yuste, *any* of his friends had died, he had been punctual in doing honor to *their* memory. — Stirling.

But I enjoy the company and conversation of its inhabitants, when *any* of them *are* so good as to visit me. — Franklin.

Do you think, when I spoke anon of the ghosts of Pryor's children, I mean that *any* of them *are* dead? — Thackeray.

In earlier Modern English, *any* was often singular; as, —

If *any*, speak; for *him* have I offended. — Shakespeare.

If *any* of you lack wisdom, let *him* ask of God. — *Bible.*

Very rarely the singular is met with in later times; as, —

Here is a poet doubtless as much affected by his own descriptions as *any* that *reads* them can be. — Burke.

*Caution.*

The above instances are to be distinguished from the adjective *any*, which is plural as often as singular.

None *usually plural.*

**424.** The adjective pronoun **none** is, in the prose of the present day, usually plural, although it is historically a contraction of *ne ān* (not one). Examples of its use are, —

In earnest, if ever man was; as *none* of the French philosophers *were.* — Carlyle.

*None* of Nature's powers *do* better service. — Prof. Dana

One man answers some question which *none* of his contemporaries *put*, and is isolated. — Emerson.

*None obey* the command of duty so well as those who are free from the observance of slavish bondage. — Scott.

Do you think, when I spoke anon of the ghosts of Pryor's children, I mean that any of them are dead? *None are,* that I know of. — Thackeray.

Early apples begin to be ripe about the first of August; but I think *none* of them *are* so good to eat as some to smell. — Thoreau.

The singular use of *none* is often found in the Bible; as, —

*None* of them *was* cleansed, saving Naaman the Syrian. — Luke iv 27

Also the singular is sometimes found in present-day English in prose, and less rarely in poetry; for example, —

Perhaps *none* of our Presidents since Washington *has* stood so firm in the confidence of the people. — Lowell

In signal *none his* steed should spare. — Scott

Like the use of *any*, the pronoun *none* should be distinguished from the adjective *none*, which is used absolutely, and hence is more likely to confuse the student.

Compare with the above the following sentences having the adjective *none*: —

Reflecting a summer evening sky in its bosom, though *none* [no sky] was visible overhead. — Thoreau

The holy fires were suffered to go out in the temples, and *none* [no fires] were lighted in their own dwellings. — Prescott

All *singular and plural.*

**425.** The pronoun **all** has the singular construction when it means *everything*; the plural, when it means *all persons*: for example, —

*Singular.*

The light troops thought ... that *all was* lost. — Palgrave

*All was* won on the one side, and *all was* lost on the other. — Bayne

Having done *all* that *was* just toward others. — Napier

*Plural.*

But the King's treatment of the great lords will be judged leniently by *all* who *remember*, etc. — Pearson.

When *all were* gone, fixing his eyes on the mace, etc. — Lingard

*All* who did not understand French *were* compelled, etc. — Mcmaster.

Somebody's else, *or* somebody else's?

**426.** The compounds **somebody else, any one else, nobody else**, etc., are treated as units, and the apostrophe is regularly added to the final word *else* instead of the first. Thackeray has the expression *somebody's else*, and Ford has *nobody's else*, but the regular usage is shown in the following selections: —

A boy who is fond of *somebody else's* pencil case. — G. Eliot.

A suit of clothes like *somebody else's*. — Thackeray.

Drawing off his gloves and warming his hands before the fire as benevolently as if they were *somebody else's*. — Dickens.

Certainly not! nor *any one else's* ropes. — Ruskin.

Again, my pronunciation—like *everyone else's*—is in some cases more archaic.—Sweet.

Then everybody wanted some of *somebody else's*.—Ruskin.

His hair...curled once all over it in long tendrils, unlike *anybody else's* in the world.—N. P. Willis.

"Ye see, there ain't nothin' wakes folks up like *somebody else's* wantin' what you've got."—Mrs. Stowe.

## ADJECTIVES.

# AGREEMENT OF ADJECTIVES WITH NOUNS.

These sort, all manner of, *etc.*

**427.** The statement that adjectives agree with their nouns in number is restricted to the words **this** and **that** (with **these** and **those**), as these are the only adjectives that have separate forms for singular and plural; and it is only in one set of expressions that the concord seems to be violated,—in such as "*these sort* of books," "*those kind* of trees," "*all manner* of men;" the nouns being singular, the adjectives plural. These expressions are all but universal in spoken English, and may be found not infrequently in literary English; for example,—

> *These kind* of knaves I know, which in this plainness
> Harbor more craft, etc.
> —Shakespeare

All *these sort* of things.—Sheridan.

I hoped we had done with *those sort* of things.—Muloch.

You have been so used to *those sort* of impertinences.Sydney Smith.

Whitefield or Wesley, or some other such great man as a bishop, or *those sort* of people.—Fielding.

477

I always delight in overthrowing *those kind* of schemes. — Austen.

There are women as well as men who can thoroughly enjoy *those sort* of romantic spots. — *Saturday Review*, London.

The library was open, with *all manner* of amusing books. — Ruskin.

According to the approved usage of Modern English, each one of the above adjectives would have to be changed to the singular, or the nouns to the plural.

*History of this construction.*

The reason for the prevalence of these expressions must be sought in the history of the language: it cannot be found in the statement that the adjective is made plural by the attraction of a noun following.

*At the source.*

In Old and Middle English, in keeping with the custom of looking at things concretely rather than in the abstract, they said, not "all *kinds* of wild animals," but "alles cunnes wilde deor" (wild animals of-every-kind). This the modern expression reverses.

*Later form.*

But in early Middle English the modern way of regarding such expressions also appeared, gradually displacing the old.

*The result.*

Consequently we have a confused expression. We keep the form of logical agreement in standard English, such as, "*This sort* of trees should be planted;" but at the same time the noun following *kind of* is felt to be the real subject, and the adjective is, in spoken English, made to agree with it, which accounts for the construction, "*These kind of* trees are best."

*A question.*

The inconvenience of the logical construction is seen when we wish to use a predicate with number forms. Should we say, "This kind of rules *are* the best," or "This kind of rules *is* the best?" *Kind* or *sort* may be treated as a collective noun, and in this way may take a plural verb; for example, Burke's sentence, "A *sort* of uncertain sounds *are*, when the necessary dispositions concur, more alarming than a total silence."

# COMPARATIVE AND SUPERLATIVE FORMS.

*Use of the comparative degree.*

**428.** The comparative degree of the adjective (or adverb) is used when we wish to compare two objects or sets of objects, or one object with a class of objects, to express a higher degree of quality; as, —

Which is *the better* able to defend himself, — a strong man with nothing but his fists, or a paralytic cripple encumbered with a sword which he cannot lift? — Macaulay.

> Of two such lessons, why forget
> The *nobler* and the *manlier* one?
> — Byron.

We may well doubt which has the *stronger* claim to civilization, the victor or the vanquished. — Prescott.

A *braver* ne'er to battle rode. — Scott.

He is *taller,* by almost the breadth of my nail, than any of his court. — Swift.

Other *after the comparative form.*

**429.** When an object is compared with the class to which it belongs, it is regularly excluded from that class by the word *other*; if not, the object would really be compared with itself: thus, —

The character of Lady Castlewood has required more delicacy in its manipulation than perhaps any *other* which Thackeray has drawn. — Trollope.

I used to watch this patriarchal personage with livelier curiosity than any *other* form of humanity. — Hawthorne.

**Exercise.**

See if the word *other* should be inserted in the following sentences: —

1. There was no man who could make a more graceful bow than Mr. Henry. — Wirt.

2. I am concerned to see that Mr. Gary, to whom Dante owes more than ever poet owed to translator, has sanctioned, etc. — Macaulay.

3. There is no country in which wealth is so sensible of its obligations as our own. — Lowell.

4. This is more sincerely done in the Scandinavian than in any mythology I know. — Carlyle.

5. In "Thaddeus of Warsaw" there is more crying than in any novel I remember to have read. — Thackeray.

6. The heroes of another writer [Cooper] are quite the equals of Scott's men; perhaps Leather-stocking is better than any one in "Scott's lot." — Id.

*Use of the superlative degree.*

**430.** The **superlative degree** of the adjective (or adverb) is used regularly in comparing more than two things, but is also frequently used in comparing only two things.

Examples of superlative with several objects: —

It is a case of which the *simplest* statement is the *strongest*. — Macaulay.

Even Dodd himself, who was one of the *greatest* humbugs who ever lived, would not have had the face. — Thackeray.

To the man who plays well, the *highest* stakes are paid. — Huxley.

*Superlative with two objects.*

Compare the first three sentences in Sec. 428 with the following: —

Which do you love *best* to behold, the lamb or the lion? — Thackeray.

Which of these methods has the *best* effect? Both of them are the same to the sense, and differ only in form. — Dr Blair.

Rip was one of those ... who eat white bread or brown, whichever can be got *easiest*. — Irving.

It is hard to say whether the man of wisdom or the man of folly contributed *most* to the amusement of the party. — Scott.

There was an interval of three years between Mary and Anne. The *eldest*, Mary, was like the Stuarts — the *younger* was a fair English child. — Mrs. Oliphant.

Of the two great parties which at this hour almost share the nation between them, I should say that one has the *best* cause, and the other contains the *best* men. — Emerson.

In all disputes between States, though the *strongest* is nearly always mainly in the wrong, the *weaker* is often so in a minor degree. — Ruskin.

She thought him and Olivia extremely of a size, and would bid both to stand up to see which was the *tallest*. — Goldsmith.

These two properties seem essential to wit, more particularly the *last* of them. — Addison.

"Ha, ha, ha!" roared Goodman Brown when the wind laughed at him. "Let us see which will laugh *loudest*." — Hawthorne.

*Double comparative and superlative.*

431. In Shakespeare's time it was quite common to use a double comparative and superlative by using *more* or *most* before the word already having *-er* or *-est*. Examples from Shakespeare are, —

How much *more elder* art thou than thy looks! — *Merchant of Venice.*

Nor that I am *more better* than Prospero. — *Tempest.*

Come you *more nearer*. — *Hamlet.*

With the *most boldest* and best hearts of Rome. — *J. Cæsar.*

Also from the same period, —

Imitating the manner of the *most ancientest* and *finest* Grecians. — Ben Jonson.

After the *most straitest* sect of our religion. — *Bible*, 1611.

Such expressions are now heard only in vulgar English. The following examples are used purposely, to represent the characters as ignorant persons: —

The artful saddler persuaded the young traveler to look at "the *most convenientest* and *handsomest* saddle that ever was seen." — Bulwer.

"There's nothing comes out but the *most lowest* stuff in nature; not a bit of high life among them." — Goldsmith.

*THREE FIRST* **OR** *FIRST THREE*?

**432.** As to these two expressions, over which a little war has so long been buzzing, we think it not necessary to say more than that both are in good use; not only so in popular speech, but in literary English. Instances of both are given below.

The meaning intended is the same, and the reader gets the same idea from both: hence there is properly a perfect liberty in the use of either or both.

First three, *etc.*

For Carlyle, and Secretary Walsingham also, have been helping them heart and soul for the *last two* years. — Kingsley.

The delay in the *first three* lines, and conceit in the last, jar upon us constantly. — Ruskin.

The *last dozen* miles before you reach the suburbs. — De Quincey.

Mankind for the *first seventy thousand* ages ate their meat raw. — Lamb.

The *first twenty* numbers were expressed by a corresponding number of dots. The *first five* had specific names. — Prescott.

Three first, *etc.*

These are the *three first* needs of civilized life. — Ruskin.

He has already finished the *three first* sticks of it. — Addison.

In my *two last* you had so much of Lismahago that I suppose you are glad he is gone. — Smollett.

I have not numbered the lines except of the *four first* books. —
Cowper.

The *seven first* centuries were filled with a succession of triumphs. — Gibbon.

## ARTICLES.

*Definite article.*

**433.** The **definite article** is repeated before each of two modifiers
of the same noun, when the purpose is to call attention to the noun
expressed and the one understood. In such a case two or more separate objects are usually indicated by the separation of the modifiers.
Examples of this construction are, —

*With a singular noun.*

The merit of *the Barb, the Spanish,* and *the English* breed is derived
from a mixture of Arabian blood. — Gibbon.

*The righteous* man is distinguished from *the unrighteous* by his desire and hope of justice. — Ruskin.

He seemed deficient in sympathy for concrete human things either on *the sunny* or *the stormy* side. — Carlyle.

It is difficult to imagine a greater contrast than that between *the
first* and *the second* part of the volume. — *The Nation* , No. 1508.

*With a plural noun.*

There was also a fundamental difference of opinion as to whether
the earliest cleavage was between *the Northern* and *the Southern* languages. — Taylor, *Origin of the Aryans.*

**434.** The same repetition of the article is sometimes found before
nouns alone, to distinguish clearly, or to emphasize the meaning;
as, —

In every line of *the Philip* and *the Saul,* the greatest poems, I think,
of the eighteenth century. — Macaulay.

He is master of the two-fold Logos, *the thought* and *the word*, distinct, but inseparable from each other. — Newman.

*The flowers*, and *the presents*, and *the trunks and bonnet boxes* ... having been arranged, the hour of parting came. — Thackeray.

The *not repeated. One object and several modifiers, with a singular noun.*

**435.** Frequently, however, the article is not repeated before each of two or more adjectives, as in Sec. 433, but is used with one only; as, —

Or fanciest thou *the red and yellow* Clothes-screen yonder is but of To-day, without a Yesterday or a To-morrow? — Carlyle.

*The lofty, melodious, and flexible* language. — Scott.

*The fairest and most loving* wife in Greece. — Tennyson.

*Meaning same as in Sec. 433, with a plural noun.*

Neither can there be a much greater resemblance between *the ancient and modern* general views of the town. — Halliwell-phillipps.

At Talavera *the English and French* troops for a moment suspended their conflict. — Macaulay.

The Crusades brought to the rising commonwealths of *the Adriatic and Tyrrhene* seas a large increase of wealth. — *Id.*

Here the youth of both sexes, of *the higher and middling* orders, were placed at a very tender age. — Prescott.

*Indefinite article.*

**436.** The **indefinite article** is used, like the definite article, to limit two or more modified nouns, only one of which is expressed. The article is repeated for the purpose of separating or emphasizing the modified nouns. Examples of this use are, —

We shall live *a better* and *a higher* and *a nobler* life. — Beecher.

The difference between the products of *a well-disciplined* and those of *an uncultivated* understanding is often and admirably exhibited by our great dramatist. — S. T. Coleridge.

Let us suppose that the pillars succeed each other, *a round* and *a square* one alternately. — Burke.

As if the difference between *an accurate* and *an inaccurate* state-ment was not worth the trouble of looking into the most common book of reference. — Macaulay.

To every room there was *an open* and *a secret* passage. — Johnson.

Notice that in the above sentences (except the first) the noun ex-pressed is in contrast with the modified noun omitted.

*One article with several adjectives.*

**437.** Usually the article is not repeated when the several adjectives unite in describing one and the same noun. In the sentences of Secs. 433 and 436, one noun is expressed; yet the same word understood with the other adjectives has a different meaning (except in the first sentence of Sec. 436). But in the following sentences, as in the first three of Sec. 435, the adjectives assist each other in describing the same noun. It is easy to see the difference between the expressions "*a red-and-white* geranium," and "*a red and a white* geranium."

Examples of several adjectives describing the same object: —

To inspire us with *a free and quiet* mind. — B. Jonson.

Here and there *a desolate and uninhabited* house. — Dickens.

James was declared *a mortal and bloody* enemy. — Macaulay.

> So wert thou born into a tuneful strain,
> *An early, rich, and inexhausted* vein.
> — Dryden.

*For rhetorical effect.*

**438.** The indefinite article (compare Sec. 434) is used to lend spe-cial emphasis, interest, or clearness to each of several nouns; as, —

James was declared *a* mortal and bloody *enemy, a tyrant, a murde-rer,* and *a usurper.* — Macaulay.

Thou hast spoken as *a patriot* and *a Christian.* — Bulwer.

He saw him in his mind's eye, *a collegian, a parliament man — a Ba-ronet* perhaps. — Thackeray.

**VERBS.**

# CONCORD OF VERB AND SUBJECT IN NUMBER.

*A broad and loose rule.*

**439.** In English, the **number** of the verb follows the meaning rather than the form of its subject.

It will not do to state as a general rule that the verb agrees with its subject in person and number. This was spoken of in Part I., Sec. 276, and the following illustrations prove it.

The statements and illustrations of course refer to such verbs as have separate forms for singular and plural number.

*Singular verb.*

**440.** The **singular form** of the verb is used —

*Subject of singular form.*

(1) When the subject has a singular form and a singular meaning.

Such, then, *was* the earliest American *land.* — Agassiz.

*He was* certainly a happy fellow at this time. — G. Eliot.

*He sees* that it is better to live in peace. — Cooper.

*Collective noun of singular meaning.*

(2) When the subject is a *collective noun* which represents a number of persons or things *taken as one unit*; as, —

The larger *breed* [of camels] *is* capable of transporting a weight of a thousand pounds. — Gibbon.

Another *school professes* entirely opposite principles. — *The Nation.*

In this work there *was* grouped around him *a score* of men. — W. Phillips

A *number* of jeweled paternosters *was* attached to her girdle. — Froude.

*Something like a horse load* of books *has* been written to prove that it was the beauty who blew up the booby. — Carlyle

This usage, like some others in this series, depends mostly on the writer's own judgment. Another writer might, for example, prefer a plural verb after *number* in Froude's sentence above.

*Singulars connected by* or *or* nor.

(3) When the subject consists of two or more singular nouns connected by *or* or *nor*; as, —

It is by no means sure that either our *literature*, or the great intellectual *life* of our nation, *has* got already, without academies, all that academies can give. — M. Arnold.

*Jesus is* not dead, nor *John*, nor *Paul*, nor *Mahomet*. — Emerson.

*Plural form and singular meaning.*

(4) When the subject is *plural in form*, but represents a number of things to be taken together as *forming one unit*; for example, —

Thirty-four years *affects* one's remembrance of some circumstances. — De Quincey.

Between ourselves, three pounds five shillings and two pence *is* no bad day's work. — Goldsmith.

Every twenty paces *gives* you the prospect of some villa; and every four hours, that of a large town. — Montague

Two thirds of this *is* mine by right. — Sheridan

The singular form is also used with book titles, other names, and other singulars of plural form; as, —

Politics *is* the only field now open for me. — Whittier.

"Sesame and Lilies" *is* Ruskin's creed for young girls. — *Critic* , No. 674

The Three Pigeons *expects* me down every moment. — Goldsmith.

*Several singular subjects to one singular verb.*

(5) With *several singular subjects not* disjoined by *or* or *nor*, in the following cases: —

(a) Joined by *and*, but considered as meaning about the same thing, or as making up one general idea; as, —

In a word, all his conversation and knowledge *has been* in the female world — Addison.

The strength and glare of each [color] *is* considerably abated. — Burke

To imagine that debating and logic *is* the triumph. — Carlyle

In a world where even to fold and seal a letter adroitly *is* not the least of accomplishments. — De Quincey

The genius and merit of a rising poet *was* celebrated. — Gibbon.

When the cause of ages and the fate of nations *hangs* upon the thread of a debate. — J. Q. Adams.

(b) Not joined by a conjunction, but each one emphatic, or considered as appositional; for example, —

The unbought grace of life, the cheap defense of nations, the nurse of manly sentiment and heroic enterprise, *is* gone. — Burke.

A fever, a mutilation, a cruel disappointment, a loss of wealth, a loss of friends, *seems* at the moment unpaid loss. — Emerson

The author, the wit, the partisan, the fine gentleman, *does* not take the place of the man. — *Id.*

To receive presents or a bribe, to be guilty of collusion in any way with a suitor, *was* punished, in a judge, with death. — Prescott.

*Subjects after the verb.*

This use of several subjects with a singular verb is especially frequent when the subjects are after the verb; as, —

There *is* a right and a wrong in them. — M Arnold.

There *is* a moving tone of voice, an impassioned countenance, an agitated gesture. — Burke

There *was* a steel headpiece, a cuirass, a gorget, and greaves, with a pair of gauntlets and a sword hanging beneath. — Hawthorne.

Then *comes* the "Why, sir!" and the "What then, sir?" and the "No, sir!" — Macaulay.

For wide *is* heard the thundering fray,
The rout, the ruin, the dismay.
—SCOTT.

(*c*) Joined by *as well as* (in this case the verb agrees with the first of the two, no matter if the second is plural); thus,—

Asia, as well as Europe, *was* dazzled.—Macaulay.

The oldest, as well as the newest, wine
*Begins* to stir itself.
—LONGFELLOW.

Her back, as well as sides, *was* like to crack.—Butler.

The Epic, as well as the Drama, *is* divided into tragedy and Comedy.—Fielding

(*d*) When each of two or more singular subjects is preceded by *every, each, no, many a*, and such like adjectives.

Every fop, every boor, every valet, *is* a man of wit.—Macaulay.

Every sound, every echo, *was* listened to for five hours.—De Quincey

Every dome and hollow *has* the figure of Christ.—Ruskin.

Each particular hue and tint *stands* by itself.—Newman.

Every law and usage *was* a man's expedient.—Emerson.

Here *is* no ruin, no discontinuity, no spent ball.— *Id.*

Every week, nay, almost every day, *was* set down in their calendar for some appropriate celebration.—Prescott.

*Plural verb.*

**441.** The **plural form** of the verb is used—

(1) When the subject is plural *in form and in meaning*; as,—

These *bits* of wood *were* covered on every square. — Swift.

Far, far away thy children *leave* the land. — Goldsmith.

The Arabian poets *were* the historians and moralists. — Gibbon.

(2) When the subject is a *collective noun* in which *the individuals* of the collection are thought of; as, —

A multitude *go* mad about it. — Emerson.

A great number of people *were* collected at a vendue. — Franklin.

All our household *are* at rest. — Coleridge.

A party of workmen *were* removing the horses. — Lew Wallace

The fraternity *were* inclined to claim for him the honors of canonization. — Scott.

The travelers, of whom there *were* a number. — B. Taylor.

(3) When the subject consists of *several singulars connected by and*, making up a plural subject, for example, —

Only Vice and Misery *are* abroad. — Carlyle

But its authorship, its date, and its history *are* alike a mystery to us. — Froude.

His clothes, shirt, and skin *were* all of the same color — Swift.

Aristotle and Longinus *are* better understood by him than Littleton or Coke. — Addison.

*Conjunction omitted.*

The conjunction may be omitted, as in Sec. 440 (5, *b*), but the verb is plural, as with a subject of plural form.

A shady grove, a green pasture, a stream of fresh water, *are* sufficient to attract a colony. — Gibbon.

The Dauphin, the Duke of Berri, Philip of Anjou, *were* men of insignificant characters. — Macaulay

(4) When a singular is joined with a plural by a disjunctive word, the verb agrees with the one nearest it; as, —

One or two of these perhaps *survive*. — Thoreau.

One or two persons in the crowd *were* insolent. — Froude.

One or two of the ladies *were* going to leave. — Addison

One or two of these old Cromwellian soldiers *were* still alive in the village. — Thackeray

One or two of whom *were* more entertaining. — De Quincey.

But notice the construction of this, —

A ray or two *wanders* into the darkness. — Ruskin.

# AGREEMENT OF VERB AND SUBJECT IN PERSON.

*General usage.*

**442.** If there is only one person in the subject, the ending of the verb indicates the person of its subject; that is, in those few cases where there are forms for different persons: as, —

Never once *didst* thou revel in the vision. — De Quincey.

Romanism wisely *provides* for the childish in men. — Lowell.

It *hath* been said my Lord would never take the oath. — Thackeray.

*Second or third and first person in the subject.*

**443.** If the subject is made up of the first person joined with the second or third by *and*, the verb takes the construction of the first person, the subject being really equivalent to *we*; as, —

I flatter myself you and I *shall* meet again. — Smollett.

You and I *are* farmers; we never talk politics. — D. Webster.

> Ah, brother! only I and thou
> *Are* left of all that circle now.
> — Whittier.

You and I *are* tolerably modest people. — Thackeray.

Cocke and I *have* felt it in our bones — *Gammer Gurton's Needle*

*With adversative or disjunctive connectives.*

**444.** When the subjects, of different persons, are connected by adversative or disjunctive conjunctions, the verb usually agrees with the pronoun nearest to it; for example, —

Neither you nor I *should* be a bit the better or wiser. — Ruskin.

If she or you *are* resolved to be miserable. — Goldsmith.

Nothing which Mr. Pattison or I *have* said. — M. Arnold.

Not Altamont, but thou, *hadst* been my lord. — Rowe.

Not I, but thou, his blood *dost* shed. — Byron.

This construction is at the best a little awkward. It is avoided either by using a verb which has no forms for person (as, "He or I *can* go," "She or you *may* be sure," etc.), or by rearranging the sentence so as to throw each subject before its proper person form (as, "You *would* not be wiser, nor *should* I;" or, "I *have* never said so, nor *has* she").

*Exceptional examples.*

**445.** The following illustrate exceptional usage, which it is proper to mention; but the student is cautioned to follow the regular usage rather than the unusual and irregular.

**Exercise.**

Change each of the following sentences to accord with standard usage, as illustrated above (Secs. **440-444**): —

1.

> And sharp Adversity will teach at last
> Man, — and, as we would hope, — perhaps the devil,
> That neither of their intellects are vast.
> — Byron.

2. Neither of them, in my opinion, give so accurate an idea of the man as a statuette in bronze. — Trollope.

3. How each of these professions are crowded. — Addison.

4. Neither of their counselors were to be present. — *Id.*

5. Either of them are equally good to the person to whom they are significant. — Emerson.

6. Neither the red nor the white are strong and glaring. — Burke.

7. A lampoon or a satire do not carry in them robbery or murder. — Addison.

8. Neither of the sisters were very much deceived. — Thackeray.

9.

> Nor wood, nor tree, nor bush are there,
> Her course to intercept.
> — Scott.

10. Both death and I am found eternal. — Milton.

11. In ascending the Mississippi the party was often obliged to wade through morasses; at last they came upon the district of Little Prairie. — G. Bancroft.

12. In a word, the whole nation seems to be running out of their wits. — Smollett.

## SEQUENCE OF TENSES (VERBS AND VERBALS).

*Lack of logical sequence in verbs.*

**446.** If one or more verbs depend on some leading verb, each should be in the tense that will convey the meaning intended by the writer.

In this sentence from Defoe, "I expected every wave would have swallowed us up," the verb *expected* looks forward to something in the future, while *would have swallowed* represents something completed in past time: hence the meaning intended was, "I expected every wave *would swallow*" etc.

*Also in verbals.*

In the following sentence, the infinitive also fails to express the exact thought: —

I had hoped never to have seen the statues again. — Macaulay.

The trouble is the same as in the previous sentence; *to have seen* should be changed to *to see*, for exact connection. Of course, if the purpose were to represent a prior fact or completed action, the perfect infinitive would be the very thing.

It should be remarked, however, that such sentences as those just quoted are in keeping with the older idea of the unity of the sentence. The present rule is recent.

**Exercise**.

Explain whether the verbs and infinitives in the following sentences convey the right meaning; if not, change them to a better form: —

1. I gave one quarter to Ann, meaning, on my return, to have divided with her whatever might remain. — De Quincey

2. I can't sketch "The Five Drapers," ... but can look and be thankful to have seen such a masterpiece. — Thackeray.

3. He would have done more wisely to have left them to find their own apology than to have given reasons which seemed paradoxes. — R. W. Church.

4. The propositions of William are stated to have contained a proposition for a compromise. — Palgrave

5. But I found I wanted a stock of words, which I thought I should have acquired before that time. — Franklin

6. I could even have suffered them to have broken Everet Ducking's head. — Irving.

# INDIRECT DISCOURSE.

*Definitions*.

447. **Direct discourse** — that is, a direct quotation or a direct question — means the identical words the writer or speaker used; as, —

"I hope you have not killed him?" said Amyas. — Kingsley.

**Indirect discourse** means reported speech, — the thoughts of a writer or speaker put in the words of the one reporting them.

*Two samples of indirect discourse*.

**448.** Indirect discourse may be of two kinds: —

(1) Following the thoughts and also the exact words as far as consistent with the rules of logical sequence of verbs.

(2) Merely a concise representation of the original words, not attempting to follow the entire quotation.

The following examples of both are from De Quincey: —

*Indirect.*

> 1. Reyes remarked that it was not in his power to oblige the clerk as to that, but that he could oblige him by cutting his throat.

> *Direct.*

> His exact words were, "I *cannot* oblige *you* ..., but I *can* oblige *you* by cutting *your* throat."

*Indirect.*

> Her prudence whispered eternally, that safety there was none for her until she had laid the Atlantic between herself and St. Sebastian's.

*Direct.*

> She thought to herself, "Safety there *is* none for *me* until *I* have laid," etc.

*Summary of the expressions.*

> 2. Then he laid bare the unparalleled ingratitude of such a step. Oh, the unseen treasure that had been spent upon that girl! Oh, the untold sums of money that he had sunk in that unhappy speculation!

*Direct synopsis.*

> The substance of his lamentation was, "Oh, unseen treasure *has* been spent upon that girl! Untold sums of money *have I* sunk," etc.

**449.** From these illustrations will be readily seen the grammatical changes made in transferring from direct to indirect discourse. Remember the following facts: —

(1) Usually the main, introductory verb is in the past tense.

(2) The indirect quotation is usually introduced by *that*, and the indirect question by *whether* or *if*, or regular interrogatives.

(3) Verbs in the present-tense form are changed to the past-tense form. This includes the auxiliaries *be*, *have*, *will*, etc. The past tense is sometimes changed to the past perfect.

(4) The pronouns of the first and second persons are all changed to the third person. Sometimes it is clearer to introduce the antecedent of the pronoun instead.

Other examples of indirect discourse have been given in Part I., under interrogative pronouns, interrogative adverbs, and the subjunctive mood of verbs.

**Exercise.**

Rewrite the following extract from Irving's "Sketch Book," and change it to a direct quotation: —

He assured the company that it was a fact, handed down from his ancestor the historian, that the Catskill Mountains had always been haunted by strange beings; that it was affirmed that the great Hendrick Hudson, the first discoverer of the river and country, kept a kind of vigil there every twenty years, with his crew of the Half-moon, being permitted in this way to revisit the scenes of his enterprise, and keep a guardian eye upon the river and the great city called by his name; that his father had once seen them in their old Dutch dresses playing at ninepins in a hollow of the mountain; and that he himself had heard, one summer afternoon, the sound of their balls, like distant peals of thunder.

## VERBALS.

### PARTICIPLES.

*Careless use of the participial phrase.*

**450.** The following sentences illustrate a misuse of the participial phrase: —

Pleased with the "Pilgrim's Progress," my first collection was of John Bunyan's works. — B. Franklin.

My farm consisted of about twenty acres of excellent land, having given a hundred pounds for my predecessor's goodwill. — Goldsmith.

Upon asking how he had been taught the art of a cognoscente so suddenly, he assured me that nothing was more easy. — *Id.*

Having thus run through the causes of the sublime, my first observation will be found nearly true. — Burke

He therefore remained silent till he had repeated a paternoster, being the course which his confessor had enjoined. — Scott

Compare with these the following: —

*A correct example.*

Going yesterday to dine with an old acquaintance, I had the misfortune to find his whole family very much dejected. — Addison.

*Notice this.*

The trouble is, in the sentences first quoted, that the main subject of the sentence is not the same word that would be the subject of the participle, if this were expanded into a verb.

*Correction.*

Consequently one of two courses must be taken, — either change the participle to a verb with its appropriate subject, leaving the principal statement as it is; or change the principal proposition so it shall make logical connection with the participial phrase.

For example, the first sentence would be, either "*As I was* pleased, ... my first collection was," etc., or "Pleased with the 'Pilgrim's Progress,' I made my first collection John Bunyan's works."

**Exercise.** — Rewrite the other four sentences so as to correct the careless use of the participial phrase.

## INFINITIVES.

*Adverb between* to *and the infinitive.*

**451.** There is a construction which is becoming more and more common among good writers, — the placing an adverb between *to* of the infinitive and the infinitive itself. The practice is condemned by many grammarians, while defended or excused by others. Standard writers often use it, and often, purposely or not, avoid it.

The following two examples show the adverb before the infinitive: —

*The more common usage.*

He handled it with such nicety of address as sufficiently *to show* that he fully understood the business. — Scott.

It is a solemn, universal assertion, deeply *to be kept* in mind by all sects. — Ruskin.

This is the more common arrangement; yet frequently the desire seems to be to get the adverb snugly against the infinitive, to modify it as closely and clearly as possible.

**Exercise.**

In the following citations, see if the adverbs can be placed before or after the infinitive and still modify it as clearly as they now do: —

1. There are, then, many things *to be* carefully *considered*, if a strike is to succeed. — Laughlin.

2. That the mind may not have to go backwards and forwards in order *to* rightly *connect* them. — Herbert Spencer.

3. It may be easier to bear along all the qualifications of an idea ... than *to* first imperfectly *conceive* such idea. — *Id.*

4. In works of art, this kind of grandeur, which consists in multitude, is *to be* very cautiously *admitted.* — Burke.

5. That virtue which requires *to be* ever *guarded* is scarcely worth the sentinel. — Goldsmith.

6. Burke said that such "little arts and devices" were not *to be* wholly *condemned.* — *The Nation*, No. 1533.

7. I wish the reader *to* clearly *understand.* — Ruskin.

8. Transactions which seem *to be* most widely *separated* from one another. — Dr. Blair.

9. Would earnestly advise them for their good to order this paper *to be* punctually *served up.* — Addison.

10. A little sketch of his, in which a cannon ball is supposed *to ha-ve* just *carried off* the head of an aide-de-camp. — Trollope.

11. The ladies seem *to have been* expressly *created* to form helps meet for such gentlemen. — Macaulay.

12. Sufficient to disgust a people whose manners were beginning *to be* strongly *tinctured* with austerity. — *Id.*

13. The spirits, therefore, of those opposed to them seemed *to be* considerably *damped* by their continued success. — Scott.

## ADVERBS.

*Position of* only, even, *etc.*

**452.** A very careful writer will so place the modifiers of a verb that the reader will not mistake the meaning.

The rigid rule in such a case would be, to put the modifier in such a position that the reader not only can understand the meaning intended, but *cannot misunderstand* the thought. Now, when such adverbs as *only, even,* etc., are used, they are usually placed in a strictly correct position, if they modify single words; but they are often removed from the exact position, if they modify phrases or clauses: for example, from Irving, "The site is *only* to be traced by fragments of bricks, china, and earthenware." Here *only* modifies the phrase *by fragments of bricks,* etc., but it is placed before the infinitive. This misplacement of the adverb can be detected only by analysis of the sentence.

**Exercise.**

Tell what the adverb modifies in each quotation, and see if it is placed in the proper position: —

1. Only the name of one obscure epigrammatist has been embalmed for us in the verses of his rival. — Palgrave.

2. Do you remember pea shooters? I think we only had them on going home for holidays. — Thackeray.

3. Irving could only live very modestly. He could only afford to keep one old horse. — *Id.*

4. The arrangement of this machinery could only be accounted for by supposing the motive power to have been steam. — Wendell Phillips.

5. Such disputes can only be settled by arms. — *Id.*

6. I have only noted one or two topics which I thought most likely to interest an American reader. — N. P. Willis.

7. The silence of the first night at the farmhouse, — stillness broken only by two whippoorwills. — Higginson.

8. My master, to avoid a crowd, would suffer only thirty people at a time to see me. — Swift.

9. In relating these and the following laws, I would only be understood to mean the original institutions. — *Id.*

10. The perfect loveliness of a woman's countenance can only consist in that majestic peace which is founded in the memory of happy and useful years. — Ruskin.

11. In one of those celestial days it seems a poverty that we can only spend it once. — Emerson.

12. My lord was only anxious as long as his wife's anxious face or behavior seemed to upbraid him. — Thackeray.

13. He shouted in those clear, piercing tones that could be even heard among the roaring of the cannon. — Cooper.

14. His suspicions were not even excited by the ominous face of Gérard. — Motley.

15. During the whole course of his administration, he scarcely befriended a single man of genius. — Macaulay.

16. I never remember to have felt an event more deeply than his death. — Sydney Smith.

17. His last journey to Cannes, whence he was never destined to return. — Mrs. Grote.

# USE OF DOUBLE NEGATIVES.

*The old usage.*

**453.** In Old and Middle English, two negatives strengthened a negative idea; for example, —

> He *nevere* yet *no* vileineye *ne* sayde,
> In al his lyf unto *no* maner wight.
> — Chaucer.

*No* sonne, were he never so old of yeares, might *not* marry. — Ascham.

The first of these is equivalent to "He didn't never say no villainy in all his life to no manner of man," — four negatives.

This idiom was common in the older stages of the language, and is still kept in vulgar English; as, —

I tell you she *ain'* been *nowhar* ef she don' know we all. — Page, in *Ole Virginia.*

There *weren't no* pies to equal hers. — Mrs. Stowe.

*Exceptional use.*

There are sometimes found two negatives in modern English with a negative effect, when one of the negatives is a connective. This, however, is not common.

I never did see him again, *nor never* shall. — De Quincey.

However, I did *not* act so hastily, *neither.* — Defoe.

The prosperity of no empire, *nor* the grandeur of *no* king, can so agreeably affect, etc. — Burke.

*Regular law of negative in modern English.*

But, under the influence of Latin syntax, the usual way of regarding the question now is, that *two negatives are equivalent to an affirmative*, denying each other.

Therefore, if two negatives are found together, it is a sign of ignorance or carelessness, or else a purpose to make an affirmative effect. In the latter case, one of the negatives is often a prefix; as *in*frequent, *un*common.

**Exercise.**

Tell whether the two or more negatives are properly used in each of the following sentences, and why: —

1. The red men were not so infrequent visitors of the English settlements. — Hawthorne.

2. "Huldy was so up to everything about the house, that the doctor didn't miss nothin' in a temporal way." — Mrs. Stowe.

3. Her younger sister was a wide-awake girl, who hadn't been to school for nothing. — Holmes.

4. You will find no battle which does not exhibit the most cautious circumspection. — Bayne.

5. Not only could man not acquire such information, but ought not to labor after it. — Grote.

6. There is no thoughtful man in America who would not consider a war with England the greatest of calamities. — Lowell.

7. In the execution of this task, there is no man who would not find it an arduous effort. — Hamilton.

8. "A weapon," said the King, "well worthy to confer honor, nor has it been laid on an undeserving shoulder." — Scott.

## CONJUNCTIONS.

And who, and which.

**454.** The sentences given in Secs. 419 and 420 on the connecting of pronouns with different expressions may again be referred to here, as the use of the conjunction, as well as of the pronoun, should be scrutinized.

*Choice and proper position of correlatives.*

**455.** The most frequent mistakes in using conjunctions are in handling correlatives, especially *both ... and, neither ... nor, either ... or, not only ... but, not merely ... but (also)*.

The following examples illustrate the correct use of correlatives as to both choice of words and position: —

*Whether* at war *or* at peace, there we were, a standing menace to all earthly paradises of that kind. — Lowell.

These idols of wood can *neither* hear *nor* feel. — Prescott.

*Both* the common soldiery *and* their leaders and commanders lowered on each other as if their union had not been more essential than ever, *not only* to the success of their common cause, *but* to their own safety. — Scott.

*Things to be watched.*

In these examples it will be noticed that *nor*, not *or* is the proper correlative of *neither*; and that all correlatives in a sentence ought to have corresponding positions: that is, if the last precedes a verb, the first ought to be placed before a verb; if the second precedes a phrase, the first should also. This is necessary to make the sentence clear and symmetrical.

*Correction.*

In the sentence, "I am *neither* in spirits to enjoy it, *or* to reply to it," both of the above requirements are violated. The word *neither* in such a case had better be changed to *not ... either*, — "I am not in spirits *either* to enjoy it, *or* to reply to it."

Besides *neither ... or*, even *neither ... nor* is often changed to *not — either ... or* with advantage, as the negation is sometimes too far from the verb to which it belongs.

A noun may be preceded by one of the correlatives, and an equivalent pronoun by the other. The sentence, "This loose and inaccurate manner of speaking has misled us *both* in the theory of taste *and* of morals," may be changed to "This loose ... misled us *both* in the theory of taste *and* in *that* of morals."

**Exercise.**

Correct the following sentences: —

1. An ordinary man would neither have incurred the danger of succoring Essex, nor the disgrace of assailing him. — Macaulay.

2. Those ogres will stab about and kill not only strangers, but they will outrage, murder, and chop up their own kin. — Thackeray.

3. In the course of his reading (which was neither pursued with that seriousness or that devout mind which such a study requires) the youth found himself, etc. — *Id.*

4. I could neither bear walking nor riding in a carriage over its pebbled streets. — Franklin.

5. Some exceptions, that can neither be dissembled nor eluded, render this mode of reasoning as indiscreet as it is superfluous. — Gibbon.

6. They will, too, not merely interest children, but grown-up persons. — *Westminster Review.*

7. I had even the satisfaction to see her lavish some kind looks upon my unfortunate son, which the other could neither extort by his fortune nor assiduity. — Goldsmith.

8. This was done probably to show that he was neither ashamed of his name or family. — Addison.

Try and *for* try to.

**456.** Occasionally there is found the expression *try and* instead of the better authorized *try to*; as, —

We will try *and* avoid personalities altogether. — Thackeray.

Did any of you ever try *and* read "Blackmore's Poems"? — *Id.*

Try *and* avoid the pronoun. — Bain.

We will try *and* get a clearer notion of them. — Ruskin.

But what.

**457.** Instead of the subordinate conjunction *that*, *but*, or *but that*, or the negative relative *but*, we sometimes find the bulky and needless *but what*. Now, it is possible to use *but what* when *what* is a relative pronoun, as, "He never had any money *but what* he absolutely needed;" but in the following sentences *what* usurps the place of a conjunction.

**Exercise.**

In the following sentences, substitute *that, but,* or *but that* for the words *but what*: —

1. The doctor used to say 'twas her young heart, and I don't know *but what* he was right. — S. O. Jewett.

2. At the first stroke of the pickax it is ten to one *but what* you are taken up for a trespass. — Bulwer.

3. There are few persons of distinction *but what* can hold conversation in both languages. — Swift.

4. Who knows *but what* there might be English among those sun-browned half-naked masses of panting wretches? — Kingsley.

5. No little wound of the kind ever came to him *but what* he disclosed it at once. — Trollope.

6. They are not so distant from the camp of Saladin *but what* they might be in a moment surprised. — Scott.

## PREPOSITIONS.

**458.** As to the placing of a preposition after its object in certain cases, see Sec. 305.

Between *and* among.

**459.** In the primary meaning of **between** and **among** there is a sharp distinction, as already seen in Sec. 313; but in Modern English the difference is not so marked.

**Between** is used most often with two things only, but still it is frequently used in speaking of several objects, some relation or connection between two at a time being implied.

**Among** is used in the same way as *amid* (though not with exactly the same meaning), several objects being spoken of in the aggregate, no separation or division by twos being implied.

Examples of the distinctive use of the two words: —

*Two things.*

The contentions that arise *between* the parson and the squire. — Addison.

We reckoned the improvements of the art of war *among* the triumphs of science. — Emerson.

Examples of the looser use of *between*: —

*A number of things.*

Natural objects affect us by the laws of that connection which Providence has established *between* certain motions of bodies. — Burke.

Hence the differences *between* men in natural endowment are insignificant in comparison with their common wealth. — Emerson.

They maintain a good correspondence *between* those wealthy societies of men that are divided from one another by seas and oceans. — Addison.

Looking up at its deep-pointed porches and the dark places *between* their pillars where there were statues once. — Ruskin

What have I, a soldier of the Cross, to do with recollections of war *betwixt* Christian nations? — Scott.

*Two groups or one and a group.*

Also *between* may express relation or connection in speaking of two groups of objects, or one object and a group; as, —

A council of war is going on beside the watch fire, *between* the three adventurers and the faithful Yeo. — Kingsley.

The great distinction *between* teachers sacred or literary, — *between* poets like Herbert and poets like Pope, — *between* philosophers like Spinoza, Kant, and Coleridge, and philosophers like Locke, Paley, Mackintosh, and Stewart, etc. — Emerson.

**460.** Certain words are followed by particular prepositions.

Some of these words show by their composition what preposition should follow. Such are *absolve, involve, different.*

Some of them have, by custom, come to take prepositions not in keeping with the original meaning of the words. Such are *derogatory, averse*.

Many words take one preposition to express one meaning, and another to convey a different meaning; as, *correspond, confer*.

And yet others may take several prepositions indifferently to express the same meaning.

*List I.: Words with particular prepositions.*

**461.**

# LIST I.

- Absolve *from.*
- Abhorrent *to.*
- Accord *with.*
- Acquit *of.*
- Affinity *between.*
- Averse *to.*
- Bestow *on (upon).*
- Conform *to.*
- Comply *with.*
- Conversant *with.*
- Dependent *on (upon).*
- Different *from.*
- Dissent *from.*
- Derogatory *to.*
- Deprive *of.*
- Independent *of.*
- Involve *in.*

"Different *to*" is frequently heard in spoken English in England, and sometimes creeps into standard books, but it is not good usage.

*List II.: Words taking different prepositions for different meanings.*

**462.**

# LIST II.

- Agree *with* (a person).
- Agree *to* (a proposal).
- Change *for* (a thing).
- Change *with* (a person).
- Change *to* (become).
- Confer *with* (talk with).
- Confer *on* (*upon*) (give to).
- Confide *in* (trust in).
- Confide *to* (intrust to).
- Correspond *with* (write to).
- Correspond *to* (a thing).
- Differ *from* (note below).
- Differ *with* (note below).
- Disappointed *in* (a thing obtained).
- Disappointed *of* (a thing not obtained).
- Reconcile *to* (note below).
- Reconcile *with* (note below).
- A taste *of* (food).
- A taste *for* (art, etc.).

"Correspond *with*" is sometimes used of things, as meaning *to be in keeping with*.

"Differ *from*" is used in speaking of unlikeness between things or persons; "differ *from*" and "differ *with*" are both used in speaking of persons disagreeing as to opinions.

"Reconcile *to*" is used with the meaning of *resigned to*, as, "The exile became reconciled *to* his fate;" also of persons, in the sense of making friends with, as, "The king is reconciled *to* his minister." "Reconcile *with*" is used with the meaning of *make to agree with*, as, "The statement must be reconciled *with* his previous conduct."

*List III.: Words taking anyone of several prepositions for the same meaning.*

**463.**

# LIST III.

- Die *by*, die *for*, die *from*, die *of*, die *with*.
- Expect *of*, expect *from*.
- Part *from*, part *with*.

Illustrations of "die *of*," "die *from*," etc.: —

"*Die* of."

The author died *of* a fit of apoplexy. — Boswell.

People do not die *of* trifling little colds. — Austen

Fifteen officers died *of* fever in a day. — Macaulay.

It would take me long to die *of* hunger. — G. Eliot.

She died *of* hard work, privation, and ill treatment. — Burnett.

"*Die* from."

She saw her husband at last literally die *from* hunger. — Bulwer.

He died at last without disease, simply *from* old age. — Athenæum.

No one *died from* want at Longfeld. — *Chambers' Journal.*

"*Die* with."

She would have been ready to die *with* shame. — G. Eliot.

I am positively dying *with* hunger. — Scott.

I thought the two Miss Flamboroughs would have died *with* laughing. — Goldsmith.

I wish that the happiest here may not die *with* envy. — Pope.

"*Die* for." (*in behalf of*).

Take thought and die *for* Cæsar. — Shakespeare.

One of them said he would die *for* her. — Goldsmith.

It is a man of quality who dies *for* her. — Addison.

"*Die* for." (*because of*).

Who, as Cervantes informs us, died *for* love of the fair Marcella. — Fielding.

Some officers had died *for* want of a morsel of bread. — Macaulay.

"*Die* by." (*material cause, instrument*).

If I meet with any of 'em, they shall die *by* this hand. — Thackeray.

He must purge himself to the satisfaction of a vigilant tribunal or die *by* fire. — Macaulay.

He died *by* suicide before he completed his eighteenth year. — Shaw.

**464.** Illustrations of "expect *of*," "expect *from*:" —

"*Expect* of."

What do I expect *of* Dublin? — *Punch.*

That is more than I expected *of* you. — Scott.

*Of* Doctor P. nothing better was to be expected. — Poe.

Not knowing what might be expected *of* men in general. — G. ELIOT.

"*Expect* from."

She will expect more attention *from* you, as my friend. — Walpole.

There was a certain grace and decorum hardly to be expected *from* a man. — Macaulay.

I have long expected something remarkable *from* you. — G. Eliot.

**465.** "Part *with*" is used with both persons and things, but "part *from*" is less often found in speaking of things.

Illustrations of "part *with*," "part *from*:" —

"*Part* with."

He was fond of everybody that he was used to, and hated to part *with* them. — Austen.

Cleveland was sorry to part *with* him. — Bulwer.

I can part *with* my children for their good. — Dickens.

I part *with* all that grew so near my heart. — Waller.

"*Part* from."

To part *from* you would be misery. — Marryat.

I have just seen her, just parted *from* her. — Bulwer.

Burke parted *from* him with deep emotion. — Macaulay.

His precious bag, which he would by no means part *from*. — G. ELIOT.

*Kind* in *you*, *kind* of *you*.

**466.** With words implying behavior or disposition, either *of* or *in* is used indifferently, as shown in the following quotations: —

Of.

It was a little bad *of* you. — Trollope.

How cruel *of* me! — Collins.

He did not think it handsome *of* you. — Bulwer.

But this is idle *of* you. — Tennyson.

In.

Very natural *in* Mr. Hampden. — Carlyle.

It will be anything but shrewd *in* you. — Dickens.

That is very unreasonable *in* a person so young. — Beaconsfield.

I am wasting your whole morning — too bad *in* me. — Bulwer.

## Miscellaneous Examples for Correction.

1. Can you imagine Indians or a semi-civilized people engaged on a work like the canal connecting the Mediterranean and the Red seas?

2. In the friction between an employer and workman, it is commonly said that his profits are high.

3. None of them are in any wise willing to give his life for the life of his chief.

4. That which can be done with perfect convenience and without loss, is not always the thing that most needs to be done, or which we are most imperatively required to do.

5. Art is neither to be achieved by effort of thinking, nor explained by accuracy of speaking.

6. To such as thee the fathers owe their fame.

7. We tread upon the ancient granite that first divided the waters into a northern and southern ocean.

8. Thou tread'st, with seraphims, the vast abyss.

9. Eustace had slipped off his long cloak, thrown it over Amyas's head, and ran up the alley.

10. This narrative, tedious perhaps, but which the story renders necessary, may serve to explain the state of intelligence betwixt the lovers.

11. To the shame and eternal infamy of whomsoever shall turn back from the plow on which he hath laid his hand!

12. The noise of vast cataracts, raging storms, thunder, or artillery, awake a great and awful sensation in the mind.

13. The materials and ornaments ought neither to be white, nor green, nor yellow, nor blue, nor of a pale red.

14. This does not prove that an idea of use and beauty are the same thing, or that they are any way dependent on each other.

15.

> And were I anything but what I am,
> I would wish me only he.

16. But every man may know, and most of us do know, what is a just and unjust act.

17. You have seen Cassio and she together.

18. We shall shortly see which is the fittest object of scorn, you or me.

19. Richard glared round him with an eye that seemed to seek an enemy, and from which the angry nobles shrunk appalled.

20. It comes to whomsoever will put off what is foreign and proud.

21. The difference between the just and unjust procedure does not lie in the number of men hired, but in the price paid to them.

22. The effect of proportion and fitness, so far at least as they proceed from a mere consideration of the work itself, produce approbation, the acquiescence of the understanding.

23. When the glass or liquor are transparent, the light is sometimes softened in the passage.

24. For there nor yew nor cypress spread their gloom.

25. Every one of these letters are in my name.

26. Neither of them are remarkable for precision.

27. Squares, triangles, and other angular figures, are neither beautiful to the sight nor feeling.

28. There is not one in a thousand of these human souls that cares to think where this estate is, or how beautiful it is, or what kind of life they are to lead in it.

29. Dryden and Rowe's manner are quite out of fashion.

30. We were only permitted to stop for refreshment once.

31. The sight of the manner in which the meals were served were enough to turn our stomach.

32. The moody and savage state of mind of the sullen and ambitious man are admirably drawn.

33. Surely none of our readers are so unfortunate as not to know some man or woman who carry this atmosphere of peace and good-will about with them. (Sec. 411.)

34. Friday, whom he thinks would be better than a dog, and almost as good as a pony.

35. That night every man of the boat's crew, save Amyas, were down with raging fever.

36. These kind of books fill up the long tapestry of history with little bits of detail which give human interest to it.

37. I never remember the heather so rich and abundant.

38. These are scattered along the coast for several hundred miles, in conditions of life that seem forbidding enough, but which are accepted without complaint by the inhabitants themselves.

39. Between each was an interval where lay a musket.

40. He had four children, and it was confidently expected that they would receive a fortune of at least $200,000 between them.

FOOTNOTES:

[1] More for convenience than for absolute accuracy, the stages of our language have been roughly divided into three: —

(1) Old English (with Anglo-Saxon) down to the twelfth century.

(2) Middle English, from about the twelfth century to the sixteenth century.

(3) Modern English, from about 1500 to the present time.

CPSIA information can be obtained at www.ICGtesting.com
Printed in the USA
LVOW01s2305050214

372490LV00027B/1252/P